FROM

DEADWOOD TO

DEEP STATE

—JACK'S OFT' DERAILED JOURNEY
BACK TO NEWBERRY

A number of very wonderful people helped me prepare this book for publication. Each of them contributed significantly.

Thank you Evie, Charity, Andy, Steve, Lora, George, Gay, John, EmaLee, and all the members of Grand Valley Artists, Grand Rapids, MI.

FROM DEADWOOD TO DEEP STATE

—JACK'S OFT' DERAILED JOURNEY BACK TO NEWBERRY

MICHAEL CARRIER

GREENWICH VILLAGE INK

An imprint of Alistair Rapids Publishing
Grand Rapids, MI

FROM DEADWOOD TO DEEP STATE—
JACK'S OFT'DERAILED JOURNEY BACK TO
NEWBERRY

From Deadwood to Deep State. Copyright 2019 by Michael Carrier.

Published 2019 by Greenwich Village Ink, an imprint of Alistair Rapids Publishing, Grand Rapids, MI.

All rights reserved. No part of this book may be reproduced or transmitted in any form or by any means, electronic or mechanical, including photocopying, recording, or by any information storage and retrieval system, without written permission from the author, except for the inclusion of brief quotations in a review.

Permission to use the special font on the cover was obtained from the artist.

Visit the *JACK* website at http:/www.greenwichvillageink.com

For upcoming books by the same author visit www.greenwichvillageink.com.

Author can be emailed at mike.jon.carrier@gmail.com.

ISBN: 978-1-936092-03-1 (trade pbk) 978-1-936092-06-2
Printed in the United States of America

Library of Congress Cataloging-in-Publication Data

Carrier, Michael.
JACK and the New York Death Mask / by Michael Carrier. 1st ed.
ISBN: 978-1-936092-03-1 (trade pbk. : alk. paper)
1. Political Intrigue 2. Novel 3.Assassination 4. Plot 5. New York.

Notes

DISCLAIMER: *From Deadwood to Deep State* is not a true story. It is a work of fiction. All characters, locations, names, situations, and occurrences are purely the product of my imagination. Any resemblance to actual events or persons (living or dead) is totally coincidental.

CONSIDER THIS: If you enjoy my books, how about writing a short review of this one. Most books are sold over Amazon or through other forms of distribution. Most of my books, including this one, are sold primarily at book signings and other personal appearances. When you buy a book on Amazon, they follow up the sale with a request for a review. I am unable to follow up in a similar fashion. That's why, if you like this book, would you please submit a nice review on Amazon? I would appreciate it very much. … And, please check out my website to find out where and when you can see me. I try to do at least one event every weekend (generally I take January off). Thanks!

Check out Jack's webpage at: http://www.greenwichvillageink.com
—Michael Carrier

What people are saying about earlier Jack Handler books

Top Shelf Murder Mystery—Riveting. Being a Murder-Mystery "JUNKIE" this book is definitely a keeper … can't put it down … read it again type of book … and it is very precise to the lifestyles in Upper Michigan. Very well researched. I am a resident of this area. His attention to detail is great. I have to rate this book in the same class or better than authors Michael Connelly, James Patterson, and Steve Hamilton. — Shelldrakeshores

Being a Michigan native, I was immediately drawn to this book. Michael Carrier is right in step with his contemporaries James Patterson and David Baldacci. I am anxious to read more of his work. I highly recommend this one! — J. Henningsen

A fast and interesting read. Michael ends each chapter with a hook that makes you want to keep reading. The relationship between father and daughter is compelling. Good book for those who like a quick moving detective story where the characters often break the "rules" for the greater good! I'm looking forward to reading the author's next book. — Flower Lady

Move over, Patterson, I now have a new favorite author. Jack Handler and his daughter make a great tag team, great intrigue, and diversions. I have a cabin on Sugar Island and enjoyed the references to the locations. I met the author at Joey's (the real live Joey) coffee shop up on the hill, great writer, good stuff. I don't usually finish a book in the course of a week, but read this one in two sittings so it definitely had my attention. I am looking forward to the next installment. Bravo. — Northland Press

My husband is not a reader—he probably hasn't read a book since his last elementary school book report was due. But ... he took my copy of *Murder on Sugar Island* to deer camp and read the whole thing in two days. After he recommended the book to me, I read it—being the book snob that I am, I thought I had the whole plot figured out within the first few pages, but a few chapters later, I was mystified once again. After that surprise ending, we ordered the other two Getting to Know Jack books. — Erin W.

I enjoyed this book very much. It was very entertaining, and the story unfolded in a believable manner. Jack Handler is a likeable character. But you would not like to be on his wrong side. Handler made that very clear in *Jack and the New York Death Mask*. This book (Murder on Sugar Island) was the first book in the Getting to Know Jack series that I read. After I read *Death Mask*, I discovered just how tough Jack Handler really was.

I heard that Carrier is about to come out with another Jack Handler book—a sequel to *Superior Peril*. I will read it the day it becomes available. And I will undoubtedly finish it before I go to bed. If he could write them faster, I would be happy. — Deborah M.

I thoroughly enjoyed this book. I could not turn the pages fast enough. I am not sure it was plausible but I love the characters. I highly recommend this book and look forward to reading more by Michael Carrier. — Amazon Reader

An intense thrill ride!! — Mario

Michael Carrier has knocked it out of the park. — John

Left on the edge of my seat after the last book, I could not wait for the next chapter to unfold and Michael Carrier did not disappoint! I truly feel I know his characters better with each novel and I especially like the can-do/will-do attitude of Jack. Keep up the fine work, Michael, and may your pen never run dry! — SW

The Handlers are at it again, with the action starting on Sugar Island, I am really starting to enjoy the way the father/daughter and now Red are working through the mind of Michael Carrier. The entire family, plus a few more are becoming the reason for the new sheriff's increased body count and antacid intake. The twists and turns we have come to expect are all there and then some. I'm looking for the next installment already. — Northland Press

Finally, there is a new author who will challenge the likes of Michael Connelly and David Baldacci. — Island Books

If you like James Patterson and Michael Connelly, you'll love Michael Carrier. Carrier has proven that he can hang with the best of them. It has all of the great, edge-of-your-seat action and suspense that you'd expect in a good thriller, and it kept me guessing to the very end. Fantastic read with an awesome detective duo—I couldn't put it down! — Katie

Don't read Carrier at the beach or you are sure to get sunburned. I did. I loved the characters. It was so descriptive you feel like you know everyone. Lots of action—always something happening. I love the surprise twists. All my friends are reading it now because I wouldn't talk to them until I finished it so they knew it was good. Carrier is my new favorite author! — Sue

Thoroughly enjoyed this read—kept me turning page after

page! Good character development and captivating plot. Had theories but couldn't quite solve the mystery without reading to the end. Highly recommended for readers of all ages. — Terry

Here are the Amazon links to all my Jack Handler books:

Jack and the New York Death Mask (Jack):	http://amzn.to/MVpAEd
Murder on Sugar Island (Sugar):	http://amzn.to/1u66DBG
Superior Peril (Peril):	http://amzn.to/LAQnEU
Superior Intrigue (Intrigue):	http://amzn.to/1jvjNSi
Sugar Island Girl Missing in Paris (Missing):	http://amzn.to/1g5c66e
Wealthy Street Murders (Wealthy):	http://amzn.to/1mb6NQy
Murders in Strangmoor Bog (Strangmoor):	http://amzn.to/1osAjJ8
Ghosts of Cherry Street (Ghosts):	http://amzn.to/1PvWfJd
Assault on Sugar Island:	http://amzn.to/2n3vcyL
Dogfight:	http://amzn.to/2F7OkoM
Murder at Whitefish Point:	http://amzn.to/2CxlAmC
Superior Shoal:	https://amzn.to/2pbM89v

From Deadwood to Deep State

Jack's Oft-Derailed Journey Back to Newberry

Part 1

Chapter 1—Fourth Tuesday of October, Current Year—in Singapore

"Hands up in the air!" Jack shouted. "Everyone! NOW!"

There were twenty-two people in the room with Jack, including Chairman Kim, the leader of North Korea, and the current President of the United States. Among the rest of those in the room were a contingent of translators and advisors who were accompanying Chairman Kim, a similar-sized group who were there to aid POTUS (President of the United States), and security personnel from both camps.

"What the hell do you think you're doing?" POTUS barked, pointing his finger at Jack. "And just who the hell do you think you are! Don't you know who I am?"

"I do know who you are, Mr. President," Jack said. "But this room is a death trap. It's booby-trapped to kill all of you. I've got to get you out of here right now!"

"What the hell are you talking about?" POTUS said. "And answer my question: who are you?"

"There is poison gas, and I believe explosives. The plan was to get all of you down here, and then to kill you. Chairman Kim as well. We don't have any time to talk about it."

"Damn it all! I still don't know who you are, and—"

Just then the Secret Service agent who had earlier been giving instructions interrupted, "Mr. President. I can assure you that we are perfectly safe in here. This room is explosion proof, and it has its own air supply and ventilation system. We are not going—"

"Shut the hell up!" POTUS shouted him down. "I'm doing the talking here. You just shut your damn mouth and sit down."

And then POTUS turned toward Jack. "Now tell me. Who the hell are you? I've asked you that three times now. And how'd you get in here?"

"Bob Fulbright, the ex-President. You know him quite well, I'm told. He sent me here to keep you alive. And that's what I'm doing. And if I'm going to be able to do that, we've got to get you out of here immediately."

"Fulbright?" POTUS snarled.

"Right," Jack said. "And my name is Jack."

"Fulbright, you say?" POTUS said. "His politics suck, but,

I'd have to say that he *is* a friend of mine. And *he* sent you? You wouldn't be Jack *Handler*, would you?"

"That's me."

"Holy shit," POTUS said. "He has a lot of confidence in you. And, he sent you here for this?"

"Right. Now, we've got to get going."

Then POTUS turned to the interpreter and told her, "Tell Chairman Kim that the man with the gun is a friend of mine, and that he is here to protect us."

Chapter 2—Second Tuesday in August

It was a nasty morning—cold and rainy. Larry Morrison, the project foreman for the construction site, was more miserable than the weather. Due to numerous issues in procuring all the necessary permits, the new hotel project was already over a month behind schedule. And everyone was well aware that Michigan's Upper Peninsula offered only six months of reasonably conducive weather for construction. Once November arrived, you'd best be able to close the door behind you and work inside, because Newberry winters were wicked—sometimes even worse than that.

"You absolutely positive that they were *human* bones?" Morrison snarled. "Not just some big buck that ran over here and died?"

"Oh yeah," Joe Crow, the dozer operator, said confidently. "It was a human skull all right. I got a good look right down into his hollow eye sockets. Creepy as all hell. Believe me. And it was down there a ways—four feet, or more. This wasn't an old cemetery, was it? Like a Native American burial ground? If it was, then we've got real problems doing any work here at all, if you know what I mean."

"She-it! Don't even talk to me about that. This was *never* a cemetery—Native American or otherwise. No records like that whatsoever. You did call the sheriff. Right?"

"Oh yeah," Joe Crow said. "Dispatcher said she'd get someone out here right away. I sent Needham out to the road to direct them back here. Or they might spend half the morning trying to find it. And I know you're in a hurry. I'd say they'll get here real soon. It's been nearly half an hour. Anytime now."

The village of Newberry was founded in 1882 and named in honor of John Stoughton Newberry, a U.S. representative. It was located approximately halfway between Lake Superior to the north and Lake Michigan to the south. While Newberry's population hovered at around 1,600, in the summer the charm of this little town drew many from Wisconsin to the west, as well as thousands of additional visitors crossing the Mackinac Bridge from the south.

Recent talk in the area was that plans were in the works for a new two-hundred-million-dollar casino to be built just south of the town. Investors hoped that the addition of a new four-star hotel might add incentive to increase the size of the casino project. Were both projects to occur as anticipated, Newberry's summer population would increase dramatically.

Investors in the hotel project knew that Morrison was the right man to carry out the construction end of the project. He had headed up large building ventures from Detroit to Marquette, and so he was well aware that in virtually every endeavor of this size and scope, timing was everything. He had no patience with anyone or anything that threatened to delay his work.

Typically, Morrison would provide everything that his men were likely to require during the entire day. In the back of his two-year-old, navy blue, four-wheel-drive crew-cab Chevy pickup he had packed two yellow and red three-gallon water containers. He knew that, depending on the size of his crew of excavators, this amount of water would easily hydrate the team for the entire day. He not only provided the water, inside the cab he stored a large supply of paper cups, which he dispensed individually as needed.

Morrison's wife would always pack sandwiches for him, and an extra dozen for those on his team who might have inadvertently failed to bring their own lunch. Because, once a man entered the jobsite, Morrison would not permit him to leave for any reason short of a physical injury.

On this day, Mrs. Morrison had packed ham-on-ryes with his usual apple and a large thermos of coffee. He never brought coffee to share. But his wife did send over a dozen peanut butter cookies to distribute at break time, which was usually around two P.M. each day. They would start precisely at seven A.M., eat lunch at eleven-thirty, break at two, and clean up the site at four. When he felt he was under the gun to get a job done, he would keep some workers until dusk.

This was one of those times—most of the team would be working late.

Before he left at night, he would diligently scour the entire area to make certain he had picked up any discarded waste. Every worker considered Larry Morrison to be the best boss they had ever worked under, despite his inherently impatient disposition.

Crow and Morrison were still standing there talking when they spotted a patrol car winding its way back to the excavation—emergency lights flashing, but no siren. It was followed immediately by a white van and another patrol car.

Two uniforms got out of the first car, and they immediately ushered both Crow and Morrison away from what they called their "crime scene."

Twenty minutes later the officer in charge, Det. Bret Nicolson, walked over to talk with Morrison.

"We do have a human body, so you will definitely have to shut down this operation. For sure we will need you to avoid this area for a day or two. You'll just have to find something else to do."

"The whole damn day!" Morrison complained. "How the hell long could it take to scoop up some bones and get them off of my construction site? I want to talk to your boss."

"That would be Sheriff Bellere. Actually, the sheriff is on temporary medical leave for a day or two. The undersheriff, Victor Brady, he's my boss right now. Would you like to talk to him?

"Hell no!" Morrison barked. "I went to school with him. The prick hates me. Just tell me—how the hell long is this going to take? Before I can get back to work?"

"I will work as fast as I can."

"Worst case scenario—how long before I can get my men back to workin'?"

"Give me a week. I should be out of here by then—probably sooner."

"She-it! A whole week? I can't sit on my hands that long!"

"I'm sure there's other work you can do. Just stay outside of the yellow tape and you'll be okay."

"You've got over an acre taped off!" Morrison said, gesturing broadly with both hands. "And it's right in the middle of my construction site. What the hell! Why do you need to mark off this much? Don't tell me you need all that?" Morrison's impatience was evolving into molten anger. He ripped off his red flannel shirt and threw it in the direction of his truck.

"Sometimes there is more than one body buried in any given location. We have to determine if our John Doe ever got lonely up here. Or if there is some additional evidence buried with him. All that kind of crap. Once we satisfy our forensic technicians that there is only one body buried up here, and that we've gathered up all the evidence, we can wind this up and move on. Like I said—most likely it'll be next week at the outside. Probably a lot sooner, if we can get busy and there's no interference."

"As long as we stay outside the tape, you've got no problem with what we do up here? Right?"

"That's right," Det. Nicolson said, preparing to toss a verbal jab in Morrison's direction. "… You still want to talk to the under-sheriff?"

Morrison sneered at Det. Nicolson, but kept his mouth shut and walked away.

After quickly constructing a makeshift morgue from a white tent, the forensic field technicians—each dressed in a full-body suit with a hood, mask, booties and gloves—quickly determined that the object of their attention was the body of a young man. He appeared to have been murdered—perhaps beaten to death in a fight, and then buried six feet beneath the surface of a sandy hillside just east of the now quiet little town of Newberry.

His wallet had been left in his pocket. It contained eighty-four dollars in cash—three twenties, two tens, and four ones. "Robbery was obviously not the motive." So declared Det. Nicolson.

In addition to the cash, his wallet contained his draft registration card, dated June something, 1917. While it was substantially degraded, after being digitally scanned under various types of light, parts of it could still be read. It described a man named William Lawrence Owens, born on August 19, 1894 in Marquette, MI. It further indicated that at the time he registered for the draft he was employed in Dollarville, MI, as a timber worker for The American Lumber Company. Much of the rest of the registration card was not legible, but the information gleaned from the intact portion proved enough to quite easily identify the victim. Because draft registrations from that era are digitalized, the team would be able to locate the original.

While Mr. Owens never married, he was survived by two sisters and a brother—all of whom were deceased years before his body was discovered. But something interesting was turned up in the possession of Claire Mansfield, granddaughter of Agnes Cross (Owens), the married name of William Owens' older sister. Tucked inside the photo album Ms. Mansfield inherited from her mother were a number of family pictures, some of which included shots of a young William—Claire's great-uncle.

But even more interesting were the other pictures and letters found among William's things after he had disappeared. These images included a snapshot of a beautiful young woman named Maria. It was signed, and it had these words written on the back: "To My Darling Billy, the one true love of my life." Along with that picture were half a dozen letters, four of which were signed "All my love Always, Maria."

No one in William's family recognized the young woman in the picture, nor could anyone even hazard a guess as to her role in William's short life. The letters, while lengthy, were not apparently posted—at least, there were no envelopes accompanying them. They had more the appearance of hand-delivered notes rather than posted mail. That conclusion was reached by family members due to the fact that they had all been folded into squares, rather than into a shape conducive to fitting into a standard envelope. Also, William's name was written on the outside of each note, in much the same way a schoolgirl would write a boy's name on a personal missive she might pass in class.

A logical conclusion could thus be drawn that the young lady probably lived near the lumber camp where William worked, and was therefore able to deliver the notes personally. Lending weight to that theory was the total lack of any accompanying envelopes. *If these notes had been mailed to the young man,* Det. Nicolson concluded, *odds are that at least some of them would have been returned to those envelopes in order to protect them. But,* Det. Nicolson wondered, *if young Maria did live nearby, why would she feel the need to write notes in the first place?*

That question was clearly answered within the text of two of the six letters. Maria had a significant other—perhaps her husband—and she was sneaking around to see William, whom she referred to as "my love."

Could her deception and infidelity have led to William's murder? It would certainly seem logical to think so—at least long enough to explore that motive as a legitimate possibility.

The case for such would most certainly have been more aggressively pursued at the time the man came up missing had it been known, or even strongly suspected, that he had come to harm. But that didn't happen.

Instead, it was just assumed that he received a better job offer and moved on to a different lumber camp. That frequently happened during the decades immediately after the turn of the century. In fact, during that time there was a lot of labor unrest in the timber industry—agitators frequently picketed timber companies trying to obtain better wages or better working conditions. If the protests didn't work, unhappy lumberjacks would simply pull up and move to another camp.

Another motivation for a lumberjack's moving to a different camp often had to do with the condition of the forest he was harvesting. Once a stand of trees had been thinned out, he would not be able to make much money continuing to work it. At that point, he might conclude that he would be able to improve his income by moving on. And often that move occurred unannounced—perhaps even in the middle of the night after payday.

And that's what William was suspected of having done. After all, he had done it before. During the two years prior to his disappearance, he had worked at four different lumber camps. He was not married, or encumbered in any other way, so if he was able to find a better job, he'd suddenly pack up and move. His boss at the Newberry lumber camp knew that when he hired him. But, he also knew William to be a good worker, so he hired him in spite of his record.

That possibility did seem logical. After all, the night he disappeared, October 17, 1924, was the same night he'd been paid. That meant that he had plenty of cash to fund a move. Had he wanted to leave the camp that was the night he'd be most likely to do it.

But, as it turns out, there was evidence which proved that was definitely not what William had done.

Chapter 3—Back in 1924

While the body of William Lawrence Owens was substantially degraded—the contents of his stomach indicated that he had eaten a large supper right before he died, and that he had not chewed much of his food very well—there remained enough of the meal in his stomach to determine that he had consumed a large quantity of beef, and a sizable quantity of what was probably pork and beans. According to records at that camp, beef was always served on Friday nights, and pork and beans frequently accompanied it. The fact that undigested beef was found in William's stomach strongly suggested that he was killed and buried that Friday evening.

One of the other things that lumberjacks were likely to do on a Friday night after they'd been paid was to get drunk.

Frequently a lumberjack would walk into town and visit one of the many taverns, and then, probably a brothel. Or, if he had a girlfriend, he just might choose to buy a bottle of hooch from the camp's resident *moonshiner*, and then meet up with his paramour at the dancehall, or someplace more private—especially if said lady was already married.

From what the family could recall about William, he liked his alcohol just about as much as he liked his women. So, given it was payday, and since it was now obvious that he had not moved to a different camp, the odds were good that he would have gone out looking for the man with the still. And, usually, there were a few of them in or around the community surrounding a working lumber camp.

This particular camp boasted a whole family who were involved in the illicit manufacture and distribution of an alcoholic beverage—corn liquor. Two brothers, Edward and Isaac Pierce, were in charge of that enterprise. Isaac managed the procurement of the raw materials, while older brother Edward oversaw the production process, and was in charge of distribution. Edward also served as the banker and various levels of security. He was what you might call a genuine badass.

Even while working in the woods, which he loved to do, he would never be found without his six-shot long-barreled .45 caliber pistol—a firearm that later was made popular by the fiction writer Ned Buntline. And, still later, was manufactured by Colt under the writer's name. The Colt version was a single action .45 caliber revolver which sported barrels ranging from twelve to sixteen inches. They were called *Colt Buntline Specials*.

Edward Pierce was not only the resident moonshiner, he was the camp's enforcer. And he had lots of help, if and when he might need it. The Pierce family was a large one, with nearly a dozen brothers and cousins who also worked in the woods—several at that camp. But, most often, Edward could solve his own problems. It just so happened that he was several inches taller than any of his brothers—and a lot meaner. Plus, he always wore his signature .45 strapped to his waist, or otherwise attached under his jacket. Family members say he even slept with it on. And, to top it all off, in his right front pocket, he always carried a shiny little device known to the men of that era as *brass knuckles*, *knuckle-dusters*, or just simply *knucks*.

It was common knowledge that no one would ever dare to approach Edward's tarpaper shanty looking to buy hooch. If a man were to shout out, or pound on the door of the shanty Edward shared with his wife Carol, his first reaction would be to fire a warning shot through the door. He would aim high, hopefully missing the visitor's head. The first shot, which would shower the unwanted visitor with slivers of shattered pine, would be followed by a verbal warning: "Get the hell outta here, or you're gonna need a new belt."

There were over a dozen bullet holes through that rough-cut pine door—all from the inside out. The unsuspecting would-be visitors never stuck around for the second shot. With a face full of splinters, they would do as told, and get "the hell outta there" as quickly as possible—sometimes on all fours and with soiled trousers.

Given the willingness to do violence, and the obvious bad attitude of Edward Pierce, and given the likelihood that young William would have been a candidate for going after some hooch on a payday night, it stood to reason that Edward would be a person of interest in a murder investigation.

However, William was not shot with a .45. In fact, he was not shot at all—nor was there any evidence that he was stabbed. He was apparently beaten to death by someone who could punch.

In boxing, the term used to describe a fighter who is particularly skilled at delivering a crushing left hook, or an effective straight right, is "the guy with the heavy hands." Such could be said about Mike Tyson. When he delivered a hook, it was as though he had taken aim at his opponent's spine, and was punching through the poor fellow's ribcage. Mike Tyson had heavy hands. Sonny Liston, and a litany of other great fighters, learned that lesson in their pugilistic encounters with *Iron Mike*—and they had the bruises to prove it.

On the other hand, boxing champ Floyd Mayweather, arguably the greatest pound-for-pound boxer of all time, did not have heavy hands. For his success—he remained unbeaten during his entire professional career—he relied on unmatched speed, immense counterpunching skills, and an innate ability to continually bob and weave more quickly than opponents could throw leather.

The evidence suggested that the man who had beaten young William to death that fateful Friday UP night punched more like a Mike Tyson than a *Money Mayweather*.

The most serious of the injuries sustained by William were about his face. While there was one broken rib on his right side, all the rest of his injuries were to the left side of his face and head. And those inflicted to his skull were consistent with what would be expected if the person delivered the blows with a very heavy right fist.

The left side of his jaw was broken in two places. The bone surrounding his left eye socket was shattered so severely a piece of it was actually driven into his brain. The pathologist who examined William's remains determined that it was likely the blow that shattered his skull beside the left eye was the punch that knocked William unconscious. While that blow would not by itself have proved immediately fatal, it was concluded that any man would have been totally incapacitated by the barrage of blows that he obviously encountered.

How he actually died—that remained a mystery. The pathologist deduced that even though the beating was severe, William might have actually been strangled to death, or perhaps buried alive.

Investigators determined that even in this soft soil it would have taken over an hour for one man to dig the grave. While the hole in which William was buried was narrow, it was deeper than most shallow graves—nearly six feet. If there were two men digging, it would obviously have taken less time. Since even a half an hour would have been a long time for a person to have remained unconscious and silent, it would not be surprising if the killer or killers strangled William before they buried him.

If the killers would have buried William while he was still alive, it might be expected to find soil in his mouth and esophagus, but because the body was so degraded, the existence of such evidence could not be positively determined. However, it could not be totally ruled out either.

All that was known or strongly suspected was that William Lawrence Owens died on Friday night, October 17, 1924, and he did so at the hands of at least one other person, and that he was buried in a grave most likely near to the place where he met his end. *Of those things,* the pathologist determined, *we can be quite certain.*

We also know that he had an attractive young woman named Maria who was very much interested in him. She sent him pictures of herself and wrote several love notes to him. We know from the contents of those missives that Maria was either married, or perhaps engaged to be married, to another man, and that she was very concerned that her significant other might find out about her affair with William. She in fact expressed substantial concern, if not abject fear, about their being found out. These are the notes/letters they left behind:

Letter One:

To My Darling Billy:

You are all I think about during the day. And when I go to bed and close my eyes, you're all I see. You own my dreams. But you already know all that. I've told you a thousand times how much I love you.

You're all I can think about today. I woke up dreaming I'm back in your arms. All day long you're on my mind. It's like my life stops until I hear your voice again. Do you understand? I love you. I think <u>only</u> of you. I am and will be faithful to you alone. You must never doubt me. Although I live under the same roof as another man, you are my true love. My very breath. My everything. My love.

Soon we must declare our love. I can't bear this much longer. He will begin to see he's lost me. I can't continue to hide it. He is a good man. But he is not, nor will he ever be, my man.

When he holds me I want to pull away. I'm repulsed at the thought of being with him. I must be with you. I can't go on. We must talk about this when we are together again. Very soon, I hope. There has to be a way. I will love you forever.

All my love Always, Maria

Letter Two:

Darling Billy:

I hope I see you when I pick up supplies. I write this note just in case I do. You say that when we're apart you're sad. Me too, my love. Always. You're unhappy that I am with my husband at night. I call him my "husband" and not by name because if this letter is ever read by another, it wouldn't do that his name be known. He really isn't my husband by any sense of law. We never got a marriage license. I think we should run off someplace together. Maybe go west. Some night after you get paid. Borrow a car and leave the camp together. I need to go to bed with you. And wake up with you. Taste your kisses when I open my eyes. Just you and me. I'm saving every penny I can. Sometimes my husband gives me money for supplies, and if I'm careful, I can keep some of it. I sold some oatmeal to Carol. It wasn't much, but it would buy us a few miles. I could leave the baby with her for the day. And we could leave in the morning. You get paid on Friday. We could leave on Monday. We would have a full day before anyone would miss us. Sleep in the car, and keep driving. We could get jobs in Deadwood. That's in South Dakota I think. I've read about that. I could cook and clean, or work in a shop. You could find a job in timber or in a sawmill. We could do it. I keep a bag packed and ready. I must be with you all the time. If even for a moment I lose hope, I break down and cry. Please. I know you love me. Please take us away from here.

All my love Always, Maria

Letter Three:

To My Darling Billy:

It pains me so to be apart. Last night I cried myself to sleep. My husband gets drunk every night. I think he might get fired. He barely crawls out of the house in the morning. Last night he threw up in bed. I had to sleep on a rug. Covered up with coats. Today Carol and I are doing laundry. I can't take this much longer. I must be with you. Lately I've been given to melancholy. I know you are sad too. I love you. Do you know what that means? I am and will always be faithful to you. You and I are nothing like my husband and me. We had to get married when I got pregnant (although we really didn't get married officially). I can't wait until we are together again. I expect it will be shortly, and I am saving up my love for you.

All my love Always, Maria

Letter Four:

To My Darling Billy:

My heart is dancing. Our time together yesterday was just marvelous. And what you said was even better. At least part of what you said was wonderful—that we must leave the camp together. Let's just do it. Let's run away from here. Two paydays, with what I've saved up, would get us to Deadwood. I know it. All we need is a car, and you can borrow one. When we get settled, we can return it and then take a train back to Deadwood. It's so beautiful there I've heard. Of course, any place on earth would be beautiful if you were there with me.

But you did make me cry too. When you doubt my love it makes me very sad. I love you with all my heart. I don't think it makes sense, but you must realize that it would not be possible for me not to love you. There is nothing you could do to make me stop loving you. You own me heart and soul. You should never be jealous, or doubt me in any way. My love for you is endless. I will always love you. It's wrong to distrust me. I have never and will never give you reason not to trust me completely. That's just the way my love is for you. There is, and will always be, no room in my heart for any other. You must believe me about that. We must be together forever. Until I take my last breath I will love you.

All my love Always, Maria

Letter Five:

Darling Billy:

My life here with my husband is becoming unbearable. I'm sure he knows that I don't have feelings for him anymore. Please, let's leave here, before he starts suspecting something. He has such a temper. And, he has a lot of friends and family—especially Edward, his brother. If he knew about you, I think he would hurt you—his brother would help him. They would hurt you badly. I know you are a big strong man. But my husband can be real mean. And even though he doesn't really love me, and he never has, he would not just let me go. He has never hit me, so I don't worry about that. But I know he would hurt you.

I don't think he suspects you and me. Not yet. If he did, he would just blurt it out when he was drunk. Which lately has been all of the time—he's been drunk a lot that is. He just says things like "Don't you love me anymore? Did I do something that made you mad?" Stuff like that. Poor man, he blames himself. Truth is, I have never loved him. Not really. He's always had a bad smell about him. He bathes every week, and I keep his clothes clean. But something about him does not smell good. Don't know what it is, but it's always been that way. I just wish to God that I would never have let him touch me. Then I would not have to leave our poor child without a mother. I know Carol will take good care of him, but it makes me sad. And I'm sure my husband will provide for him after I leave. He always has money. And he's generous. I know the child will be okay. But I won't be, unless I can be with you day and night. Soon, let's leave soon. Next week? Before he finds out. Please think about it. And then let's just do it.

All my love Always, Maria

Letter Six:

My Dear Billy:

I'm really scared. I think something is up. My sister-in-law Carol asked me questions about you, like she suspected something. Maybe someone saw us yesterday? I don't know. Maybe her husband Edward asked her about us. But she even knew your name. She asked me if I knew a man named Billy Owens, that some people knew you as William Owens. I don't like to lie, but I told her that I didn't know you. I asked her why she was wondering about you, and if she knew you. She said she didn't know you either, and then she quickly changed the subject. She seemed worried about something. Like there was something she wasn't telling me. Or maybe I am just imagining. But I don't think so. I know her pretty well. Why would she just up and ask me about you?

You get paid tomorrow. I've saved up some money. I got nearly twenty dollars. You said you had saved up eighty dollars. With what you get paid tomorrow, we'll have well over a hundred and fifty dollars. That would buy enough gasoline to get us to Deadwood, easy. I'll make up some sandwiches. So let's leave Monday morning, right after my husband goes to work. I'll ask him for money to buy supplies. I'll drop the baby off with Carol and tell her I need to go to the store. You pick me up at our usual place, and we'll just keep on going. If you're not there by nine o'clock, I'll know that you've changed your mind about us. Oh, Billy, I hope you're there. I hope that you feel the same way about me that I feel about you. I think you love me. But I will understand. It's hard for you to just pull up stakes and give up good steady work. I understand what you must be feeling. Whatever you decide, I will be at our place at nine in the morning, and I will wait five minutes. Please, my darling, please be there and pick me up.

I love you with all my love as always, your Maria

At the time, and without these letters, it was virtually impossible to piece together the details surrounding the murder of young William, particularly with regard to the other people in the camp who might have had some knowledge of the man's disappearance.

Whether due to his history of moving from one lumber camp to another, or perhaps because William had no immediate family in the area, his disappearance did not arouse much attention. After a week, his few belongings were shoved into a couple of pillowcases and stored at the company office, and a letter was sent to Mrs. Agnes Cross, William's next of kin. It indicated that:

> William has apparently left the camp with no plans to return. He did leave behind a few of his personal belongings. You may pick them up at the camp's office at your convenience. We will store them for you for the next six weeks, after which time they will be disposed of. If you know of his whereabouts, please advise him of this.
>
> According to our books, William's pay record is up to date, as he left immediately after receiving his wages. Thank you for your consideration in this matter, and please let him know that we appreciated his good work here at the camp, but would have appreciated even more had he notified us as to his plans to leave. We do wish him the best.
>
> Sincerely yours, Sherman Fox, Camp Manager.

The reason the camp boss suggested that William had moved to another camp is because that was the story circulated by those who had worked with him—primarily by Edward and Isaac Pierce. The rumor was that he had a friend who had promised him a job cutting timber downstate near Manistee, and that it was a virgin stand. The story went on that William would make more money at the new job, and that the weather would be a little less harsh during the upcoming winter months.

There was some talk initially about the possibility that William had run off with the wife of one of the other lumberjacks, but that story quickly died out when none of the women in the camp turned up missing.

One other story did percolate for months after William's disappearance. That involved the possibility that William met with foul play at the hands of Edward and Isaac Pierce, the camp's resident hooch makers. One version of it was that he had got drunk and tried to force his way into Edward's shanty, and that Edward shot him through the door.

A second version of the story also involved the Pierce brothers. According to that narrative, William had been screwing Isaac's wife, and when Edward and Isaac heard about it, they lured William out in the woods with the promise of selling him some liquor, and there they shot and killed him.

But that story did not attract many adherents because no one could recall having heard any gunfire on that Friday night. And if Edward had shot William, it would have been with his huge .45 caliber pistol, and someone in the camp would have heard and remembered the event.

Much of this information was dug up by William's sister Agnes and her husband, John Cross. Soon after Agnes had received the notification concerning her brother's disappearance, she and John set out via railroad from Grand Rapids to pick up his belongings, and to see what they could learn as to what had become of William.

After meeting briefly with Sherman Fox, and receiving two pillowcases containing William's possessions, Agnes and John headed back to Grand Rapids. It was obvious to them that Mr. Fox was not pleased that one of his best workers just up and left the camp without giving any notice, so they did not wish to stick around asking questions. In fact, Mr. Fox offered little help at all, unless moderately restrained criticism could be considered helpful. They did not even take the time to inspect the contents of the pillowcases, aside from a cursory visual examination without studying any of the individual items.

But on the train ride back to Grand Rapids, Agnes removed every article individually and examined it. She was looking for a clue as to what might have become of her younger brother.

"I'm going to inspect one item at a time," she said to John. "I will describe it as best I can, and you write down what we find. Sort of like an annotated inventory."

What she found shocked both her and her husband.

Chapter 4—1924

Because this type of project required a great deal of careful scrutiny it suited John well. He had started out his career at seventeen when he became a clerk in a grocery store on Michigan Street near Eastern Avenue. The train came through next to his store dropping off supplies and coal, he offered credit and home deliveries, and his store became one of the more popular markets in Grand Rapids. He saved nearly every penny he earned, and four years later he became a partner. After spending another six years at that job, he was able to buy out the entire enterprise. Shortly thereafter, the opportunity presented itself and he sold the store and became the chief bookkeeper at Grand Rapids Bank and Trust. And then, ten years after joining the bank, he was promoted to the position of bank president.

In the jargon of the twenty-first century, John could well be described as a human Excel file.

Once they were comfortably seated on the train to Grand Rapids, Agnes started with the pillowcase that from the outside appeared to contain only her brother's clothes. The first item she pulled out was a stack of neatly folded flannel shirts. They were held together with a piece of brown binder twine.

"I'm confident that William didn't care for his clothing like this," she said. "Obviously someone took the time to launder these items, and then to tie them in little bundles. I'm not going to loosen this string until we get home, or I might not be able to get everything back into the bag. Looks to be four or five flannel shirts. Just put 'four clean flannel shirts' on your list."

Next was a bundle of trousers—it was also tied with a similar piece of binder twine.

"Looks like there are four pair of work pants."

She set them down on top of the shirts and removed the next bundle.

"Four sets of long underwear."

"Seven pair of socks."

"Four bandanas."

The next item she pulled out was a pair of dress shoes. She sat holding them for a long moment before she said anything.

"One pair of black dress shoes."

And then she started to cry.

"Aggy," John said as he placed his arm around her to console her. "Aggy. I know what you're thinking. But we don't know anything for a fact. William was a free and easy, fun-loving sort of man. Just because he left behind his clothes doesn't mean a thing. It's true, I know that if I were pulling up stakes and moving, I would have taken my clothes with me. But William isn't me. He would do things like this—on the spur of the moment. So, don't let yourself get all worked up about something that just might not be the case.

"As it stands right now, we really do not have any evidence whatsoever—for good or ill. We just can't know anything until he writes us and lets us know where he is. And when he does, I will personally take his belongings to him. Wherever he's living at the time. You and I will take this stuff, and deliver it to him. That's all—that's *all* we can do.

"But, as far as assuming that something's happened to him— we just can't go there. We must assume the best. We have to hope for the best."

"I know William is immature," Agnes said, still crying. "But I can't imagine anyone moving to a new job, and leaving his dress shoes behind. I know he had only one pair. He absolutely would not have gone off without them. Not if he wasn't planning to return in a day or two."

"Think like this," John said. "What if he met up with someone at a tavern? Maybe an old buddy he'd worked with before. And his friend told him that there was a job opening in a nearby town, but that he'd have to jump at it right then, or they'd hire someone else. And what if the two of them drove all night so he could offer his services in person. You and I both know how convincing William could be. What if he got the job, but that he had to start that day or he would lose it.

"That is exactly how William was," John continued. "If it was something that he wanted to do, he would weigh everything, and make a firm decision. He would do it, just like that. And some time later he would show up at our house asking if old man Fox sent his belongings on to us. Because that's what he'd expect. That's why he left our address with his boss. It could be just like that. And all your crying and sadness will have been for nothing."

"You might be right. William would do something just like that. And it *was* payday. Nothing was owed him, so he could have decided to pull out and move, if that's what he wanted to do. And he might not want anyone to see what he was doing. I know you're right. It's just that it's so hard going through his clothes. I've washed and folded those very same shirts. When he moved in with us last year. I remember each of those shirts. It's all he had.

"But, if he did leave with just the clothes on his back, he's for certain going to want to get these things back. He'd need them for work. No matter *where* he was, he couldn't get along without them. All he could possibly have with him are a pair of work boots, work pants, underwear, a shirt, a pair of gloves, and his Mackinaw. That's probably it. I can't help it. I'm worried."

With that, Agnes shoved all of William's clothes back into the pillowcase, and then jammed it all, as best she could, under her seat. But, the day they got back to Grand Rapids, they removed everything and spread it out on the dining room table and carefully examined every aspect of each individual item.

Chapter 5—The Fourth Thursday of October, Current Year

"Jack," Henry said, "I want you to meet the cousin I told you about. This is Bill Pierce. He's the one who's got the questions about his family."

Jack had been sitting out by the St. Mary's River in his Adirondack chair. It was one of those beautiful nights, after a storm, and the clouds had moved on leaving pinks and oranges in the sky to delicately reflect on the water. He loved evenings like this, but could only handle so many nights of relaxing before he realized he needed a bit of excitement in his life.

"Hello, Bill, nice to meet you," Jack said. "So, you two are related, are you? Well, Bill, I promise I will not hold it against you—that you're related to this mangy Henry character."

Henry, observing that Bill was a little taken aback at Jack's comment, countered, "Right, Jack. I already warned my cousin that you were full of shit. So, you won't have to try to convince him. He already knows you're a sonofabitch."

Bill did not know how to respond. Here he was—stuck between two very powerful men, either one of whom could break him in half like a #2 pencil.

"You guys are pulling my leg? Right?"

"You could say that," Jack said, reaching out to shake Bill's hand. "Henry here is without doubt the best friend I've ever had. If you don't count Buddy, my son's retriever. But, I suppose that would be an unfair comparison. ...Anyway, Bill, Henry tells me that you've recently learned that there might be some surprises in your lineage. And that you'd like us to help you get to the bottom of it. Is that about it?"

"That's what they're telling me."

They decided to meet on the mainland in about an hour. Jack wanted to make sure his boys, Red and Robby, had dinner and were settled in for the night.

It was nine-thirty on this Thursday evening. The three men were sitting around a table at Moloney's Alley in Sault Ste. Marie. The barmaid had just served them their first round of Two-Hearted Ale.

"Why don't you fill me in on all the details that you know for a fact, and then tell me about what you suspect. Just keep the two separate."

"That's gonna mean some very boring genealogy. This goes back three, four generations."

"Not boring. I think that's what this is all about. Besides, no conversation is ever boring when you're with friends, and you're drinking a good beer. So spill it—not your beer, of course."

Jack's lame attempt at humor accomplished what he had intended—it put Bill at ease.

"This is what I know. My full name is William Lawrence Pierce. I was born in 1981 in Newberry, Michigan. My mother's name was Maggie. I was an only child. My father's name was the same as mine—William Lawrence Pierce. He was born in 1950, also in Newberry. His mother's name was Jessica. He had one sister, LucyAnne. She was stillborn. And a younger brother, George. He died in the Vietnam War. He was never married.

"My grandfather was also named William Lawrence Pierce. He was born in Rapid City, South Dakota on February 8, 1925.

His mother's name was Maria Pierce. She and her husband, Isaac Pierce, were divorced right after my grandfather was born. His name at birth was James Edwin, but his mother had it changed to William Lawrence right after he was born."

"That seems a little strange, don't you think?" Jack asked.

"For sure," Bill agreed. "I've always been curious as to why she did that. But certain events that occurred only this year might shed some light on that part of my family's strange history."

Jack at this point pulled out a small black notebook and pen from his jacket pocket and started making notes.

"Okay," he said as he leaned back in his chair, "I can see that this story is going to require at least one more Two-Hearted Ale. Henry. You're in charge of keeping full bottles in front of us. All right, Bill, let's hear your story. Just try to be as concise as possible."

"Three months ago I got this letter from a lawyer. At first I thought it was some kind of a phony promotion, so I just tossed it. And then, after another month or so, I received another letter. From that same lawyer. This one I had to sign for, so I read it this time.

"It said that this lawyer, Craig Conklin, had been retained by someone named Claire Mansfield. Apparently, this Mansfield woman had been named the executor of the estate of Agnes Owens. Agnes was Ms. Mansfield's grandmother.

"In her will—Agnes's will, that is—Ms. Mansfield's mother, Grace, and Agnes' brother, William Lawrence Owens, were originally named beneficiaries of the estate. The problem was that this William fellow went missing back in 1924. It seems as though he totally disappeared off the face of the earth."

"That's a hell of a long time ago," Jack said. "What could your involvement possibly be?"

"That was my question. I don't trust lawyers. Every time I've had to deal with one, I ended up getting my pocket picked. I didn't want to respond to the letter, so I didn't.

"But then, I got a call from this Claire Mansfield herself. She asked to meet with me. She said that it was possible that I was somehow related to her, and that she would like to find out for sure, one way or the other.

"Before I'd talk to her I asked her if this was going to cost me anything. I'd heard about these scams that tell a person they have inherited some money, but that they had to pay someone in order to get it. I didn't want anything to do with that sort of deal. But, she assured me that it would cost me nothing, and that she'd even pay for the coffee.

"I told her that I'd be happy to pay for my own coffee, and that I'd be willing to sit down with her. And so we did. We got together at a coffee shop in Munising. We had a coffee and a donut at the Falling Rock coffee shop and bookstore there on the main drag."

"I know where that is," Jack said. "And, when was this? Do you know specifically?"

"Two weeks ago. Thursday the tenth. We met at one-thirty in the afternoon. After the lunch crowd."

"So, what did she tell you?"

"She said that her grandmother, Agnes Owens Cross, had a brother. His name was William Lawrence Owens. Of course, that got my attention—my name being William Lawrence, just like his. And it seems that he had disappeared in 1924. At the time he was working at a lumber camp over by Newberry. After a few years most people thought that he had died. Maybe got drunk and fell in a river. Or got himself killed in a poker game—something like that. But there never was a body to prove it.

"Agnes, the sister, was not willing to believe that her brother was dead. She always thought that he had moved to another lumber camp, or maybe out west someplace. But she wouldn't accept that he might have died—not until someone actually found his body. She always held out hope. She died in 1950, never finding out what had become of her brother.

"But then, this Mansfield lady told me something very interesting. Just recently contractors found his body—William Owens's body. They were excavating for a new construction development near Newberry, and there he was. And it turned out to be that he had been murdered—probably the same day he had disappeared. The spot where he'd been buried was actually on the site of the original lumber camp. That was a couple years ago, Ms. Mansfield told me. When the body was discovered."

"Well," Jack said, "I'd say that the man who killed him definitely got away with it. What's that been, now? Whoever it was that did the murder—by now he's been dead a generation himself. Not sure how you think I can help you."

"There's more to this story. A *lot* more. We haven't got to the good part yet."

"Henry," Jack said. "Another round. Okay, Bill, let's hear the *good* part."

"Well, apparently the news about the brother being murdered renewed Ms. Mansfield's interest in her great-uncle's case. So she started doing some investigating herself. Sometime earlier her grandmother had given her an old photo album that had belonged to William. And she found that one of the covers on the album was thicker than the other—I think it was the back cover. She said it looked like it had been made that way, with a slot on the top where a person could hide some pictures or letters, and no one would find them without doing a real careful examination.

"It was in that secret pocket that she found a signed picture of a beautiful young woman, and a note from that same woman. She had a copy of it with her and she showed me.

"It seems that this William had won the heart of a married woman named Maria Pierce—same last name as me—and that he had got her pregnant. She, Ms. Mansfield, gave me a copy of that note. Would you like to see it?"

"Why don't you just read it to me," Jack said. "The lighting in here isn't so great. Is it a *long* letter?"

"It's just a note. One page. It's not very long. I'll read it. All of the notes start out in a similar fashion. Ms. Mansfield let me read them all. But the one I copied and brought with me, that is the only one that she believed was relevant to our current situation—question.

> To My Darling Billy:
>
> You are all I think about during the day. And when I go to bed and close my eyes, you're all I see. You own my dreams. But you already know all that. I've told you a thousand times how much I love you.
>
> You're all I can think about today. I woke up dreaming I'm back in your arms. All day long you're on my mind. It's like my life stops until I hear your voice again. Do you understand? I love you. I think <u>only</u> of you. I am and will be faithful to you alone. You must never doubt me. Although I live under the same roof as another man, you are my true love. My very breath. My everything. My love.
>
> Soon we must declare our love. I can't bear this much longer. He will begin to see he's lost me. I can't continue to hide it. He is a

good man. But he is not, nor will he ever be, my man.

When he holds me I want to pull away. I'm repulsed at the thought of being with him. I must be with you. I can't go on. We must talk about this when we are together again. Very soon, I hope. There has to be a way. I will love you forever.

All my love Always, Maria

"That's it. Ms. Mansfield suggested that the baby she was expecting might be my grandfather—William Lawrence Pierce."

"That's quite a jump," Jack said. "How do we get from Owens to Pierce?"

"Ms. Mansfield told me that her grandmother found out that there were two men who left her brother's camp suddenly. Just like her brother. They were brothers, Edward and Isaac Pierce. She found out that the brothers left the next week with their wives, and moved to Deadwood, South Dakota. And here are some of the interesting parts—Isaac Pierce's wife was named Maria, and she was said to be a very beautiful woman.

"And, these brothers were both troublemakers. The older one always carried a long-barreled .45. Now, I realize that the body of the man that was found apparently was not shot, but the gun part does demonstrate the state of mind these brothers reflected. Also, the two of them were moonshiners—again showing that they were not law abiding.

"Ms. Mansfield was thinking that Maria might have been pregnant at that time. That could have been why the brothers and their wives left the camp so abruptly. She considered that there might have been some question as to who got her pregnant. She, Ms. Mansfield, thought that the father might have been her great-uncle—William Lawrence Owens. And that immediately before or after her baby was born, Maria might have divorced her husband, and then moved back to the UP. Back to Newberry, to be more specific. Since that's where she was originally from.

"I always wondered about my name—William Lawrence. I was told that, officially, my *great*-grandfather's name was Isaac Pierce. But, as far as I know, prior to Isaac, there were no other *William Lawrences* in my family's history. At least none that I could find. And I do know that my great-grandparents did split up just about the time my grandfather was born. But I didn't know about any of the specifics.

"My grandfather did eventually move south from Newberry, settling in the Grand Rapids area. Which is, as you know, in the Lower Peninsula. That's where my great-grandmother—Maria—remarried. Her new husband's last name was Schwartz—Roland Schwartz. My grandfather kept the name Pierce. But, my grandfather's sibling—his older brother—took Schwartz for his last name."

"That's all very interesting," Jack said. "But just how badly do you want to get to the bottom of this? There are websites, you know. You can plug in a name and for a small fee it will kick out your lineage. That would be a hell of a lot cheaper than engaging your cousin Henry and me. We will be as generous with our time as possible, but it is going to cost money."

"Yeah, I know all about that. I even gave it a try. From what I learned, it is entirely possible that my great-grandfather was this William Lawrence Owens. But, nothing can be documented regarding his lineage. At least, not yet. That's where I thought you might help me."

"And finding this out, definitively. Just why would that be so important to you?" Jack asked.

"I'm not a rich man," Bill said. "But, there seems to be enough evidence, at least on the surface, that I am a direct descendant of William Lawrence Owens. But, nothing beyond that—nothing suggesting that would connect me to William Lawrence Owens. That would require further investigation. By someone who is good at it. Because, if it can be proven that I am the great-grandson of this William Lawrence Owens, I stand to inherit a great deal of money."

Jack glanced up from his beer and stared into Bill's eyes. He then exchanged a smile with Henry. Jack finished off his beer and set the bottle on the table. "Okay, you've got my attention. Tell me more. Tell me more about that potential inheritance."

Chapter 6

The three men, Jack, Henry, and Henry's cousin, William Lawrence Pierce, remained at Maloney's Pub until closing. The single topic of discussion was anything and everything William could recall regarding his family history.

"Like I explained," Jack said. "If Henry and I dig deeply into this matter, there's going to be some substantial cost to you. We would be happy to take a look. To see if we thought it would warrant a more thorough investigation. For that, we would not charge you.

"But, if it looks like there might be good reason to think that your grandfather just might be the son of this lumberjack who went missing, this William Lawrence *Owens*. Then, at that point, we will begin logging billable hours, plus expenses.

"And then, if it turns out that Henry and I are confident that we can prove lineage, we will expect to be paid."

"That sounds very fair," Bill replied.

"Just so we know what we're getting into," Jack said. "What sort of inheritance would that proof earn for you? It seems a little strange that this Mansfield woman would be seeking out someone to *split* her inheritance with. Because, isn't that what this would mean? If we are able to demonstrate that you are a legitimate heir, would that not require her to split her inheritance with you?"

"In a sense, yes it would," Bill explained. "But, there's a stipulation in the will that has limited her ability to collect the total that might be due her."

"Okay, Bill," Jack said. "Explain that to me. And tell me just how much *you* might expect to receive. Because I can tell you upfront, even at a substantially discounted rate, Henry and I could easily rack up a $30,000 tab. Especially if we have to travel out to South Dakota to investigate. Is there enough in it to warrant that kind of costs? As I said, if we accept this job, and if it turns out that we cannot definitively prove that you're related to this William Owens fellow, then there will be no cost to you at all—aside from legitimate out-of-pocket expenses. We will do what we can to hold them down. But, like I said, they could still be substantial.

"If, however, we can successfully establish your right to the inheritance, and you are able to collect it, then you would pay us up to that $30K, plus expenses. Does that sound fair to you?"

"More than fair. What you're saying is that you'd be willing to take a look at my situation, and if it looks promising, you'd take a closer look. But, if you were not able to connect the dots in such a way so as to convince you that you might win my inheritance, then you'd not charge me anything. Is that about it?"

"That's it," Jack said. "At that point all we would have invested is some of our time. No charge for that. But, you still haven't told me if you stand to gain enough to warrant the type of expenditure we're talking about. It could be thirty large, or possibly even more. Five hundred dollars a day, times two. That's our family rate. Plus expenses. We'll provide a weekly list of charges. The thirty grand would reflect our charge if totally successful. Does that line up with what you expected? Just how much do you stand to gain if all of this works out in your favor?"

"Millions."

Jack looked over at Henry and said, "I'd say your cousin answered my question. What do you think, Henry? Do we have time for one more round?"

Henry turned and glanced over at the bartender. He held up three fingers. The bartender nodded.

"So," Bill asked, "what's first on your agenda?"

"Not quite so fast. First, I need you to put in writing everything you know about your family history. And I do mean *everything*—names, dates and places. Qualify each entry in one of three ways. Tag it with an *A* if you're ninety percent certain that it's accurate. A *B* if you're only fifty percent sure. And a *C* if you suspect it might be rumor."

"That's gonna be a hell of a lot of work," Bill complained. "It's gonna take a while."

Jack allowed Bill's words to sink in for a moment.

And then he said, "How much do you earn in a week?"

"It depends. I'm a service technician. I repair household appliances. I have my own business. I average between ten and twenty service calls a week. Maybe I make fifty on each. Sometimes nothing. Maybe a couple hundred. It depends."

"Okay. Say you have ten calls in a given week. And you make a hundred dollars on each of them. That would be an even grand. One thousand dollars.

"Now, I told you that even at a reduced rate, if successful, our charges will likely be in the range of thirty thousand dollars—more or less a few grand. If you spend ten or twenty hours putting together your family history, it might be a little unpleasant for you, but it sounds like it might cost you five hundred or so in lost fees. But, it could save you several thousand dollars in our time saved."

"Yeah," Bill chuckled. "Sorry about that. I understand. It's just that my handwriting sucks, and I don't have a typewriter. I'm a little embarrassed about it."

"Do you have any children?" Jack asked.

"My daughter is a whiz on the computer. I'll have her type it up for me."

"There you go. That would be perfect. When you have your daughter type this up for you, have her load the file on a thumb drive. And, I would suggest that you not get into too much detail about the financial ramifications. She could get the wrong idea. Just leave that out altogether."

"Right."

"But, I would like you to tell Henry and me just how this whole story looks to play out—financially. You should spell that out right now. But don't commit it to writing. Okay? Explain it to us, as simply as possible, just how it is that this Mansfield woman might have this much money to throw around?"

Chapter 7

"It's not like Ms. Mansfield wants to throw money around," Bill said. "She's a pretty level-headed woman as far as I can see. And, in this case, she doesn't make the rules. It was her grandmother who set the system up. Agnes Cross—formerly Agnes Owens, the sister of William Lawrence Owens—the fellow who went missing in '24. I guess she planned the whole thing out."

"Approximately how much money are you thinking that this would end up being for you? You suggested millions. Were you exaggerating?"

"I don't think so. John Cross, Agnes's husband, was a very astute businessman. He was a banker and business owner. He invested in several businesses. Made a *lot* of money. But when he died, Agnes sold everything except for the family home in Grand Rapids, and a small department store. And she invested all the rest of the money in stock—namely DuPont stock.

"She lived well into her late nineties. And she ran the little store in Grand Rapids right up until she passed. In her will she named her granddaughter Claire, and her brother, that would be Agnes's brother, William, as the beneficiaries. Claire's mother, Grace, had died giving birth to her only child—that would have been Claire. And even though Agnes's brother hadn't been heard from in several decades, she never gave up on him.

"She stipulated in her will that upon her death, Claire would receive half of the estate immediately, but Agnes's brother, William, his half would remain invested in stock until he came forward to claim it, or until it could be proven that he was no longer alive.

"And, she further stipulated that William's body must actually be found and positively identified in order to qualify as proof of his passing. And even if it could be demonstrated that William was deceased, if William had children, then his inheritance would pass on to his offspring.

"However, if neither William nor his children ever turned up, then, when the last of Claire's children died, William's share would be divided up among a group of charities. She listed them specifically as well. But, if Claire or any of her children are still living, and William's body turns up, and it cannot be adequately demonstrated that the brother left any children, then, Claire would receive William's share of the inheritance."

"Really?" Jack blurted. "That is just about the most convoluted bunch of BS that I have ever heard."

"That's because I put it in my own words," Bill said. "The will itself spells it out quite clearly. Very detailed. I could even understand it. I can get you a copy of it if you wish."

"No need. It's on file I'm sure. But the part I find confusing is this Mansfield's motive. Seems like if she were just to let it run its course, she would be in a position to claim William's share uncontested."

"That's what I thought, too. But something else happened that threw new light on the whole thing."

"Damn, just when I thought it couldn't get more complicated," Jack said through a broad smile.

"That's right," Bill agreed. "It does get a little crazy."

"What happened?"

"As soon as William's body was unearthed, a woman came forward with an interesting story. Her name was Nellie Francis.

She said she was the granddaughter of Maria Schwartz. She said her grandmother's name had originally been Maria Pierce, and that she had remarried. The new husband was named Roland Schwartz.

"She said that before she had died, Maria had told Nellie's mother a very interesting story. She said that she had been married to a man named Isaac Pierce, and that she had become pregnant and had a baby while they were married. But that Isaac was not the real father, and that her husband had at some point figured that out—that Maria had not been faithful to him—so when the baby was born, he kicked Maria and the baby out.

"Nellie wasn't exactly sure about the timeline, and maybe her grandmother got kicked out of the house even before the baby was born. At any rate, Isaac Pierce did kick Maria out either before or right after the child was born.

"Maria had explained to Nellie's mother that when she was young she had fallen in love with a man her husband worked with at a lumber camp near Newberry. But she wouldn't say what this man's name was. And that this lover was actually the father of her baby.

"Apparently, Nellie's grandmother had moved from Newberry to South Dakota when she was pregnant. Nellie recalled that her mother had told her that the baby's name was William Lawrence Pierce. She, Maria, had decided to keep the legal family name of Pierce for the baby, but to give him the name *William Lawrence.* No one understood where she came up with that name—William Lawrence. And then, at some point, she took the baby and moved back to Newberry.

"In retrospect, Nellie thinks that Maria went back to Newberry in an effort to see if she could find her lover—the real father of the baby. She would not have known that he was dead. Besides, she really had no place to live—being kicked out and all.

"So," William continued, "when this body turns up in Newberry, with the names so similar, Nellie puts two and two together and concludes that this dead guy just might be the father of her grandmother's baby.

"Apparently my granddad did not remain close to his sister—that would have been Nellie's mother. So, since Nellie did not know how to reach her uncle, she went to the sheriff and told him her story. The sheriff then contacted the attorneys who were executing Agnes's will—and, that's how I come into the story.

"They did a search for men named William Lawrence *Pierce*, and they found me. Actually, they found my father first. That was his name. I was named after him."

"But," Jack said, "I still don't fully grasp the reason Ms. Mansfield is so aggressively trying to prove that you are an heir. How can that possibly work to her advantage?"

"That's because there was an additional stipulation in Agnes's will. It states that should it be demonstrated that her brother had a child, and if that child dies before inheriting his share, half of that inheritance would go to that child's offspring. And, the other half would pass on to her—Agnes's—offspring.

"What that means is this: if Claire can prove that I am a direct descendant of William Owens, because my father has already passed away, she would be in line to receive half of whatever is left in the estate."

"Wow!" Jack marveled. "That sure was an involved set of requirements. Are you pretty confident you understand them all correctly?"

"Oh, yes. I spent an afternoon with the lawyers and Ms. Mansfield. They explained it to me six ways to Sunday, and I got it. I might not have explained it very well, or entirely accurate. But that was the gist of it.

"If we can show positively that I am a direct descendant of William Lawrence Owens, I will receive eleven million dollars. At least that would be half of the current value of the stock. And Claire Mansfield will also receive an equal amount. Otherwise, it all goes to charity—twenty-two million dollars. The latest records are from two years ago. So, it should be a little more than that by now."

"On second thought," Jack said, "why don't you have a copy of that document—the will—sent to me. Include it with your report, or your history—whatever you want to call the paper you're going to put together. Just include a copy of what you received. We need to make sure that there were no changes made."

"I will take care of that right away," Bill said. "And there was one more thing. Another stipulation. There is a time limit involved."

Chapter 8

Jack and Henry were getting tired. They wanted to wind up the discussion and go home. But, the last words that had just come out of Bill's mouth got Jack's attention.

"*A time limit?*" Jack asked. "What exactly does that mean?"

"I have ninety days to file my proof of lineage, or I lose the money—actually, we *all* lose the money."

Jack looked over at Henry and said, "Ninety days. That's a pretty long time, as long as we get going on it right away."

"That was ninety days from the date the body was positively identified."

"And how long ago was that?" Jack asked.

Bill looked at his watch.

"It's one A.M. right now," he said. "As of right now, we have nine days, plus twenty-three hours. At least that's what I'm counting after all those beers. I think nine days."

"You have to be shittin' me!" Jack complained. "Why the hell did you wait so long?"

"Like I said, at first I thought it was one of those scams. I really didn't take it seriously. Not until Ms. Mansfield called me. Then I began to think there might be something to it."

"Hey, Buck," Jack yelled over to the bartender. "Send two more bottles of Two-Hearted Ale over here."

"You mean three?" the bartender asked.

"No. Just two. My friend Bill here—he's done drinking for the night. Make it four. Two for me and two for Henry. And we might need to stay here while you clean up. We've got a little work to do."

Jack then laid his phone down on the table and told Bill to give him a call.

"I want you to tell me *everything* you can remember about this whole matter. Forget about identifying what parts you know for certain, and what you might be guessing about. Just spill the whole story. *Everything*. And I'll record it. And give me every phone number and email address where you can be reached. I want everything you can think of—right here and right now."

Even though the three men remained at the bar until closing, they wasted no time. Before Jack and Henry headed back to the Handler's Sugar Island Resort they had wound up squeezing out of Bill all of the information he had, including a possible contact in Deadwood. When they got back to the resort, they immediately packed a couple duffels and locked it up.

"Enough to last us a few days," Jack advised Henry. "That's about all we've got."

It was two-thirty in the morning by the time they hit the road.

"I'll drive until I get tired," Jack said. "You get some sleep first, and I'll wake you up when I need to be spelled.

"I'm thinking I should be good at least until we hit I-94 in Wisconsin—that's maybe three hundred miles. You could take over then and get us through Minnesota and into South Dakota and I'll get a little rest. I want to head straight into Deadwood. We'll get our business done and see where it takes us."

"Deadwood," Henry said. "Isn't that where Hickok got shot in that poker game?"

"Aces and Eights—the infamous 'Deadman's Hand.'"

"Right. Did you catch any of those episodes of *Deadwood*? That TV drama. With Timothy Olyphant?"

"No, I didn't," Jack answered. "Were they good?"

"Olyphant's a pretty good actor. I think he did a great job with it. But the interesting thing about the show was the nature of the dialog. For me, it took a little getting used to. At first I thought it seemed stilted. But then, once I'd watched a couple episodes, it struck me as being almost Shakespearean except for the cussing. Never heard so much cussing."

"You need to get some sleep, my friend," Jack said.

"You're right. Excuse me. I'll see you in a few hours."

Jack had taken this route west before: I-75 south to M-28, follow it through Newberry and Marquette. Catch US-41and head toward Green Bay and Appleton, and then all the way down to I-90. Jack knew that would take them through Rapid City and Sturgis, and finally to Deadwood—over eleven hundred miles in all.

If all went well they should arrive in Deadwood around eight the next evening.

"What are we lookin' to find in Deadwood?" Henry asked after nearly an hour of silence.

"What the hell!" Jack blurted. "You're supposed to be getting some sleep."

"Can't," Henry said. "At least not right now. So, where to first?"

"I thought we'd have a drink at Seven Stallions Saloon."

"Really?" Henry said. "Isn't that the very place where Hickok was shot?"

"That's the story."

"Why'd you pick that place?"

"I didn't. We're meeting a fellow there. And it was his idea. Bill's."

"Oh. And who would this fellow be?"

"He's the guy your cousin alluded to in his story. Remember

him?"

"Yeah," Henry said. "When did you get a chance to talk to him? We just learned about him a few hours ago."

"Right. But what did Bill say about him?"

"Something about this old guy who hung out …"

"Who hung out at that saloon. Well, this is Friday. We'll be in Deadwood today. If he hangs out at one of the bars, chances are he will be at this saloon, or one of the other ones. So, there's a good chance we will locate him, or someone like him, either tonight or tomorrow night. If you want to learn the history of a small town, these are the guys who know it. Or at least they know one version of it. Talk to a few of them, and you soon are able to piece together what just might be the true story.

"I've been playing back in my mind everything that your cousin told us. That Nellie woman. She would have been your cousin's great-aunt. What a piece of work she was. Coming forward like that. Maria must have confided in her family for a reason. Probably wanting them to keep their eyes and ears open, just in case her missing lover ever turned up. And the picture she painted of her husband and his brother—moonshining gunslingers. She knew that something bad happened to her boyfriend. She knew it, and wanted to make sure her family knew as well.

"So, if we can locate this fellow that Bill described, he will be able to tell us something about these two young men—gun-toting men—who moved into Deadwood in the mid-twenties, and started making and selling home-brew. Because that would be exactly what these guys would have to do—make hooch.

"And, we've even got names—Edward and Isaac Pierce. Of course, they could have changed their names. Especially if they were concerned that the body might have turned up. But, my guess is that they had relatives there in Deadwood. Maybe a brother, uncle, or a cousin. Someone to move in with until they got settled. We'll find some local historians who will know something about it. Or be able to point us to someone who does."

"So, how do we handle this?" Henry asked. "Do we work together, or split up?"

"We can cover twice as much real estate if we each work different bars. We'll get in town early enough to hit them all, or most of them, yet tonight. We'll then get some rest, and go back out Saturday.

"By Sunday night we'll have learned as much as we're going to. We'll decide then if we stick around to visit the courthouse on Monday to look up records. Or, if we will want to just head back and break the bad news to your cousin.

"Be nice to find the record of birth of your cousin's grandfather. If it was even recorded."

"Whether or not we find what we're looking for by Monday, we'll then head back to Newberry?" Henry asked.

"Maybe," Jack replied. "But, remember, what we believe to be the case is that Bill's grandfather was raised by his mother. And that after apparently spending time in the Newberry area looking for her boyfriend, Maria and her son somehow ended up in Grand Rapids.

"Anyway, those are some of the questions we might be able to get answered this weekend."

"It's obvious that our work is cut out for us," Henry said. "I suppose I'd better get some sleep. Sounds like you've got a full night's work planned out for us once we arrive."

"Yeah," Jack said as he took a careful look in his rearview mirror. "Better get some rest."

Less than a minute after Henry put his seat all the way back and closed his eyes, Jack shouted, "Holy shit!"

And then the collision.

Chapter 9—Friday

Jack and Henry had barely got started on their trip. They were still travelling west on M-28 between Munising and Marquette when the truck hit them.

It could have been much worse—especially given the fact that the huge semi-tractor was moving thirty miles per hour faster than Jack's Tahoe. Immediately upon impact, the vehicle seemed to leap into the air and come down into a series of three-sixties—so many, in fact, Jack was unable to count them. His black Tahoe had just been in for the routine oil change and the guys at the dealership were always trying to talk him into the latest black Corvette, but considering the extreme winters, he would just tell them maybe next year.

When it seemed to Jack that he was going to be able to pull out of it, the truck hit them again. This time it was on the driver's side front quarter panel, just in front of Jack's door.

"Damn!" Jack shouted as the truck struck. "He barely slowed down."

Jack was right. The driver of the truck never touched the brakes. In fact, when the vehicles came together for the second time, the driver of the truck appeared to accelerate after impact in an attempt to inflict maximum damage.

Finally, after pushing Jack's Tahoe sideways down the highway for nearly one hundred yards, one of the seventeen-inch rear wheels of Jack's vehicle caught in the loose gravel on the shoulder and it flipped over on its side. It then careened off the road on the north side and slid through a ditch, ending up over a hundred feet off the roadway.

The semi slowed down slightly as though the driver wanted to inspect, but then sped off.

"Henry," Jack rhetoricized with a smile, "hope I didn't make you spill your coffee."

"What the hell just happened?" Henry asked. "I just closed my eyes and all hell breaks loose."

The Tahoe had come to rest facing east and lying on the passenger's side. Jack powered his window down and then turned the engine off.

"Careful when you crawl out of here," Jack warned, "it's sitting at a pretty precarious angle. It's almost ready to roll back on its wheels. On second thought, just sit tight for a minute. I'll see how stable it is. In fact, stay put until after I check it out."

Jack pulled himself up through the open window, stepped on the back of the seat, hoisted his legs out, and then slid down to the ground.

"Yeah, Henry. I think I might be able to roll it back onto its wheels. Turn the ignition key on and put it in neutral, but don't start it. And then make sure your seat belt is on."

Jack pushed on the roof of the Tahoe. It moved about six inches. And then he let up.

"Looks like I might be able to roll it back," Jack said. "Hang on."

He pushed again and it moved a little farther, and then he pulled back. He repeated the exercise four times, gaining a little more momentum with each effort. And then he shoved it as hard as he could. For a moment it appeared as though it was going to roll back to where it started out, but he gave it one more hefty push. At the same time Henry threw his upper body onto the seat across from him, and the Tahoe dropped down on its wheels. When it did it began rolling backward into the ditch.

"Hit the brakes!" Jack shouted.

Henry reached down and applied the brake with his left hand.

"Great! Great!" Jack said loudly. "Now put it in park, and see if it starts."

Henry turned the key, and after the engine cranked over a few times it started.

Henry sat back up in his seat and powered his window down.

"Need a ride, mister?" he asked with a big smile. "This taxi's headed to Deadwood. The home of famous saloons and gambling houses. And I suppose a brothel or two."

Jack slapped the hood twice as he waded down into a few inches of ditch water. He slid behind the wheel, fastened his seatbelt, engaged the four-wheel-drive, and slid the shifter into gear.

"And I always thought you had that roll bar installed just so I'd have something to bump my head on," Henry quipped as they pulled around and headed back west on M-28.

Henry did a once-over at the inside of the Tahoe and said, "We didn't even get a window broken. Looks to me like it's all intact."

"Right," Jack agreed, "but we could sure use a carwash. We've got mud and grass hanging from everything."

"What do you suppose that was all about?" Henry asked after having sat silently for nearly ten minutes.

Henry—whose real name was Chuchip Kalyesveh—was typically on the quiet side. However, this recent event seemed not only to get his heart racing, but also his communication suddenly increased. He grabbed his worn Detroit Tigers cap from the floor and pulled it low over his brow. His hair was long, black and straight.

Both his mother and father were Native Americans from the Hopi tribe in Arizona. His deep-toned skin and dark eyes seemed to penetrate right through the night, giving chills to anyone who did not know him. His huge muscular frame—nearly two hundred and fifty pounds—along with immense survival skills and a keen awareness of his surroundings made him a perfect complement to Jack and his adventures.

"Damned if I know," Jack replied. "Maybe that was one of those self-driving trucks."

"Do you think," Henry asked with a laugh.

Just then Jack slowed down abruptly.

"What's up?" Henry asked.

"That was our truck we just passed. Parked along that side road. At least, I'm pretty sure it was. Let's go back and take a look."

Jack made a double U-turn and pulled in closely behind the truck. Jack grabbed a flashlight as they slid out of the Tahoe and walked up to the cab—Jack on one side, Henry on the other. Both were armed.

Jack stood on the running board of the semi and opened the driver's side door. It revealed a littered cab, with a tagged key in the ignition, but no driver.

"Don't touch anything," Jack ordered. "I'm going to see if I can get some prints off it." He walked back to the Tahoe and retrieved his briefcase.

Jack always packed so as to be prepared to investigate a crime.

After putting on a pair of latex gloves, he dusted the steering wheel and the shifter knob. He then announced in disgust, "It's all been wiped down. We're not going to find any good prints here. Unless maybe a thumbprint on the key."

He placed the key in a plastic bag and slid it into his pocket.

Feeling the side of a fast-food cup, he said, "This is still cold. Might get something off of it."

He poured the rest of the drink out on the ground and slid the empty cup into another plastic bag along with the straw.

He then jumped out of the truck and walked around in front of it.

"Take a look at this, Henry," Jack said. "He went to a lot of trouble just for us."

Jack shone his flashlight on a fully inflated spare tire that was tied to the front bumper.

"I haven't seen anything like that in a long time. He wanted to make sure he didn't drive over the top of us and maybe get himself hung up. This was pretty well planned out."

"Still don't have any idea who might be behind it?" Henry asked.

"No. None. I suppose it might have something to do with this job we just signed up for with your cousin. But I can't think of anyone who would take it this far. This bastard tried to kill us."

"I've no doubt you'll get to the bottom of it," Henry said. "And sooner than later."

Chapter 10

Both men were dragging by the time they reached their hotel in Deadwood. Henry was able to nod off for a few hours as they passed through Wisconsin and Minnesota. And just before they reached the South Dakota border, Jack pulled into a do-it-yourself carwash and began hosing the Tahoe down.

Whether it was the sound of the water splashing against the side of the passenger window that woke Henry up, the occasional spray that found its way around the damaged doorframe, or the bright South Dakotan sun, he jumped out of the Tahoe, stretched heartily, and then made his way toward the coffee machine.

"Don't bother with that," Jack said. "I picked up a Starbucks for you. It's in the center console. Can you take it the rest of the way?"

"Sure. Just plug the hotel into the GPS, and I'll go on autopilot."

It was nine-thirty P.M. by the time they had showered and put on some clean clothes.

"Not a bad time to hit the bars," Henry commented. "Still think we should go solo?"

"I think so. We can cover a lot more territory that way. Besides, who's to say that these local historians are going to stick to a single watering hole. It'd be no problem if you and I were to hit the same bars. Just as long as we can get what we're after.

"Take some of these with you," Jack said, handing Henry a dozen business cards. "They've got a phone number on them. I'd make sure the bartenders each have one."

"What exactly should I be looking for?" Henry asked. "What

sort of questions should I be asking?"

Jack reached into his pocket and took out a wad of hundreds. He peeled ten off and gave them to Henry.

"These might help as well."

"Some things will stick in a man's memory, even if he heard it second- or third-hand. Like the big old .45 Edward Pierce carried. And that they made and sold hooch. People would remember something like that—so much so that they just might have told their children about it.

"And, like I said before, they might remember their father, or uncle, talking about these brothers who moved to Deadwood in the twenties, making and selling corn liquor. There might even be stories about them shooting or threatening someone who didn't pay up. Never know what kind of trouble those boys got themselves into while they lived here.

"They were lumberjacks. The big thing around here was mining. They might have got a job in the mines, but I think it more likely that they lived with relatives, and sold hooch.

"If you're able to find someone with a story, and it sounds like it might be our guys, find out about family. They must have had family here. It just figures."

The first place Jack visited was Seven Stallion Saloon. It was nearly ten o'clock when he arrived. He took a seat at the bar and surveyed his surroundings. He was wearing his black jeans, brown leather cowboy boots and a Stetson with an antiqued Concho leather band he had brought along for the occasion.

"Never saw you in here before," the bartender said. "You just visiting?"

"You could say that," Jack said. "But it's more like business. I'm working for a family who is looking for one of their relatives. He stands to inherit some money, if I can locate him."

"Really? Who would that be? Maybe I know him."

"Last name is Pierce. Got any of them around here?"

"Deadwood's a curious little town—emphasis on *little*. Strangely, our population has shrunk through the years."

"That's what I've heard," Jack said. "At one time, at the heart of the Gold Rush, I think there were five thousand people living here. Isn't that about right? But now, what do you think? Maybe two thousand?"

"Try thirteen hundred. And that's down a hundred or so from ten years ago."

"But, you do a nice tourist business. Right?"

"We do. And there's quite a few saloons in Deadwood, and in the surrounding areas—like Sturgis. That's where they have the annual motorcycle rally. There will be five hundred thousand bikers around here for that."

"I'm sure that brings in a lot of revenue."

"For sure. It's huge. But, that's not really what you're interested in. Unless the fellow you're looking for is a biker. And if he is, it's likely that he won't be here until the first week of August."

"The fellow I'm looking for has been dead for some time. At least that's most likely the case. I'm looking for a pair of brothers with the last name of Pierce—Edward and Isaac Pierce. They were probably in Deadwood for only a short period of time. That would be in 1924. But they would have stood out. They were lumberjacks from Michigan's Upper Peninsula. But that's not what would have made them stand out. They would have made a living by making and selling corn liquor—moonshine. And it's quite possible that they would have lived with relatives in the area."

"We've had a few of those here from time to time. Moonshiners, that is. And there are some Pierces living in the area. Might not mean anything, though. A lot of money's at stake, you say. How much, approximately?"

"Several thousand dollars, I would think," Jack said. "Don't know exactly how much. But the ones I need to track down are some fellows named Edward and Isaac Pierce. Brothers. One of them would likely be a direct ancestor of the man I need to find. Got any ideas?"

All the while Jack was talking, the bartender was busy drying and polishing shot glasses that he had just removed from the sanitizer. He would hold each one up to the light to be sure there were no lipstick stains or watermarks.

While Jack was still talking, he slipped the bartender two crisp twenty-dollar bills.

"Really?" the bartender said. "That's mighty generous of you. Thanks. Now, you must keep in mind that I've only worked here for the past six months. But, there are a couple regulars who might be able to help you. Old-timers. They usually show up on Fridays about this time, or a little later. Sometimes on Saturdays. They're vets. Vietnam. They know the history of the area pretty well. Sometimes Harry stops in and has a beer with them. He's a little older. He goes back to before the Korean War, I think. … They've lived in Deadwood all of their lives, and they know the history—especially the family histories. They pride themselves on that. They tell me stuff. I never know if they're shittin' me or not. But I doubt that they are. I think if one of them was feeding me BS, one of the others would set them straight. They usually start out at the bar, have a beer, or two. They just drink beer. And when their favorite table opens up, they slide over there, until closing, or whenever they're ready to leave. It's the table over there in the far corner. I'll let you know when one of them comes in. I'm sure they'd talk to you. They like to show off their knowledge of Deadwood. Especially Deadwood from back in the day. Can I get you something to drink?"

"What's your most popular beer?" Jack asked. "In a bottle."

"Most of my regulars drink Coors."

"That's good. I'll have one of those."

"Light or regular?"

"Regular."

The bartender drew out a cold bottle and popped the top off.

"Want a glass or do you drink it out of the bottle?"

"Don't need a glass," Jack said as the bartender set the beer down in front of him on the bar.

"The stubby," Jack commented. "How's that going over?"

"I get a lot of crap tossed at me when I pour it. But I think they'd complain about anything. Same beer. I don't know what the beef's all about. People just don't like change, I think. Especially when it comes to something as personal as their beer. But that's okay with me. I'd rather have my patrons bitchin' about the stubby versus the long neck than complaining about politics. That's been the subject for the past year or so. I hate politics. Actually had fights break out about it. At least no one gets *that* riled up about the physical dimensions of their beer bottle—not riled up enough to want to fist it out. Unless they prefer the long neck as a handle when corking somebody over the head."

Jack further examined the bottle, and then took a long swig.

The bar had been remodeled into a sports bar with 23 flat screens hanging from the ceilings. However, the architect decided to leave the original stonewalls and hardwood floors. Wagon wheels and black and white pictures from the turn of the century filled every open wall surface. The bottoms of whiskey barrels were cut off and turned into tabletops. Both the bartenders and servers wore red plaid flannel shirts and blue jeans covered by long black aprons with the logo from the bar on the top left corner.

"There ya go," the bartender said. "Walt just walked in. He's one of the group of local experts. After he orders his beer, I'll ask him if he'd be willing to share some of his knowledge with you."

"Don't bother," Jack said. "I'll introduce myself. Just tell him I'm buying his beers tonight. What's his last name?"

The bartender had to think about it for a moment.

"Hell, I never had occasion to call him by his last name. But it's Silverman, I think. Walt Silverman. Just call him by his first name—Walt."

He then popped the top off another Coors stubby and headed down to where the old man was sitting. By the time he had explained that Jack was buying his drinks, Jack was already walking up to the bar stool beside him.

"Mr. Silverman. My name's Jack Handler. Would you mind sharing a little bit of your knowledge about Deadwood with me? The bartender told me that you are the local expert."

"That *Mr. Silverman* business sounds pretty formal to me. You some kinda cop?"

"No. Definitely not."

"You trying to find someone who skipped out on his bond? Like this Dog the Bounty Hunter?"

"Not that either. I just have a friend who was named in a will. If I can document him as a legitimate heir, then he can claim his inheritance. It's not a big deal. A few thousand dollars. But he's a veteran. He could use the money."

"A vet, you say. So am I—Vietnam—'67 to '69. I'm always happy to help a fellow warrior. And I do appreciate your buying my beer. That's mighty nice of you. But my knowledge has to be worth a little something. Besides the price of a beer or two. Don't ya think? I am on a fixed income, you know."

"Absolutely," Jack said, sliding a folded twenty over to the old man. "Wouldn't have it any other way."

Walt took a look at it and tucked it into the breast pocket of his blue and white flannel shirt.

Walt had the worn out look of a vet that had seen too much too young. He sported a three-inch unevenly trimmed white beard, and steely blue eyes. His hands trembled a bit when taking the money.

As he teared up a bit, he said, "Thank you. That's just really nice of you. I appreciate it. Now, what did you say your name was?"

"Handler. My name is Jack Handler. And please call me Jack."

"Jack. It would be absolutely fine for you to call me Walt. No one's called me Mr. Silverman since the judge, when I got arrested for drunk and disorderly. Please do call me Walt. Now, just what sort of information is it that you're looking for? I'll see what I can do to help you."

Chapter 11

Jack gave his guest a few minutes so that he could take several long slugs on his drink.

"Here's the deal. The story is that these two brothers moved from Michigan's Upper Peninsula to the Deadwood area. This was back in the early twenties. We think it was 1924. But that part is supposition."

"Hell. That's a long time ago. Way before I was born. I wouldn't have no direct knowledge about stuff that long ago."

"Right. I understand that. But these brothers were quite unusual. You might have heard stories about them. And even that could be helpful."

"Well, tell me what you know, and see if it rings a bell."

"Like I said, it would probably have been in 1924. Their names were Edward and Isaac Pierce. They were lumberjacks in Michigan. But they might have tried something else in Deadwood. Maybe worked in the mines."

"Well, we do have some Pierces in the area. And they've been around a long time. Since long before the twenties. So, *they* wouldn't be your guys."

"We think that the brothers might have moved here because they had family in the area. So, what you tell me fits in. I've heard that they had cousins here. And maybe even a brother. But, there are some additional facts that you might find interesting. They might have had some run-ins with the law. They had a reputation in Michigan. No reason to think that they would have changed. Another thing—they were known for making and selling corn liquor in the lumber camps."

"No shit!" Walt said. "Now you're talking. Jimmy Jackson, one of my buddies, who is also a vet. The Korean War. Some still call it a conflict. But a lot of good men fought and died over there. So, in my book, it was a war, even though it was never declared. Jimmy's people came to Black Hills after the Civil War. In the late 1870s. They came for the gold. The Black Hills Gold Rush, it was called. They worked their claim for several years, and then it petered out. They operated a small hardware store here in Deadwood after that. And they then opened a tavern. Even though the town was no longer a boom town, they were still able to eke out a living.

"Some of the Jackson clan raised pigs. They did all right. Grew the corn on their farms, too.

"But, they really earned their money turning that pig corn into liquor during Prohibition. Story goes, according to Jimmy, that the family closed the tavern, but turned the back room of the hardware store into a gambling hall, and served up their hooch. That's where they made their money.

"So, if your guys came here during the twenties, there's a fair chance that Jimmy might have some info on that. I'll give him a call. He usually comes over for a few beers on a Friday night. If I can get ahold of him, I'll have him bring some of his photo albums with him."

"One more thing," Jack said before the old man could call his friend. "One of the brothers, Edward, carried a side arm. All the time, I've heard."

"That's nothin' new. Back then everyone carried a gun."

"But this wasn't the average run-of-the-mill pistol. It had a long barrel. Fourteen inches I'm told. Something like the one Wyatt Earp used to carry."

"No shit!" the old man said. "A Buntline Special. That's what they called that gun. It was made by Colt. Actually, I don't think there's any real evidence that Earp used anything like that legendary pistol. More likely that it was purely the invention of Ned Buntline, the novelist who popularized the Wild West stories. But long-barreled pistols did exist back then. I'll see if Jimmy is comin'. He'd be the one to talk to about this."

"Jimmy. You plannin' to come over tonight?"

Jack took the break in conversation to call Henry.

"Henry. Looks like we might be on to something over here at Seven Stallion. How're you doing?"

Henry informed Jack that nothing appeared to be happening at either of the bars he'd been to, so he agreed to join Jack.

"Before you head over let me run it by my new friend here. Hang on for a minute."

Jack waited until Walt had finished talking to his friend.

"Any luck?" Jack asked. "Is your friend able to make it tonight?"

"Oh. Yeah. He'll be here. He's feelin' a little under the weather, but he wouldn't pass up an opportunity like this. He is the king of BS. Loves to hear himself pontificate. Even more when he has someone to listen to him. No one pays much attention to him anymore. None of the regulars. They've all heard his stories."

"Then you don't think he'd mind if my assistant sat in."

"Oh hell no. The more the merrier."

"I'll let Henry know."

"Henry," Jack said in a voice loud enough for the old man to hear. "Yeah. Come on over. We've got two sages over here who are knowledgeable about the history of Deadwood. I'm sure you'd find it enlightening."

"Where's your buddy right now?" Walt asked.

"Just down the street. At another local bar."

"We don't call this a bar here in Deadwood. It's Seven Stallions to the locals. Jimmy's gonna bring along some pictures. He's got lots of them. Some of them printed on metal. They call them tintypes. They were pictures printed on sheets of iron. There actually wasn't any tin used. None. But most of what would interest you will be the letters and pictures from the twenties. He has plenty of that stuff too. And he loves to show it off. Don't be surprised if he keeps talking until Billy, the bartender, kicks us out so he can get the place cleaned up. That's just how Jimmy is."

"Sounds fine to me," Jack said.

"But don't offer to pay him," Walt said. "He will be offended. Very proud man. He will help you as much as he can. And he'll love every minute of it. Like I said. Expect to be here until closing. But don't try to pay him like you did me. Hell. I'm not proud. I can use the money. But Jimmy would be offended."

"Thanks for the advice," Jack said. "But, how about I buy the beers tonight? Would your friend have a problem with that?"

"Oh hell, no. *That'd* be fine. Be fine with me too."

"Then that's what I'll do," Jack said as he stood to his feet. "Excuse me for a minute, I'll inform the bartender that the drinks tonight will be on me."

"Hey, buddy," Jack said to the bartender. "Here's a couple Franklins. This should cover the beers tonight for me and my friend. Two more gentlemen will be joining us. Whatever we don't use tonight, carry it over for the old man, and his friend Jimmy. For another night.

"And here's a little for your effort," he said handing the bartender a couple twenties.

"Thanks," the bartender said. "I'll take care of it."

"It could be a while before Jimmy gets here," Walt said as Jack rejoined him at the table. "He doesn't drive. Says he's too old. And he's right about that. He can't see a thing. Not really. So, he walks from his apartment. Sometimes he gets a ride from a friend. He has a buddy in his apartment building who drives. So, sometimes they will drive over. But, his friend is getting a little muddled upstairs. You know what I mean? Up here," he continued, pointing at his bald head. "I don't really like it when he brings Harry—that's his friend's name. Not really his friend. More like his free ride. Harry doesn't add anything to the conversation. But he does like his beer."

"You think Harry will be with him tonight?"

"No. Jimmy wants center stage tonight. He will not want to share it with anyone. Not even for a free ride. Besides, he already told Harry that he wasn't coming to the Seven Stallions tonight. Because he wasn't feelin' well. So, he'll be by himself. I'm sure."

"Henry could be walking in at any moment. You sure that won't be a problem for your buddy? I could have Henry sit at the bar until you introduce me to him."

"It'll be fine. I'm sure. Jimmy's that kind of a guy. He loves an audience."

"Now, you said he's a bullshitter," Jack said. "Does that mean that we can't be sure what he is saying is the truth?"

"No. He's not *that* kind a bullshitter. Jimmy tells the truth. But it is the truth as he remembers it. He's old, and he's told these stories hundreds of times. And, along the way, he tends to embellish them a bit. So, just be prepared to peel what he says down to the core. You'll find there is a kernel of truth to all of his stories. But you can't buy what he says hook line and sinker, if you know what I mean."

"There's my friend now," Jack said, waving Henry over to their table.

"Walt, let me introduce you to my associate, Henry Kalyesveh. Henry, this is Walt Silverman. Walt is very knowledgeable about the city of Deadwood."

"How do you do, Mr. Cail-yes-e-vah?" Walt stood and said. "I hope I didn't butcher your name too much."

"Henry. Just call me Henry. And don't worry about mispronouncing my name. It's even a mouthful for me sometimes. Especially after a couple beers."

"And just call me Walt. Nobody calls me by my last name either."

"Walt. It's a real pleasure to meet you. Jack here tells me that you are a local historian. I would just like to be considered an expert at anything. It's really pretty cool that you've taken the time to study your community's history."

"It's not *that* big a deal," Walt laughed. "All you have to do is retire young and live to be old. But I'm not the real expert on Deadwood. That would be Jimmy Jackson. Not only is he as old as dirt, his whole family, on both sides, goes back a very long time. And, he has the records and pictures to document it. He's coming over to the saloon to talk to you fellows. He should be here any time now."

Walt then stood and looked toward the front entrance.

"In fact, speak of the devil and he shall appear," he said, motioning for his friend to join them. "Jimmy. We're over here."

Chapter 12

Jimmy took a moment to size up the assembly, and then he walked slowly over to their table.

"What the hell is that you're pullin'?" Walt asked as his friend approached. He was referring to the twenty-inch rolling carry-on travel case the man was dragging behind him.

"You said you wanted me to bring some of my pictures and letters from the twenties. So, that's what I did. I didn't know what your friend would be looking for, so I grabbed up a couple photo albums. And a few letters. Not a lot—just a few."

Henry had not yet seated himself. Jack stood with them to greet the *expert*.

"Jimmy, this is the man I told you about. His name is Jack, I think I forgot your last name."

"Hello, Jimmy," Jack said, reaching out to shake hands. "My name is Jack, Jack Handler. Your friend Walt has told us a lot about you. And this is my associate, Henry. We are very grateful that you are willing to share some of your expertise with us."

"Walt told me a little bit about what you looking for. Maybe you could fill me in on just why you're wanting to know about my family history."

"Absolutely," Jack said as they sat down. "Happy to do so."

Before Jack could begin his explanation, the bartender walked up with four stubby Coors.

"You can just put mine on my tab, Mikey," Jimmy said to the bartender.

"All taken care of," the bartender said. "Jack here has taken care of your beers for the whole evening. With some left over for another day."

"Well thank you very much," Jimmy said. "Now, why is it you are so interested in my family's story? You were about to tell me, I think."

"Right," Jack began. "We're not looking to poke into your *private* business, Jimmy. What we would like is some help in locating or identifying the family history of a friend of ours. He would have been born in Deadwood, we think, in or about 1924. Walt thinks that it is possible that your family might have had some dealings with our friend's family. He said that you had pictures and letters from that period in Deadwood's history."

"So, it's not so much about *my* family, then?"

"Right. Only when and if our guy's paths crossed with those of your ancestors."

"And, why is it you're trying to track him down?"

"The descendants of our friend stand to inherit some money—not a lot, but a few thousand dollars—if we can successfully trace his lineage back to a specific branch of the family tree."

"So, it's not like you're some kind of skip-tracer then?"

"No. Nothing like that. No one has anything to lose. We're not trying to get anyone in trouble."

"Well, I have to say that you two fellows look a lot like cops to me. You're not cops, are you?"

"Very astute observation," Jack said. "I did, years ago, work as a detective in the City of Chicago. But now my daughter and I run a small resort in Michigan's Upper Peninsula. And Henry here is our assistant. It's his cousin that stands to inherit. We're doing this as a favor to help him out. He could use the money, if it is legitimately his. That's what this is all about."

"So, nobody goes to jail on the basis of what I tell you?"

"Promise you that. If we're successful, Henry's cousin will be able to send his daughter to college for a year or two. With a little pocket change left over. That's it, pure and simple."

"Well, tell me your story, and I'll see what I can do."

"We have only one picture," Jack said, sliding the five by seven portrait of Maria out of the brown Manila envelope. "This is a picture of the baby's mother. Her name was Maria."

"Damn," Jimmy said as he turned the faded glossy around so he could see it better. "She was quite the looker."

Walt adjusted his position to get a better view.

"What can you tell me about the rest of the family?" Jimmy asked. "Walt said you knew something about a pair of brothers who moved here around 1924. From Michigan. There they made and sold hooch. Would you tell me if there's anything that you know or have heard about them?"

"This is what we think," Jack continued. "Henry and I believe that there were two brothers— Edward and Isaac. The younger one, Isaac, he was married to this woman, Maria. She had a baby. But, we think that Isaac was not the biological father. We think the brothers moved to Deadwood when they learned that there was another man in Maria's life. We think that man's name might have been William Lawrence Owens."

"Never heard of any *Owens* around here," Jimmy said.

"The boy's last name was Pierce, we think. Same as Isaac's. It seems likely that Isaac kicked Maria out of the house when the baby was born. And that she soon thereafter moved back to Michigan with the young baby."

"If you know all of that, how is it you think I can help you?"

"We've made the calls," Jack said. "And we can find *no* evidence to suggest that the birth of any baby was registered to Maria Pierce during that whole decade. So, if it did indeed happen, then the baby must have been delivered at home—probably assisted by friends or relatives, or possibly a midwife. It would not be surprising if the family preferred that there not be records, if the baby was thought to be illegitimate.

"Now, that was certainly common practice at that time—birthing at home, that is. If there was family, it would not be a stretch to think that a baby could be delivered by a family member. Especially if the identity of the biological father was in question. The family might want to keep the delivery very private."

"I still don't see how I can help you."

"It's possible that the brothers were living under a different name. They might have been trying to hide out. You see, they appear to have pulled out of Michigan suddenly and without warning. And the biological father of the baby—he went missing at the same time."

"Did he move to Deadwood as well?"

"No. He stayed in Michigan. Not by choice, however. In fact, it appears as though he was murdered at about the same time as the brothers moved their families to Deadwood. His body was recently unearthed just outside of Newberry."

"Murdered! The boy's father was murdered? And how do you know that?"

"It appears he was beaten to death, and buried in the woods. Near the lumber camp where he worked."

"Well, by now you can be sure that whoever murdered the father back in 1924—it's for sure the killer is dead too. So you can't be trying to solve *that* crime. And if you are trying to solve it—to what end? They're all dead."

"What I told you is the truth. All we are out to do is establish that the murdered man was the biological great-grandfather of Henry's cousin. If we can do that, then he can collect his inheritance."

"Why can't you use DNA? I don't know much about it, but I've heard it works."

"The body was highly degraded. Plus, the family had the remains cremated."

"I see. So, there's no DNA to work with?"

"Right. The body fit the description. Plus, it was found near where the man had last been known to have resided. And there was sufficient evidence in the wallet for it to be identified—driver's license, draft card, family pictures—enough to satisfy the family, and the sheriff. So, once they had determined the body was that of Mr. Owens, they had the remains cremated."

"Okay," Jimmy said. "I'll be happy to do what I can, but I'm not sure I can be of much help."

"Anything that you've got—pictures, letters. And anything that you've heard that might have occurred during that period of time might be useful. But, let me first tell you what I know about the brothers, and you see if any of it relates to what you know.

"First of all, the brothers would have arrived without a lot of money. They might have had what they had earned for the week. Odds are they would have left Newberry with their wages for two weeks, or a combined total of a couple hundred dollars, more or less—probably not much more. So they would have been looking for employment—some way to make a living.

"The two things that they were experienced at were lumberjacking, and making corn liquor. That's what they did in Michigan. I understand that your family had a history of making hooch during that time as well. It was during Prohibition."

"Yeah, they sure did. They ran a tavern and a hardware store, raised pigs, grew corn, and made hooch."

"These two brothers might have done business with your family. It's possible that they worked in the woods, but lumbering in Deadwood wasn't what it was in Michigan. And the Gold Rush was over by then. So, they might have lived with some family members and made moonshine."

"I never heard talk of them. But my dad probably wouldn't have had much to say about a couple young men from Michigan. Especially if they kept to themselves, and lived with family members."

"One other thing about them that might have set them apart was the gun the older one carried. Edward. In Michigan he always carried a very distinctive sidearm. It was a long-barreled .45 caliber Colt. It had a fourteen-inch barrel."

"That sounds a lot like the famous Buntline Special," Jimmy said with a smile.

"That's what I said," Walt chimed in.

"I doubt that there were too many of them around," Jack added. "So, maybe you could check your photos and letters and see what you might find."

"I didn't know you had all these," Walt said as he fingered through some of the materials Jimmy had brought with him.

"This isn't everything. Just what I thought your friends might find interesting. I've got twice this much at home."

"And we really appreciate it," Jack said. "Is it okay if we take a look at what you've got here?"

Jack made that request mostly just to show respect for the effort the old man had made to accommodate him. He knew that Jimmy would not have lugged the suitcase over to the saloon unless he was very eager to show off its contents.

After nearly an hour of looking through the pages of crumbling, smelly snapshots of Jimmy's remarkably large family, Jimmy closed the last of his albums and said, "I'm sorry I couldn't be of any help to you fellows. But it looks like our family did not have any social contact with the two brothers you're wanting to find something out about. At least, no one in my family took a picture of them."

"That stands to reason," Jack said. "Photo opportunities were generally reserved for family members and their close friends. Besides, if these boys were responsible for the death of Mr. Owens in Michigan, it seems unlikely that they would want to have their pictures taken. And if you don't recall reading anything in your collection of correspondence about a couple of guys competing with your family's moonshine business, then chances are that we're not going to find much that is helpful to us. I do sincerely appreciate your bringing all of this fascinating information over here for us to see. How long have you been accumulating historical memorabilia? You could write a book based on it, I would think."

"Since I was a boy. I think I've always had a hankering for collecting stuff like this. You could say it's in my blood. My father used to have boxes of old copies of the *Black Hills Pioneer*—that's the local newspaper. It's been around since the Civil War. He, my father, kept the newspapers stored in our attic. But in the winter of 1952, while I was serving in Korea, there was a fire in the family house, and all those newspapers were ruined. But they weren't really necessary anyway. The *Pioneer* is still publishing, and I'm sure they've put most of their publications on a computer. I don't know that for a fact, but I suspect it's so.

"Then there's the BKHN. Stands for the Black Hills Knowledge Network. It's located in Rapid City, but you can look stuff up on your computer, too. They have an enormous amount of information. If what I brought doesn't answer your questions, you should try them. My shit is mostly about my family. But they've got books and newspapers—all sorts of historic shit."

"It's on my list," Jack said. "Monday morning I—"

"Hey," Jimmy interrupted. "Sorry to butt in like this, but I just had an idea. You suggested earlier that the two brothers you're looking for might have been bootleggers. And if they were, then if they made corn liquor, they would have cut into my family's business. Right?"

"Makes sense," Jack said.

"Now, one of my father's cousins was a Lawrence County sheriff's deputy. And *his* uncle, my great-uncle, was a local politician. And, as I said, my family owned the hardware store. All people of influence. So, if my family found these Pierce brothers were disrupting their moonshine business, they might have resorted to drastic measures, such as turning them in to the authorities.

"I don't know if the court records would turn much up, but if the law was after them, there might have been a notice tacked up at the local post office. And my great-aunt ran the post office. I have a whole brown Manila envelope filled with old wanted posters—a hundred or more of them. Maybe even a hundred and fifty.

If I'd thought about it, I'd have brought them with me. I can run back to my apartment and pick them up if you think you might be interested. They're awful fragile, so I don't show them very much. But for this, they might be our best bet."

Jack glanced over at Henry and said, "If you wouldn't mind. I'd sure appreciate it. Maybe we can send Henry over to pick them up."

"No. No. No," Jimmy said. "I may be old, but I can still get around pretty well. I'll just finish off my beer and be off."

Jimmy drained the last of his Coors and sat the bottle down firmly on the table.

"I really don't mind these stubby bottles. I think they're harder to knock over. And I even think that they might stay cold longer."

"That's all BS, Jimmy. I think you just guzzle them down faster," Walt said, laughing at his friend.

"That's not bullshit. What do you think about it, Jack? Doesn't it make sense? There's less surface glass on the stubby bottle, so why wouldn't it stay colder longer?"

Not wishing to engage in the controversy, Jack said, "I never give mine a chance to get warm in the first place, so I wouldn't be the expert on *that* subject."

"Yeah, right. Well, I'll be back in a few minutes. I'll leave my stuff here. Feel free to look through it while I'm gone. Maybe you'll run across something of interest to you. Be right back."

After Jimmy disappeared through the door on the way to his apartment, Jack opened and began to carefully examine the pages of the largest of the three photo albums.

"What's this?" Jack asked, pointing at an old farmhouse. "Is that the old Jackson family homestead?"

Walt took a careful look at it and said that it was.

"That's where Jimmy grew up. He lived there right up until he went off to war. That was the house that had the fire. Didn't burn it down, but it did a lot of damage. Like Jimmy said, it destroyed whatever was stored in the attic."

"And this?" Jack asked, pointing at a picture of a man and a woman with two children standing in front of a log cabin. "Do you know what this might be?"

Walt took a long look, and then shrugged his shoulders.

Jack turned it over and read the back: "1904 John and Mary Jackson, with William and Netta."

"My guess is that would be Jimmy's great-uncle and aunt, and two of their children. That's just a guess. It's not his parents, though."

"Like you said, it sounds like he had a lot of family around Deadwood."

"One of the oldest and biggest. He probably doesn't even recognize them all, there's so many of them."

"Let's leave that one out for now," Jack said. "I'd like to ask Jimmy about it when he comes back. If I'm not mistaken, that picture is the only reference to those particular members of his family. I wonder why that was. Does Jimmy still have a lot of family in the area?"

"Some. Not like it used to be. There's not a lot of industry around Deadwood. Gambling is the big deal now. Only about thirteen hundred people actually live here. So most of Jimmy's family moved on. Some moved to Rapid City. But a lot of our former residents got out of the state altogether. I don't have much family left either."

All three of the men at the table turned their faces toward the door at the same time.

"Holy shit!" Walt blurted out. "I ain't seen him move that fast in years."

He was referring to the way Jimmy was hurriedly lumbering toward them.

"Jimmy," Walt said as he neared them. "You'd better slow down. You're gonna pop a blood vessel."

"You're going to love this," Jimmy said as he sat down. "I took a minute to look through these before I came back, and I found something very interesting. *Very* interesting."

"Take a gander at this," he said, sliding a yellowed and crumbling wanted poster toward Jack. "Careful with it. It's falling apart. But you can still read it just fine."

"Okay," Jack said as he began studying it. "What have we got here? You're right. This *is* very interesting."

Jack turned the wanted poster so both he and Henry could see it. He read it out loud:

Notice

Reward of $500
Is offered by the city of Deadwood
for the capture of
Edward Smith and his younger brother
Isaac Smith.
Wanted for bootlegging
And attempted murder.
And they are suspected in other murders.
Edward is 6 feet tall, and Isaac
Is 5 feet 10 inches.
Edward is known for carrying
A long-barreled six-shooter.
He sometimes carries it in a holster sewn to his vest.

> Although he is right handed, he wears
> It on his left side, and cross draws
> In John Wesley Hardin fashion
> They have been known to work as lumberjacks.
> Both men should be approached with great caution.

After Jack had finished reading the poster he looked up at Jimmy and said, "This is a *real* wanted poster, right? It's not one of those novelty ones?"

"It's as real as they get. It had been posted in my great-aunt's post office."

"Good. Good," Jack said. "The men in the picture certainly fit the description of the men we're looking for, as far as we know. They were brothers, the right age, they at least used the same *first* names. And they were bootleggers. But, it's the gun—the long-barreled revolver. That's the biggest clue. Not likely there were that many of those pistols floating around."

"But," Henry said, "It does give us something else to think about. If these brothers actually did change their last names—why did they do it? And at what point did they start calling themselves *Smith*? Was it before or after Isaac booted Maria out of his house, and out of his life?"

"Let's think about this for a minute," Jack said, "for the sake of this discussion. Let's assume that once the baby was born, Isaac determined, for whatever reason, that the baby was not his. And he kicked his wife and the baby out. Then later, he changed his name.

"At that time, blood testing was not very effective for determining paternity—maybe thirty percent accuracy."

"Maria might have just come out and admitted that Isaac was not the real father," Jack offered. "Sometimes it's just that obvious.

Maybe that was the situation in this case, so she just confirmed the husband's suspicions. We'll probably never know *why* it happened as we suspect, but it seems likely that it did. She left with the boy, and the name. And the brothers changed their names—quite possibly to escape their past."

Jack then stood up and set his cell phone to the camera app. "Is it okay if I take a picture of this?" he asked.

"Sure," Jimmy said. "There's no date on it, but I'd put it to be during the time you speculated. She quit, my great-aunt, that is, she quit the post office right before the Great Depression. So we know that it would have been before 1929."

"Perfect," Jack said. "I will check into this possibility. One more thing …"

Chapter 13

After Jimmy's *Show and Tell,* Jack noticed one particular picture and set it aside.

Jack showed the picture to Jimmy and said: "I found this picture interesting. It shows a couple standing outside a log cabin. I pulled it out of one of your albums. I might be wrong, but I think this is the only picture of them that you showed us. Can you tell us a little more about *these* folks?"

"Sure," Jimmy said, first studying the picture and then turning it over. "Oh, yeah. That would be my grandfather's brother and his wife, and their two children. Very troubling about them. The story is that the four of them just up and moved on. Disappeared without a trace. No one knows what happened. They packed up some clothes and took off. My father told me that his father suspected foul play, but he couldn't prove anything. Back then stuff like that happened, I suppose. You know, people just pulling up stakes and movin' on. Houses were simple. Log cabins. Dirt floors. All you needed was a crosscut saw, a sharp axe, and a few bucks to buy an acre of land. And you could build a new house in two or three weeks."

"How about their car? I see the front end of one in the picture. Did it disappear as well?"

"I asked my dad about that. He said that it was broken down, so it would have been useless to move with. They were missing for a week or so before anyone checked up on them. When they did they found two couples living in the log cabin. They had a signed quitclaim deed to the property."

"What did they do for a living?"

"Raised pigs."

"Then I suppose they probably ran a small farm," Jack suggested. "Those pigs liked to eat. They had to feed them."

"Corn. They would have raised corn for the pigs. And they had a garden for their own needs."

"You wouldn't know the names of the family who moved into their house, would you?"

"No. Dad never mentioned anything about them. Their names would be in the court records as owning that property. That is, if they ever registered the quitclaim. Dad said that the log cabin burned down a couple years after his cousins moved out."

"What about the law?" Jack asked. "Wouldn't they have thought it suspicious? Pulling out and leaving a successful farm. How about the stock. Who took the pigs?"

"I asked Dad about that. He didn't know. But it seemed that it would all be covered in the deal—in the quitclaim deed. The new owners would receive the cabin, the property, the crops, and the stock. Apparently it was in John's own hand, or it wouldn't have been considered legal."

"If they were to have *moved on*, as you put it, how would they have done that? Without a car."

"They would have had a horse and wagon—everyone did. Or, they could have taken a train. The railroad ran through Deadwood."

"Or," Jack offered, "the people who moved into the log cabin might have forced them to sign over the property, and then killed the whole family. Maybe they buried all four of them somewhere in the back forty."

"I see where you're going with this. Anything's possible, I suppose."

Jack silently studied the picture for a long moment, while Jimmy, whose interest was morphing into nostalgia, continued to page through the largest of the albums.

Finally, Jack spoke.

"I'm wondering if the two couples who bought your *great-cousin's* homestead, could they have been the ones pictured on the wanted poster? It does suggest that they were suspected of murder. Could it have been this family that they were supposed to have killed?"

Just then Jack's cell alerted him. It was from Roger

Chapter 14

"I've got a problem. Going to need your help. *Immediately.*"

Jack scrutinized Roger's text. Generally, the shoe was on the other foot—Jack seeking out Roger's help.

Jack was well aware that whenever he reached out to his friend, Roger *always* came through—and without hesitation.

At the time of the disturbing text, Jack was still sitting in the bar with his good friend Henry, along with the two Deadwood sages. The four of them had just spent the past two hours analyzing the collection of pictures and letters dating back to the early 1900s.

The second Jack read the message, his countenance changed dramatically. Henry had seen that happen before.

Something big's up, Henry thought. *I'd say this meeting is over.*

"Please excuse me for a minute," Jack mumbled disconcertedly as he stood. "I've got to take care of this."

He looked over at Henry and said, "You take over here. Not sure what this might entail—or for how long."

By the time he responded, Jack knew that he would be flying someplace within the hour. He just didn't know where he would be headed, nor did he have any indication as to why his services were deemed necessary.

"What's up?" Jack asked as Roger picked up.

"What the hell are you doing in South Dakota?" Roger barked. "I thought you'd be sitting on your Sugar Island pier smoking a Havana and nursing a JD. Whataya got going in of all places—Deadwood?"

"A job. I'm running down some leads on a murder. One that

took place in Newberry almost a century ago."

"Newberry," Roger said. "That's up by where you live. Right? In the UP. Look, Jack, you know I wouldn't be rattling your cage if I weren't in a bind."

"Of course. How can I help?"

"Can anyone at your end listen in on our conversation?"

"I'm just now approaching my truck. No one's around. We're good."

Jack knew that unless another person were physically within earshot, his conversation with Roger would remain private. That was because Roger had earlier installed an app on Jack's phone that would scramble both ends of the conversation with RSA-2048 encryption.

"Something up with Allison?" Jack asked.

Because Roger was permanently attached to former first lady Allison Fulbright's Secret Service detail, it was only logical for Jack to surmise that Roger's dilemma would most likely involve his charge, especially since in the past Allison always seemed to challenge both Roger and Jack in the most unconventional of fashions.

"You know," Roger replied, "I really can't answer that question. She actually might be involved. I just can't say for sure. But, at this point, I can truthfully say that I have no reason to suspect that she is. The whole matter, however, is much broader than Allison and her personal aspirations."

Both Jack and Roger were well aware of Allison's obsessive desire to go back to the White House—this time as President, rather than first lady.

"How about Bob?" Jack asked. "Is he involved?"

The *Bob* Jack was referring to was Bob Fulbright—the former

President, and Allison's quasi-estranged husband.

"No," Roger said. "About that I'm *quite* certain. In fact, Bob is the source for all of this alarming information. He laid the whole matter out for me. At least as much as he was at liberty to talk about."

"The *whole* matter," Jack repeated. "Just what is this *matter* that you're so concerned about? It sounds a bit ominous."

"Bob recently became aware that there is a credible plot to assassinate the President of the United States."

"Bob *told* you that?" Jack asked.

Jack knew the former President well. In fact, during the early years of the Fulbright presidency he had worked very closely with then President Fulbright. Back then, whenever circumstances presented the President with a particularly unpleasant situation, he would regularly turn to Jack to fix it. So, if Bob Fulbright concluded that there did actually exist a real threat of a presidential assassination, Jack would be the first to consider it credible.

"Shit," Jack groused. "If both Bob and you think this is happening, then I'm sure there has to be something to it. But, isn't this a job for the FBI? Or the Secret Service? Why would you guys think that I could help you out when you've got all these special agents at your disposal? We're talking about a *presidential* assassination. Right?"

"That's just it, Jack," Roger said speaking slowly. "The Deep State *is* the problem. They're behind it."

Chapter 15

Jack was shocked. He just sat silently in his Tahoe pondering Roger's words.

Finally, he spoke.

"You can't be serious! The FBI *and* the Secret Service? You're thinking that they are both involved?"

"Bob spelled it out pretty clearly to me. He wants to talk to you as well. He has still-loyal contacts deep within those agencies, and he told me that the threat is totally credible. In fact, he's scared shitless about it. I've never seen him like this. You know how he is. Always in control. On top of every situation. But, that's not the case this time."

"I can see why," Jack said. "If one of his spooks spelled this out to him, then someone must think that he's sympathetic. Otherwise, he would not have been approached. So, if it gets back to whoever is heading this thing up, that Bob is not all in, then he'll have to be neutralized as well."

"Exactly how he sees it."

"Assuming that this is a legitimate threat, do you or Bob have any idea how—or when it's to be carried out?"

"Yes to both."

Jack paused for a moment while he digested his friend's short answer. Recognizing Jack's consternation, Roger did not interrupt the silence. Finally, Jack spoke.

"Let me see if I've got this right. You know who it is that's cooking up this plot. And you know both where and how they intend to pull it off. Is that about right?"

"Pretty much," Roger confirmed. "We know who the main

players are. Maybe not the specific assets who will be in the field. But we do know the ones who are behind it. And we know where and when it's going to happen."

"Then it seems pretty simple to me. Look, all you'd have to do is pull the President out of that particular situation. If you know it to be that dangerous. Or at least dramatically up the protection."

"That's the rub. The location chosen for the hit is Singapore. Next week."

"Holy shit! Are you saying that the hit is going to be at the summit?"

"Exactly. That means we can't pull POTUS out. We simply can't change venues—"

"And," Jack interrupted, "there's absolutely *nothing* you can do to provide adequate protection over there. *Nothing.*"

"That's the dilemma. The plan is to make it look like it's the work of the NoKos."

"What are they going to use?" Jack asked, somewhat in jest. "Are they going to drop a mortar round on him?"

"Pretty much. They're going to use a black-market cruise missile."

"That's a helluva lot of firepower to take out one man. Why not something more discreet? Like maybe a .50 cal?"

"They're not trying for tidy. They intend to take out everybody at the table. It's supposed to look like a NoKo *coup d'état*. With POTUS as collateral."

"How the hell do you protect against something like that?" Jack asked. "It'd be impossible. It's like putting your head inside a croc's mouth—you're going to get it ripped off. Best way out would be to use a sacrificial double. It'd be messy, but POTUS would survive."

"We suggested that. But POTUS would have none of it. This summit is too important to him. He sees himself as a cross between Winston Churchill and Mahatma Gandhi—if you can imagine that. And maybe a little Audie Murphy tossed in for good measure. "

"Yeah. Right. But that was *To Hell and Back*. Not sure I could even write the 'and back' part of this story. Then POTUS knows about it?"

"Not exactly. Bob explained to him the security nightmare this meeting presented for the Secret Service. But he's too stubborn to walk away from the talks. Even though that seems to us like the only sensible thing to do, the President will have none of it."

"How is it that these players approached Bob in the first place? What was that all about?"

"They did it under the guise that they knew that Bob did not like POTUS, and thought that he might be willing to step into the vacuum the assassination will create.—unofficially, of course."

"That doesn't make sense. What about the Vice President?"

"The plan is to impeach him. Apparently they've got some serious dirt on him and are just waiting until the most propitious time to drop that bomb. The conspirators believe that Bob's popularity, his gravitas, would provide them the cover they will need until they can get someone of their liking installed. There's even talk that the UN might get involved."

"Maybe I've not read the Constitution lately," Jack quipped, "but I don't think that this is how the founders intended transitions to take place."

"Hell, all they want to do is get through this without a full-blown revolution."

"And Bob is playing along?"

"What do you think? These spooks have the power to screw you over six ways from Sunday. If they even *suspec*t that he is not all in, Bob's a dead man if he doesn't comply."

Jack did not immediately respond. Instead he just leaned back in his seat and closed his eyes.

I'm not likely to survive this job, he reasoned. *If I succeed, or if I fail, I'm probably going to die. And I'm sure Roger and Bob fully appreciate what's at stake. The Deep State can't let any of us live.*

"Is there any way to thwart it from the inside?" Jack finally asked. "Can some sort of deal be struck with these actors?"

"We don't think so. And anyone who might move forward with that notion, Bob and I are pretty sure they would meet with an unpleasant end. When one of the original plotters tried to work out a deal, his tongue was cut out and mailed to his ex-wife. It sent a very clear message."

"So," Jack said. "Just how do you boys expect me to fix this? I've grown rather fond of my tongue—and every other part of my anatomy, for that matter."

"Bob wants to see you in New York right away," Roger said.

"I figured that. I have my go-bag in the truck. But I don't know about the next New York flight out of Deadwood. I'll head to the airport right now."

"I'll probably beat you there. I'm cleared to set down at RAP in twenty minutes. It'll take you the best part of an hour to get here."

Chapter 16

Jack phoned Henry and told him that he'd been called away, and that he should remain with Jackson and Silverman until he was convinced that he had gleaned all the information that the two old men might have regarding the late William Lawrence Owens and his mother.

"And take a lot of notes," he said.

Jack also told Henry that he would need to hire an Uber to take him to Rapid City International Airport so that he could pick up the Tahoe.

"Keys at the front desk?" Henry asked.

"Right," Jack replied. "And, of course, there's an envelope there for you as well."

Henry knew that Jack always kept a spare key in a waterproof magnetic stash box hidden under the vehicle. The envelope he spoke about was tucked inside a banged-up plastic box that contained a half-empty dispenser of Kleenex tissues. Inside that envelope were one hundred twenty-dollar bills and a debit card.

Henry was determining that the cash and keys were in their regular hiding places—*Keys front desk?* was code for just that.

Once Jack had Henry squared away he boarded the plane.

"Heading directly for New York?" Jack asked Roger.

"No, not exactly," Roger said. "Bob is routing us to Westchester County Airport. He's arranged to have us picked up and brought to his compound. That's all tentative, however. Officially, we're supposed to land at LaGuardia. But Bob thinks it would be safer for us to divert to Westchester."

"Any specific reason for that?" Jack asked.

"You know how Bob thinks at a time like this. He's convinced that he is under surveillance, and he suspects that we will be as well. And, he's probably right. Let's face it. From the moment you got on this Piper with me, your life has been changed. You can be sure of that. You might as well have a target painted on your back. And that's the way it will be until this whole matter is behind us. Or, until we're dead."

"Sobering thought," Jack replied. … "Will we have new names for this job?"

"You'll stay Jack Handler, and I'll be Roger Minsk."

A thousand thoughts rushed through Jack's mind as he contemplated just what challenges the next few days might pose for him. Any operation of this magnitude, operating under his own name, must be considered a one-way trip.

"What do you think might be the ramifications for Kate?" Jack asked. "And the two boys? I'll need to make some special provision for them."

"All taken care of," Roger said. "You'll have to notify them—the two boys, that is. But I've already arranged for them and Buddy to spend the next two weeks, or at least until further notice, at Bob's compound. Or possibly at one of his safe houses. His compound has to be the most secure location in the world. Under any normal condition. This final decision will remain Bob's call. All you have to do is notify them. Let them know that they should go with the agents I have dispatched to accompany them. I think they are staying with your good friends, Millie and Angel Star."

Roger then handed Jack a handset and said, "You can call them from this SAT phone. You might want to have Millie and her daughter go along with them. The four of them would have a great time—especially with Buddy along. And, it would be a lot safer for them all. Half of Bob's residence is built under a mountain. It's definitely the safest place to be, given the current circumstances. You should even consider having Kate join them. It could be like a family outing. Not exactly Disneyland. But you'll be amazed at just how cool his place is."

Jack took the phone and called Millie.

"When will your guys be there to pick them up?"

"As soon as you give me the word. They're waiting on my orders as we speak."

"In that case, I think it would be best to have them drive themselves. Do you really trust the agents assigned?"

"I don't trust anybody but you and me," Roger said, laughing. "Bob picked them himself. But, they are Secret Service agents, and we all have supervisors. You're probably right. They might be safer traveling in obscurity. I say do it your way."

Once Jack was confident that Millie, Angel, Buddy and the boys were safely on their way, he called Kate.

He informed his daughter regarding the possible threat, but she decided to remain on the job, at least initially. She thought she might be more useful to the operation were she to be able to access directly all of the resources of the New York City Police Department.

"What the hell is that?" Roger barked as he examined a blip on his radar.

"Is that a plane?" Jack asked.

"It's too small for a plane. It looks like it's standing still. Hovering."

"A drone? Can your radar detect drones?"

"Yes. We're equipped with a new advanced radar system. And I think that's what we've got. A drone dead ahead. Looks like it's probably a large one."

"Can you divert and miss it?"

"Should be able to."

"What's our altitude?"

"Ten-five. I'll drop it to nine, and bank right. We'll see how that works for us."

"That's about a mile," Jack said. "Right?"

"Yes. A little less now."

"That's not standard radar. Is it?" Jack observed. "Wouldn't be picking up a drone with standard equipment."

"It's definitely military grade—part of the Advanced Aerospace Threat Identification Program. Picks up small objects like drones, but this is set up so that it tracks only if the object presents a danger if it headed directly in our path."

"So, it still might be tracking us? Even though you've changed course?"

"That's right," Roger said, turning off his transponder. "No use helping it track us. If it locks on to our position, it could be closing in. Unlikely, though. We're moving along quite quickly here. For it to maintain itself as a threat to us, it'd have to be equipped with AI, and have some sort of rocket assist, or—"

"Hell fire!" Jack blurted out as he spotted the exhaust trail of an approaching rocket at eleven o'clock.

Even though there was no warhead in the air-to-air missile, the high-velocity impact was so devastating it destroyed the entire front of the Piper M350, including the windshield. Shrapnel from the damaged plane exploded into the cockpit, striking the two men and rendering them both unconscious.

Immediately the nose of the plane dipped and the predictable dramatic descent ensued.

Chapter 17—Saturday

Henry was ready to leave the bar. He was pleased with the amount of information he and Jack had gleaned from their meeting with the two old men. And, he was eager to Uber out to the airport to pick up the Tahoe. So, unless he could find a good reason to prolong the meeting, he would look for a gracious way to end the evening.

"Am I missing anything?" he asked. "Is there something else about these brothers that you fellows could add?"

"Well," Walter Silverman said, "You might want to take a look at the grave markers in the cemetery. That can often be illuminating. You've got another name to check out: Smith. Might be that these fellows stayed around the area long enough to get themselves killed. Never know. And, it might be interesting to see if there were other members of their family living around here at the time—people with the last name of *Pierce*.

"Jack had suggested that they might have had family here, and that was the reason for their moving here in the first place. I would check out Mount Moriah."

"Mount Moriah Cemetery," Henry said. "I've heard of it. With relation to Seven Stallions, where would that be?"

"Just east of here," Jimmy said. "On the side of the mountain. It overlooks the town."

"While you're up there," Walt added, "check out the celebrity section. A lot of notables came to Deadwood to die."

"I think I know about Hickok and Calamity Jane," Henry said. "Who else you got up there—that I might know?"

"That's actually about it," Jimmy chuckled. "Of course there's

Madam Dora DuFran, and Seth Bullock. He was pretty famous around here. There's a hotel named after him. But most people just want to take pictures of the grave markers for Wild Bill Hickok and Calamity Jane. I haven't been up there in the last fifty years. But whenever tourists come to town, they always want to see those two gravestones. Hickok's even got a statue, or so I've heard. Costs money to go through it. Through the cemetery itself. Two dollars, I think. Unless they've raised it. Supposed to cover the cost of maintenance. I think they just want to make money. How much could it cost to mow that grass once a week? Not *that* much. I'm sure that some days they pull in a couple of grand. But, that's okay. Those tourists can afford it. And we can use the money."

"Damn, Jimmy," Walt said almost laughing out loud. "That's the most I've ever heard you talk at one time."

"Is this Mount Moriah the historic cemetery? Do you know when it was started?"

"It wasn't the first in Deadwood," Walt said. "Originally the dead were buried at Whitewood Gulch, or Boot Hill, which was a little closer to town. When that area was needed for development, the bodies were moved to Mount Moriah. Hickok and Calamity Jane were originally buried at the earlier Boot Hill. I think that's when one of the city fathers announced that Deadwood was such a healthy place to live you'd have to start killing people to fill up Mount Moriah. But, we did eventually fill it up. No more plots are available.

"But, to answer your question. Yes, Mount Moriah is the historic cemetery. While Whitewood Gulch Cemetery actually did precede it, if you were to go to the original Boot Hill site, you'd be standing in the middle of Jackson Street or Taylor Avenue. The whole thing was moved up the hill. That all happened in the late 1800s. So, if you're looking for evidence that might relate to your guy from the twenties, Mount Moriah is the only place to look—at least around Deadwood."

"That's *basically* the case," Jimmy said through a smile. "But, if you brought your shovel, you might be able to unearth some additional Deadwood pioneers … ones that never made it up the hill."

"What does that mean?" Henry asked.

"Go ahead, Jimmy," Walt said. "Tell Henry the whole story."

Henry could see that Jimmy wanted to talk again, so he said, "Yes, Jimmy, I'm eager to hear about it."

"Well," Jimmy said, "It all started back around 2012 when a home owner at 66 Taylor Avenue applied for a permit to repair an old retaining wall that was beginning to crumble. The city issued the permit, but requested that the archaeologists out of Rapid City monitor the excavation. And, sure enough, right off the bat they unearthed a body—one that did not get moved back when they closed the original Deadwood Cemetery. Apparently most of the grave markers had been made of wood and they had rotted off, so that no one knew where the burials actually were.

"Needless to say, it dramatically slowed down the construction of the wall. For the following five years scientists from all over the country worked at reconstructing the body, they even put together a face for the skeleton. Good lookin' lad, with red hair and brown eyes. How they determined all that I don't understand. I think they just made it up. One interesting thing about it was that the young fellow had three or four gold teeth. That just might have been the last of the gold to be dug up in Deadwood.

"Anyway, Henry. The fact that there most likely remain dozens of unearthed bodies beneath the streets of Deadwood should not affect the information you're seeking, 'cuz they're going to date back to the 1870s, or before. That's when they moved the cemetery up the hill—1878."

"My friends," Henry said. "Your help has been priceless. I cannot thank you enough."

Henry then stood to his feet as though preparing to leave. When he did he observed an awkward glance exchanged by his two new friends, and he knew he needed to thank them again.

"Before we break up this very helpful meeting," he said as he prepared his cell to take pictures, "Like I said, Jack and I are both deeply grateful to you for all your help. I would invite you two gentlemen to stay as long as you wish, and lift as many beers as you'd like. My friend Jack has them covered. So, please avail yourself of this opportunity. Jack would be disappointed if you didn't.

"He regrets having had to leave us, but he's very pleased with all the information you two gentlemen shared with us. But, before we officially wind this up, I would like to take a couple shots of some of the materials you showed us. Would that be okay?"

"Sure," Walt assured him. "That's why we brought it over here. Take as many pictures as you like. We're in no hurry to leave. It's Friday night. We've got to help Mickey close this place up. Right, Jimmy?"

"It's our tradition. There's a few of our buddies eyeing us, just dying to find out what this has all been about. We might have to come back tomorrow night just to answer *their* questions."

Henry smiled broadly and began snapping pictures of some of the more interesting images and documents.

When he had finished, he slid two twenty-dollar bills into the last of the photo albums, thanked the two men again, and excused himself. On his way out he stopped at the bar to say goodbye to the bartender.

"Thanks, Mickey," he said as he slapped a twenty on the bar. "Hope to see you again. Great bar."

Henry did not wait for a verbal response from the busy bartender.

"I sure as hell hope they've got a well-developed Uber network in Deadwood," he mumbled to himself on the way to the door. "I'm just too damn tired to deal with much more before my head finds a soft place."

Chapter 18

Henry's trek out to the Rapid City Regional Airport to pick up Jack's Tahoe was quick and easy—at least reasonably so, considering that the airport was located an hour away. One hour and ten minutes after having texted his Uber, Henry was behind the wheel of the Tahoe and heading back to the hotel.

Before he turned in for the night Henry decided to do a little online research. He centered his efforts on a search for three specific family names: Pierce, Owens and Smith, and more specifically for the markers that not only contained one of these names, but that were dated within twenty-five years after the date in question—1924.

His search of the database for those buried under the name Owens yielded nothing. He did, however, locate a deceased with the last name of Owen, but no Owens. Henry had no reason to think that he would find anyone of that name in Deadwood, but thought it still worthy of consideration. From there he concentrated on the Pierce name. He found that there were a few Pierces, but none named Edward or Isaac.

Also, he reasoned, *if Edward and Isaac Pierce had family well established in Deadwood, it figures that there would have been a significant number of them who would be buried under that name in Mount Moriah Cemetery.* Since that was not the case, Henry decided to broaden his search.

It seemed logical to him that the name Smith might be significant. Not only was that the name that the brothers apparently assumed, but when he did a search for burials bearing Smith as a last name he discovered that there were eighteen men, women and children interred there under that surname.

Sure, Henry thought, *Smith is a very common name. So it would only be logical that there should be a significant number of Smiths buried here. That's probably the case with all cemeteries. Still, if the Pierce boys did eventually assume the Smith name, there might very well have been an actual connection with it. All this is pure speculation,* he reasoned, *in this regard, there's no real evidence at all.*

By ten the next morning Henry had devoured his breakfast of eggs, bacon, hash browns, orange juice and coffee at the Lee Street Station Café. Tami kept Henry busy with her humorous banter until he had almost lost track of time.

Melanie, the owner of the quaint restaurant, had told Henry that he could easily walk the short distance up to the cemetery. "Just head south on Main Street until you hit Cemetery Street," she'd told him. "And then follow the signs east on up. The hill is a steep one, but you look like you can handle it."

So that's what he did.

By the time Henry reached the cemetery he found himself in complete agreement with Melanie's tempered warning. By far the hardest part of the short journey was the last two hundred steps—the steep hill that led into it.

Of course, he initially submitted himself to his tourist instincts and checked out the markers for Wild Bill Hickok and Calamity Jane. Once he had snapped a few images of those gravestones, he expanded his effort to encompass the entire five-acre facility.

For the next two hours Henry meticulously made his way through the cemetery, capturing headstone shots of every marker that he thought might provide some information about the Pierce brothers, or perhaps a clue as to where one or both of them migrated after they left Deadwood. That is, if they ever did leave Deadwood.

In the back of Henry's mind lingered the thought that they might have been killed by someone seeking to claim the reward. And were that to have happened, and if Henry could locate the place of their burial, it might be possible to exhume the body and extract some DNA.

If it did turn out that Isaac was the biological father of Maria's son, then that would render moot the whole question of inheritance passing on to Henry's cousin from the Owens' estate via the bloodline of Maria's son. While Henry would prefer to establish his cousin's right to inherit, his foremost interest was to the truth no matter where it happened to lead.

"Wonder why I haven't heard from Jack yet?" Henry mumbled so that only he could hear. He had thought that Jack would have called him by then to check up on his progress, and perhaps to fill Henry in on just what it was that he was up to with Roger. So Henry called Jack.

But it went immediately to voice mail.

He tried it again, and the same thing happened.

"That's weird," he said to himself.

Jack should have arrived by now, he figured, *at wherever it was that he was headed. And he should have checked in with me. He's always good about that.*

Henry's next call went to Kate. She picked up.

"Hey, girl. What's up with your dad? He's not answering his cell. Have any idea where he is and what's going on?"

"No. I was hoping you could tell me. Dad did call last night and warn me to watch my back—that he and Roger had gotten themselves involved with some particularly tricky stuff. That's saying a lot for my dad. He also said that he'd be getting back to me to fill me in on some details, but I didn't hear anything else from him."

"I'm sure he's fine," Henry said trying to encourage her. "He was probably at some DC party all night and tied one on."

"Not likely," Kate said. "Not after what he did with the boys."

"Red and Robby? What's that all about? What do you mean?"

"Initially he was going to have Secret Service pick them up from Millie's house. They were staying with Millie and Angel. They were going to round up all four of them and secrete them away to someplace safe. Instead, he had them drive off on their own—he thought that would be safer. Dad was really concerned about the situation he was getting himself into. I'm surprised he didn't fill you in."

"He couldn't. He and I were meeting with a couple of Deadwood elders when Roger's call came in. Jack immediately left the meeting and called me to pick up his truck from the airport. But no further instructions. Said he'd explain later. How long since you've heard from him?"

"Not since last night. He told me he was flying into New York with Roger, but that was the last I heard from him. He was just taking off out of Rapid City. And that was it. No further communication."

"Shit. That's not like him at all. Seems like he would have touched base with one of us by now. What do you think we should do?"

"You're still in Deadwood, right? How much longer do you

think you've got there? What is it, exactly, that you guys are investigating? You are there on business? Right? Dad didn't really tell me much."

"Well, right now I'm standing over the graves of Wild Bill Hickok and Calamity Jane. We're trying to get to the bottom of a murder case that occurred back in 1924."

"Really? I understand that the statute of limitations never expires in a murder case, but wouldn't that make the perp a bit too old to stand trial?"

"Funny. The whole point is to find out if the victim was the biological ancestor of a man who stands to inherit a bushel of money if it can be determined that he is a legitimate heir of the victim. And that potential heir would be my cousin. Jack's doing me, my family, a favor. Not sure what else I can do here. Would like to talk to Jack. See what—"

"Hang on, Henry. I've got a call coming in. I'll take it and call you back."

Chapter 19

"Kate?" the voice at the other end said. "This is Bob Fulbright. I'm a friend of your father's."

"Yes. Of course."

"I'm trying to reach your father. I was supposed to pick him up from the airport, but he never arrived. Must have been diverted for some reason. Don't get me wrong—there's no evidence of a problem. It's possible that they are just otherwise engaged. I was wondering if you have been in contact with him."

"No, I haven't. In fact I was on the phone with Henry when you called. He's been trying to reach Dad as well. You say you were going to pick him up at the airport? Which airport was that?"

"He was flying in from South Dakota. Or so Roger informed me. He flew into Rapid City last night to pick Jack up. I do know that he refueled there, and did locate Jack. And that he did take off headed, I thought, to New York. But that was the last I heard from him."

"Oh my God!" Kate blurted out, clearly beginning to cry. "What was he in? What sort of plane was Roger flying?"

"Piper M350. It's not a big plane, but nothing is more reliable. I wouldn't worry, darlin'. You and I know Roger very well. He's an excellent pilot. And both of them are very resourceful. I'm sure they're just fine. I don't know what or how much your father might have shared with you about the job he was working on."

"Nothing," Kate said. "I don't know anything. Except that it was going to be a very dangerous job. He had the two boys, Millie and Angel—the boys' good friend—take off to go someplace safe. And he warned me to watch my back. That's not typical of my father. He is always careful, but I don't ever recall him going to this extreme. Having the boys put in protective custody. I thought that was pretty radical."

"Radical's not the word, Kate. There is some very heavy shit coming down the pike. Big stuff. Bad stuff. Unprecedented. At least in our lifetime. Roger was picking up your father at my request. He is working on a job for me. Hell, for the whole country. I really can't talk about it. And neither can your father. It's one of those times. But, you did say that Jack had told you to watch your back. Trust me, Kate, this is one of those times. Shit is about to start flying from all directions. Nobody is going to be safe. What Jack did with the boys was the right thing to do. Hell, it was the only thing to do. My advice to you would be to just disappear. *You are also in danger.*"

"Dad told me a little. He said that he might need me to be available at the office. That he might need to use my contacts within the police department. But, like I said, he told me to watch my back. I take his warning very seriously."

"Yeah. Well. Just know that there will be no one around to protect you. Your boss will have no knowledge of the severity of the matters at hand. To him, it will be business as usual. And it has to stay that way."

"I get it. I'll be as careful as I can. But, that doesn't solve Dad's disappearance. What do you think is happening?"

"It doesn't look good. I have to be honest with you. The plane just disappeared. No trace, at this point. But on the positive side, there have been no reports of any planes going down. Satellites have not picked up anything that looks like a plane crash. That's very good as well. If the plane suffered engine failure, it could have gone down. But Roger always carries parachutes. So, they would have had plenty of time to jump."

"I'm concerned that we haven't heard anything from them," Kate said. "They should have contacted someone. You, me, or the nearest airport. We should have heard *something* from them. Don't you think?"

"Yeah, that's my worry too. I've got planes searching for them right now. If they stayed on course, we should be able to locate the—the wreckage very soon. It would have been in a very desolate area. So it could be difficult to get out with a cell phone. But their SAT phones should still be working. We'll just have to be patient—for now."

"The plane was equipped with a transponder. Right? Can't that be traced?"

"Roger was using a portable GPS flight monitor. We think that there was a catastrophic—dramatic might be a better word here—a sudden dramatic event appears to have occurred that caused the device to cease working. Or, he might have turned it off for some reason. We have nothing at all from the aircraft after that point."

"Oh my God!" Kate cried. "Can't we get a rescue chopper in there?"

"We've got a search plane up there now. A chopper. But so far nothing."

"Could weather have been a factor?"

"They did have some very strong winds—gusts over sixty knots. But that's it. Nothing that would qualify as an *extreme condition*. We're all surprised that nothing's been spotted. And the locator—for some reason it seems not to be working. It's almost as though the plane just disappeared from the face of the earth."

"And no radio communication?"

"Right. I'll admit that's a little disturbing. I'm not troubled that neither of them was able to get through with their cell phones. There are no towers at all in that area—only mountains and forests of ponderosa pines."

Neither of them spoke for several long seconds. It was obvious to each of them that they really didn't have a lot to add to the topic, and that neither one of them wanted to end the silent conversation.

Kate was Jack's daughter—his only child. Kate's mother, Beth, was murdered by professional gangsters who were attempting to kill Jack. At that time Jack was a young cop working in Chicago. Kate was still in her first year of life. … She later studied law and became a successful lawyer working in Chicago. And, from there, with Jack's blessing she went on to join the New York City Police Department where she now served as a lieutenant homicide detective.

Finally Kate spoke.

"What can you tell me about this project that Dad is working on? Just how dangerous is it?"

"I cannot give you any details. The whole matter is Top Secret. And I am not using that designation loosely."

"On a scale of one to ten?"

"Kate," Bob said slowly, carefully choosing every word. "There is really not a rational way to measure the severity of the situation we, as a nation, are facing. And there's not even a standard protocol to apply to it, either. Without a doubt, Kate, what we are facing poses the greatest potential threat to this country that we have ever faced. Hell, it's more than a potential threat—"

"Then this is all bullshit, Bob," Kate said, interrupting the former President. "Pure bullshit. If it is, as you say, such a big damn problem, why did you stick my dad in the middle of it? You've got the Secret Service, the FBI, and the National Guard. … Hell, if it's that big a deal why don't you sick the U.S. Army after whoever it is that's trying to destroy us? Doesn't make any sense. Are you sure it's not just one of those bimbos you're trying to silence? I know all about them. I know that you had Dad working overtime when you were in the White House doing just that. Trying to keep a lid on your philandering. The whole country knew that you couldn't keep it in your pants. Is that what this is all about now? Just another bimbo eruption?"

"Kate. I understand completely why you are so upset. But you should believe me about this. It is just a fact—a situation exists that threatens our way of life. Honestly, I can't say any more about it. I'm sorry that your father had to be drawn into it. But, frankly, he and Roger are the only two people I feel I can trust to handle it. They are special people, with a unique set of skills. They are the men we need at this time. If you press me on this, I will have to terminate this call."

"Okay," Kate said after forcing herself to calm down. "If this all shakes out. If you haven't already killed my dad. You and I are going to have a little talk. If you've been lying to me. If I even think you've been lying to me. If you have unnecessarily put my dad in harm's way, I will shoot you right in the balls. Trust me on that. You had better not be shittin' with me in *any* way. Do you understand me?"

"Kate, I am telling you the truth. You have to beli—"

"I don't *have* to do one damn thing for you. I asked you a question. Do you fully understand what I just said to you? If you get my father hurt—or killed—for some stupid, selfish reason, I will kill you. Do you understand?"

Former President Bob Fulbright was not used to being talked to in this fashion. It took him a little time to gather himself up. Finally, he said, "I understand."

"Good. Damn good you do. Because if you screw with my father, I will extract full payment from you in blood. Or die trying. Okay, now that we've reached an understanding, what can I do to help?"

"First things first. We've got to extract your father from South Dakota—if he's still stuck there."

"I can't do much from New York."

"How about Henry? He was in Deadwood with your father. Right? I would assume he is still there. Is that also right?"

"He is. Shall I have him join the search?"

"Maybe."

"What did you have in mind for him? Or me, for that matter?"

"The last reading we have from the plane was not that far from Rapid City. If ... *when* we locate the plane, there's a good chance that it will be relatively close to that location."

"Should I have Henry head there now?"

"Yeah. I think that would be a good idea. If Jack and Roger were forced down, they're likely to need some help on the ground. I hate to ask you this, but I have to. Is Henry armed?"

"If he's not, I'm sure Dad has something hidden in the Tahoe. He always does. Then you think that there might be some people trying to make sure that Dad and Roger are permanently put out of action?"

"That would make sense. I'm sure that there are those out there who would believe that, at this point, the only way to ensure their success would be to eliminate both Roger and your father."

"I'll get Henry on the way. Right now. But, I have to ask you again. Why the hell don't you enlist the services of the FBI? As I see it, that would only make sense."

"Damn it, Kate. I told you that I can't talk to you about this. Believe me, if I could send the FBI out there to protect your father I'd do it in a heartbeat. But I can't. I can't, because it is the FBI that is after them. Not the rank and file. But those in charge. The problem we're facing is the Deep State. And I don't know just who all is involved. I don't know who I can trust. This is one big shitass problem."

"Tell me where I should send Henry. Give me all the info you can, so that I can inform him. He needs to know at least a little bit about the shitstorm he's getting into."

"You can tell him everything I've told you. He might be able to accomplish more from the ground than we can from the air. … That area has some very treacherous terrain. Here are the coordinates from the last time we had a transmission from the locator: 43.525046, -100.938663. That will give him something to work from. And, Kate, don't talk to anyone else about this. I don't know who we can trust at this point."

Chapter 20

While Kate did not hang up on the former President, she did abruptly end her conversation with him, and she called Henry.

"Kate," Henry said. "Somethin' up?"

"Yeah. Sure is. It looks like Dad and Roger might have gone down east of Rapid City last night. Bob Fulbright would like you to head over there and conduct a covert land search."

"Holy shit! What happened?"

"Bob wouldn't give me much information about the mission. Only that Roger had flown out to pick Dad up, and they were headed back to New York when something happened to their plane."

"Same one as Roger generally uses?"

"Yeah. At least I'd assume so."

"Can you be more specific as to location?"

"Bob gave me these coordinates: 43.525046, -100.938663. That is what he had from the last transmission of Roger's transponder. There is a search underway. But, so far, nothing's been found. There were no explosions reported, and nothing spotted from the air or by satellites. It's like they just disappeared."

"What have we got out there?" Henry asked. "Specifically? I'm pretty sure there are a couple Native American reservations in that general area. What else can you tell me?"

"You're right. I just brought it up on Google Maps, and it looks like it would be a little north of the Rosebud Reservation. Are you familiar with it?"

"No. Not really. Just that it would be part of the Sioux Nation. As far as the terrain itself—that area is sparsely populated, and pretty rugged. Still, it seems unlikely that a plane of any size could go down there without someone seeing or hearing it—even at night. I'll head that way right now. Should get tribal permission, at least let them know that I'm poking around. It's possible that they might have some useful information."

"See what you can come up with," Kate said. "I'm on my way to Rapid City as soon as I can catch a plane."

Chapter 21—Back to Jack

The immediate drag on the damaged plane had been enormous—mostly because of the missing windshield and exposed engine compartment. At first Roger remained unresponsive. The blow to his head had rendered him unconscious. Jack, however, quickly recovered.

"Roger!" Jack barked. "We're goin' down! Pull the chute!"

Recognizing that his friend was totally incapacitated, Jack reached over and pulled the Ballistic Recovery System lever, thus deploying a fifty-foot orange full-plane parachute. The forty pounds of pressure exerted on the "pull" ignited a small rocket, which in turn positioned the BRS safety device above the plane until it captured enough air to fully open. Once that happened, the Piper M350 jerked to a near standstill, up righted itself (with the help of the chute, of course), and then began a much slower descent to earth.

Even though the airplane did not belong to Roger, he had flown it so many times that he had developed a sense of ownership. So, when he invested nearly thirty thousand dollars in additional safety equipment, which included the cost of an updated radar system and an aftermarket BRS, none of his friends thought anything of it.

Jack's only remark when he learned about it was, "The way you fly, my friend, and the enemies you make, you shouldn't even think about taking a plane up without a soft way to get down in an emergency."

There was a strong wind blowing out of the northwest—forty

knots, with gusts up to sixty. So, instead of a relatively straight vertical path to the ground, the plane rode the wind and drifted dramatically to the southwest.

Because it was dark, and because all of the instruments were knocked out by the impact of the missile that had been fired at them by the drone, Jack had no notion as to when he might expect impact.

Finally, after what felt like an eternity, the plane began striking the tops of enormous ponderosa pine trees. Initially it felt to Jack like they might become lodged high up in the branches of the forest, but a firm gust of wind dragged the parachute along until the plane slashed sideways between the trees. It crashed to the ground with the end of the right wing absorbing most of the shock as it crumbled under the weight of the plane.

As soon as it was clear to Jack that it would fall no farther, he jumped out of the hole left by the smashed out windshield and began cutting the parachute lines. Not only did he wish to prevent the plane from being dragged along by a gust of wind, he knew that somebody would soon be looking for them, and most likely that *somebody* would have bad intentions. And he knew that the huge orange parachute would serve as a target on his back.

Gathering it up as rapidly as he possibly could, he began shoving it into the cockpit through the gaping hole where the windshield had been.

"Roger," he said loudly. "You still taking a nap? Hey! Buddy! It's time to wake up."

"What the hell happened?" Roger finally moaned. "Jack. What happened? Where the hell are we?"

"Trump Tower, of course. Shall I have breakfast sent up?"

"Cut the bullshit! Where are we? What happened? What time is it? How long was I out?"

"Only ten minutes or so. Just long enough for that BRS to earn its keep."

"We crashed?"

"I suppose you could call it that," Jack said. "It was more like a bumpy ride on a Chinese elevator."

"Did I pull it? I don't remember anything about it. Or did you?"

"You didn't respond immediately. So I pulled it for you."

"Damn!" Roger feigned a complaint. "After all that money—I wanted to be the one who deployed it."

"Next time," Jack said, laughing. "The next time we run into an AAM, I'll try harder to wake you up so you can pull out the chute."

"So, I guess it must have worked. Right?"

"Like a charm."

"How about the plane? Judging by the angle—there's got to be some significant damage, I'd guess. Probably totaled. What would you say?"

"I'd say it'd cost more to clean up the mess than the plane's worth, at this point. I hope *you're in good hands*."

"Bob's going to get the bill for this."

"Double it. And then buy yourself a Beechcraft turboprop. If you get the Beechcraft, I can borrow it from you."

"I might do something like that," Roger said, slowly getting his bearings. "I doubt that I'll be borrowing anything from my buddy anymore—not after this. But, I think I'd prefer the TBN 700. Need only twenty-five hundred feet of runway. And you can forget about borrowing it. Not going to happen."

"Okay," Jack said, after crawling back into the cockpit. "Time to get you out of this wounded bird. We've got a lot of fuel still spilling out. It could ignite. Not likely, though. Nice the engine had time to cool down before we broke that wing off. But we've still got to get you out of here. What do you need to gather up before we move on? Got any broken bones that I need to watch out for?"

"I don't think so. I've got a splitting headache. Might have a concussion. But everything else seems intact."

"Then I'm going to let you lower yourself through the window. Tell me if you need some help. Now, what all do you need me to collect?"

"Nothing that can be traced," Roger said as he removed the battery from his cell phone. "No radios. Grab my SAT phone and power it down. Bring my go-bag, and the charts. Leave everything else."

Jack had already removed the battery from his phone. Both men knew that their cell phones would be useless because there was a dearth of towers. And when they were to approach a tower, they would still have to exercise caution because by using their phones they would leave themselves open to cell tracking devices.

Jack carefully retrieved their bags, Roger's SAT phone, and a large piece of nylon camo he found stowed behind the rear seat. He then made his way out of the plane.

"What do you think?" Jack said. "Are you up to putting some distance between us and the plane?"

"I'm fine," Roger said. "I'm sure Bob's got his people out looking for us. The only problem is, whoever it was who shot us down—they're going to be conducting their own search."

"I think our best way out is through Henry. But it could be a real trick getting him out here. I'm not even sure about where *here* is. Might do better commandeering a vehicle and making a run for it. Where the hell do you think we are?"

"Somewhere between Deadwood and Deep State," Roger chuckled. "Actually, given the fact that we encountered that drone less than forty minutes outside Rapid City, I'd say we're probably still in South Dakota, maybe on some reservation. There's a few of them around here."

"Do you think there's anything we can do to hide the plane?" Roger asked. "You know. Somehow camouflage it?"

"The way it sliced down between the trees," Jack said. "We couldn't have done a better job of hiding it if we'd tried. Like that plane that went down near St. Ignace twenty years ago. It was just found. After all that time. Same thing with this. Without that orange chute advertising our location, no one's going to visually spot the plane … not without a ground search. Or sophisticated sensing devices. I found some camo in the back. If we use it to cover up the shiny objects, it'd be safe to say it'll take them a little time to find it."

"I think you're right," Roger replied. He was slowly regaining his strength and senses.

"Let's create some distance between us and the wreck," Jack suggested. "And then figure out our next step. That is, if you're fit to travel."

"Don't give me that shit, Jack. I'm *perfectly* fine—at least from the neck down."

Chapter 22

Even though Kate had already enlisted Henry's help, she was not about to sit back and wait. She caught a cab to Kennedy International and purchased a ticket to Rapid City.

Well east of Chicago, through the window on her Delta one-stop, she spotted the familiar cloud of urban pollution.

Henry wasted no time either. Before Kate had even boarded her plane he had checked out of his hotel and was well on his way east on Interstate 90.

Using his Garmin, Jack set about obtaining their bearings.

"Our crash site is forty-three degrees, twelve point six minutes north," Jack announced, "and one-hundred one degrees, point twenty seven minutes west. Be nice to get a snapshot from a satellite—just to get the lay of the land."

"I like to think of it as *our landing site*," Roger admonished through a bit of a tight grin. "Best not to turn *my* GPS on. I've got a tracking device built into it. Only transmits when activated."

"According to the map," Jack said, "we came down in a very opportune location—right in a very narrow line of green shit. Couldn't have done better had we placed the plane there by design. Appears to me that if we want to create some separation between ourselves and the plane, we should follow the tree line north and east for a mile or so. Looks like a dried up creek bed—for the most part. If we stay under the cover of those trees, it should bring us safely up to a two-track that runs west off of BIA Road 5."

"What's that BIA stand for?" Roger asked.

"That'd be the Bureau of Indian Affairs designation for that particular reservation road.

"When we get there—to the two-track. If it looks like a secure location, we could message it to Henry. And have him make the extraction there."

"That'd be assuming that Henry was already nearby," Roger said. "Because, once we fire up the SAT phone, it's likely that we'll have company within minutes. They'll be looking for it."

"For sure they know we're down," Jack added. "What's unknown is what sort of info they have regarding our current status."

The men, agreeing that it would be best to move southeast along the tree-covered creek bed, slogged through dips, mounds, streams and ponds until they believed they had covered enough ground to make finding them difficult even with the benefit of dogs.

"What do you think, Roger?" Jack asked. "We should be far enough from the plane to make finding us difficult, even if they happened to stumble upon it. What say we hole up for a while—at least until daybreak. That way we can get a better look at the surrounding terrain. I figure that two-track we spotted on the map ought to be within sight, once we have some daylight. When the sun comes up we might even see a better way. Maybe even come up with a superior method to facilitate extraction."

"Bob will begin missing us within a few hours," Roger said. "If he hasn't already."

"What will he do?"

"He'll contact the South Dakota Highway Patrol," Roger said. "Normally, he'd contact the FBI. But not in *this* case. The Highway Patrol will call around on the reservations, and other local law enforcement. I intentionally disabled the ELT, so they will not be able to hone in on it. And if we don't power up the SAT phone, or cells, they will have to go out and manually find us. Bob's calling the Highway Patrol will cover any contingency should the plane have been observed crashing, or bursting into flame. But that didn't happen—we just sort of slid out of the sky. Perhaps not elegantly, but at least we made it down safely.

"As soon as he is convinced that we were forced down he will call Kate. She'd be the logical choice given these circumstances. Who else can he trust? Right now you and I are it and Kate by extension. He knows Henry. Not well, perhaps. But he recognizes the fact that both you and Kate are totally good with him, so he will assume that Kate will get Henry on the case."

"That's how I see it, too," Jack agreed. "Kate's first call will go to Henry, and then she will catch a plane. But, that leaves us a few hours to keep our heads down. Don't want to give our location away before we're fairly confident Henry is in the area. Let's go over it again. Just what is it that Bob thinks I can do for him?"

"He'll have to spell it out for you personally. I know he has some specific ideas, but, as I understand it, he's relying on your special talents to come up with a working plan. I'm sure he'll not delay. The project is time sensitive. He's undoubtedly busy with this as well."

"Nice to have some idea as to the pedigree of that cruise missile. They've been around a long time. If it's an older version, like the Tomahawk, it might be easier to develop countermeasures. Am I to understand that only one of these missiles is to be employed?"

"All great questions, my friend. But Bob is going to be the only one who can answer them with any authority. And I think that even he is a little unsure of just exactly what we can expect."

"Do we know what sort of platform is being used—land or sea? And, if there is to be more than a single launch, can we expect there to be a single general location? Do you have *any* of that information?"

"I don't. At least not much. Bob did seem to suggest that it was to look like a rogue action. So that no finger would be pointed at any of the Deep State players. For it to work as planned, it has to look as though it was carried out by the NoKos. That's why it has to be something that might have been sold through the black market."

"Like those suitcase nukes that were reputedly made available to arms dealers after the Soviet Union broke up?"

"Exactly. But back then only the U.S. had a decent cruise missile. So, I think logic suggests that you might expect it to be an older version of the Tomahawk."

"It's almost impossible to take a cruise missile down. Much easier to attack the launch site before it's even fired."

"Left of launch," Roger offered. "I think that type of defensive tactic is called *left of launch*. That is, hitting the missile platform before the cruise missile is even fired."

Slowly the orange-red sun broke through the eastern sky and illuminated the South Dakota horizon.

"Well I'll be damned, Jack," Roger said, pointing to the north. "There's our route of escape that you've been talking about. Not much of a road, but I'm sure Henry can get through on it. Do you think it's too soon to give him a shout?"

Jack, who had busily been calculating and taking notes, responded, "Let's do it."

Chapter 23

"Hey, buddy," Jack said, speaking into Roger's SAT phone. "Take this down: P-O-N-O T-O-G-F E-F-D-M I-J-Z-Y D-M-M-L I-H-M-K M-P-U-T. Did you get it?"

"Got it," Henry replied.

And then, after a few minutes, Henry said, "WLS. And I have to fuel up."

With that Jack disconnected.

"What was all that bullshit?" Roger asked.

"I was explaining to Henry where we were, and he told me how long it'd be before he arrived."

"You and your cryptograms," Roger moaned. "What's Henry got, anyway, some kind of Jack Handler Decoder Ring?"

"Something like that."

"So, Dick Tracy, when does your private Uber arrive?"

"He's eighty-nine miles out right now. So, if he averages even forty-five miles per hour, and stops for gas, he should be here in two, two-and-a-half hours—give or take."

"That's just about how long it's going to take for …" Roger hesitated. "For the *black hats* to arrive. For lack of a better term, we can just call them the black hats. We might have only two hours—less, if they get lucky."

"Maybe we can improve our odds," Jack said. "Come on, Roger. Get off your lazy ass and let's create a little diversion."

"Sounds good. What do you have in mind?"

"Leave some shit here. Candy wrappers or something. And grab everything else. Let's head out to the main road."

Once they neared it, they dropped down behind some brush and Jack keyed the SAT phone again.

When Henry picked up Jack said in his best Cockney brogue, "The rain in Spain stays mainly in the plain."

To which Henry chuckled, "Got it, boss," and disconnected.

"That should do it," Jack said as he removed the battery from the SAT phone, and plugged the battery back into his personal cell phone. He then walked out onto the road and scattered his belongings out on the asphalt.

"Here," he said to Roger. "When a vehicle stops to help me, send my cell along with them. They'll be paying attention to me and not even see you."

"Yeah. Sure," Roger said reluctantly. "You know, Jack, we're signing their death certificate by doing that."

"We're not debating this," Jack barked. "Just do what I tell you."

Seldom did Jack assume that posture with his friend. But, in Jack's mind, the life of the President of the United States rested on the success of their every effort. *If one or two innocents have to be sacrificed to make my plan work*, he reasoned, *then so be it. Hell, I don't know what Roger's moaning about. Right now our odds don't look very good no matter what we do. Here we are with half the smartest people in the country hell-bent on killing us, and Roger is concerned about the welfare of a couple of strangers. Good chance we'll not live to see the next sunrise. But, that's just the nature of this game. When we're called upon to put our chips back in the box, they bury the box. Enough of this shit. I hear a truck coming from the south.*

Jack's subterfuge worked as planned. The driver of the truck, a middle-aged Native American, stopped nearly fifty feet back from where Jack was lying, and directly in front of where Roger was hiding. The driver waited behind the wheel. Jack watched him talking with his young teenage son. *Probably trying to figure out what's going on,* Jack thought. *He's telling his son to wait until he sees that everything is okay. Maybe he'll have him slide into the driver's seat so he can make a mad dash for it in case it all goes south.*

And that's exactly how it went down. After a few long moments the father gingerly stepped out of the truck, while his son slid over behind the steering wheel. They kept the engine running as the man walked toward Jack.

At the same time, Jack watched as Roger sneaked over and behind the truck. Carefully he laid Jack's cell phone in the bed of the pickup.

"Mission accomplished," Jack said to himself.

"Hey, mister," the man said. "You okay? Djoo fall down?"

Seeing Roger safely return to his hiding place, Jack pushed himself up to his elbows and moaned, "What happened? I musta taken a little tumble."

"Are you hurt?"

"I, I don't think so. I think I'm okay. Oh. I must be blocking you. I'm sorry. I'll just get my stuff picked up here and get outta your way. I'm really sorry."

"No problem. I just want to make sure you're not injured. Did you bump your head when you fell?"

"No. Really. I'm sure I'm just fine. Probably tripped over my big feet. I'm just clumsy. I'll get my shit picked up and get outta your way. I'm sorry about this."

"Here," the man said as reached under Jack's arm to help him the rest of the way up. "Let me give you a hand."

"Thank you. Thank you."

"Can I give you a lift? My son and I can drop you off somewhere, if you like."

"That's very kind of you. Very kind. But I'm expecting my son any minute. He's supposed to be picking me up anytime now. He's really gonna be worried if he sees you helping me. He worries about everything. Says I'm not able to take care of myself. Shit like that. The best thing you could do for me right now would be to let me keep walking down the road. Otherwise he's gonna want to talk to you and ask questions.

"I want to thank you for your help and concern, but I really should be getting on my way. I will be more careful. I promise."

Jack then produced his best Sean Connery smile, and reached out to shake the man's hand.

"Well," the man said. "If you're sure you'll be okay."

"I'm just fine. I'll watch my step better from now on."

Just then Jack spotted a vehicle speeding toward them from the south.

"There," he said, pointing at the oncoming dark SUV. "That's probably him now. Thanks again for your help. Now, if you don't mind, it'd be best for me if you'd leave before my son gets here. He's gonna have questions. If you don't mind."

"I understand. As long as everything's okay. You take care now."

"Thanks again," Jack said as he stepped back off of the road.

The father got back in the truck and drove off in the same direction as the approaching SUV.

As soon as the truck pulled out Jack bolted over to where Roger was hunkered down.

"That's probably going to be them," Jack said. "The black hats."

"See if they turn to follow the pickup," Roger said. "Or pull off here. I say they've got a fix on my SAT phone, and that they'll pull right in here."

"We'll soon find out," Jack said. "You're probably right. Unlikely that they've been able to ping that cell yet. My bet is they'll be searching right about here."

The SUV Jack and Roger had been watching went about five hundred yards past their position, and then slowed. After a minute the vehicle turned around and headed back toward them.

"What'll we do if they head right back here?" Roger asked.

Jack did not answer. Instead he opened his duffel and removed a zippered camo bag containing a broken down 6.5 Creedmoor compact sniper rifle.

"Well," Roger said as he pulled out his Glock. "I guess that answers my question."

Once it was assembled, Jack peered down the scope of the Creedmoor until he located the black SUV.

"Looks like they might be coming back," he said. "If they get close enough we'll take them out with our side arms. But, if need be, I can plunk them off from a thousand yards. What'd you see when they went past us?"

"Very tinted side glass, but I'm pretty sure there were only two of them."

"That makes sense," Jack agreed. "This is exploratory for them.

They don't know for a fact if that was us on the SAT phone. They'd likely only send two men to investigate. When we take them out, we'll want to do it quickly. Don't need anything like a firefight. Can't give them a chance to call it in."

"You're going to have to use the rifle, Jack. Unless they decide to walk right in on us."

"Be ready. Looks like they might be pulling in."

Slowly the SUV proceeded along the edge of the road, traveling no more than five to ten miles per hour. But, instead of driving back into the brush, the driver pulled off the road and stopped. They were about a quarter of a mile away from Jack's position—perhaps a little less. Two men leaned forward to look out of the SUV. Jack followed them with the Creedmoor.

"That's going to be it," Roger said. "They're stopping. Think you can get a good shot?"

Jack did not respond.

Slowly the driver emerged from the SUV, followed by the passenger. Both of the men then walked to the front of the vehicle and stood. They appeared to be surveying the wooded area off to the west.

And then it happened. The passenger stepped up until he was directly beside the driver. And then he pointed at something in the woods.

Jack fired.

Both of the black hats fell to the ground.

"Did I really see what I think I saw?" Roger blurted out. "Did you *actually* take them both out with a single shot?"

Jack did not respond immediately. Instead, using the scope he continued to observe the two men lying on the ground in front of the SUV. Finally, he spoke.

"Looks like it got 'em both. At least neither of them seem to be trying to get up. Superb ballistics. I really like the way this Creedmoor spits out those 6.5 rounds. The driver was a pretty well-built dude. And even with tumbling, and ribs, that round had enough speed to take out his number two."

"Must not have been wearing vests," Roger said. "That seems odd."

"I caught him at the shoulder. So number one makes sense—even if he had a vest. But, number two. Can't explain that. Not from here."

"That was either a great shot, or pure blind luck," Roger chuckled.

"You think? Whichever—I'll take it."

"Doesn't look like anyone's stirring in the back of the SUV," Roger said. "Shall we go take care of business?"

Jack then broke down the rifle while Roger briskly made his way toward the SUV. Jack stood and followed after he had returned the 6.5 to his camo bag and loosened his Glock in its holster.

By the time Jack had reached the SUV Roger had already tossed the driver in the back of the vehicle and was dragging the second man over as well.

"Let me give you a hand," Jack said, grabbing the dead man's legs. "Let's just squeeze him in there enough so that we can close the door. We got to get the hell out of here. Did you check the ground? Did they drop anything?"

"I picked up the driver's cell," Roger said. "Got it in my pocket. Thought we'd want to pull the numbers off it. That is, if it isn't locked. What are we going to do with the SUV? Should get it out of here, don't you think?"

"Yeah. That's what I'm thinking. You drive. Give me that cell."

"I've got a better idea," Roger said. "If that cell is locked you're going to need my help."

"Right."

Jack slid in behind the wheel and backed out onto BIA 5, spun around and sped off to the north.

"Well," Jack said. "What have you got?"

"It's locked."

"Can you get into it?"

"Yeah. Should be able to. As long as it powers up—and it does, I can read it with my cell and pull all the data off. Won't take more than a minute or so. There, I got it."

"Your cell—can it be tracked?"

"It's highly encrypted. And the number changes randomly. If someone were scanning the whole spectrum, they'd see mine as well. But they couldn't monitor my calls. But to do what I'm doing right now, copying the data off this guy's cell—I'm not sending a cell signal to a tower right now. So, we've still got privacy.

"How far we headed? And how are we going to hook up with Henry now?"

"We need to create some real estate between this vehicle and ourselves," Jack said. "And quickly—it's probably got a tracking device on it. We'll park it someplace a bit out of the way, and borrow somebody else's SUV. We're going to need an SUV. If you see a suitable candidate, give a shout."

"I'm looking," Roger replied quickly. "I hate the smell of brain matter and blood. Not to mention, one of these assholes shit himself. Trust me, Jack. I'm looking."

"There!" Jack blurted out. "How about that Jeep?"

"Looks fine to me."

"Have you finished with the cell phones?"

"Just the driver's. Do we need to copy the other guy's as well?"

"Let's call it good," Jack said. "More important that we ditch this truck and head back to the meetup—ASAP. Let's see if you're still any good at this. I'll time you."

Jack was referring to the amount of time it would take Roger to successfully bypass the security system and "hot-wire" the ignition.

"It's an older model. You should be able to get it rolling lickety-split."

"Don't hold your breath. I'm a little out of practice. It might take me a few minutes."

And that's just about how long it did take him—one minute and twenty-six seconds, to be exact.

As he finished, he jumped out of the Jeep and winked at his friend. Jack gave him a congratulatory thumbs-up.

Jack watched as Roger pulled the license plate off and switched it with that of a pickup truck parked three vehicles down.

As soon as Jack saw that Roger was headed back behind the wheel, he pulled out of the parking lot and sped back north. Roger was close behind.

Five miles farther up the road Jack turned off and onto a seldom used two-track. Once out of sight from highway traffic, he pulled off far enough so as not to be visible even from the dirt road.

Roger followed, turning the Jeep around when he saw Jack stopping.

"Head directly back to meet Henry—right?" Roger asked.

"Yeah. Time-wise, that should work out pretty well. Don't want to hang him out to dry waiting for us."

No one spoke for the next five minutes. And then Roger finally broke the silence.

Chapter 24

"I was right, you know," Roger said.

"Right. Right about what?"

"Your number two. It *was* blind luck."

"Really? Explain yourself."

"Your shot. It caught number one in the shoulder—which is just what you'd thought. But the round. It looks to have ricocheted off of some bones, and then exited through the driver's neck. Must have had enough upward trajectory to catch number two in the temple. Your single round closed two sets of eyes."

"Well I'll be damned," Jack chuckled. "Both of them were wearing protective vests, and somehow that round sneaked around it all. That's just how I planned it."

"Blind luck!" Roger retorted.

"Hey, buddy. You can think what you like. But, years from now, if we're going to survive this mission, we'll be talking about that shot. One round—two dead. Great shot. Excellent ballistics. End of story."

"And I'll still be chalking it up to blind luck."

"You, maybe. But Henry and I—you can just bet that we'll have a little different take on it."

"Bullshit! Henry wasn't even there."

"No. But he is now. He made good time, don't you think?"

"Hey, guys," Henry greeted them. "Nice Jeep. Where'd that come from?"

"Have you heard from Kate?" Jack asked, ignoring his question. "Where is she now?"

Looking at his watch, Henry replied, "She should be arriving shortly in Rapid City."

"Can you round up another plane?" Jack asked Roger.

"Wouldn't be wise to go through my regular channels," Roger warned. "That didn't work out so well the first time around. We have no way to know who we can and cannot trust. Right now, you're a lightning rod. Too many people in the intelligence community know you and Bob are tight. Look what just happened."

"What did happen here?" Henry asked. "Roger fall asleep?"

"Henry," Jack warned, "the less you know the better for you."

"No matter how we go about it," Roger said, "if we lease a plane, we're going to have to provide a flight plan, and show ID. That could be a problem. Same thing with a charter. They'll be watching for us."

"*Who's* gonna be watching for you?" Henry asked.

"Jack's managed to attract attention," Roger said. "That's how we ended up out here in the middle of South Dakota. We got ourselves shot down."

"No shit!"

"I need to find a quick way to get to New York," Jack explained. "Under the radar, so to speak."

"I might be able to help you out," Henry offered after thinking about it.

"How's that?"

"I have a friend who has a plane," Henry said. "He flies out of Pine Ridge. It's about an hour and a half from here. There is a small airport near here. In Rosebud. But the airport in Pine Ridge is much larger. Accommodates commercial jets."

"An hour and a half?" Jack asked. "What sort of plane does your buddy have? Need to get close to New York."

"Last I knew he was flying a Gulfstream G550. But he was shopping for a new one, last I heard."

"Nice plane—the Gulfstream. How sure are you that you can round it up and get us on it?"

"If he's in town. Rather, if his *plane* is in town and ready to go, it'd be a pretty good chance. I could give him a call."

"Why would he be willing to do this?"

"Because you're gonna write him a very big check. He's a businessman. Look, I didn't say it would be cheap."

"We're not looking for cheap. We just need to get the hell out of here, and as quickly as possible. It's got to be anonymous. Can't have our real names logged anywhere. Can he do that?"

"I can find out. Shall I make the call?"

"Sure. Find out if it's feasible," Jack said. "And then we'll make a decision. Use Roger's phone to make the call. His can't be traced. For right now, let's get rid of this Jeep. Follow me."

Jack and Roger jumped into the Jeep and tore off through the sandy terrain until they reached a point where they could be relatively certain that the Jeep would not be found right away. Henry followed right on their bumper. Jack then jumped out of the Jeep and quick-walked over to Henry.

"Made your call yet?" Jack asked, as Henry got out and took the seat behind the driver's, allowing Jack to slide behind the wheel of his Tahoe.

Henry did not answer as he searched his wallet for his friend's phone number.

"Galvin. This is Chuchip. How are you?"

"Chuchip. Long time since I heard from you. How are you, my friend?"

"Well. Doing well."

"And your daughter—Lily, is it?"

"She's growing up."

"Where are you? Are you still working in Michigan?"

"Most of the time. Right now I'm in South Dakota—not far from Pine Ridge, actually."

"Then you must come see me. Are you on vacation, or is this business?"

"Business, Galvin. That's why I'm calling you. Do you still have that Gulfstream?"

"Yes. Yes I do."

"Is it ready to go?"

"It could be. Do you need me to fly you somewhere?"

"My boss does. He and his associate need to get to New York as soon as possible. They'll be happy to pay whatever you want. It just has to be soon. And very privately. Can you help us out?"

"Chuchip. Of course. How many will be flying?"

Jack could hear both ends of the conversation. So, without speaking, he held up two fingers for Henry to see.

"There will be a total of two passengers—my boss and his associate. I won't be going."

"How does ten thousand sound to your friends?"

Jack gave Henry a *thumbs-up*.

"How soon can they leave?"

"How soon can you be here?"

"An hour and a half—give or take."

"The pilots should be good to go by then—or close to it."

Henry grabbed Jack's shoulder and asked him, "Then we're good with it?"

"We're good," Jack said. "Give me the directions."

"Galvin, will we see you there, or just the crew?"

"I'll be there to see it off. Maybe you and I can chat for a while. If you have time."

"Great. See you soon."

Just as Jack pulled out on the road and got up to speed, he spotted a tribal police car approaching from behind at a high rate of speed—lights flashing.

Chapter 25

"Oh, shit! We don't need *this*." But when Jack pulled over to stop, the car just sped past him and continued north on BIA-5.

"Looks like you dodged that one," Roger said. "Wonder what it was all about."

"He obviously didn't want *us*. Must have something else on his mind."

By the time they had driven another five miles, two more cop cars came up from behind them. And again they passed the Tahoe when Jack pulled it over.

"Three out of three," Roger said. "This must be your lucky day."

"Something's up. Has to be. They wouldn't be sending the whole tribal police force out to investigate a stolen Jeep. They must have found the bodies."

"Bodies!" Henry blurted out. "What bodies? And, what happened to you guys? How'd you end up out here in the middle of nowhere?"

Jack's hands fidgeted on the wheel as he weighed his words.

"Henry, I don't know where this is going," Jack said. "Or how much I should tell you. This whole thing could end up in court down the road. And the less you know might just work to your advantage. So, I'd like to keep this on a *need to know* basis. …Suffice it to say, we've got some really bad actors trying to kill us right now. For lack of a better term, Roger and I are calling them the black hats."

"The bodies you're talking about—can I assume that they were some of these black hats?"

"They were," Jack answered. "And there's a whole hell of a lot more of them. You can't even imagine how many of them there are. They are highly trained. Many of them trained by our very own military. I suppose they'd been thinking that Roger and I were dead. That is, right up to the time that we took two of them out."

"They caused your plane to come down?"

"Shot it out of the sky."

"How the hell did you survive that?"

"That's a long story too," Jack said. "For right now, why don't you grab my bag out of the back and assemble the Creedmoor. I think you're going to need it."

Henry spun around and reached behind his seat. As he did, he spotted what had attracted Jack's attention. Speeding up from behind was a black SUV. It was still nearly a quarter of a mile back, but it was closing the distance rapidly.

Chapter 26—Millie and the Kids

Jack had a passion—perhaps, even an obsession—when it came to providing safety for Red and Robby. Long before this current situation arose, Jack had established an emergency escape protocol to be followed by Millie Star. The plan went like this: Millie would pick up the boys with the dog and then she, along with her daughter, Angel, would head out of town. Jack always saw to it that the boys were prepared for emergencies—even when staying at Millie's house. Packed and stored there were several one-gallon containers of water, an adequate supply of non-perishable food, and three small duffels—one for each of the boys, and one to be shared by Millie and Angel.

The boys' bags included enough clothes to last a week, and some emergency electronic equipment. Red's bag was a little larger than Robby's because it contained several packages of dog food.

The third bag, the one shared by Millie and Angel, contained only electronic equipment.

From Millie's house in Sault Ste. Marie, MI, the four of them, along with Buddy, would head south on I-75, across the Mackinac Bridge, and proceed south to M-23 in Flint. They would then head south on M-23 until they hit I-90 East. However, before embarking on their journey, the four of them powered down their personal cell phones, and then removed the batteries—all according to Jack's established protocol.

Once on I-90, or wherever they decided to spend the night, they would open up all three bags, retrieve the four burner cells that Jack had packed for them, and bring the cells' batteries up to full charge. But, they wouldn't initiate a call. They would wait for

Jack or Kate to call them.

If, however, Millie or the boys sensed an overwhelming need to reach Jack, then, in that special circumstance, it would be okay to make the call.

If their departure occurred in the morning, then they would push through until they had reached Cleveland. There they would find a hotel.

If Jack had ordered their departure in the afternoon, or later, then they would seek lodging in Gaylord, Flint, or Ann Arbor—whichever worked to their advantage.

Since this exodus occurred so late at night, Millie opted for the group to spend the night in Gaylord, which is located in the Lower Peninsula about sixty miles south of the Mackinac Bridge. Once settled in, they unpacked and powered up the cell phones. But they would not initiate a call. They would wait for Jack to call them.

When ten o'clock rolled around, Millie sent all three of the teenagers to bed.

Reluctantly, they acquiesced to her wishes. Their argument was that they wished to stay up and wait to hear from Jack or Kate. To which Millie replied, "Request heard and duly considered, troop. Now hit the sack—all three of you. Buddy needs his rest."

While Millie seemingly dismissed their request out of hand, she, too, was anxious to hear from Jack. She just did not reveal her anxiety to the kids.

Millie was bright, savvy and in her late thirties. By working out daily and eating healthy, she was able to maintain her one hundred and twenty pounds—which was the goal she set the month after Angel was born fourteen years ago. Any day of the week, and regardless of the terrain, Millie could run ten miles in under seventy minutes—a rate that would make most men envious. In her younger days she took boxing classes and later karate, where she worked her way up through the ranks to brown belt. But, right after Angel turned ten, she decided to give up boxing and the martial arts in order to concentrate on parenting.

Jack had met Millie barely a year earlier—an event that, even though recent, dramatically changed her life for the better. It was he who discovered that a sizable inheritance had been secretly set aside for her by her deceased husband. Jack not only helped her successfully navigate through all the legal complications associated with obtaining her inheritance, it was also at his suggestion that she took the exam for a concealed-weapons permit. He felt that given the tumultuous events surrounding her inheritance, and the fact that she was now a very wealthy single mother, she should be able to protect herself and her daughter.

On this day, she was wearing her skinny cropped jeans with a black tee shirt and a gray hoodie. She kept her life simple with a touch of mascara and a bit of lip-gloss. Her sparkling, unaffected smile matched nicely the youthful enthusiasm in her eyes. In her small black leather purse she carried her hammerless .38. Sometimes she would slip it into a pocket, but seldom did she do that because she considered the pocket bulge an eyesore. The same was the case with her ankle holster. *It just doesn't look good,* she thought. So she almost never used the holster.

Millie considered it necessary to always look good, and to blend in—especially when it came to the clothes she chose to wear. But, when it came to a special occasion, while she maintained her *looking good* motto, she dropped the whole concept of *blending in*. When dressing for an extra special date she would pile her red hair on top of her head, break out the stilettos and be prepared to dance the night away in her little black dress.

None of these qualities escaped Jack's attention. Often he would observe her from a distance and be reminded of the way he felt when he would be in the presence of his young wife, Beth, when they first got married. While Millie did not physically resemble the love of Jack's life, she did carry herself in much the same way. At first Jack fought those feelings, because they would only remind him of the day Beth was killed on the sidewalk outside their Chicago home—and worst of all, by a bullet meant for him.

However, the longer he knew Millie, the more accustomed he grew to her natural beauty, and the more appreciative he became of it. "If only I were younger," he said to himself—at first. But now he no longer considered their age difference. And neither did she, he surmised.

Tonight, however, Millie was all business. She knew that she was the safe harbor between these golden kids and the rest of the world, and at this moment in time that was all that mattered to her.

"I wish Jack would have at least let us bring our Xboxes," Robby said. "But, I get it. He wants us to use nothing that goes online. Nothing that can possibly be traced. What all did he pack? Must be *something* in there that's fun."

Red and Robby shared a room, so they did enjoy some degree of privacy with regard to Millie and Angel. After doing a bit of napping on the drive, neither of the boys were at all tired at ten P.M., so they were now eagerly seeking something fun to do.

Of the two boys, Red was demonstrably the more independent. Having been orphaned at an early age, he found he could basically take care of himself and thrive in most any environment. Before he met Jack and Kate, at various times in his young life Red lived in backwoods huts he had constructed with his own hands on Sugar Island, and then wintered in vacant cottages into which he had broken. While in these cottages he would pay his way by making repairs and cutting firewood. He would hunt and fish for food, and in emergencies he would raid the cupboard. Before he would leave a borrowed cottage, he would clean the building thoroughly, and stock the woodbins with wood he would split. If he felt he had used an exorbitant amount of the owner's food, he would then sell some of the firewood and replenish the cupboards.

The owners always knew what was going on and never seemed to mind. Red had an amazing head of red hair, with curls that framed his young face. At fourteen, he was always full of energy and fresh ideas. Even though due to a vocal impairment—sustained in a faulty foster home—he was physically unable to talk, his fair skin and blue eyes were captivating, thus giving him the advantage when he needed to express himself. While Red never owned very many pieces of clothing, those who actually would spot the pre-Handler Red would always describe him as the red-headed kid with tattered jeans and a Northern Michigan wildcats hoodie.

A light went on behind Red's eyes. Grabbing his go-bag as he jumped out of bed, he headed into the bathroom as though shot out of a cannon. Buddy, the boys' golden retriever followed at his heels, with Robby right behind him.

"Great idea," Robby said. "I always wondered what all Uncle

Jack packed in these bags. Must be something in here that isn't so boring."

The first thing that Red pulled out was a sealed five-pound container of dog food. Robby saw him do it and quipped, "I guess that's *your* lunch for tomorrow. Let's see what's in mine. Uncle Jack knows I like to keep busy. Wonder what he sent along with me to occupy my fertile brain."

Robby and Red were stepbrothers. Some people would refer to them as *foster* brothers, but Jack, who knew the boys preferred to be thought of as stepbrothers, would quickly set them straight. Jack was raising them together at the resort because neither of the two boys had living blood relatives.

Robby had brown hair and brown eyes, and was just one inch taller than Red, however, the boys weighed almost the same. Jack had given each of them LSSU hoodies for their last birthday. The boys loved the hoodies so much that they made them their go-to piece of clothing.

Red groaned and rolled his eyes. He missed not being able to fire back a message to counter Robby's abuse. He then opened a small paper sack containing dog treats.

"Oh, crap!" Robby complained. "Looks like Uncle Jack is taking better care of Buddy than he is us. There must be *something* fun in our bags."

Just then Red reached in and pulled out a deck of cards and a box of poker chips.

Robby spotted the cards and asked him where he found them. Red tipped the bag opening toward Robby and pointed toward a well-hidden side zipper.

Robby spread his bag open and slid the contents to the side

until he found the zippered pocket.

"Well, this could be fun," he said, removing four Ziploc bags.

"Let's go," he said heading out of the bathroom. He spread the four Ziplocs out on the bed for Red to consider. "We haven't played these in a long time. What do you think?"

Red examined the first—a folded fabric chessboard and pieces. The second contained a game of Monopoly. The third—Risk. And the fourth—Stratego.

"So, what'll it be? What would you like to play first?"

Red looked back up at Robby and held up the box of poker chips.

"Really? That surprises me. Poker is the *only* game that I can sometimes win against you. You're just having pity on me, aren't you?"

Red smiled and shook his head.

"Okay. Poker it is. But don't expect me to go easy on you. Should I see if Millie and Angel want to play?"

Red furrowed his brow and shook his head.

"Right. If Millie finds out we're playing games she'll make us go to bed right now."

Red nodded.

The two boys picked up the other games and stuck them back into Robby's bag, and then divided up the chips equally.

Their game continued until two in the morning—that's when Millie overheard Robby laugh loudly after winning a large hand.

She knocked on the door separating the rooms and told the boys to, "knock it off and go to bed."

And that's what they did.

* * *

The next thing the boys heard was Millie knocking on their door again, this time telling them that it was time to get dressed so they could go down for breakfast. Red examined the clock on the small table between their beds.

He moaned loudly when he discovered it was ten minutes to ten.

By the time the four of them made it down to the hotel restaurant it was nearly eleven.

Breakfast was served only until eleven, so Millie made sure they made the cutoff time.

The delightful hotel breakfast room was painted in cool tones—blues and teals—and had small tables with four comfortable chairs around each. On top of the tables were bright colored mums—yellows, reds and whites—with sprigs of baby's breath tucked into mason jars with burlap bows. Each high-back chair was painted a different pastel color. Around the room were Fairview leather chairs in a soft gray with small tables, containing the daily newspapers from up and downstate. Breakfast was along the north wall, offering eggs, bacon, sausage, waffles, orange juice, coffee and oatmeal. At the end of the food table was a large selection of fresh fruit. A refrigerated cooler offered yogurts, milk, other juices and drinks.

The walls were decorated with artwork depicting scenes of Michigan Lakes—sandy beaches, tangerine sunsets and waves crashing onto the rocky shores of Lake Huron. If you closed your eyes you could almost hear the gulls and feel the winds of the summer shore.

As the boys finished their second stack of pancakes, heaped with soft yellow butter and rich pure maple syrup, Angel leaned toward her mother and whispered, "What do you think's up with that girl over there?" She signaled with her eyes toward a girl who was looking uncomfortable at a nearby booth. Even though sitting, the pretty brunette appeared to be tall for a teenage girl, and probably about Angel's age, or perhaps a little older.

Millie slowly stole a glance in the girl's direction. While the thin, dark-haired beauty did not look up at Millie, it appeared to her that the girl was not only aware of the attention, but that it made her even more uncomfortable.

She was wearing a soft pink tee-shirt with white shorts. She had brown leather sandals and a small leather backpack on the floor by her feet. She had a look about her that made you believe she was fiercely independent but with a bit of anxious insecurity mixed in. She kept jotting something in a small notebook that she had taken out of her backpack, and nervously monitored the door to see who entered. Then, suddenly, she pulled her legs up to her chest and put her feet on the edge of her chair. She then wrapped her arms around her legs as if she were chilled.

After a fairly lengthy inspection, Millie turned back to Angel and spoke softly.

"She looks upset. I wonder how long has she been there."

"Since before we sat down. I noticed her when we walked in the door. She seemed to check us out as the hostess seated us. I didn't see her eating anything. Just sipping on that glass of water. I'd like to talk to her and see if she's okay. What do you think?"

"Go for it. All she could do is refuse to talk to you. She might need help."

The boys were busy finishing up their breakfast, so they seemed oblivious to the situation until Angel slid her chair back and walked over to the young dark-haired girl.

"What's up with Angel?" Robby asked Millie. "Does she *know* that girl?"

"Not yet," Millie replied. "But she's just about to get to."

"Great. Maybe she can introduce her to Red. She looks like his type."

Red promptly kicked Robby in the shin without looking up.

"Ow!" Robby groaned. "What was that for? You know you like her."

Red flashed a stare at Robby signaling for his friend to cease and desist.

"Why's Angel talking to her?" Robby asked.

"We thought the girl looked like something might be wrong. She's been sitting there since before we had breakfast. Angel noticed and thought she might offer some help."

The two girls talked for several minutes. Millie and the boys were sitting too far away to hear any of their conversation, but it became clear to Robby, who was the only one who had a clear view of the girl, that there was something wrong.

"The girl just started crying," he whispered as he leaned close to Millie. "Angel just reached over and held her hand. Something's not right. Should we go over there and see if we can help?"

"Let's give Angel some time to figure this out. If she needs us, she'll let us know."

After another ten minutes Angel slid out of the booth and rejoined her mom and the boys.

"Mom. Can I ask Jessie to join us? She's got a very interesting story."

As soon as Angel suggested to her mother that she would like to have the girl join them, Red stood up and looked around until he found a spare chair from an empty table. He carried it over and slid it under the end of their table between Angel and Millie, and then he returned to his seat.

Millie smiled her approval.

Angel then looked up at her new friend and motioned for her to join them.

The girl picked up her backpack and slowly made her way over and stood behind the empty chair.

"Are you sure you want to hear my sad story?" Her eyes were red from crying.

Chapter 27

After introducing herself and the boys to Jessie, Millie said, "My daughter told us that something's troubling you. Why don't you share what's going on in your life."

Angel sensed that the girl might need a little help getting started, so she jumped in.

"Jessie spent the night in the hotel with her parents. At that point everything seemed normal to her. But then, this morning, they had a surprise visitor—someone she had never seen before. Her parents seemed to recognize the man, but she didn't. They appeared to be afraid of the man, and so they sent her down to the restaurant to pick up a couple of cups of coffee for them. Jessie, why don't you pick it up from here?"

At first Jessie said nothing. Instead, she just stared down blankly at the dishes on the table, and took a long deep breath. There was a long moment of silence before she began speaking.

"I knew my parents wanted some time to talk to the man in private, so I grabbed a water and just hung out down here for maybe thirty minutes. And then I poured their two black coffees in the paper coffee cups. And I headed up to the room. But when I knocked on the door, no one answered. So I knocked again. Louder. And I called out to them. Loud enough for them to hear me. Even if they were sleeping. Or at least I think it was. But no one came to the door. I didn't know what else to do."

"Do you have a key card to get in?" Millie asked.

"No. Two came with the room, but I left the second card on the desk in the room. I didn't want to stand out there and knock all day, so I just left the coffee by the door and came back down here. I went up twice, but the coffee was still sitting by the door. And each time I knocked again, but still no one came to the door."

"Tell Mom about the car," Angel prompted her.

"The last time—about forty minutes ago—I checked their car. To see if they had gone someplace without me. I thought I remembered where they'd parked it, but I couldn't find it."

"Cell phone?" Millie asked. "Do you have a cell phone?"

"I have one. But I was so nervous about the stranger being there, and the way he seemed to set my parents on edge. I forgot my cell and left it in the room."

"Well," Millie said, "they would have no way to get hold of you without that cell phone. We've got to go up there and get it for you. And then call your parents. Everything is likely just fine. They're probably sitting around someplace waiting for you to pick up. Let's go get the phone."

"Will they give me another card? Or will they just let you in?"

"No," Millie replied. "But we'll think of something. First let's take a look in the parking lot and see if we can find your parents' car. Maybe they just moved it. Just take a deep breath. Everything's going to be just fine. Okay, kiddo, you lead the way."

The five of them left the restaurant and began heading for the area where Jessie thought the car should be parked.

She stopped and looked around.

"Over here," she said. "I remember setting my bag on the cement right here under that light post. I'm almost positive that's where we were parked. But, that's not our car now. When I looked before, the spot was empty. Now this car is parked here."

"Were you pulled in frontward?" Millie asked. "Or did your

dad back in? Do you remember?"

"He backed in. He always backs in."

Red walked around to where the rear passenger door on the driver's side would be if a car had been backed into the space. And he began looking around. He then checked on the pavement behind that door. And he spotted something. He bent down and more carefully examined it.

Robby had followed him.

Red gripped his friend's forearm and pulled it toward the pavement until Robby acknowledged Red's finding.

"Blood," Robby said softly. "Just one drop, or did you find more?"

Red held up one finger. He then signaled with his head that Robby should go tell Millie what they had found.

Carefully, so as not to alert the young girl, Robby walked over and tugged on Millie's sleeve.

She got the message.

"Excuse me for a second," she said. "I need to get this call."

And she walked down a couple of parking spaces, and there feigned a phone call.

Robby, who had followed her, whispered softly, "Red found a drop of wet blood right by where the rear door would have been. But we didn't see any blood on the door of the car that's parked there now."

"You sure?"

"It's blood all right. Just a single drop. But we didn't look around to see if there was a trail, or anything like that. Just a single drop is all we saw."

Millie looked around at the side of the hotel, and then at the light posts.

"I don't see any cameras. Do you?"

Robby shook his head.

Millie promptly turned and walked back to where Jessie and Angel were standing.

"Let's go up to your room. Maybe your parents are already up there and waiting for you."

As Jessie led the way, Red and Robby walked behind them scrutinizing the parking lot for additional signs of blood.

Finally, after they had walked about fifty feet, Red grabbed Robby's arm again, and pointed.

There on the black pavement were three drops of blood—a large bead of wet blood, and two much smaller nearly dry ones.

Red looked at Robby with raised eyebrows and a tight, affected smile.

Robby caught up with Millie and held up three fingers.

She slowed down and whispered, "You found three more drops of blood?"

Robby nodded.

A cloud of concern dropped over Millie's face as she quick-stepped to catch up with the girls.

"Stairs or elevator?" Jessie asked.

Millie was in great shape. So her comment surprised Angel.

Once all five were on the elevator, Millie hit the *Close Door* button, but did not select *Second Floor*.

"Okay," she said. "Let's figure out how we're going to do this. Jessie, you don't have a key card—right?"

"That's right. I left the extra one inside on the little desk."

"Then, if your parents aren't there, we've got to have an alternate strategy. Jessie, do you have any ID on you? Anything to prove that you're their daughter?"

Jessie thought for a minute, and then shook her head.

"Nothing."

Millie looked over at the boys and said, "I wish your Uncle Jack were here. He'd get us inside in two seconds flat."

Millie then, noticing a puzzled look on Jessie's face, said, "Red and Robby's uncle, Jack Handler, he has a solution to everything. I'm sure he'd figure out what to do without hesitating."

"Well, what are we waiting for?" Millie said as she hit the button for the second floor.

"Is your room on the parking lot side or the back?" she asked.

"Dad parked so he could watch his car. It's here on the left."

Jessie walked up to the room and double-checked the number. "Two-fourteen," she said.

Using her hand like a mallet, she pounded loudly on the door.

"Mom! Dad! It's me—Jessie."

She waited ten seconds and then repeated her effort.

She started to do it again, but Red reached out and gripped her hand with his to stop her.

He held up an index finger indicating he would like her to give him a minute.

While his taking her fist in his hand startled her, she immediately understood what he was intending. She smiled, nodded, and stepped back from the door.

Their eyes met, and he returned the smile.

Red then grabbed Robby's arm and pulled him toward the stairs.

Robby followed, but took a second to excuse himself.

"You must have inspired Red," he said. "I think he's got an idea he wants us to check out."

"Don't say anything to the front desk," Jessie warned. "That wouldn't be good."

Red heard her admonition, turned and flashed a big smile and a thumbs-up.

The boys covered the stairs four steps at a time. Red was on a mission.

When they reached the bottom, Robby turned to enter the hall to the lobby, but Red grunted his sound for "No!" Both boys then exited the hotel.

Once outside, Red took a few steps out onto the parking area and then looked back up at the windows. He studied them for a minute, counting the number of rooms between the exit door and room two-fourteen.

He counted a second time, and then smiled broadly.

Robby understood exactly what his friend had in mind.

Each of the rooms had a sliding glass door with a small balcony. And the door to Jessie's room was open about six inches. What the boys had in mind was for Robby to hoist Red up high enough for him to get a grip on the railing of the deck. And then, with Robby's help, Red would pull himself up and over the railing. He would then enter the room and let Millie and the girls in.

It did not, however, go exactly as planned.

When Red tried to push the door open farther, it hit something that stopped it.

Dang, Red groused to himself. *The door's got a safety latch on it.*

He stood back and stared at it for a few seconds.

"What's up?" Robby asked, but barely above a whisper.

Red did not want to draw attention to his burglary, so he just turned to Robby and placed his index finger over his lips.

Robby got the message. He turned around and walked over to the other side of the parking lot and began picking up scraps of paper as though it were his job. He did, however, keep a watch on Red out of the corner of his eye.

After another few seconds Red seemed to have a plan. He lifted the door. He was pleased that it moved over half an inch.

This might work, he mumbled, again to himself.

He removed his pocket jackknife and flipped open the blade. Kneeling down he reached it in as far as he could and slid it under the slider as close to the middle of it as he could. And then, wrapping his leg around the door through the six-inch opening, he stepped on the handle of the knife. Using the knife as a lever and a fulcrum, he lifted the door as high as he could, while balancing it on the knife.

With a firm shove, he managed to force the bottom of the door to slide inward out of the track. While the safety latch was still preventing the door from sliding open any farther, he was able to force the door in at the bottom enough to gain leverage and to pull the top of the door out of the track.

He was in!
His euphoria, however, was short-lived.

Chapter 28

Robby remained in the parking lot awaiting Red's direction. He was running out of scraps to pick up.

As soon as Red had squeezed past the forced door he turned toward Robby and gave him the thumbs-up.

And then Red turned around.

The room was destroyed.

Chairs were turned over. Luggage had been opened and clothing was strewn all over the floor.

But the mess was not the disturbing part. What shook Red was the blood. It was on the walls. It looked to him like someone was repeatedly shoved, face first, onto the top of the desk, and into the wall beside the desk.

Red counted the towels. There were four of them—all appearing as though they had been used to blot blood off from someone's face and hands.

Red stood silently surveying the apparent carnage.

"Must not touch anything else," he mumbled indecipherably. "This is what Uncle Jack would call a *crime scene*. Somethin' really bad just happened here."

Slowly Red pushed the bathroom door open and looked inside. He then carefully stepped into the room and examined the shower.

"No bodies," he said to himself. "Thank God."

He made sure not to touch anything except for the sliding glass door. He considered wiping it down, but decided against it, as that would make his actions more suspicious than they already were.

How do we break this to Jessie? he wondered. *We can't let her see this. Robby. I need him up here.*

Red hurried over to the sliding glass door and peered out looking for his friend, but couldn't find him. He then stepped out onto the deck and looked over the edge of the railing.

There he spotted Robby standing and waiting for Red's direction.

"Come up," Red grumbled, using a hand signal to make sure his intentions were known.

Even though Robby was more adept at understanding Red than was anyone else, often he too had difficulty interpreting Red's vocal communications without some sort of auxiliary gesture.

Carefully Red made his way to the hall door. He waited at the peephole until he spotted Robby approaching. He then opened the door and guided Robby inside, but did not allow Millie or the girls to enter. Reluctantly Robby slid through the half-open door, not fully comprehending Red's refusal to let the others past.

Once inside, however, it quickly became clear to Robby why he had blocked the door.

Red closed the door behind them.

"What happened in here?" Robby exclaimed in an emphatic whisper. "That's blood on the wall—right?"

Red nodded.

"Oh my God! It looks like somebody might have been killed in here. Did you check out the bathroom?"

Again Red nodded. The neutral colors of carpeting and wall paint were graphically stained with the blood red horror of the mystery that had transpired earlier.

"We," Robby started to say. "We have to be careful not to touch anything. This looks like a crime scene. And you know what Uncle

Jack says about that. We need to get out of here and call the cops. Right?"

Red nodded.

"Millie and the girls. What shall we do? Jessie shouldn't see this. Right? But we have to let Millie in. She's in charge."

Red nodded and walked toward the door.

The two boys cracked the door open enough for them to squeeze out, but not wide enough for the girls to see inside.

"Millie," Robby said. "We have to show you something. But right now the girls should not enter. Okay?"

"What's this all about?" Angel said, not pleased to be left out.

"We'll explain in a minute," Robby said. "But for right now, we have to show Millie something."

"This is my room," Jessie said, attempting to push past Red and Robby.

"No," Robby said. "Millie first, and then she'll decide. She's in charge. Sorry, but it has to be this way. It *has* to."

"This is *my* room, not yours!" Jessie was beginning to border on anxious rage.

"Honey," Millie said in her soothing tone, coming to Robby's aid. "I don't know what this is all about, but if the boys say this is how it has to be, then that's what we're going to do. Just hang on for a minute. Be a little patient. And we'll get this figured out. Okay?"

"Listen to my mom," Angel said, trying to calm down her new friend. "Mom will see what's up, and let us know. Give her a second."

"This is my room! You're not the boss of me. Are my parents in there? I want to see them. Now!" Jessie was loud and becoming impossible to pacify.

"No one's in the room," Robby said. "No one at all. But we need to have Millie come in, and then she'll make the decision about what we do next."

"This is just ridiculous!" Jessie complained. "I don't know why I even talked to you crazy people in the first place. This is *my* room. I'm calling the cops. That's what I'm gonna do."

"Just give us a minute," Robby said. "Millie will come back out and explain what's happening, and then, if you want to, you can call the police. Just one minute. Please."

"I don't understand this either," Angel said. "But let's give them a chance. My mom will explain everything in a minute. I trust them. Give them a chance."

"Is my key card in there?" Jessie asked. "Would you look on the desk to see if it's there?"

"I'll look for you," Millie said as she took a step toward the door.

Jessie jerked her body around and stormed over to a comfortable looking bench located about twenty feet up the hall. She abruptly sat down on it and looked away from Angel.

"This is all a bunch of BS," she said, finally turning to face Angel. "You people are preventing me from entering my own room. My parents paid good money for that room, and you won't let me go in it. I think this is kidnapping. It's got to be against the law. I want the police to come here and arrest you crazy people. I never asked for your help to begin with. I was just sitting there in that restaurant minding my own business, and you stick your noses into my private business."

Angel did not respond.

Millie took one step into the hotel room and immediately closed the door behind her.

"Oh! Dear God!" she said. "Someone's been murdered."

Red shook his head.

"No?" she asked. "I suppose you're right. We've got to think positive."

"Red looked in the bathroom," Robby said. "And there's nothing there."

"And the blood on the parking lot would have been left there by someone walking. Not dead. So, chances are her parents at least left the hotel on their own power. One of them, or both of them, got pretty beat up. But they left here alive. We must not touch anything."

"Red and I were very careful."

"You're sure no one's in the bathroom?"

Red nodded.

"How do we break this to Jessie?" Robby asked.

"Straight up," Millie said. "We have to be totally honest with her. And, we need to call the police."

Red pulled a pad of paper from his pocket and began to write.

"She's going to want to see room," he wrote. "It's a crime scene. She'll track blood and corrupt it. I say we carefully take a look around now. And then leave. Lock door."

He then showed what he'd written to both Millie and Robby.

"You're right," Millie agreed. "But, reporting this to the police could also be a problem. Jack wants us flying under the radar. We call the police, there's going to be a report. Our cover would be blown. I just wish Jack were here to advise us."

Robby studied Red for a moment. It was obvious to him that

Red was deep in thought.

"What do you think, Red?" he finally asked.

"I say we clean the place up," Red wrote. "Wash the walls down. Throw away everything that can't be washed down. And get out of here. That's what Uncle Jack would do."

"No one was murdered here," Millie added. "There's no body, and we know that whoever was hurt was able to walk to the car. What's up with that slider? Is it broken?"

Red quickly pulled his knife out and lifted the door and put it back into its track. He then turned and gave Millie a smiling thumbs-up.

"Okay," she said. "Let's get busy and clean this place up. These towels will not clean up well enough to save. We'll use them to scrub down the wall, and the floor, and then we'll have to throw them away. The hotel will just bill their card—Jessie's parents."

The clean-up took just under fifteen minutes. Each of them attacked a different part of the room and worked feverishly until every obvious drop of blood was cleaned up.

"Not good enough to avoid forensics," Red wrote after they'd finished. "But probably good enough for housekeeping. Let's call the girls in."

"What do we do with these towels?" Robby asked.

Red opened the closet and removed the plastic laundry bag—the one hotels place in rooms for just that purpose.

They wrung as much water out of the towels as they could and shoved them into the bag, and then tied off the opening.

Red walked out onto the deck and looked around. As soon as he was certain that no one was watching, he dropped the bag of wet towels down into a large bush below. The weight of the bag caused it to slide through the branches until the bush had entirely swallowed it.

"Are we ready for Jessie's inspection?" Millie asked.

Robby said, "I think so." And Red offered his patented expression of acceptance—palms up, shrugged shoulders, furrowed brow, and tight smile.

"Well, then," Millie said. "Here goes."

She opened the door.

Chapter 29

As soon as Millie had announced her permission to enter, Jessie didn't hesitate. She charged past Millie like a hungry puppy, her wide eyes scouring the room as she plowed through.

"So," she said after peering into the bathroom, "what's the big deal? Why all the secrecy? My parents are gone. The room is empty. I don't get it."

"Sit down on the bed, kiddo," Millie said. "We've got to have a talk."

"Why? What's going on?"

"We've got to talk about this, and then we need to get out of here."

Jessie sat down on the bed like Millie had ordered.

"This is what the boys found when they entered," Millie told her. "They found a little blood on the wall, and some on the floor. It looks like someone might have cut himself shaving. Not a lot of blood. But enough to rouse attention."

"I don't see any blood. And Dad uses an electric shaver. He *couldn't* have cut himself shaving. What are you suggesting?"

"And, we found a little blood where you said your parents' car was parked. Not a lot of blood, just a couple drops."

Jessie stared straight ahead as her beautiful blue-green eyes filled with tears.

"Those men. They did it. They did something to my parents. I knew there was a problem. My dad was scared of them."

"I thought you said there was only one man."

"There was only one of them in the room. But on my way to

the restaurant, I saw a second man all in black standing in the hall. His eyes were all over me. Not like some perv. Not like that. He just watched me until I got on the elevator. I just knew he was with that other man. This one—the one standing in the hall—he looked really tough. And mean. I knew something bad was up. I shouldn't have left my parents alone with them. It's all my fault they got hurt."

At that point the tears began flowing.

Millie sat down on the bed next to Jessie and put her arm around her.

"No, honey. Nothing's your fault. Your dad knew that something was up and that's why he had you leave. He was looking out for you. Had you stayed, who knows what might have happened."

"Do you think they're okay?" Jessie asked, as Angel handed her a tissue. "My parents, do you think they're okay?"

"We've no reason to think otherwise," Millie said in a calming voice. "If those men had wanted to do them *serious* harm, this room would have looked a whole lot worse. There was obviously a disagreement. Between the men and your parents. And, for some reason, they wanted to take your parents with them. We need to determine what the problem was all about, and see if we can figure out where they might have taken them. And why. What can you tell me?"

"I'm not supposed to talk about it."

"What does that mean?"

"My parents. No one's supposed to know where they are, or where they live. Stuff like that."

"I don't quite understand."

"Dad said that bad things could happen if I talked to *anybody* about us."

"Bad stuff has already happened. It looks like your parents might have been abducted. I'll tell you what this sounds like to me. It sounds like your family is in the Federal Witness Protection program. It's called WITSEC—witness security. Does that sound familiar? It's operated by the United States Marshalls Service."

"Honest. I can't talk about it."

Millie knew from the way Jessie was avoiding the subject that her parents were most likely involved in either the WITSEC Program, or one of the similar state-run programs.

"Do your parents have enemies that you know about? People who might want to hurt them?"

Jessie didn't answer verbally. She did, however, while looking down to avoid eye contact, slowly nod her head.

"What sort of work did your father do? When he made these enemies? What was it that he did to make these fellows come after him like this? Do you know *why* they are so angry with your father?"

Jessie hesitated, and then she moved to a large overstuffed chair. It gave her room to breathe deeply and collect her thoughts. Finally, she looked Millie in the eye. Sensing that Millie was someone she could trust, she began to share some of her story.

"I don't know everything. My parents didn't actually tell me anything—not really. We used to live here—in Gaylord. I went to school here. My friends lived here, too. We hung out a lot at the movie theater. My dad was an accountant. He did the books for some people. Bad people. I just figured it out—at least I think I did. Dad was also a pilot. Not for an airline, though. He had his own plane, and did charter flights. One of the people who hired him to fly for them was one of the men here this morning. The one who came to the door. I've never seen the one who stood in the hall. Not before this morning. But I remember the one who knocked. He's the one who scared my mom and dad. As soon as they saw him they sent me down to get them coffee. I knew they just wanted to get me out of the room."

"Do you know what kind of business the man was in? What your father did for him?"

"He had a business down in Texas, I think. He imported stuff, I think. And he hired Dad to fly it in. I think from Mexico, but I don't know for sure."

"Was it legal?"

"I don't think so, because Dad had to testify against him. I read about that in the paper. And Mom and Dad sometimes talked about it. They didn't actually come out and tell me anything, I just sort of figured it out on my own. We never discussed anything about it—not directly."

"Do you live around here now?"

"No. Our home is in Oregon. For the past couple years."

"What brings you back to the Midwest?"

"Dad thought we should take a vacation. And we used to live near here."

"Did you get permission to travel here?"

"No. My parents were very nervous about coming here. But, they said it was time that they visited the old neighborhood. I overheard them talking about it. It was Dad who wanted to come here. He said we would be in and out before anyone knew. I think there was something here that he wanted to pick up. Money, maybe."

"Whose money? Did your dad have a lot of money?"

"No. Not that I knew about. We were really quite poor, living in Oregon. My dad and mom both worked. In stores. Dad didn't fly anymore, so he didn't make much money. We barely had enough to get by. I had a job, too—babysitting. I wasn't certified, but I made enough to buy my own clothes."

Red, Robby and Angel had all approached and had been listening in on the conversation.

Finally Red wrote a message to Jessie. It did not surprise her that he wrote his thoughts out. Even though no one had actually informed her of Red's inability to talk, she assumed something was amiss with his verbal situation, and she was fine with it.

"Do you remember your address when you lived in the area?" Red had written.

"Yes. Twelve-fifty Cathedral Street. It's not far from here."

Red immediately grabbed Millie's arm and signaled that they should go.

And that's what they did.

With Red leading the way the five of them bolted for Millie's car.

"Shall I go get Buddy?" Robby asked.

"Yeah," Millie replied. "But make it quick. I think Red is in a hurry."

Millie understood what Red had in mind. He figured that Jessie's father had some money stashed at their old house, and that the two men who had abducted them were after the cash.

Maybe if we get there quickly enough, Red calculated, *we can rescue Jessie's parents before those two men hurt them any further.*

Red was seated in the front with Millie. Robby and Angel were sitting behind them in the rear passenger seats next to the doors, with Jessie in the middle. Buddy found a comfortable spot in the back.

Millie had plugged the address into the car's GPS and asked it for the best route.

"Looks like we're only ten minutes away," Robby said. "Did your dad keep a lot of cash around the house? Did he have a safe?"

"I never saw a safe," Jessie said. "But sometimes he did have a lot of cash. Once I saw a whole suitcase full of one-hundred-dollar bills. But that was just once. Usually I didn't see anything like that."

Red grabbed his notepad and wrote, "When he had a lot of cash, where did he keep it? In the house?"

He held the notepad up for Jessie to read.

"I saw the suitcase with the money in it. Dad had it in the house that once. But he had an office above the garage. He had an alarm system in it and everything—but not in the house. He just had an alarm in his office. That was all back when we lived here."

"Did your parents sell the house?" Millie asked. "Or do they still own it?"

"We don't own it anymore," Jessie said. "The Feds made us sell *everything*. The plane, the house, everything. Even our cars. We had to sell both cars. We had two Escalades. And they made us sell them. Now we own an ugly brown Chevy Impala. It's five years old. And ugly. The windshield is even cracked. We bought it used when we moved into the program. We used to be rich. Now we're poor. I hate being this poor."

Millie pulled up to the curb and stopped suddenly.

Chapter 30

The house at twelve-fifty did not look like any of the other houses on the street. It was a very large stone house. Red raised his eyebrows and nodded his head. It appeared to him to be the most expensive-looking house in the neighborhood.

The fieldstone had been carefully laid, one stone at a time with skilled, strong hands, taking care in keeping the walls level and straight. The fact that no cracks were visible indicated that the rocks were placed on a firm foundation.

The house—a massive two-story—had a wrought iron fence around it, with freshly-planted red roses in dark brown mulch skirting the perimeter. The roses were attempting to use the black fence as a trellis for climbing. You could see tendrils of stems and leaves reaching upwards and wrapping themselves around the iron as if they knew that there would be another Midwest winter, with winds and gales, and that they would need to hang on for life.

Beyond the front gate, there was a wraparound porch filled with a few rocking chairs and hanging plants. The double doors in the front entry had side panels with leaded oval glass in each. A beveled glass arched transom crowned the top of the entry. The doors themselves had been freshly sanded and stained, showing off the grain of the lush mahogany. Like the side panels, the oval-shaped windows in each of the matching doors were leaded as well. The whole assembly gave the home a majestic entrance.

Attached to the house was a two-stall garage. Red pointed at it as Millie slowly pulled her car along toward it.

"No," Jessie said, recognizing that Red was asking her if that was the garage where her father had his office. "There's another building behind that garage. We called the one in back *our* garage. And that's where Dad's office was—in the attic of the rear building. The steps up to it were inside our garage. That was the only way to get into his office. Dad had an emergency aluminum ladder in case of fire. You know—one of those that kinda fold up and store under the window until you need it. He made me go down it just so I would know how. I guess he wanted to make sure I wasn't scared. It was a little scary, right at first. Taking that first step out of the window. He had me do it twice."

As they pulled closer to the house Red signaled for Millie to stop. He had noticed some unusual activity back by the office-garage. The gate to the driveway had been left open. He studied it for a moment, and then took action. With his left foot, Red shoved Millie's foot off of the gas pedal, He then slammed his foot down on the gas pedal and yanked the steering wheel to the right. The car sped up the driveway and around toward the garage.

"Red!" Millie screamed. "What are you doing?"

Red didn't respond or slow down. As they approached the garage door Red hit the button on the dash that deactivated the passenger side airbag, and immediately thereafter he unsnapped his shoulder harness. He aimed directly for the center of the garage door. Once confident that the car would strike close to middle of the door he pressed the side of his face and his chest against the cushioned dash of Millie's car. At impact, they were moving over twenty miles per hour, the bottom three horizontal panels of the door snapped like number two pencils. Neither Red nor any of the other occupants even sensed the initial collision. But, when they struck the back of the late-model dark-blue Malibu inside the garage, Millie's airbag inflated, as did the airbags in the Malibu.

The force of the crash shoved the car that contained Jessie's parents and their two kidnappers into the rear wall of the garage with such force that it knocked a Malibu-sized hole through it. The car, with the engine still running, ended up balanced like a huge teeter-totter on the foundation blocks. The two kidnappers were momentarily trapped in the car and were knocked virtually unconscious by the impact of the airbags. Their doors were blocked by the garage wall so that even had they been able to move about under their own strength, they would still have been trapped inside the car.

Red did not hesitate.

He leapt from the Suburban and ran over to the side of the Malibu. He opened the door and virtually pulled out the bloodied and beaten body of Jessie's mom. She was so stunned that when her feet hit the concrete floor she stumbled and started to fall. Fortunately, Jessie was there waiting and she steadied her mother.

"This way," she said firmly as she led her mother back to the Suburban. "Come with me. You'll be safe here. Let's hurry."

Red then pulled Jessie's father across the seat and out of the only door that would open.

All this time, which was only a matter of seconds, Millie remained behind the wheel—her body severely traumatized by the impact of the airbag. Slowly she began to realize what had just happened.

"Angel!" she mumbled without turning around. "Are you okay?"

Even though Angel was unable to hear her mother because she was already out of the car, she nonetheless answered by hurriedly scampering over to where Red and Robby were attending Jessie's father—there Millie could observe what was going on.

The two boys dragged the nearly unconscious man around and strapped him into the seat just vacated by Robby.

The two boys then secured the mother in the middle seat beside him, with Jessie sliding in beside her. Angel and Robby jumped into the back of the Suburban, while Red again took the seat beside Millie. He began removing the remnants of Millie's now deflated airbag. Red then placed his hand on her shoulder and signaled with his thumb that she should back out of the garage. She got the message.

She slid the shifter into reverse and began backing out through the destroyed garage door.

As the vehicle cleared the opening, Red, Robby and Angel all gazed transfixed at the swirling mass of one-hundred-dollar bills blowing around amid the broken car parts and other debris on the garage floor. Red looked back at his friends and raised his open palms in disbelief. But he made no sound.

Jessie continued to comfort her parents.

"Oh, Mom. I'm so very sorry. This was *all* my fault. I know it. I'm so sorry."

Her mother did not say anything at first. She just slowly shook her head.

Finally, she spoke.

"No, Jes. None of this was your fault. *None* of it. Your dad and I brought this on ourselves. We got what we deserved. That's *all* that happened. We got what we deserved."

Angel looked first at Red, and then at Robby. Her eyes were asking the question, "What just happened, and are those one-hundred-dollar bills real?"

Robby's jaw dropped as he silently shook his head in disbelief.

Once it was clear that Millie had the Suburban under control, Red turned his attention back to the two abductors. They were busying themselves by frantically scooping up the loose cash and shoving it into a badly-damaged cardboard box. One of the men glanced back at Red for a moment, and flashed an angry middle finger.

Only Red witnessed it. And, in an inscrutable manner known only to him and his closest friends, he laughed out loud.

Robby and Angel heard the articulations he was making, but did not understand what precipitated them.

When Millie had reached the street, Red signaled that they should escape by heading away in the opposite direction.

While that thought did not initially occur to Millie, she complied with Red's directive.

Angel observed that they were not leaving the way they came in, and asked Robby, "What's this all about? That's not the way we came in."

"It's better this way," he said to her. "No point showing yourselves twice to the same potential witnesses. Besides, we might find out where they stashed your parents' car. That wasn't it in the garage, so it must be around here someplace."

"Oh my God!" Angel suddenly said. "That could be it. Old Chevy. With out-of-state plates. I can't tell what state. … Jessie. Is that your car?"

Jessie looked up and said, "Yeah! That's it!"

Red snapped a glance back and gestured turning an ignition switch.

Jessie thought for a split second, and then said, "Yes. Dad kept a spare key in a little magnetic box behind the back bumper, underneath. On the passenger side."

Red grabbed Millie's arm right after they passed the car and had her stop.

He then jumped out and ran back to the vehicle. He quickly lay down behind it and slid his face under the back bumper.

"Ahh!" he growled, as he peeled the muddy little container from the frame. He threw it to the pavement to jar off the mud. He repeated his effort until most of concrete-like mud had chipped off. Finally, the little box popped open and a single Chevy ignition key went flying. Flashing a huge smile, he picked it up and jumped behind the wheel.

The car started immediately.

Red put the car in drive and pulled out from the curb and past Millie. As he did so he signaled that they should follow.

Even though he did not know the city at all, after driving a few dozen blocks he managed to find a neighborhood that evidenced some decay. He pulled the Chevy into an opening directly behind a vehicle that appeared abandoned. The windows were covered with the sort of residue that accumulates on a vehicle left unattended for weeks if not months. He removed the key from the ignition, and looked back for Millie. She drove up as he was getting out.

"What was that all about?" she asked as Red jumped in and buckled up.

Red looked back at Robby.

"Red doesn't want the police to locate the car right away," Robby explained. "Not until we can make some sort of arrangements for Jessie's parents. Now the car will get stripped and eventually towed. It could be weeks before anyone reports it. If we'd left it where we found it, it would have got reported and the cops would have investigated it right away—it would probably be reported today. What Red did just buys us some time."

Millie was not pleased about all that had just transpired. But she did not scold Red. Instead, she turned her attention toward Jessie's parents.

"We've got to get you two to the hospital," she said as she looked at them in her rearview mirror. "You both look pretty rough."

"No!" Jessie's father vehemently insisted. "We're *fine*! We *can't* go to a hospital. Neither one of us is injured. Not seriously. We just got ourselves slapped around a little. We're not hurt. I don't know what Jessie's told you, but we can't go to the police, and we can't go to a hospital."

"I told them a little," Jessie said. "I told them that you had testified against some bad people, and that they wanted to hurt us. So the court changed our names, sold our house and cars, and put us in a program. And that it was all a secret."

"Yeah," he said. "That's about right. That's what those two men were all about. They were going to kill us. You guys saved our lives."

"What were you doing at your old house?" Millie asked. "Seems to me like you could have stayed back in Virginia, or Oregon. Wherever that was that you left. If you had, maybe you'd not have been found out."

"That's my fault," Jessie said, beginning to cry. "They came back for me. That's why it's all my fault."

"Nonsense," her mother said. "You did nothing wrong. We're the ones who screwed up. Not you—"

"No," Jessie interrupted. "It *was* my fault. *All* my fault. I ran away last year. I moved to Chicago. Sometimes I lived on the streets. Sometimes in vacant buildings. I ended up getting sick. *Real* sick. Now the doctors tell me I need a very expensive surgery. A liver transplant. And they're *very* expensive. We have insurance, but the deductible is over ten thousand dollars. The government had said that if I ever ran away without permission they would remove the whole family from the program. And Dad's afraid that if he tries to have them help pay for my surgery, they might find out that I had run away.

"So far, they've not said anything about it. But Dad thinks that they will eventually figure it out if he pursues trying to get them to help cover my expenses.

"That's why we came back here. My dad had secretly hidden some money away in the attic of his office. Actually, it was lot of money. Probably enough to cover my surgery."

"But it wasn't my money," he said. "It belonged to the guys I worked for. When the cops first arrested them, the money was in my possession. And I just kept it. I didn't think they knew that I still had it. But when I came back into town, someone must have spotted me and reported it to them. That's probably how they found me.

"So, this morning two of their men showed up at the hotel. They wanted the money. They even knew *exactly* how much there was. One point six mil. They demanded I give it to them. But they also wanted to punish me for testifying against them."

Jessie's dad looked very beaten at this point—both physically and emotionally. His daughter and wife were his life. He could not lose them. He was a tall, thin man. His hair was prematurely graying. Life had been hard on him—particularly the last few years of it. His face was creased with worry lines that should only be seen on a man twice his age. He had been nattily dressed, wearing a new pair of Levis, a Levi jacket, a plaid flannel shirt, and brown leather boots. But now, his shirt and jacket were torn and stained with his own blood. One of his boots was totally missing.

"I told them I'd take them to the money but only if they let Jessie and my wife go. They agreed to spare Jessie, but not my wife.

"After I brought them to where I'd hidden the cash, and turned it over to them, I'm positive they were still gonna take us out and kill us. I'm *sure* that's what they had in mind. You guys saved our lives. No doubt about *that*. But, now, we can't go to the police. If that's what you have in mind, just drop us off here. We can't let anyone else know we're back in town. I've got *too* many enemies here."

"We're not going to just leave you here," Millie said. "Where would you go? And how would you get there?"

"I'll figure somethin' out. I just know that I *can't* stay here. Can't even go back to the hotel to pick up our stuff. They'll be watchin' for us now. Hell. They know you've been helping us. You might have a problem when you go back to the hotel. How about you? You got all your stuff?"

"We'll be fine," Millie said. "I'm sure they didn't see me—"

Red started shaking his head, and reached over and touched Millie on the arm. He then pointed at the front of their badly damaged truck.

Robby knew what Red was thinking.

"They saw you *and* us," Robby said. "And, for sure, they'll remember the Suburban that rammed them."

Robby then took a piece of paper that Red had been writing on, and he read it out loud, "Angel gets an Uber."

And then Robby said, "We don't think that anyone will recognize Angel. *She* could get an Uber, go back and clean out our rooms."

"Yeah," Angel said. "I'm sure they didn't see me. I could just sneak in and sneak out. It'll be okay."

"Not as easy as it sounds," Millie retorted. "I don't have the Uber App on the burner Jack gave me. And I don't dare activate my other cell. We'll just do a taxi and pay cash."

Dirk Westin was waiting in the parking lot of the hotel. Engine running. He had been sent there to keep an eye on the room occupied by Jessie's parents—Ellen and Rod Childress. He worked for the same crime organization as did Craig (Baldy) Robinson and James Richards, the two men who had abducted Jessie's parents. Baldy had called and told him to wait out at the hotel and watch for Ellen or Rod to come back for their things.

"And when they do," Baldy told him, "Kill them both. You already know what they look like. Kill 'em. And they might just send the girl. Their daughter. They might send her back to get their shit. You'll recognize her easy enough. She's very tall, for a girl, skinny, and she has curly dark hair. If she shows up, don't introduce yourself. Just follow her when she leaves. She'll lead you back to the parents. And then do all three of them.

"I'd be on the lookout for her. I doubt that either of the Childresses will be showin' their faces around there.

"But, there is something else to look for. When they showed up at their old house, they had a whole shitload of people with them. I spotted two young boys, and a *thirtyish* woman. At least.

There could have been more. But I'm sure about the kids and the woman. And a dog. They had a golden retriever, too. Like I said, there was a whole shitload of people. So, be on the lookout for *anyone* heading up to the hotel room. I'm pretty sure they're gonna want to get some of their stuff. Just don't know who they might send to do it. But, my guess is that it will all go down pretty soon, because the maids are gonna want to clean the room pretty soon. Be alert to any activity around that room."

Chapter 31

At the same time that Dirk Westin was scrutinizing his surroundings in order to secure the most advantageous position from which to monitor the Childresses' room, Henry, Jack and Roger were heading north on BIA-5 on their way out of the Rosebud Reservation. They were aiming for the Pine Ridge Native American Airport on Highway 87 near Whiteclay. The sun was well into the South Dakota sky. The trailing SUV that was troubling Jack now filled the telescopic sight of Jack's 6.5 Creedmoor. Henry's finger was teasing the trigger.

"Driver, radiator, or left front tire?" Henry asked.

Jack did not hesitate answering Henry's question.

"Try to take out the left front first," he ordered. "If they're running some sort of *runflats*, then go for the radiator."

As soon as Jack had spoken, he hit the button to open the custom rear window. As soon as the sound of the power window motor stopped—*BANG.*

"DAMN!" Roger barked. "Try giving us a—"

BANG!

Roger was trying to say, "Try giving us a little warning next time." But his admonition was cut short by a second blast from this compact sniper rifle.

"Damn you, Henry!" Roger again complained. "You did that on purpose. My ears are going to be ringing for a week!"

Roger then looked over at Jack.

"And you're worse than your damn buddy is!" he said. "Here you are steering this truck with your knees so you can cover your ears."

"I'm sorry, Roger," Jack quipped in his Sean Connery brogue. "Were you talking to me?"

"Runflats," Henry said. "I saw it drop and lurch, but that was it. It's gonna take a few minutes for the coolant to leak out. At least we slowed them down a bit with the tire shot. Do you even suppose they felt the impact of the shot in their engine?"

"I think they would have," Jack said. "Doesn't matter at this point. It's not like they're going to call the cops on us."

"Perhaps not the cops, exactly," Roger said. "Maybe just their buddies in that Apache helicopter."

Jack cranked the wheel to the left and shot off of the road.

"Bail! Fast! Get out!"

All three men jumped out of the black Tahoe before it had even stopped rolling.

"Over here!" he shouted. "Get in here!"

What Jack had found was a four-foot culvert that ran under the road. It was designed to be large enough to handle flash flood waters that were the result of the frequent torrential rainstorms common to parts of South Dakota. Henry was the last one to make it into the huge runoff drain. He was slower because he took the time to gather up Jack's duffel and sniper rifle.

"Give that bitch to me and get down on your face!" Jack barked.

Both Roger and Henry leapt face first into the coarse bed of rocks that lined the bottom of the culvert. Jack, however, grabbed Henry and his munitions bag, and the two of them darted on their hands and knees on through the pipe until they had reached the far end of it.

There they waited for the inevitable.

The explosion was phenomenal.

The Apache had fired a Hellfire missile into the Tahoe. Fortunately, the vehicle had rolled nearly a hundred feet away before the blast occurred. Even though the explosion did not injure Jack or the other two men, the fireball it generated still blew through their cylindrical bunker, singeing their eyebrows and hair.

Carefully Jack peered out at the Apache that was then stationary at seventy-five feet above the road.

"Dammit!" he growled as he drew his Glock and stepped up and out of the culvert.

"Deploy the drone!" he shouted to Henry.

What had garnered Jack's immediate attention was the rope that he had spotted dropping from the helicopter.

"They're fast-roping us!" he barked as he drew his Glock and waited. "Get that drone up *now!*"

Both men knew the drill. They had rehearsed this technique many times. One of them, probably Jack, would station himself as near as was feasible to the fast-rope target, while the other would launch a drone.

When a landing is not possible due to rugged terrain, there are two basic methods used to deploy fighters from a helicopter: rappelling and fast-roping. With rappelling, one fighter at a time lowers himself hand-over-hand from a rope until he reaches the target's surface.

With fast-roping, a single larger braided rope is used, with the fighters allowing the rope to slide through their hands and legs, thus completing their landing more rapidly. Fighters being deployed using this method must wear special gloves. Sometimes two pair of gloves are necessary due to the buildup of heat.

The major advantage of fast-roping is that it can deploy a large number of fighters in a short amount of time—nearly one per second.

Jack became acutely aware of the danger as soon as he had spotted the single large braided rope. He knew that within seconds there would be six well-armed black hats shooting up the neighborhood.

"Henry!" he shouted again. "Get that damn bird up there! NOW!"

These words had barely escaped his mouth when he heard the familiar sound of the five rotors of his drone whirring above his head. Using a joystick and CCTV monitor, Henry shot the drone up under full power until it reached an altitude of two hundred feet. It used the airspace a few hundred feet off the left side of the Apache to avoid the enormous downdraft created by the Apache's rotor.

Once at an altitude of five hundred feet, he armed an explosive device that was attached to the drone. That bomb consisted of a metal box containing two pounds of C-4. He then drifted the drone toward a position directly over the Apache.

As soon as Jack observed the drone taking a position over the Apache's rotor, and before the fighters could begin dropping down the fast-rope, he started firing at the helicopter with his Glock. While he was well aware that the rounds from the Glock would make no significant impact on any of the critical components of the Apache, he also knew that no fighters would be sent down the fast-rope as long as he was firing.

Once the drone was over the Apache, Henry eased off on the power, and the downdraft created by the Apache's rotor immediately began sucking the drone toward it. At that point both Jack and Henry made a beeline back into the culvert.

The first explosion was loud, but the second blast was deafening.

Initially, when the drone hit the chopper, the bomb attached to it exploded on contact. It took out the rotor, causing the Apache to dip to the side and then drop to the ground. The crash caused the ordnance onboard the Apache to explode with the ferocity of a night in London during World War II.

While Jack, Henry and Roger were well protected from the actual explosion, they were all knocked off of their feet by the blast wave it caused. The earth quaked so violently that yards of soil and damaged roadway became dislodged and cascaded over each end of the culvert.

"Let's go!" Jack shouted. "Now. We gotta get outta here now! Move! Let's go!"

The three men bolted back out of the culvert and sprinted toward the cover of nearby trees on the west side of BIA-5.

"What now, boss?" Henry asked.

"Unless you've got another drone in that bag of yours," Roger said, "one big enough to fly us out of here, we're going to have to steal another vehicle."

"Henry," Jack said pointing north. "Roger and I are going to move up the road here a thousand yards or so. You see if you can sweet-talk someone into giving you a ride. And then pick us up. Think you can do that?"

"Why me?" Henry asked. "Don't you think Roger's much cuter than me? Well, probably not. But he *is* a fast talker."

"These black hats have never seen or heard of you. I think you can pull this off. Anyway, you are our best shot. See what you can do. And, remember, we're supposed to meet up with your friend in a little over an hour. Better get going. Hit your four-ways so we'll know it's you."

"Sure thing. I'll do my best."

"You're armed, right?" Jack asked.

"My Glock's still in the Tahoe," Henry said. "I didn't have a chance to grab it before we got hit."

"Well, I'd say that your Glock's not doing so well right now," Jack said as he reloaded his pistol's magazine. "Here, take mine. You might need it."

Jack and Roger immediately headed north following BIA-5 for what felt to them as though they had separated themselves from the crash site by a little over half a mile.

"Let's get ourselves in a little closer to the road," Jack suggested. "Wouldn't want to miss the bus."

The two men stretched out on the ground under a small tree and waited. Finally, they spotted a tribal police car headed their way from the south.

"What's that all about?" Jack asked. "They've got their flashers on. Shouldn't it be lights and sirens? If they were running on something? Not just their hazards. Right?"

"I would think so. Do you think that could be Henry?"

"Damn," Jack moaned. "I can't imagine Henry stealing a *cop* car. But, it does appear to be stopping. Or, at least slowing down. Let's take a walk over there and check it out. Slip me your Glock, Roger. No point in you going down should this whole thing go south."

As the two men walked toward the stopped patrol car, Roger handed his pistol over to Jack.

Jack slid in behind Roger for cover as he verified that the magazine was fully loaded. After he had checked it, he tucked the Glock under his belt and pulled his shirt over it.

"We'll soon find out what this is all about," Jack said as he neared the patrol car. "What can you make out? Anything? Can you spot Henry? I can see two people in the car. One appears to be in uniform. Shit! This could really get messy fast."

Just then the passenger door opened, and out stepped Henry.

"Jack. Roger. It's cool. Officer Olson has offered to give us a lift to the airport. He's friends with my friend, Galvin Thorpe. In fact, his father works for Galvin. We gave Galvin a call, and he verified that we needed to fly out of Pine Ridge right away. So, he very kindly volunteered to drive us. As long as we paid for the gas. Wasn't that kind of him?"

"Very much so," Jack agreed, handing the officer a one hundred-dollar bill. "Will that cover the gas?"

"Oh, yes it certainly will," Officer Olson said. "That will definitely cover the gas. But, this will have to be considered *personal use of a tribal vehicle*. When we use a patrol car for personal use it costs us extra—one dollar a mile. I think it's about one hundred and thirty miles. So it would be an additional one hundred and thirty dollars."

"Times two," Jack added. "You'll have to pay for bringing the car back as well. Right?"

"That's right."

"So, that'd be one hundred for gas, and another two hundred and sixty for use of the patrol car. How does it sound if we just round it up to four hundred dollars?"

"That would be great. That would cover it just fine."

"Cash work for you?" Jack asked, peeling off three more crisp one-hundred-dollar bills.

"Cash would be very good."

"Great," Jack said. "Now, if you don't mind, we should get a move on. We've got a plane to catch."

Jack did not mind paying for the ride to the airport. But he always bristled when he felt he was getting hustled. This was one of those times.

Jack leaned in toward the driver, his steel-blue eyes knifing through Officer Olson's glib expression. "Okay if we get going now?" he asked with an air of anger as he firmly gripped the officer's shoulder.

"Absolutely," Officer Olson said. "I can turn my siren and flashers on, too. That should get us there a little quicker."

"Don't do that," Jack commanded. "Leave the lights off. And turn those damn four-ways off too. Just get us to the airport in a reasonable amount of time. Can you do that? No sense in attracting unnecessary attention. Does that work for you?"

"Yes. I can do that."

Officer Olson, who was still pinching the four one-hundred-dollar bills in his right hand, tucked them carefully into the left breast pocket of his well-worn jean jacket, and pulled out onto the road.

Jack turned the radio on and adjusted the volume to a click above what was necessary for it to be heard in the rear seat.

"Mind if I turn that down a notch?" Officer Olson asked as he reached toward the volume knob. "I've got very sensitive ears."

Jack intercepted his arm before he could accomplish its mission. Squeezing the officer's wrist tightly, and twisting it at the same time, Jack said, "Leave it where it is."

The officer cringed.

Not receiving an immediate response, Jack kicked up the pressure on the officer's wrist.

"Yeah. Sure. I don't care. Leave it where it is. If everyone else is okay with it. It's fine with me."

But Jack was not satisfied with Officer Olson's response. "You don't get it," he said, still not letting up on the pressure. "I don't give a damn if they like it or not. I just want to know if you are ready to keep your damn hands off the radio. Are you?"

"Yes. I'm fine with it. You can play the radio as loud as you wish. No problem."

"Roger, let me see your cell," Jack said as he released his grip on the officer's wrist. But before Roger could respond to Jack's request, Officer Olson jerked his hand back and sneered his disgust.

So, instead of receiving the cell Roger was trying to hand him over the seat, Jack instead landed a straight left to the officer's temple, knocking him unconscious. And then, with his right hand Jack pulled the officer's foot from off the gas pedal. With his left hand, Jack steered the car to the side of the road.

Once stopped, Jack asked Henry to take over behind the wheel.

"I've had enough of that asshole's shit," Jack said. "Think you can find this place?"

"Yeah. I've been there before. Should be easy. It's pretty much straight west on 18. Should be a piece of cake. What should we do with Officer Olson? Do you think he's dead?"

"Not yet," Jack said as he opened his door and slid the unconscious officer over to the passenger seat. "He'll be fine right here where I can keep an eye on him. Hopefully he doesn't crap his pants."

Once he had strapped the officer up, Jack opened the rear door and asked Roger to slide over.

"Okay, driver," Jack announced with a smile. "Let's get on our way. Time is wasting. Now, where's that cell phone? Get me the most secure connection you can, and ring your buddy Bob."

Roger fingered his phone through a few steps. When Bob Fulbright answered, he said, "Bob. I've got someone here who wants to talk to you."

Chapter 32

"Hey, Bob," Jack said in a tone he'd been saving for this moment. "How's it going at your end?"

"Jack! Damn. I thought you were, er, might be dead. What happened?"

"Very long story. Best save it for a beer and a cigar. Right now, I'm looking for an update. We still on in New York?"

"Where are you? According to what I'm seeing, you're on Roger's phone, and it's somewhere out in the middle of nowhere?"

"Southern South Dakota. You know—out here where someday they'll be carving your profile into the side of that mountain."

"Right. How long is this vacation of yours going to last? I've got you booked to be flying out of Kennedy in about two hours. I take it you're not going to make it?"

"Private or commercial?"

"Charter."

"Then you can hold it for me. Right?"

"Given you're the only passenger—I think I can arrange a little delay."

"I'd like to take Roger with me. Can you work that out?"

"Does he know about this?"

"He does now."

"Does he know that the odds are really stacked against you, or the two of you—if he decides to go with you? I don't know what your chances are, but I'd have to say that I wouldn't bet on your safe return. Does he know that?"

"After what we've been through this past day, I think he's got a pretty good idea about what's at stake."

Bob Fulbright thought about Jack's request for a few seconds, and then said, "Hell. I suppose if he *wants* to go with you on this mission—this death mission, I won't stand in the way. But, I was under the impression that if you wanted to have a sidekick on this trip, you'd want to take Henry. He's younger, tougher, and seems to read your every move before *you* even do. Why not Henry?"

"Henry has an eleven-year-old daughter. Enough said."

"Then Roger it is. I'll make arrangements with Allison. I'll tell my wife that Roger is going on a fishing trip to Canada and won't be back until he catches his limit. Or something like that."

The reason Bob Fulbright needed to clear Roger's absence with Allison, former first lady Allison, was that Roger was the head of Allison's Secret Service detail responsible for protecting her.

"We'll be flying out of here in about two hours. We'll fly directly into Kennedy. If we leave immediately, I won't have time to gear up properly. How's that going to work?"

"Trust me, 007, you'll have everything you could possibly want or need—and more. Half the shit I'm sending on the plane with you hasn't even been field-tested. It's all brand new."

"Sounds great. But are you confident that it will all work? And, how will I know how to use it?"

"You're a smart guy. You'll figure out which end stings. And which doesn't. If not, then you're the wrong man for *this* job."

"I think that's what I've been trying to tell you, Bob. I'm getting too old for this kind of horseshit. Send somebody else next time. Why don't you?"

"Go to hell!" Bob blustered back. "You just get here. And, Roger, buy a couple boxes of Depends—if you think you boys will need them. Just keep in mind. If this mission goes south, it very well might mean the end of the United States of America. As we know it. It could all be over—the Grand Experiment. All done. Think about *that*."

Jack did not respond as he disconnected.

Henry had heard enough of Jack's end of the conversation to know that he would not be engaged in at least the initial part of Jack's mission.

"What do you want me to do, then?" Henry asked. "Shall I continue on with the Deadwood matter?"

"Exactly," Jack said. "We're up against the clock on that already."

"Sounds good. And how about Kate? She'll be arriving in Rapid City soon, if she hasn't already."

"Pick her up at the airport and bring her up to speed on the Owens case. If she's got some time, that is. Maybe she can give you a hand until I get freed up. Besides, that way you two would be easy to reach if I should end up needing a little help with this job."

About fifteen miles outside the Pine Ridge Airport Jack noticed that Officer Olson was beginning to stir.

"Officer Olson," Jack said. "Have a nice nap?"

"Oh! God! What happened?"

"You apparently dozed off while you were driving. Whatever happened, we helped you slide over here and had Henry finish the trip. I'd say you've been out for about an hour. Feel better now?"

The officer did not respond. Instead he moaned and rubbed a large knob on his right cheekbone.

Jack and Roger arrived at JFK at three-twenty in the afternoon. Bob was there waiting for them.

"Be prepared to depart at sixteen hundred hours," Bob said.

"Get as much sleep as you can on the plane. Your schedule will be pretty tight once you set down."

"And when will that be?" Jack asked.

"The trip will take about eighteen and a half hours, which will put you into Singapore at about ten-thirty A.M. New York time. That would be ten-thirty P.M. there. Twelve hours' difference."

"And when does POTUS arrive?"

"They're not announcing his specific arrival time for security reasons. Besides, it's subject to change, anyway. What is critical is that the next day, at nine hundred hours, he will be making a speech. That will be at twenty-one hundred hours in New York—prime time. In his speech he will be announcing the total normalization of diplomatic relations with North Korea."

"Denuclearization?" Jack asked. "The NoKos are finally destroying their nukes?"

"That's right. And the dismantling of all of their nuclear facilities—their reactors, centrifuges—everything."

"Damn," Jack said. "I never thought we'd see that happen. His daddy and grand-daddy must be turning in their graves. What's he getting in return?"

"I haven't heard all the details," Bob said. "POTUS is holding all the specifics for his speech. But, it's been hinted that young Kim and POTUS are forming a partnership to turn the whole southeast section of North Korea into a major vacation and recreation haven—from Wosan in the north, to Mount Kumgang National Park in the south. They're going to develop the whole southeastern seaboard into golf courses, condos, and corporate headquarters."

"Corporate headquarters?" Jack asked with a sneer. "How could that be? North Korea is a fascist regime. No need for corporate headquarters."

"That's the old North Korea. POTUS and Chairman Kim are transforming the whole political structure of the North. The tax structure they are setting up is going to make North Korea the new Hong Kong."

"Well, I can see how that has made POTUS a Deep State target. Can't have that kind of success—not by an outsider. So, do you anticipate the assassination attempt before or after the speech?"

"None of that is known," Bob said. "But, in my opinion, I'd say that the likelihood would be right during the speech—while he is delivering the early introductory comments. Before the meat of the talk. That would guarantee the largest audience. They're estimating that over a billion people, worldwide, will be tuned in. Possibly the largest audience ever to watch a single event since the 2008 Olympics. Some are even saying it could go substantially higher than that. Kim will joint POTUS on the stage, I'm told. For the first ten minutes both leaders will share the podium."

"That would be the most opportune moment to pull it off," Jack said. "That's how it would seem to me. Especially if the goal is to make it look like a NoKo attempt on Kim's life. You going to show me around the plane? Roger and I'd like to familiarize ourselves with some of the special toys you were telling me about. I see you've got Air Force One here waiting on the President. But is our plane here yet?"

"That's going to be your transportation for the mission. Technically, it would not actually be called Air Force One unless the President is on it. But that is his plane. And we're referring to it as Air Force One just as though he were on it. We're taking him over using a little different plan."

"Roger and I are going to Singapore on the President's plane? Air Force One. Is that the idea?"

"Right."

"So, that would make us the decoys? Right?"

"You could say that."

Jack looked over at Roger and winked.

"That'd be fine with us," Jack chuckled, "as long as the bar is well stocked."

"I'm sure you'll find everything you might want. Shall we board?"

"Sure," Jack said. "I do have a question for you. It really has nothing to do with the mission. It's just a question that came to mind as we were talking. Do you mind?"

"Let's hear it," Bob said. "No guarantees about my answering your question, but you can feel free to ask."

"Why now? Why is North Korea making this move now? Other presidents have tried to get them to the table for decades. And nothing worked. Why was POTUS successful this time?"

"Oh. Hell. What you're saying is, why couldn't I ever get them to budge. God knows I tried."

"No. That's not what I'm saying. But, you have to admit that he has had more success than any earlier president enjoyed. There has to be some good reason. Unless, of course, Young Kim is just yanking POTUS's chain. Is that what's happening? Is Chairman Kim just trying to snooker the leader of the free world?"

"I think he tried that. But that's not what's happening this time. This deal is for real. It has become very clear that this is really happening this time."

"Why? Why this time?"

"There's three—probably four reasons."

"And they are?"

"I've got to get you on your way. There's really no time."

"One-word answers. Whatever you can tell me. Quickly."

"First of all, the optics. POTUS showed the young leader what his country could look like. He showed him a video. Got him thinking."

"I saw that. Are you saying that's what got the deal done?"

"Partly. But there is more. POTUS treated him like a man. Not like a teenage despot. POTUS showed the man respect. They genuinely do like each other. It's a fact. Just like POTUS has said."

"You said there were four reasons. What are the other two? Are you referring to the sanctions?"

"No doubt the sanctions played a part. But all the time you had Russia and China working around the sanctions. So they were not as effective as they might have been. Even South Korea was making side deals with their neighbors. The sanctions had an effect, but when you're dealing with a totalitarian regime like the NoKos, sanctions don't mean that much. What's the population going to do? They can't fight back. No, the third reason for Chairman Kim to make the deal now is that he believed that POTUS was actually going to blow him up. No one had ever talked to him the way POTUS talked to him. POTUS respected him, but he believed the threats POTUS threw at him. And, you know what, Jack, I believed him too. I think that POTUS meant every word he said."

"I can see that. And the fourth reason?"

"This is the one that I probably shouldn't be telling you. But, nothing would have happened had POTUS not ordered it."

"Well, what is it? What's the big secret?"

"That's what it is. A secret. You can't talk about it. Ever. If I tell you, will it go to the grave with you?"

"Damn, Bob, I wish you'd quit talking like that. Of course we'll keep our mouths shut. But, don't give us any state secrets. Nothing that could get us tortured."

"It's not one of those things. Both the Chinese and the Russians know all about it. And I'm pretty sure the Israelis are aware of it as well. They know more about us than the VP knows. Pretty sure about that. But, it's not the kind of secret that could get anyone tortured. It's just that if it ever got out, it would serve to embarrass Chairman Kim and, probably the Chinese and the Russians. No point in doing that, now that things are going so well."

"You going to spill it?" Jack asked. "I have to take a pee, and it's chilly out here on the tarmac."

"Sure. Here's the deal. Do you recall when the mountain caved in on their underground nuclear facilities? Remember that?"

"Yeah. I read about it. One of them caved in and ruined it."

"More than one. Several suffered from the same problem."

"Oh my God! What are you saying?"

"Yeah. That's it. Smart bunker busters. Not particularly huge. But they were stacked, one after another, dropped from the stealth bombers. One would penetrate thirty or forty feet and blow. The next one another thirty or forty feet. And then another, and another. Finally, it brought the whole mountain down on their heads. Everyone of their so-called *secret sites* suffered the same fate."

"No shit!" Jack said. "Did they use nukes or conventional?"

"Yes, and yes."

"Yes to both?"

"That's right. They softened it up with several rounds of conventional with the B-2 Stealths, and then delivered a B-61 low-yield thermonuclear bomb using a different delivery mechanism."

Jack glared into Bob's eyes.

"Why the hesitation? What are you saying? You're not suggesting that they dropped the nukes from an F-35, are you? That upgrade's not supposed to be ready for another few years."

"Well, it's ready now. POTUS ordered it to be put on the front burner, and here we are."

"We blew up their nukes with nukes?" Jack queried. "DAMN! What did Russia and China think about that?"

"Their reaction was not what you might think," Bob said. "There was no official reaction. At least as far as what I've heard. But the scuttlebutt is that they were not happy that we could pull it off without their even knowing anything about it until well after it had occurred."

"Then we were able to penetrate their defenses with both the B-2s and the F-35s?"

"That's right. They were unable to get *anything* off. Hell, no one even suspected that we had conducted the bombing until the Chinese found peculiar isotopes at all four locations. They knew then that it had to have been us, and that we had to have delivered it with the stealth bombers. But they made no official announcement. So, what were the NoKos to do? We destroyed everything they had in one night. Thankfully, all that radioactivity is buried hundreds of feet beneath solid rock. At least most of it is."

"So, that means that Chairman Kim really doesn't have any bargaining chips left?"

"Did he ever?" Bob retorted. "Think about it. Everyone knew that he really did not have a bomb that would work. He was bluffing. POTUS knew that. His biggest weapon, if you can call it that, was his ability to do significant damage to South Korea with long-range artillery, and all the troops he had amassed at the border. Were he to get off an initial attack, he could possibly kill a lot of South Koreans, and American soldiers, but he could be beaten back. His leverage was his perceived nuclear capability. But it was never really there.

"POTUS called his bluff. And here we are. I think you could say that he called out Russia and China, too. We got in, and out, and no one knew. They are undoubtedly upset about the cavalier manner POTUS demonstrated in his attack. And his success. But, they actually seem relieved to get the nukes out of North Korea. Neither of them is really disappointed about *what* we did, just the way we did it. And the fact that we caught them flatfooted. They were not happy about that to say the least.

"But, not everyone is happy that POTUS neutralized North Korea. Our intelligence community—the Deep State—they are mad as hell. In their eyes POTUS just set them back twenty years. And they are not about to let it stand. Not if they can help it."

"And the only way they feel they can deal with it," Jack offered, "is to take POTUS out. Is that about it?"

"And Chairman Kim," Bob said. "Don't forget about him. He failed to stand up to POTUS. So, he has to go, too. In their eyes, he is equally to blame for what they perceive as their failure. And that is how they view it—as *their* failure. More than ever before. The Deep State establishment now feels threatened—totally boxed in. In their eyes, something has to give."

Just then a car drove up and stopped. Jack and Roger looked at each other, and then at Bob.

"Okay," Bob said. "Enough of this chatter for tonight. Colonel William French is here. I hadn't told you about him. He's the weapons expert. He will accompany you to Singapore and brief you further on the mission. He is highly trained in the use of all the weaponry that you might need. Believe me, this plane is loaded with some of the most sophisticated shit you could ever imagine. And Colonel French knows more about it than anyone else. In fact, he has been instrumental in the development of much of it. Let me get you guys settled in and on your way."

"But, Bob," Jack said. "We weren't planning on taking anyone else with us. We don't know anything about this Colonel French. Who the hell is he?"

"He's a former Army Ranger," Bob said as the man approached. "Gentlemen, I want you to meet Lieutenant Colonel William C. French, Retired. Colonel French, these are the men I told you about: Jack Handler and Roger Minsk. Colonel French will accompany you throughout the mission. He will brief you with regard to all the specific details of the mission. He is responsible for all the weapons onboard this plane—or as Jack refers to them, the *toys*. Colonel French is a trusted friend, and an accomplished weapons expert. As your plans are developed, once you get a lay of the land, I'm sure you will find that Colonel French will prove invaluable to you—his knowledge is unique. He will also serve as a liaison between you and me—in every respect. So, regard him as such."

"Now," Bob said to Jack, "I believe the colonel has something for you. Right, Colonel French?"

Col. French was a no nonsense man—which can be said about all Rangers. Not only was he meticulous about the way he looked, he was a man thoughtful with regard to precision and intelligence. When he set about to accomplish a mission he attacked it with speed and ferocity, sticking to his effort until he had accomplished the mission, even when it took him into the most hostile environments imaginable.

Today this former Ranger was wearing green camo pants with a black short-sleeved shirt and black combat boots. He stood six foot three inches, and every muscle was toned and firm. Even after his Ranger days, he continued annually in the Ranger School training program. The program is a grueling ordeal due to the long hours of walking with your gear, sleeping in the field and eating one or two meals less a day than normal. Many rookie students lose twenty to thirty pounds during their fifty-six-day training program.

"Yes, gentlemen," Col. French said as he handed new cell phones to both Jack and Roger, "from now until this mission is completed, we want you to use these devices for all communication. These units are pre-programmed with all the numbers you will need for the mission. All communication associated with them will be encrypted to the highest degree possible. They are indecipherable to all the bad actors, at least as far as communication with any of the pre-programmed contacts. However, if you call anyone outside this network, your call could be heard—both ends of the conversation. But your location would not be compromised, unless you divulge that information verbally. As I said, inside the network, your communiqué is entirely secure.

"Now, if you would leave your current cell phones with me, I will return them to you when you get back. If something should happen to you, and you do not make it back, all personal items will be presented to your next of kin."

"I don't think so," Jack responded.

"We certainly don't think anything bad will befall you," Col. French said, responding to Jack's concerns. "But, as is the case with any mission like this, there always is a substantial level of danger, and something bad could happen. And should that be the case in this instance, we will see to it that—"

"That's not what I am saying. Of course you will return all of my personal items to my family. But I am not about to give you my cell phone. I will remove the battery, which I always do in this type of situation. But my cell phone stays in my possession all of the time. The same goes for Roger. We will keep our phones."

"I'm sorry," Col. French said. "That's just not the way we do it. We take and hold personal phones, and then return them to—"

"Don't worry about that," Bob interrupted, "The men keep their phones if that's what they want. Just make a note on your *personal-property voucher* that they are keeping their personal cell phones. That's all you have to do."

"Now, gentlemen," Bob said as he prepared to leave, "It's time for you guys to shove off. The colonel will show you around. Get some rest. And, do your best to save the free world. I look forward to debriefing you personally on your return. Godspeed."

"Sorry about the confusion," Col. French said in a quasi-apologetic tone. "I have my orders, and they are to follow protocol. That's all I was doing. Nothing personal."

"Of course," Jack replied. "We get it."

"About those personal cells," Col. French said as they were beginning to board the plane, "I would appreciate it if you would remove the batteries at this time."

"We're all set there," Jack said.

Once on board, Col. French introduced Jack and Roger to the pilots and the crew, and then showed them to the common area.

"Thank you, Colonel," Jack said, pointing at a full-sized refrigerator in the corner of the area. "See that refrigerator over there? May I assume that there are some cold beers in it?"

"It should be well stocked. This *is* the main living area."

"I'm not looking for energy drinks. A simple Bud Lite would do the trick."

"Help yourself to whatever you see. And, when would you like me to give you the full tour?"

Jack opened the refrigerator and removed three glass bottles of Two-Hearted Ale, and the same number of Ore Docks.

"I know the President does not drink any alcohol. So I do appreciate that this ice box is stocked with my favorite beer."

"You're right. He doesn't drink. When it was determined that you were going to perform this mission Bob had the plane fitted to suit *your* needs. Unfortunately, you and Roger will be sharing this area for your trip. But the sheets are clean, I suppose you could say."

"No problem," Jack chuckled. "I'll share a couple of bottles with my buddy. How about cigars? Got any of those?"

"Check the humidor."

"So, that is a humidor. I suspected it was, but I've never seen one quite like it."

"Dottling, I believe. German made."

"Any Cubans, by chance?" Jack asked.

"I've heard they're excellent. But I don't believe that they come with a *country of origin* stamp. We do ask that you not smoke anywhere except in the smoking room."

"You've actually got a smoking room on this plane?"

"I doubt that it appears as such in the specs. But there is a room where people do go to smoke. I'll show it to you on our way through."

As the trio moved around in the four-thousand-square-foot interior of the plane, Jack noticed the leather furniture and the nineteen flat screens. Col. French pointed out the operating room and the on-staff physician who flew every mission—"Not that you'll be needing it," he commented through a slight grin.

As they circled around they re-entered the common area.

"Take a look at this, Roger," Jack said pointing out the exquisite humidor. "I think we should have one like this up on Sugar Island—at the resort. What do you think?"

"I'll bet it's got a pretty big price tag," Roger said. "What would you say, Jack? Maybe two or three thousand dollars? Maybe more. Take a look at those instruments. They look expensive. And that leather. It just feels like money."

"Try twenty grand," Colonel French said, quite proud that he had that information. "I'm not sure about it, but I heard that it cost over twenty thousand dollars. But it was purchased by the President with personal funds. No tax-payer dollars were spent on it."

"Well, that's good to hear," Jack said, as he pulled his new cell phone out and prepared to make a call. "That is, it's good to hear that the President values his cigars. That's all I was getting at."

"Colonel," Jack continued. "Would you show Roger around the smoking room while I step out and make a personal call? Thanks."

The colonel was not used to being ordered around like a sleeping car steward, and his demeanor changed.

Chapter 33

"I would be happy to do that," Col. French replied to Jack's command. "But, I would remind you that any personal calls you make, even on this phone, are subject to monitoring, provided the person you're calling is under surveillance. Your location can't be determined, but the contents of your conversation could be compromised."

Jack threw the colonel an instinctual smile and an equally automatic nod. He was already well aware of the phone's limitations, but remained eager to talk to his daughter.

"Kate," he said when she picked up. "Careful what you say, we might have someone listening in."

"I understand," she replied. "What's on your mind?"

"Can I assume that you've made contact with Henry?"

"Yes, he's right here now. He picked me up from the airport. He told me a little bit about what you're up to. At least, as much as you'd shared with him. He suggested that I should help him on the case you two were working on in Deadwood. And that we should be available should you need us with—with something else."

"Exactly. Don't know how long my other job will take, or even what it might involve. But, I will try to keep you in the loop as much as is feasible. For now, our conversations regarding this project will have to be strictly on a *need-to-know* basis. Are you good with that?"

"Absolutely. I'll hang out with Henry in the meantime."

"Pass the phone to Henry. I need to tell him something."

"Sure."

"Hey, boss."

"You're headed back to talk to the old guys at the bar, right?"

"That's what I was planning to do."

"That's the right plan. Now, as far as reaching me, it would be best if you allow me to initiate all communications. If something comes up, and you must get a message to me, send a text to this number. I'll get it eventually."

"Sounds good," Henry replied. "Since I've got you right now, let me fill you in on a very strange text I received just a short time ago."

"Yeah, this is a good time," Jack said. "Fire away."

"Do you recall Claire Mansfield?"

"Sure. She's the one who got this whole thing started."

"Right," Henry said. "She, along with the lawyer, Craig Conklin, wants to have a sit-down."

"Really? That's strange, don't you think? At this time? Especially given the stringent time constraints we're working under. Any idea what might be prompting this?"

"Somewhat. She said that there was another witness that we should interview. That he might shed some light on the whole matter."

"What sort of witness?"

"Apparently our friends in Deadwood have been talking."

"Walt and James?"

"Right. And it seems that they've turned over a stone—Walt and James, that is—and another old guy from Deadwood crawled out from under it. And he contacted the Mansfield family, and

Claire called her lawyer."

"What kind of information does this new witness have that could have prompted all this attention?"

"Well, I don't know all the details, but it looks like this new witness, Roger Hornsboro. B-o-r-o, or b-o-r-o-u-g-h—not exactly sure how it's spelled. This new guy is the son, or perhaps grandson of a man who is thought to have hung out with the brothers."

"That's interesting."

"Yes," Henry agreed, "It really is. Because there's more to this story than we had ever imagined."

"What does that mean?" Jack asked.

"Those brothers, according to what this Hornsboro guy shared with Ms. Mansfield, they were into a lot of illegal activity. At least during the time they spent in Deadwood. A *whole* lot of shit. That's how Mansfield described it. I'm not sure what that might mean. And, I don't think she has all the details either. But apparently this guy did not want to talk on the phone. Gave her just enough info to whet her appetite. He wanted to meet with her directly. Personally. But her lawyer said that it would be best if you and I met with the witness. I didn't say anything about your not being available right now. But, I thought if it was okay with you, Kate and I could meet with him. What do you think?"

"By all means. Do it. See what he can tell you."

"Right. I've got a phone number. I'll give him a call right now and set something up."

"Great. I'll try to contact you when I get a chance. Best if you don't reach out to me unless there is an emergency. And, in that case, go through Bob."

After Henry had disconnected, he said to Kate, "I'm sure you caught most of that. Your dad wants us to go ahead and contact the new witness. Ms. Mansfield told me that this guy lives just west of Deadwood, in a town called Lead, which is spelled L-e-a-d, but pronounced *Leed*. It is located just off the CanAm Highway."

Henry, who was driving, then handed the phone to her and said, "The phone number is listed under *New Witness*. Why don't you give him a call and set something up for tomorrow—or even for today. We'd have time."

"Sure. I can do that," she said as she clicked onto the number.

After the fourth ring, a man answered, "Hello."

"Is this Roger Hornsboro?" she said.

There was some hesitation. And then the voice said, "Yes. Who's calling?"

"This is Kate. You don't know me, but I think you do know Claire Mansfield. I'm calling on her behalf. She asked my partner and me to set up a meeting with you tomorrow—that you might have some new information for us concerning a matter she was interested in. Can we get together tomorrow? At your convenience, of course."

Kate was eager to follow up with this new lead. She had pen and paper ready for more information. She had also checked her laptop and cell to be sure they were fully charged and ready to go.

As for clothes—she was intentionally traveling light. Today she was wearing her navy blue Yankee Baseball cap with its distinct *NY* insignia—she was proud of New York. She'd pulled the bill low over her eyes to block the glare of the South Dakota summer sun. Her long-sleeved white button-down shirt, tied at her thin waist, along with her dark denim skinny jeans and hiking boots, gave her the options she needed to be comfortable yet be able to handle her mission with a look of confidence.

Google had *told* her that the nights in South Dakota could provide considerable drops in temperature, so she also packed her fashionable light leather jacket.

"Sure," the man said. "I suppose. But what exactly is *this matter* you're talking about?"

That response caught Kate a little off guard.

"I'm sorry," she said. "But didn't you recently give Ms. Mansfield a call telling her that you might have some information she would be interested in? She authorized me to offer you a cash incentive if the information proved credible. Wouldn't you like to talk to us tomorrow and we can discuss it in more detail?"

"Yes, I most certainly would, Kate. And what did you say your last name was?"

"My name is Kate Handler."

"I see that this is not a local number. Are you from Deadwood?"

"No. My partner and I, like I said, have been contacted by Ms. Mansfield. But, while I'm not from Deadwood, I am in Deadwood tomorrow. And I could meet you at your house, or wherever you wished."

"Okay, Kate Handler. Why don't we get together at my office. This is Sheriff Miller, Sheriff William Miller. I'm sheriff of Lawrence County. My office is in Deadwood. On Sherman Street. Why don't you stop in around ten A.M.? I would really like to talk to you."

"*Sheriff?* You said you were *Roger*. Roger Hornsboro. He's the man I'm supposed to meet. Why did *you* answer the phone? Would you please put Mr. Hornsboro on? If he's there. Put him on, please."

"Oh, he's here all right. But he can't come to the phone."

"I can wait."

As soon as she had uttered those words she suddenly realized that something serious was wrong.

"Is he okay?" she asked.

"I regret to inform you that Roger Hornsboro is dead. That's why I want to talk to you tomorrow in my office. At ten. For right now, can you tell me where you were earlier this morning?"

"Dead? We just learned today that he wanted to talk to us. What happened?"

"That has not yet been determined. I'll ask you again. Where were you earlier today?

"I just flew into Rapid City. Not more than an hour or so ago."

"From where?"

"New York. I flew in from Kennedy."

"What were you doing in New York? Were you on vacation? Or Business?"

"I live and work in New York. I've never even been in South Dakota before. I'm a New York City homicide detective. And from your question, it sounds like you suspect foul play in this case. Is that right?"

"Somebody shot Mr. Hornsboro. Actually, he might have shot himself, I suppose. Or, he might have had some help. All I can say for sure right now is that he's dead from a gunshot wound to the head. I should know more by the time I talk to you tomorrow. Now, you said *we*. That means you're with someone. Just who might that be?"

"My friend Henry picked me up from the airport."

"Henry. What's Henry's last name?"

"Actually, Henry's real name is Chuchip Kalyesveh. Everyone calls him Henry."

"Please spell that for me."

"C-h-u-c-h-i-p K-a-l-y-e-s-v-e-h."

"Is Mr. Kalyesveh from New York as well?"

"Henry is from Michigan."

"Michigan. Well I'd say that he's also a long way from home. Did you say that Mr. Hornsboro was expecting to see you both?"

"Henry is a friend of my father. My father is a private investigator. He was asked—that is, *my father* was asked—he was asked to investigate the identity of a body that was recently discovered in Michigan. They think the body was buried back in 1924. We suspected that some of the people that knew the victim might be living in or around Deadwood. That's what we were checking up on. And the client told us that Roger Hornsboro had called her indicating that he might have some new information on the party in question."

"Bring him, this Henry guy, with you tomorrow. When you visit me at my office."

"We could do that," Kate said. "But I have another idea. We're just around the corner from you. How about we just stop in and you can question us right now?"

"That works. Why don't you do that?"

Henry quickly rummaged through the center console until he found a map.

Kate took it from him and located Lead on it.

Kate, like her father, was quick thinking and observant. She could sense a bit of deception in this conversation, although she could not exactly place her finger on it. "Sheriff," she said. "Maybe you can help me. We were told that Mr. Hornsboro lived just off 85. I was calling to get specifics. What is his address, exactly?"

"He's living in a motorhome. Actually, it's a pickup truck with a camper. Looks like he's been here a while. It's parked on Park Avenue just east of Enos Street. You should be able to find it just fine. Look for the patrol cars and the ambulance. Right there at Park Avenue and Enos Street. I'll be looking for you as well."

"How far out are we?" Kate asked after she had disconnected.

"We're not exactly just *around the corner*," Henry said as he stepped on the gas. "But, we're not more than an hour out. You can blame me for the delay."

For the next five miles, the two of them sat without speaking.

"You know what," Henry said, finally breaking the silence, "We need to get hold of Claire and tell her about her witness."

"Right. And it could also be telling to see how she reacts at the news. If somebody capped that guy, and that appears to be what the sheriff is thinking, she might have a good guess as to who that might be."

"Is there any reason to think that the sheriff knows about Claire and the lawyer? Like, maybe something other than what we just shared with him?"

"If he did, he didn't let on," Kate said. "Do you want me to call her, or do you want to?"

"*I* should make that call," Henry said. "She's about to learn that her new witness just got murdered—I think she might handle it better if she hears it from me. You ring her up and I'll give her the news."

Claire Mansfield picked up on the second ring.

"Henry?" she answered, recognizing the caller ID.

"Yes, Claire. It's me. I'm afraid I have some bad news for you."

"What? Tell me. What has happened?"

Kate had leaned over so that she could listen in on the conversation.

"I'm sorry to tell you this," Henry said. "But your Mr. Hornsboro is dead."

"Dead! What? Oh my God! No! How do you know that?"

"We just called the number you gave me, and the sheriff answered. He informed us that Roger Hornsboro had died earlier today."

"How did he die? He was not that old. Was he? What happened to him?"

"The cause of death has not yet been determined. But, I understand that a gun was involved. So it does not appear that his age would have been a factor."

"He was murdered?"

"Can't say. All we know is that Mr. Roger Hornsboro received a single gunshot to the head earlier today. Now, sometimes a gunshot to the head can be self-inflicted. That's how many people commit suicide. But, it's also possible that he had some help—that somebody killed him. I would say this, however: In many cases, when a separate shooter is involved, generally the victim is shot more than a single time. But we will know more later.

"I would like to ask you, and have you think about it. Do you know of anyone who would want to see Mr. Hornsboro dead? Did you know him pretty well? And, for how long have you known him?"

"I've never actually met him, you know—face to face. I've talked to him on the phone a few times."

"When was this?" Henry asked. "When did you talk to him?"

"My lawyer gave me his number a week or so ago. Right before I talked to you the first time. He, Craig Conklin, my lawyer, he had said that Mr. Hornsboro might have some information that could be useful to me in learning about my Uncle William—actually, he would have been my *great*-uncle."

"Then," Henry said, glancing briefly over at Kate, "you knew about this Hornsboro fellow before you initially talked to me?"

"Yes. I had talked to him on the phone, but he didn't think he knew anything that could help me at all. That's why I never bothered to tell you about him."

"Given your limited knowledge about Mr. Hornsboro, can you think of anyone who might want him dead? What sort of new information did he have? What do you know about him?"

"I don't have any ideas about who might want to do him harm. He seemed very nice to me. Maybe a little evasive. But I didn't know him. Just a couple of phone calls. He never mentioned anyone that sounded like an enemy. As far as I know, he wasn't afraid of anyone.

"Here's pretty much what he told me. He said that he'd heard that there were some men in town asking questions about Edward and Isaac Pierce. I would assume that the men asking questions would be you and Jack Handler. So that's what I told him. I gave him your names."

"Aside from that, did he tell you that he had some new information?"

"Right. That's what he said. He told me that since he'd talked to me earlier, he'd learned some things about the Pierce brothers that

I would find very interesting."

"Like what?" Henry asked. "Did he give you any clues as to what he wanted to talk to you about?"

"He had some old letters. I'm sure—at least I'm pretty sure that he wanted some money for his information. When I told him that you'd be the one who'd be meeting with him, he asked me if you would be paying for information. I told him that I didn't think so, but he could ask you himself. I thought that would be a good way to get him to meet with you."

"He must have told you *something*. He obviously managed to get your attention. Anything you give me might be helpful. What can you remember about your conversation with him?"

"The first time we communicated with him," she said, "… that would have been over a week ago. He then told my lawyer and me that he knew something about the two Pierce brothers. He, of course never actually met them, but his father and his grandfather, they knew of them. But, that's about all he said at that time. His name had come up, Roger Hornsboro's name, that is. My lawyer came across the Hornsboro name when he was cross-referencing families that lived in Deadwood back in 1924 with the names of current residents. That's how he found him. There were Hornsboros living in Deadwood at the time, and this guy, Roger Hornsboro, was currently living in or around Lead. So, my lawyer called him.

"At that time this guy seemed a little hesitant about talking to us without cash. But, finally, he agreed to sitting down with us. Unfortunately, he did not seem to have any concrete information at all. He did agree to keep his ears open and to ask around. My lawyer left his phone number with him in case he were to find out anything.

"And that, in a nutshell, is where we're at right now. Except the poor man's dead."

"Then, can I assume that he did not tell you anything specific, anything at all, in order to coax you into setting up the meet with me?"

"He only made mention of those letters that had come into his possession."

"Okay. Tell me what you can about them."

"He didn't discuss anything specific about them, though. He didn't mention content."

"Must be something you can remember that he did say about them. How did he obtain them? And, who were the parties involved? Was there anything along that line that came up?"

"His grandmother. The letters were addressed to Hornsboro's grandmother."

"And who sent them?"

"That's the part that I don't know. He wouldn't tell me who had sent them to his grandmother. Just that they were from some other woman. They weren't from a man. I thought that it might have been the woman that knew my great-uncle. While he refused to tell me her name, he said that it was a name that was very common back then."

"Shit! I'll bet the letters might have been from Isaac's wife! Why else would he have contacted you? Or even thought that he might use them to extort some money out of us? Damn! Having them could have been huge. Did you get the impression that he kept them at his—at his house? Those letters must still exist—somewhere. Maybe they're still at his house."

"He didn't let on where they were. All he wanted to know was if we'd be willing to pay him for them. While he wouldn't tell me what exactly it was that was in them, he did say that I would find the subject matter *very* interesting, and that there were some very interesting postmarks on a couple of the envelopes."

"Really? Postmarks? Wonder what that could mean? Well, Kate and I are approaching the scene. I'll let you know what I find out."

"Kate? Who's Kate?"

"It's Kate Handler. Jack's daughter. She's in from New York. She'll be working with us for a while."

"Is Jack with you too?"

"Jack had an errand to run. He'll be away for a day or two. But I'll be keeping him updated. If you hear anything at all, be sure to let me know. Okay?"

"Yes. Of course. Let me know what the sheriff says about Mr. Hornsboro's death. If it was suicide or something else."

"Right," Henry said as he disconnected.

"Did you catch most of that?" he asked Kate.

"Pretty sure I got most of it."

"What do you think?"

"For someone who was not personally acquainted with the guy, she sounded like she was unusually surprised to learn about his death," Kate observed. "Did you get that impression? Did her reaction to the news strike you as how you would have expected her to react? Maybe that's just the way she is. You would have a better handle on this than I. What I am getting at is, did she seem to you to be a little bit over the top?"

"I don't know her well at all," Henry said. "So I wouldn't know what to expect. What are you suggesting? Like maybe she had something to do with the guy's death. For all we know right now, he might have offed *himself*."

"I don't know—I'm not suggesting anything," Kate said. "It just seemed like her reaction to his death was a little affected. We'll probably know a lot more after we talk to the sheriff."

"So, he wants us to meet him at his office tomorrow," Henry said. "He might not welcome us with open arms today. After all, he's still busy processing that potential crime scene."

"You're not chickening out, are you?" Kate said. "We need to crash his party. We're bound to learn something."

"Cold feet?" Henry said. "Absolutely not. I can't wait to check this out."

They had no difficulty finding Roger Hornsboro's camper. All they had to do was look for the strobes.

"That's a pretty shabby camper," Kate observed. "Looks like this guy could have justifiably used some extra cash."

Roger Hornsboro's "house" was old and faded, and the brown 2010 pickup truck it was sitting on was rusty. But, even though it had the appearance of having been driven around the world several times, it looked as good as was possible. *How in hell does he manage to Simonize that truck with all of the rust?* Henry was thinking. *And the camper—it looks amazingly well too, in spite of its age.*

Henry pulled in as close as he could to the newest-looking patrol car. As he and Kate got out, a tall distinguished gentleman walked down the three steps leading out of the camper.

Henry said as they headed in his direction, "He's younger than I anticipated."

"And better looking than I expected," Kate added. "Not your typical county sheriff. Bet he's the son or nephew of a former sheriff, or of some other local political figure."

"And who might you folks be?" the sheriff asked as he approached them.

Chapter 34

Henry walked ahead of Kate as they approached the camper and Sheriff William Miller, sheriff of Lawrence County, South Dakota.

"My name is Chuchip Kalyesveh, but everyone calls me Henry. And this is Kate Handler. She had talked to you a short time ago. We were expecting to meet with Mr. Hornsboro this afternoon."

"Oh, yes," the sheriff said. "So, Miss Handler, you're a New York City cop—is that right?"

"Yep, that's me."

"Well, maybe you should be in my shoes today," Sheriff Miller said. "I think I even heard that you are a *homicide* detective. Is that also right? You look awfully young to be a detective."

"I will take that as a compliment," Kate said as she flipped her bag open revealing her badge.

"Lieutenant! Oh my God. I never made that rank. Not before I ran for sheriff. I'm *really* impressed. So, you're a lieutenant in the New York City Police Department, Homicide Division. And you look young enough to be right out of the academy."

"I'm not that young. I actually had almost five years under my belt as a prosecutor—that was before I joined up."

"Well, all I can say is that it is a real honor for me to be standing right here now, on a bona fide murder scene, talking with a professional homicide detective."

"Murder?" Henry said. "Then you've determined that it was *not* a self-inflicted gunshot wound?"

"Right. Murder. The doctor found a second GSW. Not many people manage to shoot themselves twice. Usually one shot to the head does it."

"Do you mind if we take a peek inside?" Henry asked.

"Hell yes, I mind," the sheriff replied indignantly. "Now, she may be a big city homicide detective and all, but this is *my* crime scene, and, as far as I know, you have not been invited to this party."

"Of course," Henry said. "We get it. But would it be okay if we just took a quick looksee through the door? We'll stay outside and not touch anything?"

The sheriff took a long look at Kate, who was smiling in what could be described as a flirtatious manner.

"Put these on," he said, handing each of them a pair of latex gloves. "You may take a quick look inside, but you may not enter. I would appreciate it if you would not allow any DNA transfer. That is, do not lean in and deposit any hair. And, before you leave, I will have to have a technician take your DNA swab just in case—for elimination purposes, you understand. But, if all that is okay, go ahead and take a gander in there for yourselves."

"Thanks, sheriff," Henry said as he put on the gloves.

Kate did not verbally respond, but she and the sheriff did again exchange smiles.

As Kate and Henry walked toward the camper door, Sheriff Miller collared one of his technicians and told him to swab Henry and Kate before they left.

Kate arrived at the camper first. She leaned in slightly and spoke to a man who was examining the body.

"Excuse me, doctor. The sheriff said there were two wounds to the victim's head. Any exit wounds?"

"And who might you be? Please stand back and don't even

breathe in here. Who the hell said you could be corrupting my crime scene, anyway? Does the sheriff know you're poking around?"

"Sheriff Miller said we could take a peek inside, as long as we didn't bother you."

"Well, that's a first. Who the hell are you?"

"My name is Lieutenant Kate Handler, New York City Police Department—Homicide Division. And this is my associate, Chuchip Kalyesveh."

"And the sheriff gave you permission to fart around with my crime scene? What the hell's a big-time New York City cop doing out here in the sticks?"

"I'm sorry, Barry," Sheriff Miller said looking over Kate's shoulder. "These folks are my friends. They just wanted to get a quick look inside. They are investigating a different matter, and I wanted them to take a quick look at our victim and see if they can verify the identification. And perhaps provide some additional information. They will only be here a few minutes. And I promise I won't let them mess anything up for you."

The camper was very rundown, with torn curtains, old blue shag carpet, a small flat-screen and a pile of dishes in the tiny sink. The smells wafting from the open door were nauseating. "Sure, sheriff. Just keep them well outside. I don't want them screwing this up."

"You got it, Barry. Got anything really interesting, yet?"

"No," he blurted back loudly.

"What do you think, Kate? I'm sure you see a lot more of these in any given month than I will during my whole career."

The sheriff then looked over at the doctor and said, "Kate here is a homicide detective in New York City."

The doctor then stopped what he was doing and stood to his feet.

"She already told me that. New York is a long way from Lead," he said. "Are you here to tell me how to do my job?"

"No. Certainly not. I'm here on a totally different matter."

Kate then turned to the sheriff and said, "It's just that Henry and I were asked to talk to your victim. But, it looks like we're a little late for that. Would you mind if I asked *you* a couple questions? And then we'll get out of your hair."

"Sure. Fire away. But I do intend to hold you to your promise. Two questions, and then you'll get the hell outta here—for good. So, ask away. But, before you do that, if you two don't mind, I'd like to run your driver's licenses while we talk. Would that be okay with you?"

"No problem," Henry said as he pulled out his license and handed it to the sheriff. Kate then did the same.

The sheriff studied them briefly and handed them off to a deputy. "Deputy Corker, please call these in and get them back to me quickly," he said. "My friends here are eager to be on their way."

Once she again had the sheriff's attention, Kate said, "I can see that at least one round was fired into the right temple. It looks like a small entry wound. Perhaps a .22 caliber. Or maybe a .32. Where did the second shot strike him? And are there any exit wounds, or stippling?"

"You don't miss much, do you, Kate Handler? There are two entry wounds, but neither one appears to have exited. The one on the side of the head looks to have been fired from at least two feet—judging by the minimal degree of stippling. And the spread.

The second round appears to have been fired nearly pointblank—right into the brainstem. Might have expected an exit wound for the second shot, given the point of entry. So my guess is—and it's just a guess at this point—my guess is that it was fired into the victim as he was slumped forward. I say that because the pattern of stippling suggests that the shot was fired at an upward angle, with respect to the neck and head alignment. It caused the round to bounce around inside the skull. Instead of exiting through the mouth, or through the softer tissue of the neck. Like might be expected if the victim were sitting erect for the second round."

"So," Kate said. "Forensics might have one or two bullets to work with."

"That would seem to be the case," the doctor chimed in. "It could be that one or both of them could yield some good ballistic evidence. Or, the rounds might have just bounced around inside the skull until they broke up. My guess is—actually, experience tells me, that we will end up with something useful."

"Any casings?"

"No casings."

".22 or .32?"

"Probably a .22. Hell, by the looks of it, the shooter almost certainly used a .22 caliber pistol."

".22 caliber with no casings," Kate observed. "That means the shooter most likely used a revolver. Sounds to me like it could have been a professional. Is that what you're thinking?"

"Okay," the sheriff interrupted. "I'm pretty sure that you got the two answers I agreed to. So, if you could kindly move along and wait until Doc issues his report. I'm sure it will answer more of your questions. We need to let the doctor get on with his work here."

"Thanks, doctor," Kate said as she prepared to leave.

But the doctor did not respond.

As the three of them stepped away from the camper, Kate asked, "Looks like somebody tossed the place looking for something. Any idea what they might have been after?"

"I thought you might be able to answer that question for me," the sheriff said. "Why are you here, anyway? What are *you* looking for? Why did you want to talk to my victim in the first place?"

Hum, Kate was thinking. *That tells me that the sheriff was not the one who tossed the camper.*

"My father and Henry are working on a case," she said. "My dad's a licensed private investigator, and Henry works with him. And their client suggested that your victim, Mr. Hornsboro, might have some information that could be helpful."

"What sort of info are you talking about?"

"Not too sure about that. He had called our client and told her that he had some new information regarding an individual we have been investigating. But he would not give her any specifics. He wanted to get paid before he talked. So she did not learn much."

"Here you go, guys," the sheriff said as one of his deputies approached. "I'd like to have my technician take a little sample from your hands, in addition to the DNA swab. I'm sure you wouldn't mind. It's just standard procedure. This is to see if either one of you have been shooting people in my county today.

"Now where exactly is this client of yours—Claire, what did you say her last name was?"

"Her last name is Mansfield," Henry said. "Claire Mansfield."

"And where does she live? Is she from Deadwood?"

"Grand Rapids. She lives in Grand Rapids, Michigan."

"Is she in this area right now? Visiting, perhaps?"

"As far as I know she might be in Munising at the present time. But I don't know that for sure. When I talked to her earlier, she didn't say anything to make me think that she wasn't still at her house."

"Can you give me that number? Ms. Mansfield's phone number?"

"It's in my cell. Would you like me to text it to you?"

"Yes. Please do that. And text me your boss's number as well. You said his name was Jack? Is that right? Jack Handler? Tell me again why it is that he can't be here today? Is he busy in town?"

"I'm not really sure where he is. But I do know that he is not in town. Last I saw him he was catching a plane to New York."

"Wow. What's he doing in the *Big Apple*?"

"I have no idea. He has clients all over the country. I assume he is meeting with one of them right now."

"Was he in this area earlier this morning?"

"No. He flew out of Rapid City last night."

"There were no flights to New York out of Rapid City last night. I think the last one to New York was around five P.M. Is that the one you meant?"

"I think he was on a private plane. But I'm not sure. I just know that we hung out in the tavern last night until about eleven P.M. And that's the last I saw him."

"Did you text his number to me too?"

"Yes. I texted my number, Kate's number, Claire's and Jack's. You've got us all."

"Can you tell me where you were between eight and eleven A.M. this morning? That goes for both of you."

"You're asking me if we have an alibi?"

"That's right. It's what I do, you know. I'm a cop. I try to eliminate as many people as I can. And, whoever is left at the end—I either arrest 'em, or shoot 'em. Just kiddin', of course. But, where were you two?"

"I left early this morning. I'm staying at a hotel in town. I left early and drove to Rapid City to pick Kate up. She got in this afternoon, I picked her up, and here we are."

"Kate, Miss Big City Homicide Detective, is he lying? Or can you substantiate his alibi?"

"All I know is that I got in from JFK about an hour and a half ago. Henry was there waiting to pick me up when I got off the plane. And, here we are. We left from the airport in Rapid City and drove directly here."

"But you don't have any knowledge as to where your friend Henry was earlier this morning? Is that correct?"

"All I know for sure is just what I told you."

"Then, Henry, do you mind if we take a look at your GPS and see where you've been today?"

"That'd be fine with me," Henry said. "But I don't know how much good that would do you."

"Really? For one thing it'd tell me if you drove here earlier—to pay Mr. Hornsboro a visit."

"That's the problem. This Taurus I'm driving now doesn't belong to me. I just rented it. This morning I was driving Jack's Tahoe. I left it with a friend of his and rented this 2019 Taurus."

"Who's your carrier?" the sheriff asked, not pleased with Henry's convoluted story. "I might want to have them get your GPS history for me."

"My cell carrier is Verizon. You've already got my number."

The sheriff made a note of Henry's carrier, and then turned to his forensic technician, "Are you all set with the tests? Did you get a DNA swab as well as test for GSA?"

"Did both tests, sheriff. And I did get both of them—Mr. Kalyesveh and Ms. Handler."

The sheriff then handed their driver's licenses back to them.

"Well, my friends," the sheriff said, with a two-palms-up gesture, "I think we're all done here. I look forward to talking with you at my office, tomorrow morning at ten."

Henry looked over at Kate as though to send her a message. He knew that the sheriff would be more inclined to entertain some questions from another officer of the law than from a civilian.

"Sheriff," Kate said. "Henry and I have some additional questions. I will make them brief. Do you mind?"

The sheriff stared at her with his steel gray-blue eyes and put his right hand on his gun—a gesture of power.

"More questions?" he said, looking down at his watch. "I'll give you two minutes. Not one second longer. Fire away."

"Thanks," Kate said. "We can see that the camper was obviously tossed. Can we assume that is the way you found it?"

The sheriff flashed her an irritated scowl and said, "You can."

"Do you know who did it? Who tossed it, I should say."

"Not yet. But it seems pretty clear that the killer was looking for something."

"Do you have any idea what they were looking for?"

"No."

"Does the victim bear any evidence of trauma? Other than the two gunshot wounds."

"Are you asking me if Mr. Hornsboro was *tortured*?"

"Yes. In a nutshell, that's what I'm asking."

"Forensics will have to determine that. But, aside from the two bullet holes, I didn't see any other wounds. By the way, either one of those gunshot wounds would most likely been fatal. But that's all the *trauma* I could see with the naked eye. We'll have to wait until we get the autopsy back for any further details. Okay, your two minutes are up. I will see you two tomorrow."

"Thanks, sheriff," Kate said as she smiled and started to turn toward their car.

Henry reached out and shook the sheriff's hand.

"We'll see you tomorrow," he said. "Thanks for your help."

"*Lieutenant* Kate Handler," the sheriff said slowly, carefully enunciating the title. "What's the name of your commanding officer there in New York?"

"Captain Spencer," she replied. "Midtown precinct. If you talk to him be sure to say I said *hi*."

"Got a number?"

"Just call the main number and ask for him. He won't pick up your call, but if you leave your number, and the fact that you're another cop, he will call you back when he has time. Reference your call to me. That will get his attention. You might get him to call you back more quickly if you say it's related to me. But good luck. Cap is a very busy man. See you tomorrow."

As soon as they were seated in their car, both Henry and Kate carefully glanced back at the sheriff.

"He's making a call," Henry said. "Wonder if it has to do with us. My money says it does."

"Doesn't really matter," Kate said. "We didn't kill the guy."

"Oh, it matters," Henry disagreed. "I'm sure I have some GSR on my hands. He'll have the lab results back in by ten tomorrow. It promises to be a very interesting meeting."

To that point Henry had not told Kate about what had transpired before he had picked her up at the airport. He had not provided any details about how he had earlier shot the engine out of the vehicle that was pursuing Jack's Tahoe. Nor had he explained to her that her father's Tahoe had been destroyed by an Apache helicopter, or how he had subsequently used a drone to bring that chopper down.

Right now, Henry felt it was enough to say that he had recently discharged a firearm. Kate could draw her own conclusions from that. And, she could start preparing herself for the disaster that he knew might befall them the next morning.

Kate thought about asking a question or two about Henry's comment, but then thought better of it. *Why should I press him?* she asked herself. *If he thought I should know more he'd tell me. Best for all of us if I can plead ignorance—especially if there were laws broken.*

"Henry," she said. "Why is it you and my father always seem to get in trouble whenever I'm not around?"

"Kate," Henry replied. "You're my friend. And so this might come as a surprise to you, but I'm here to tell you that you suffer from a severe case of selective memory."

"And how's that?"

"Think about it. Can you think of a single instance, in the past couple of years, when you and your dad got together, when one of you didn't end up capping someone? Be honest."

Kate thought about it for a full minute, and then she said, "Christmas. Last year. I came home to the resort and cooked that turkey."

"That had to have been two or three Christmases ago—before I had even met your father. Last Christmas we were all in New York dealing with that drug kingpin from Queens. The one who had been giving you trouble."

"Oh. Yeah. I think you're right about that. But, if I remember correctly, you were the one who ended up taking care of Peaches—that was the dealer's name. Peaches."

"Right. But you were there too," Henry said. "Look, I'm not pointing fingers here. I just think you know that pretty much every time you and your father get together, it's business. And the business Jack engages in more often than not involves someone getting seriously hurt. I'm just saying—it's not by accident that trouble seems to follow your dad around. And, by the way, did you spot that Chevy that's tailing us?"

Chapter 35

Millie had reservations about sending her daughter to the hotel to retrieve the personal items from the two suites. But she knew that if the task were to be successful, Angel was the right choice to accomplish it.

Red and Robby both liked the idea as well. But, before Millie could arrange for the taxi, Red wrote a note to her: "Should buy two burner cells—one for her and one for you. In case she runs into something."

Millie concurred.

When Angel arrived at the hotel she had the taxi drop her off directly in front of the main office entry. *No point trying to hide the cab,* she reasoned. *They're going to be looking for anything that appears out of place. Might as well sneak around here out in the open.*

"Here's a fifty," she told the driver. "There'll be another one for you if I find you here when I come back out. Shouldn't be more than twenty-five minutes or so. Okay?"

The driver thoroughly examined the fifty-dollar to be sure it was legit.

"You'll pay me another fifty when you come back out? Aren't you checking in?"

"Right. I will give you another fifty within the half hour. I'm not checking in. I'm checking out. You wait here and I'll hurry as quickly as I can. Can I count on your being right here in half an hour?"

"I'll be here. But I can't wait all day. You've got half an hour."

"Terrific," Angel said.

As she walked in through the main office entry she made it a point not to allow her eyes to wander for fear of alerting anyone who might be looking for any unusual activity. Once inside, she immediately commandeered a luggage cart and headed for the suite she and her mother shared with the boys and Buddy.

Before she had left on her mission her mother had told her to limit what she remove from their rooms to what would fit into two suitcases, and to do the same when packing up the Childresses' belongings.

"Check everything out as rapidly as possible," Millie had told her. "Stuff that looks important to you, stick it in the bags and get back out. You must act quickly. Whatever you choose to leave will be fine. *Stuff* can all be replaced. Just hurry. And remember—the most important thing is to remove anything that could lead these guys back to the Childresses' witness protection location. That's the main thing you're going back for."

Angel checked her watch after she had packed up the first set of rooms.

"Ten minutes flat," she said out loud as she briskly pushed the cart toward the Childresses' suite. "So far so good."

When she reached room two-fourteen she parked the cart against the wall adjacent to the door. "Whoa! That's weird!" she muttered to herself.

The reason for her surprise was that the door was ajar.

"Now that doesn't make any sense at all."

Carefully she opened the door and peered inside.

At first she did not see anything, except that the two beds were made up, and what appeared to be all the contents of the rooms was stacked up neatly on the dresser.

"Hello," Angel said loudly as she stepped through the door. "Is anyone here?"

"Oh," a voice said from the bathroom. "Was this *your* room?"

The voice was immediately followed by the appearance of a very neatly uniformed young lady. She stepped out through the bathroom door and smiled at Angel.

"Yes," Angel responded cautiously. "I know I'm a little late. I just stopped in to pick up the rest of our stuff. Is that okay?"

"Yes. Of course. Our regular checkout time is noon, and so my boss sent me in to clean up the room. I saw that you hadn't entirely moved out yet, so I put all of your stuff on the dresser. I'm really glad you're here to pick it up. It will save me a lot of trouble. You'll find it's all there. I checked twice to be sure I got everything."

"Wonderful," Angel said. "Thank you. Sorry I'm so late getting back. My parents took me sightseeing. We haven't been back in Gaylord for years. Not since I was a baby, actually."

"Oh. Are you originally from this area?" the maid asked.

Nuts! Angel was thinking. *I should not have started this conversation.*

"My *parents* were. I was born and raised in the Upper Peninsula—in the Curtis area. But my parents used to live just south of Gaylord."

"Really. My parents have a place on Otsego Lake. Where did your parents live?"

Angel quickly realized that she needed to get going, so she faked receiving a call.

"Sorry," she said as she removed the burner cell from her bag. "Excuse me. I've got to take this call."

"Hi, Mom. I'm *almost* done. Just have to pack up a few things and get going. The nice people here set all our stuff on the dresser, so I can just grab it and get going. I'll be right out. Bye."

"Thanks so much for picking it all up. My mom thanks you too. But I really have to get going."

"You're welcome," the maid said. "Glad it all worked out."

These people were not travelling light, Angel groaned to herself when she scrutinized the large amount of belongings the Childresses had left behind. *I'm gonna have to take it all or it will look suspicious. Dang!*

"Okay if I toss these suitcases on the bed while I pack the rest of it up?"

The maid had managed to stuff most of their belongings into the suitcases, but there were a few items she had picked up as she cleaned, and had not yet packed up.

"Sure, no problem," the maid said.

"Thanks."

The maid, who had disappeared into the bathroom for a couple minutes, then stuck her head out and asked Angel a question: "I really like those shoes. The ones that are red on the bottom. The stilettos. I don't mean to be rude, but are they *really* Christian Louboutin?"

Angel had not yet tucked them away.

"You know," she said. "I think they are genuine. My grandmother lives in New York. She's *really* rich. *We're* not rich—but she is. And once a year she sends Mom and me a *care package*. She sends us some of her clothes that she has grown tired of. And she has very expensive tastes. Mom says she only sends us stuff when she gets drunk. I hate to say it, but I hope she doesn't stop drinking. It's nice to get those packages. It's kinda funny, but Mom doesn't call Grandma up anymore to thank her because Grandma never remembers sending them in the first place."

It was then that Angel realized that all the shoes in the Childress suite were two sizes larger than she wore. *I'll bet that the maid has tried on all of these shoes,* Angel was thinking. *This nosey maid's gonna realize that none of them would fit me. I've gotta get my little lyin' butt outta here—and right now.*

"I really have to run," Angel said.

By that time she had managed to stuff as much as she could into the two large soft-sided suitcases that belonged to the Childresses. But she still had a few things left to pack. She glanced over by the door. There she spotted a department store tote that was not being used. Without asking, she quickly appropriated it and shoved what remained into it.

"Thanks again for your help," Angel said as she wheeled the two huge bags and the tote out of the door. "I really appreciate it."

"You're welcome," the maid replied without emerging from the bathroom. "Good luck."

Angel then loaded the bags on the cart and headed down the hall to the elevator.

The driver of the taxi popped open the trunk as she approached. "Just toss them in the back, if you would," he said as he remained behind the steering wheel. "I've got to talk to my office."

Angel did as he suggested, and then returned the cart to the service counter.

"Okay, darlin'," the driver said as he flipped on the meter. "Where to?"

That comment caught Angel by surprise. *What could he be talking about?* She wondered. *And why did he turn the meter on? Doesn't he remember our deal?*

"Just take me back to where you picked me up," Angel said.

"Oh, darlin', help me out. I have a terrible memory."

"Sure," Angel said, figuring out that the man driving now was not her original driver. "I'm sorry. Just pull out on West Main Street and head west. I'll tell you where to turn."

"You got it," the driver said.

Angel had arrived at the hotel from the east. So, by telling the driver to head farther west she was directing him away from where she needed to go.

I've got to find a way to escape, she was thinking. *I need to play along with this guy until I can think of something. I need a plan.* Suddenly it came to her. She carefully dialed her mom's phone. She turned the volume as low as it would go.

"How far down this way do I have to go?" he asked.

"Stop at Meijer's. The gas station. Mom's supposed to meet me there."

"Okay. The gas station at Meijer's."

Initially Angel's mother could not figure out why her daughter did not respond to her. *Must have called me by accident,* she reasoned. *Maybe I should just hang up.*

But then she detected something that did not compute. The voice of the man who was talking to Angel had a bit of an East Coast accent. *That doesn't sound like the taxi driver who picked her up,* Millie observed. *Why would she switch drivers? And how could she switch? She doesn't have a credit card.* So, Millie listened in silently.

"Excuse me," Angel said. "Why did you replace my first driver?"

The man driving the taxi took a look at the picture ID of the real driver, and said, "Miguel's wife called him. There was a family emergency and she needed him. So he asked me to take care of you."

Angel looked down at her cell phone and saw that she was still connected to her mother.

"Oh no! I hope it's nothing serious."

"Nothin' new. This happens about once a month. I think he has issues with his kids."

"That's too bad."

"Yeah. Well, here we are. Do you see your people here? Or, did we beat them?"

"I don't see her car. Maybe she's parked around back. I'll go in and see if I can find her."

"Sit tight," the driver said as he locked the rear doors. "I'll drive around the station and you can look for her car."

Millie figured it out. She placed her hand over the mic on her phone, jumped up and sought out Red and Robby.

"We've got a problem," she said when she found them. "Somehow they found out that Angel was clearing out the rooms, and now they've got her in the cab at Meijer's gas station."

Red motioned for the car, and all three of them hurried off in its direction.

"What're we gonna do?" Robby asked. "When we find her. How're we gonna get her away from them? Do we know how many of them we have to deal with?"

"We don't know that," Millie said. "As far as I know there's just one. At least I only heard one."

Red presented a palms-up gesture and uttered, "Huh?"

"Angel called me but didn't talk. She wanted me to listen to what was happening. Apparently someone replaced the regular taxi driver, probably while she was picking up the luggage and stuff. And I heard her say that she was to meet me at the Meijer's gas station. They're there now, I think."

Millie was driving, and both boys were riding in the rear seat.

Red closed his eyes and sat back in the seat. He was thinking.

After only a couple minutes Red lunged forward. He grabbed Millie's shoulder and signaled for a paper and pencil.

Millie handed her bag back to him.

He rummaged through the bag until he found a pen and paper, and then began writing. When he had finished he handed it to Robby.

"Must get driver out of taxi," Robby read aloud, "and distract him. Divert his attention, somehow. Then one of us will let the air out of one of his rear tires.

"When he comes back to car and opens trunk to get spare, we'll surprise him. Get the luggage, and the keys, and lock him in it."

"He's gonna have a gun," Robby said. "Right? How do we get it away from him? Or do we even try? If we knock him unconscious, he couldn't use it, anyway."

"That could be dangerous," Millie said. "Never know what can happen when you hit a person on the head. I have pepper spray—that would work better. That would be better than hitting him on the head. We don't want to cause permanent injury."

Red nodded.

Robby concurred.

"I'll let the air out," Red wrote. "And spray him when he comes out to fix it. Robby, can you distract him?"

"How?"

All three of them thought about it. But no one had an idea.

"Here we are," Robby said. "Let's just do it. I'll think of something."

Millie removed the pepper spray from her bag and handed it to Red.

"Ever use one of these before?" she asked.

Red shook his head.

"Neither have I. Can't be too difficult. I think you just flip the guard over and push the button. Be sure it's not pointed at *your* face when you shoot it. Now, how is this going to work?"

Both Red and Millie looked at Robby for the answer.

"I'm gonna create a distraction to get the driver out of the taxi. Once he's out, Red's gonna let the air out of his tire. He will eventually come back and discover he has a flat. When he opens the trunk to get the spare, Red will spray him with pepper spray. We will grab the suitcases and toss him in the trunk, and close it."

"Shouldn't we get his gun first?" Millie asked.

Red affected a tight smile and gestured by rocking his hands.

"I'm just not sure about how concerned Red is about that. Might not be that easy to get the gun. Right, Red?"

Red nodded.

"I think the rest of it should work pretty well. Just don't know about grabbing the gun. Might just want to lock him in the trunk with the gun. And then duck."

Red grinned and nodded.

"All we need is a couple minutes to load up the luggage in your car and get outta here before the driver escapes. The pepper spray should blind him for a while, at least long enough for us to get away."

"There they are," Millie said. "Over there by the LP gas. I'm going to park over here and wait."

"Give me five bucks," Robby said, holding out his hand to Millie. "I've got an idea."

Millie did not ask any questions. She gave him a five-dollar bill, and he walked into the store.

Four minutes later Robby came back out carrying a gallon of pasteurized milk. Right behind him walked the clerk who was working the counter.

"Do you have an empty?" the clerk asked.

"No," Robby said. "I'll have to buy one of yours."

"Okay," the clerk said. "But you should know that the new tanks are not cheap."

"Yeah," Robby said. "That's okay. Mom needs it."

As the clerk unlocked the Propane cage containing the full tanks of gas, using his jack knife Robby poked a good-sized hole in the gallon of milk. And then he set the rapidly hemorrhaging container on the hood of the taxi.

At first the driver didn't notice the white liquid pouring out onto the car. But, eventually, he realized what was happening. He jumped out of the taxi and shouted, "You little asshole! Get that shit off of my car. Get it off! Now!"

By the time Robby lifted the milk container off of the hood, two-thirds of the milk had already poured onto the taxi, much of it leaking onto the grill, with some even running down into the windshield drain.

While the driver was yelling at Robby, Red sneaked up and, using his jackknife, cut off the valve stem from the right rear tire.

"Is there a car wash around here?" the angry driver asked the clerk.

"Sir, yes there is. It's just east of here on Main Street. Down there on the left. But, if you wish, you can drive around back. There's a hose there, and you can wash that milk off. What do you say? Would you like me to show you where it is?"

"Hell no! I'll do the car wash."

"And you," he said pointing a finger in Robby's nose, "you little fart. You're lucky I don't have the time right now; otherwise I'd smash your skinny little face in. Now get the hell outta my sight! Move!"

Mumbling to himself as he jumped back in the taxi, Westin started the engine, shoved it in reverse, and gunned the engine. The taxi shot backwards, making a terrible noise as it did.

"What the hell was that?" he yelled. He put the shifter in drive and pulled back up to the curb.

"Damn it all!" he yelled when he saw the flat tire. "What the hell is goin' on?"

He quickly walked back to the ignition switch and removed the keys.

Red observed the action and got in position behind a pickup truck that had just pulled in.

Westin singled out the proper key and unlocked the trunk.

Red then made his move.

"Where the hell did he hide the tools?" Westin grumbled.

"I'll bet they're under here," he said, sliding the suitcases over so he could look for a trap door to a storage space.

"There it is. At the bottom of all this. Damn it! I'm gonna have to move all this crap before I can get at it!"

And so he began setting the four suitcases and the tote bag out onto the paved parking surface.

When Millie saw what he was doing, she started her engine and slowly headed in his direction.

Just as he had set the fourth suitcase down, Red arrived.

I've got to make this guy turn around so I can hit him with the pepper spray, Red thought.

"Urrugg," Red blasted. It sounded like something one might expect to hear coming out of an old man who had just had the neighbor kid run over his foot with a bicycle.

"Holy shit!" Westin shouted as he turned to face Red.

That was Red's opportunity—and he didn't miss it.

"Pssshhhht."

The stream of burning liquid streamed into Westin's face for a full seven seconds.

Even though the man tried to protect his eyes with his hands, his efforts were futile.

Red did not even have to push Westin into the trunk, because when he tried to escape the dreadful fury that was assaulting his senses, he toppled into the trunk all by himself. And as he did, the .38 caliber pistol he had tucked under his belt became exposed just long enough for Red to snatch it out.

He flicked the cylinder over and dumped the six rounds into his hand. "Dang!" Red mumbled as he slid the six rounds into his pocket. "My fingerprints are now on the gun." So he quickly wiped it down with his shirt and tossed it back into the trunk.

Westin had felt the pistol striking his leg. Instinctively, he tried to sit up to reach for it. But when he did, Red slammed the trunk down on his head.

"Oh! Damn! My head! You little sonofabitch! I'm gonna kill you!"

Red slammed the trunk a second time.

Again Westin barked some profanity.

The third slam caught the man's fingers as he was trying to crawl out.

"Ow!" he screamed. This time sounding more like a little boy in pain than the scary monster he thought he was.

Red's fourth attempt at closing the trunk was the charm. It latched.

Angel observed the whole show from her seat. Once she was sure Westin could no longer harm her or anyone else, she bolted over the back of the front seat and out of the taxi.

"Great job, Red!" she shouted. "That was fun to watch. But, oh my gosh! The air—it *stinks* out here! My eyes are burning like fire!"

Red looked at her as if to say, "stop complaining and help me get this luggage loaded into your mom's car."

It went very quickly. Within twenty seconds all four of the suitcases and the tote were shoved indiscriminately into the back of Millie's white Suburban. Red and Robby were the last to climb aboard.

Just as they were driving off Angel spotted the keys on the pavement beneath the back of the taxi. She had Millie stop so she could retrieve them. The driver was shouting loudly and kicking the trunk from inside.

"Do you think you could help my poor friend here?" Angel said to a middle-aged man who had just walked over to see what was going on. "He's the driver. This is his taxi. He accidently shot himself with pepper spray, and then, for some crazy reason, locked himself in the trunk. I don't know where the keys are. Maybe he has them in his pocket. If you have a cell phone, maybe you could call a locksmith to get him out. Or, better yet, the police. That's what we need to do. You could call the police. Do you think you could please help?"

While the man, who Angel thought might be a tourist, was searching for the keys, she sneaked away and got back in the Suburban.

"Hey, buddy," the tourist said as he knocked on the trunk door. "Are you okay? Do you know where the keys are? Do you have them on you? I just want to help you."

Westin's throat was so irritated by the pepper spray that he was unable to utter a word. He tried, but all he could do was to woof out an uncomfortable cough.

"Hey, mister," the helpful man said again. "I smell—I think I smell pepper spray. It's pretty bad. That can't be good for your lungs. You need to get out of the trunk and get some fresh air. Did you know that there is a release lever inside the trunk? It has a glow-in-the-dark handle. Can you see it? All newer cars have it. Just find it and pull it, and the trunk will pop open."

Even though Westin's eyes were killing him, he was still able to open one enough to locate the general area of the trunk latch, and eventually he did successfully feel around until he detected the little handle. He pulled it, and the trunk popped open.

And as soon as a little fresh air hit his lungs, he literally broke down in grateful tears.

"Here," a new voice said, "Let me give you a hand getting out of there."

"Thanks, mister," Westin said. "I can't see a thing."

"That's okay," the man who had lifted him out said, "you won't have to see to know what I'm about to do."

"What do you mean?"

"Just turn around and put your hands on the car."

"What?"

"You, my weepy friend, are under arrest for—for a whole boatload of crimes. Kidnapping possibly being one of them. At least, for being in possession of a stolen vehicle. And a firearm. Do you have a permit for that? I suspect not. So, whatever your name is, you have the right to remain silent. You have …"

"Good job, Angel," Robby said as Millie drove east on Main Street.

Red gave her his biggest smile and two thumbs up.

"Red agrees with me that you did a great job," Robby said, "but he can't quit crying. I guess he's a little too broken up to personally congratulate you."

With that comment, Red forced one eye open just enough to locate Robby's arm and to land a monstrous right hand just below the shoulder.

"Ow!" Robby moaned. "Ow! Dang it, Red. That *really* hurt!"

"That's *enough*, boys!" Millie barked. "Straighten up back there or I'm calling Jack right now!"

Both boys stopped immediately. Red forced his eyes open a little, and the two boys looked at each other in disbelief. Never before had they ever heard Millie raise her voice at anyone.

Angel, who was sitting in the front passenger seat, turned and smiled at them. While she did not say a word, her smile conveyed both her gratitude, and the sense that it would be wise right now not to further rile Millie—that perhaps she'd seen this side of her mother before, and that this situation would pass if not stoked.

The boys smiled back at her, and then slouched down in their seats as if to avoid Millie's attention altogether.

Millie saw their heads drop below her line of vision in the rearview mirror. She could not block a faint smile from capturing her face. But while her attention was drawn to the plethora of flashing red and blue lights highlighting the success they had just enjoyed, she did not notice the shiny black Mercedes G-65 that pulled out behind her from the gas station. And she also did not observe it turning with her east onto Main Street—fifty feet off her rear bumper.

Chapter 36

Back in New York, Jack's flight began taxiing to take off. It left within moments after the three passengers—Jack, Roger and Col. French—had boarded.

"After we lift off, shall I show you men the rest of the plane?" Col. French asked. "It is a big one, and there's a lot to see."

"That won't be necessary," Jack replied. "We need to get some rest. But, before we turn in, Roger and I would like to get a handle on some of the *toys* Bob is sending with us."

"I thought you might want to see what we've got for you in that regard," Col. French said. "Bob indicates that you refer to them as *toys*. But I think you will find that they are anything but toys."

As soon as the pilot okayed their moving around the plane, Col. French handed them an inventory sheet and said, "If you gentlemen will please follow me, I will now show you the marvelous *tools* we've got for you." Col. French then led Jack and Roger through the dining room, which had a twelve-foot-long table complete with fruit plates, croissants, meats, cheeses and chocolates, with a huge ice bucket of flavored waters and fruit juices. And, finally, they entered into the staff's quarters.

"Bob had us remove the furnishings from the staff and secretarial section in order to display and transport the smaller weapons," he explained. "As you may have already noticed, all the cabinetry you see here is on wheels. That will allow us to expeditiously remove the tools and weaponry and transfer them to a van. They, along with some of the larger pieces of equipment, will all fit into a single Mercedes Sprinter—one of those tall vans. It is fully armored, I assure you. If the situation dictates it, that van just might be the safest place in all of Singapore."

"Nice to know," Jack said as he walked down the first of three rows of weapons of various sorts. "Much of this looks pretty pedestrian—.50 cal., assorted Glocks, looks like a few .308s. I would assume these pens are capable of firing a round. Would that be the case?"

"Some are pretty self-explanatory," the colonel said. "Others not so much. That one, for instance," he said removing a ballpoint pen from its container. "There are a total of four identical units just like this one. If you squeeze and twist the clip—which I'm *not* going to do right now. But if I were to, I could then point it at a target. And when I released the pressure, it would fire a poisoned dart using compressed CO_2. Virtually silent. The weapon has an effective range of twenty-five feet. I'm told it will actually shoot much farther than that, but with less accuracy. The effect of the poison paralyzes the victim in fifteen seconds, and kills within a minute.

"The beauty of this piece of equipment is that not only does it kill quietly, and quickly, but the victim does not even know he has been targeted. The tip immediately injects a small quantity of anesthetic, much like that of a mosquito, so that the victim does not even suspect he is under attack, or that he is dying.

"As I explained, much of what you see here is self-explanatory—that is, merely variations of weaponry you have used before. One of the principal differences, with regard to firearms and ammunition, is that these units have all been manufactured to the highest possible standards. The same holds true for the ammunition—especially that designed to be fired in the various sniper rifles.

"There are depleted uranium and explosive rounds for the .50 cal. The MPADS we've sent are barely beyond the prototype stage of development. If it continues to prove itself in the field, and so far it has, it will replace all current versions. It is lighter and more accurate—it's actually scary accurate. And, because it employs an incredibly smart integrated guidance system, it is virtually impervious to all standard countermeasures. It has an effective range of ten miles. The missiles it fires have ten times the punch of those currently available. That means you could use it to take out any tank on the ground, as well as a jet flying at forty thousand feet. So, be *very* careful with it. Not only can it actually penetrate tank armor, the shrapnel it produces has nearly the ballistics of a military-grade rifle at short range.

"Everything you see here represents the most deadly munitions on the face of the earth. And, what we've assembled down below, while it is less portable, it is even more lethal."

"Do you have some sort of spec sheet or operation manual for all this shit? So we can familiarize ourselves with it before we have to use it?"

"Yes, sir. I will provide that for you when we're finished here."

"That would be terrific," Jack said. "I'll read a copy of that manual, grab a snack and retire. How about you, Roger, anything else you need to see before we turn in?"

"I'm good."

Col. French then handed them each a copy of the manual and directed Jack and Roger back to their seats.

"I trust you'll understand that you'll not be spending the night in the Presidential Suite. *That* is, of course, always reserved for POTUS."

"We assumed that," Jack chuckled. "These reclining sleepers will do nicely for us. But, if you cut the main lights on your way out, that would be appreciated."

"Will do. And, keep in mind, this is a fully-equipped Air Force One. Those leather recliners open into beds. If you think of anything else you need, we have two flight attendants—Becky and Jill. They will be happy to help you."

"Nice to know," Jack said.

After the colonel had left, Jack looked over his reading glasses and said to Roger, "What do you think of the arsenal they're sending with us? I'd like to keep what we don't use. But I doubt that will happen."

"Have you checked out page three of the inventory?" Roger said, not directly responding to Jack's rhetorical question. "If Che and Fidel would have had this much firepower they would have overthrown Batista in a single day. There is one helluva lot of very lethal shit in the belly of this plane."

"Apparently it'll all fit in a single Mercedes Sprinter. I hope the colonel wasn't just blowing smoke up our ass about that puppy being armored."

"I'm sure it is," Roger said. "But can you imagine how it's going to stand out in Singapore? Maybe they're supplying two of them."

"The colonel said there would be *one*," Jack said. "There could be a second, I suppose, but it'd have nothing to do with the munitions he discussed. And, I'm sure *fitting in* isn't at the top of his priority list. Anyway, what he didn't indicate was whether or not we would have a driver."

"I think we can assume that there will be no driver," Roger said. "But we'll for sure find out about that in a few hours. I'll tell you what I find interesting. I think it's very curious that they've got us flying in Air Force One, while POTUS is arriving on a helicopter."

"Right," Jack quipped. "Our arrival on this monster 747 will certainly stand out. I wonder which one of us is the more likely to get shot down?"

"Precisely," Roger agreed. "That most certainly was by design. Just in case the enemies of the state decide to simply follow the most direct route to take POTUS out—to forgo the subterfuge."

"I'm sure the Russian S-400 would get through to take this bird down," Jack said.

"Yeah. And they could do it from 250 miles out to sea."

"But I have a lot of confidence in Bob's intel," Jack said. "If he thinks that our biggest concern is that the Deep State will launch their attack using black market weaponry, then that's most likely how it will go down."

"As long as they don't know we're onto them," Roger added.

There was a long pause after Roger's comment.

"Well," Jack finally said, "at this point, the only thing I can say for certain is that the next thirty hours promise to be the most exciting thirty hours of our lives. And, at the end of that time, if we're lucky, we'll be able to go home. Hopefully, as *passengers* on *this* plane, and not in the belly of some air transport."

Roger contemplated what Jack had just said, and then he spoke: "What is this—time wise? Singapore is twelve hours ahead of New York time. How do we keep it straight? Whether it's day or night?"

Jack thought about Roger's question and said, "If my eyes are closed, it's night."

Those were the last words either man spoke for the remainder of the trip.

It was eight A.M. when their plane landed at Changi International Airport in Singapore. By nine they were on their way to the Sentosa Gateway Bridge, which would take them to their destination—the newly constructed Miami Beach Hotel, on the west end of Sentosa Island.

The previous meetings between POTUS and Chairman Kim had been held at the Capella Singapore Resort. While all parties involved were pleased with the accommodations, the Secret Service believed that this time it would be advisable to conduct the meetings at the new Miami Beach hotel, located west of Universal Studios on the Singapore Strait between Fort Silaso and Tanjong Rimau.

The newly completed facility was every bit as luxurious as the Capella, but it was chosen not for its opulent accouterments, but rather because it afforded a more conducive scenario for security.

The Miami Beach Hotel provided two virtually identical fourteen-room presidential suites—one at each end of the sixth floor. Because the suites were of equal quality, neither POTUS nor Chairman Kim would be able to boast that they enjoyed the superior accommodations.

All the perimeter walls of the two presidential suites were constructed of twelve-inch-thick steel-reinforced tempered concrete. The same was true for the ceilings and floors, except the concrete utilized for them was only nine inches thick. All outside windows were bulletproof. The doors leading out of the suites, which were fire rated for one hour, were constructed of two sheets of three-eights-inch steel sandwiched around one-hour rated fireproof insulation. The doors were covered on each side with one-inch-thick decoratively carved mahogany. As a result of their excessive weight, they required electronically-initiated hydraulic door openers.

As a further security provision, each suite was equipped with a self-contained *safe room*—a virtual vault within a vault. And, in the second basement, was a special executive security bunker. It was designed to provide extended protection against an all-out attack on the building. In an emergency it could comfortably accommodate up to twenty individuals. Like the sixth-floor executive rooms, the walls were constructed of tempered concrete; but what made the executive bunkers unique was their ability to provide air, food and water to last up to thirty days. That was a significantly longer period of protection than any other commercial hotel in the world could provide.

But, the aspect about the Miami Beach Hotel that most excited the Secret Service was the fact that the two world leaders would not have to venture out of the hotel during the entire summit. That was the case because the hotel boasted its own world-class conference center, complete with dozens of meeting rooms, as well as state-of-the-art telecommunication capabilities, which included provisions for numerous satellite uplinks.

Initially, Chairman Kim had planned to stay at the St. Regis Singapore. But U.S. security convinced him that since the quality of the accommodations at the Miami Beach Hotel was comparable to what the St. Regis offered, and that greater security could be provided, after arrival, neither he nor POTUS needed to venture outside the hotel to conduct the summit. It would therefore be advisable for both parties to reside at the Miami Beach Hotel.

In short—the Secret Service drove home the point that limiting exposure necessitated by travel around the city would be a good thing.

As was the case with earlier summits between the two leaders, even though it was widely speculated that POTUS offered to pay the cost for the summit, the city of Singapore insisted that it foot the twenty-plus million-dollar bill for the entire meeting. The city's leaders said, "We believe that it (the cost of the summit) is a reasonable investment toward world peace, and we're happy to make it."

The plan was for Jack and Roger to arrive at the Miami Beach Hotel by nine A.M. And then, using the special Secret Service credentials that they both had been issued by the director of the agency, as per a directive by POTUS, they would inspect and thoroughly sweep the presidential suite that would be occupied by POTUS. This effort would precede the arrival of POTUS by three hours. If they found nothing alarming, they would inform POTUS' regular Secret Service detail that they were satisfied from a security standpoint. Of course, the regular detail would conduct their own security sweep of the suite as well.

And after all the security experts had finished their work, the cleaning crew, which was flown in from the U.S. with POTUS, came through to prepare the suite for occupancy.

"Check this out," Roger said as he pulled the bedding off of the bed. "Bet you've never slept on a sheet that felt like this. At least I know *I* never have."

Jack, who had been sweeping the bookshelves in the master bedroom looking for microphones and transmitters, walked over to the bed and slid his hand across the fabric. "What would you say this was?" he asked. "Maybe one thousand thread count. Is that what you'd say? Egyptian cotton? I think there's an American company who makes sheets like this. Boll and Branch? I think that's it."

"I suppose," Roger said. "Shall we take a look at what's under them? The POTUS crew will bring their own. I don't know why they go to all this trouble making up the room, only to have us come through and take it apart."

"They're just following orders," Jack said. "Like you and I are doing today."

"By the way, did you discuss with Bob what we're getting paid for this mission?" Roger asked.

"Getting paid?" Jack teased. "You're Secret Service. You're already drawing your regular paycheck. What the hell makes you think you should get paid any extra? If I were you I'd be more concerned about the status of my life insurance policy than the nickels and dimes Bob might be offering."

Roger just grumbled at Jack's comment, and then began stripping the bed.

A few moments later Jack commented on a reading he was receiving when he scanned various pieces of hanging art.

"All of these wall hangings have wireless security transmitters. They've all got to go. I counted seven of them. I suppose the fastest way to get security up here to take care of it would be to just pull one off the wall. If they come in with drawn guns I'm going to tell them you did it."

As soon as Jack lifted a tastefully-framed Chagall from its hanger, a siren sounded inside the suite.

Forty-six seconds later two armed security guards burst

through the door—with guns drawn.

"Holy shit, Rambo," Jack said greeting them. "We're U.S. Secret Service. And these alarms have to go. We can have *no* transmitters of any kind in here. Okay? I hope it's okay. Otherwise, talk to your boss. But these alarm transmitters have to go right now."

"I don't think he speaks English, Jack," Roger said. "Maybe you'd better show him your special badge. But, I'd be real careful if I were you. He looks to me like he wants to shoot you."

Chapter 37

"I speak English just fine!" the guard in charge barked at Roger. "You must not touch the art. It's against the rules. Should you do so, I will have to turn you in to the Singapore Police. I have no choice."

"You have a choice," Jack thundered back. "And you'd damn well better put that Glock away before I take it from you and shove it down your throat!"

Just then a nattily attired middle-aged man walked through the door.

"Put the guns away," he said as he laid his hand on the guard's shoulder. "Everything is fine. Relax. Holster your weapon and leave. I'll take it from here."

After the uniformed guards had left, the gentleman in the suit introduced himself to Jack and Roger.

"My name is Tony Khoo," he said as he reached out to shake Jack's hand. "I'm one of the managers here. What seems to be your concern?"

"The wireless transmitter on these pieces of art. I'm going to have to have you remove the batteries and take them off line. We can't have that type of electronics transmitting around our President. Does that present a problem? If it does, I'll be happy to remove the art and the alarm transmitters. It's up to you. But the transmitters have to go."

"No problem," the manager assured him. "I'll send someone right up to take care of it. No problem at all."

"It has to be right now," Jack said. "Otherwise I will pull them out myself. Okay?"

The manager smiled and turned away while he made a call.

Seconds later he turned back to Jack and said, "The technician is on the way up right now to take care of it."

"He must remove all the batteries entirely," Jack reiterated. "And if there are any other wireless transmitters in the suite, they will have to go as well."

"He absolutely will remove all batteries. I am sorry for this inconvenience. Is there anything else?"

"Not right now," Jack said. "But if you could stick around for a bit in case something comes up. We should be winding this up shortly. If it's convenient for you. Might save us both some aggravation if you were around to deal with any question we might have. Can you do that?"

"Absolutely. Happy to do so."

"By the way, Mr. Khoo," Jack said. "What's the deal with all the equipment connected to the toilet—that porcelain throne? Does it have a purpose?"

What Jack was describing was the refrigerator-sized piece of equipment located beside the toilet.

"Sir. This is the *presidential suite*. Visiting dignitaries from all over the world stay in these rooms. In some cases it is important to these leaders that they not leave behind anything that could be used against them. Therefore, we make a provision for them to collect and take with them any fecal matter and body fluids. Apparently, in the past, opposing interests have dispatched agents to collect such materials in order to examine them. I guess they put them under a microscope. This device serves that purpose for guests."

"I had heard that both Khrushchev and Gorbachev discovered

later that their shit had been stolen by the CIA," Jack said through a large grin.

"But it doesn't really matter," Khoo said in a slightly sarcastic tone. "The word is that both leaders will be providing their own toilets. That's fine. Makes our job a little easier—less to clean up when they leave."

Seeking to change the subject, Khoo added, "Have you seen all the rooms in the suite? Each has a small gym, an office, and of course the living and dining rooms. All the rooms have very high ceilings—over four and a quarter meters. That would be about fourteen feet. As you can see, the walls are tastefully finished in white, charcoal, and teak woods. The main living and dining areas have beautiful white marble fireplaces, with crystal chandeliers. And the floors in these two areas are constructed of imported black marble. I'm sure you'd agree that the glass and gold furniture is absolutely exquisite. The safe room—"

"I see you've removed all the TVs," Jack said. "How about that Steinway ebony grand piano. Is that an electronic piano?"

"No. It's a standard analog piano."

"Good. I read that the suite comes with butler service. Is that right?"

"We were told to cancel the butler for this visit."

As Jack was talking, Khoo's men were pulling down the paintings one at a time and disabling the transmitters that protected each piece. And then afterward re-hanging them.

"Well, Roger," Jack asked. "Are we ready to wrap this up?"

"I'm finished," Roger said.

"Then, Mr. Khoo," Jack said. "We will be getting out of your hair. Thanks for your good help."

The manager was not sure how to interpret Jack's idiomatic *hair* comment, but he did understand the *thank you* part. He acknowledged both Jack and Roger by shaking hands with each of them as they left.

Waiting for them outside the presidential suite stood a fidgeting Col. French. Checking his watch before speaking, he declared, "You're cutting it close. POTUS arrives any second now."

While neither Jack nor Roger responded directly to Col. French's comment, Jack did toss a disgruntled Sean Connery sneer in Roger's direction.

"Duly noted," Roger grumbled so only Jack could hear.

Col. French led the way down the corridor and onto the elevator.

As soon as the door closed behind them, Col. French tried to continue his speech: "I allowed one hour for your sweep of the presidential suite. You two were—"

That was all the words he got out. Jack, who was standing behind the colonel, placed his left hand on the Col. French's shoulder and gently turned him around.

"Excuse me," the colonel said, clearly not pleased that Jack had placed his hand on him.

As soon as Col. French was facing him, Jack gripped his belt in his left hand, and the knot of his red tie with his right, and hoisted the colonel off the floor and slammed him backwards into the elevator door.

"What the hell are you doing?" Col. French vehemently protested. "You take your hands off me right now! I'm reporting—"

"Let's get one thing straight, Colonel," Jack interrupted, as he slammed the colonel into the doors a second time. "*You're* not in charge of this mission. *I* am. If timing isn't as it should be, that means *you* screwed up. So *you* should fix it."

"I'm going to call—"

Jack pulled the colonel a few inches off the elevator door, and then slammed him a third time back into it. Col. French's head banged loudly against the stainless steel. He winced.

"You can do anything you wish," Jack said. "I'd prefer that you just do your job and keep your snide comments to yourself. *I* am in charge here. You get that straight, and do your job right, we'll get along just fine."

Col. French opened his mouth as if to say something.

"Ah. Ah. Ah," Jack said. "Your next words could get you seriously injured. How about you just say, 'Yes, Jack. That sounds good to me.' Can I assume that's what you were going to say?"

The colonel did not respond verbally. Instead he nodded slowly his resentful acquiescence to Jack's terms.

"Wonderful," Jack announced as he quite carefully repositioned the colonel on his feet and straightened his suit. "Now, then, I suggest you let Roger and me get on with our job. Where to next?"

Once squarely on his feet, the colonel turned to face the elevator door.

"We're headed to the tower," he said. "We should arrive there in fifteen minutes, if all goes well."

"We're going directly to the *tower*?" Jack asked. "How about our equipment?"

"It's already in place. The tower is closed to the public. I've already had my men offload everything we brought with us onto the main observation deck. So we can go directly to the tower and you can perform the final setup as you wish."

"Terrific."

The elevator had stopped, but the door had not yet opened. Col. French turned to face Jack and said, "Jack, I want to apologize for—"

"Enough said," Jack interrupted for the third time. "We're good. Let's just get on with what we have to do."

The tower the men were referring to was the Tiger Sky Tower. Located centrally on Sentosa Island, it afforded the best vantage point in all of Singapore. As it stood three hundred and sixty feet above ground level, with a viewing height of around three hundred feet, Jack had earlier requested the exclusive use of the tower for his base of operations.

More specifically, Jack not only wanted total control over the tower during the summit, he had asked that the glass be removed from the viewing cabin. The tower had been closed to the public since December, 2018—this provided the perfect opportunity to make use of the structure without inconveniencing or endangering the public. By having the glass taken out, Jack realized he would not only be granted a full three hundred and sixty degrees of unobstructed view of the surrounding geography, he would also obtain full operational access to the airspace above that same geography.

While Jack could not be certain that the attack on the summit would come through the air, the intel provided to him by Bob Fulbright strongly suggested that the weapon of choice was to be an older model cruise missile—one sporting a conventional warhead. Since it would be utterly impossible for him to guard against every conceivable mode of attack, he was convinced that his best bet for success would be to prepare himself for an attack utilizing one or more of the older Tomahawks. *I would sure like to have some sort of confirmation regarding my assumption,* Jack reasoned, but I have to prepare on the basis of the information received. And, generally speaking, when the former President speaks, he is usually correct.

The limo that delivered Jack and Roger at the tower was driven by one of the male attendants that had accompanied them on the flight from JFK. Jack found that fact comforting; *the fewer faces the better,* he reasoned.

Col. French was also in the vehicle, but he did not offer any conversation. *Must be the colonel is still pissed off at me,* Jack thought. *I know I would be if some strange asshole jerked my chain like I did his. Hell! I'd probably have killed any sorry SOB who'd dare do what I did. But, I wouldn't have pulled that horseshit if he wouldn't have acted like that. It is what it is.*

As they arrived Jack spotted the Mercedes Sprinter parked adjacent to the boarding doors of the viewing cabin.

"There it is, Roger," Jack said. "Our wardrobe on wheels. So far, everything's going as planned."

Roger turned to Jack, but did not immediately speak.

Finally, after nearly a minute, Roger said, "No mission ever goes without a hitch. I'd just as soon get our bad fortune out of the way. You've got to know it's going to slap us in the face eventually. I wouldn't mind if it would rear its ugly head sooner than later. Everything can't go perfectly. Not from start to finish. It *never* happens like that."

Both Jack and Col. French heard what Roger had said, but neither one of them was eager to respond.

Sensing that Roger's declaration did warrant some sort of reply, after a few long, awkward moments, Jack finally offered this: "Roger, old man. If I didn't know better I'd think you were trying to jinx our mission. Good thing I'm not superstitious."

"No, that's not at all what I had in mind," Roger quickly rejoined. "It's just that never does everything go as planned. There's always something. And so far, this leg of the mission has gone pretty well. I'm just saying."

"Damn, Roger," Jack said. "What the hell's wrong with you? Are you developing some kind of early-onset issues? First we had our plane shot out of the sky. And then we had to deal with that badass Apache chopper. We've already had enough calamity piss on us enough for *two* missions."

"But that was all yesterday, Jack," Roger said. "This is a new day."

"Well, if it would make you happier, maybe we'll find the Sprinter empty. Or, we might break the key off in the door."

Col. French heard both ends of their conversation, but again, he did not respond.

Chapter 38

The mood in Millie's Suburban was somewhere between euphoric delight and simple relief. All the boys could think about was the sight of that crabby old man tumbling into the trunk, and his frantic cries from inside that eye-burning tomb. Their plan had worked perfectly, and their sense of self-satisfaction thoroughly reflected that success.

Angel, on the other hand, while thankful for her rescue, was not able to totally identify with the overwhelming joy that the boys were obviously reveling in. Even though she had pulled off the amazing feat of retrieving not only their personal property, but all the seemingly lost possessions belonging to their new friends—the Childresses. *Sure,* she was thinking, *I did it. I managed to do everything Mom sent me to do. But I ended up getting myself kidnapped. And that's exactly what happened to me—I got kidnapped. And I had to be rescued. I came close to succeeding, but I just made one mistake too many. I wonder—what could I have done differently?*

Millie had a totally different take on what her daughter and the boys had just accomplished. She was not at all pleased about anything that had just transpired. While she was very proud of her daughter, and of the two boys, she regretted all her recent decisions in the most powerful way. *Never in this life should I have put these kids in that kind of danger. And that's what I did. Jack would not be happy that I gambled with their well-being.*

First of all, I should not have allowed the situation to develop to where I would even be tempted to permit these people to lead us down that type of rabbit hole. I should have rejected the Childresses' requests and turned the whole thing over to the cops. Just who did

I think I was—Jack Handler? I could have got these kids killed. I had no business allowing this whole incident to unfold the way it did. And then, I take my frustration out on those two heroic boys by screaming at them. Shame on me. It was all a big damn shame. And I'm to blame. Not these kids. It was me who was wrong.

"Boys," Millie said loudly enough for them to clearly hear, "I apologize for yelling at you. You guys did a great job—what you accomplished was absolutely wonderful. Your Uncle Jack would have been *very* proud of you. I am sorry. I never should have raised my voice at you."

Angel was relieved that her mother had a change of heart. *I knew she would come around sooner or later,* she said to herself. *It was only a matter of time.*

Her mother's conciliatory words to the boys helped Angel to overcome her nagging sense of failure. She sat up in her seat and whipped her head around.

"Yeah! You guys were just *terrific*," Angel said. "I can't wait to tell Jack and Henry what you did."

And then she started to chuckle.

"Red, you look absolutely pathetic."

"Mom, Red's eyes are swollen nearly shut. We need to get him in the shower."

"You think he looks bad," Robby said. "He's stinkin' up the whole back seat with that pepper spray. My eyes are burning too."

Just then Angel's eyes glanced above the boys' heads and out of the rear window. She had spotted something behind them that got her attention.

"Mom! Turn down the next street. Do it!"

"What's up?" Millie asked as she braked hard and turned left in front of oncoming traffic. "Why are we turning?"

Angel did not answer her. Instead her eyes scoured the floorboard, both in front of her and behind her seat.

"Okay," she said. "Turn right. Now!"

Millie did as Angel said.

"Now speed up a little. Speed up a lot."

"Tell me what's going on!" Millie said as she hit the gas.

"Now turn right again. And stop."

This time Millie just did as her daughter commanded without asking questions.

As the car screeched to a stop, Angel reached back and grabbed the two bottles of sparkling grape juice that Millie had earlier purchased at the Meijer's store. She jumped out of the Suburban just as the Mercedes G-65 SUV approached from behind them. Taking one of the bottles by the neck she flung it like a Nazi grenade at the skidding vehicle. The glass of the bottle struck the windshield with such force it shattered both. She then threw the second bottle. It obliterated what remained of the treated safety glass.

The fine glass needles produced by the virtual explosion of the laminated windshield temporarily blinded both the driver and passenger. So, while they were attempting to get a fix on what had just transpired, Angel ran back to the Suburban.

"Let's get outta here while we can!" she suggested in her most commanding tone.

"What was *that* all about!" Millie protested, as she gunned the Suburban.

Even though Robby was not aware that they had been followed, he quickly, and correctly, surmised what had just transpired.

"Mrs. Star," Robby said as he pulled himself forward using the back of the front seat, "Haven't you ever seen your daughter act out like this? That's the way she behaves at school every day."

Red tried so hard to contain his laughter at his friend's comment he farted loudly. With that, all three teens burst forth in half-restrained sniggering.

Millie did not verbally acknowledge Robby's comment, nor did she comment about Red's accident. But she could not block the smile that crept across her face.

Once the laughter had subsided, Millie asked, "How many people were in that Mercedes? More than one?"

Robby looked to Red for a possible answer, but none was forthcoming.

"We don't know," he said. "By the time we checked out what was back there, Angel had punched that poor car in the nose. And then we couldn't see anything."

"How about you, Angel?" Millie asked. "Do you know if there were more than just the driver?"

"The only one that I saw was the driver," Angel said. "That's what I remember. It happened so fast. My only thought was to smash the windshield out right in front of the driver. I didn't even glance at the passenger side until after I'd thrown that first bottle. And then, when I threw the second, if there *was* a passenger, he'd of been ducking, so I guess I really wouldn't know whether or not there was a second person in the car.

"Do you think it really matters how many people were in that car?"

"It might," Millie replied. "But, whatever, you did a great job. I'm proud of you."

Chapter 39

Henry and Kate did not want to give the driver of the car that was tailing them the opportunity to escape, so they quickly hatched a plan to reverse roles.

Henry clicked on his left-turn signal. They were just leaving Lead—heading east on Highway 85. The car behind them slowed down as soon as Henry had signaled for his turn.

"You're right," Kate said, sneaking a peek out of the rear window. "They're hanging back so we won't know they're following us. What have you got in mind?"

"This looks like a bit of a side street," Henry said. "Short Street. That's its name. It even sounds like a side street. I'm gonna pull off here and see if we can circle around behind them somehow. Whoa! Would you look at that!"

Henry had spotted a widened and graveled section of the street on the left. He hit the gas and cranked the rental vehicle into it, forcing it into a controlled power skid. As the rear of their vehicle spun around, the tailing Chevy passed them and continued down Short Street.

Henry then gunned his way back onto the street and rapidly caught up with the Chevy.

"Are you ready for this?" he asked Kate, while at the same time unsheathing his knife in order to hasten the deflation of the anticipated airbag.

"Ready," she said, switching her airbag off.

And then, holding her Glock in her right hand and placing her left hand on her seatbelt latch, she said, "Let's do it."

"Crunch!"

Henry slammed into the rear of the car with smashing force. His vehicle bounced off as the Chevy was shot forward.

"Defective airbag!" he mumbled, tossing his knife on the floor.

Henry hit the gas again. This forced his front bumper into the trunk of the car causing it to careen slightly to the right. Henry kept his foot on the gas, this time striking the vehicle just behind the right wheel, sending the Chevy into a full spinout, causing it to veer off the street and head on into a large pine tree.

"Go! Go! Go!" Kate yelled as she bolted out of the car and ran toward the passenger door of the crashed Chevy.

Henry headed for the driver's side.

Kate arrived first—Glock in hand.

"What the hell!" she blurted out. "Where'd he go?"

The car's engine was still running, but the windshield was entirely popped out and the driver missing.

"Did you see him take off?" she asked Henry.

"I didn't see a damn thing after he smacked that tree. Looks like he flew right out of the window, and then took off."

Kate quickly opened the passenger door and surveyed the inside of the car. She scooped up a half-eaten Snickers candy bar from the floor, a paperback book entitled *Murder on Sugar Island*, several empty candy wrappers, various scraps of paper, and two soiled tissues. She opened the glove box and grabbed what looked like the vehicle's registration, and stuffed it all into an empty plastic grocery store bag.

"We'd better get the hell out of here," she said. "Before the sheriff decides to have us in early for that meeting."

Henry took one last look off to the east, and then turned back to his car.

As he approached it he took a long glance at the damaged left front quarter-panel and grumbled, "Shee-it! That's gonna be a tough one to explain to the rental company."

After Kate had buckled herself in, she tied together the handles of the bag of rubbish she'd scarfed up from the crashed Chevy and tossed it onto the rear seat.

"What did you find?" Henry asked. "Anything interesting?"

"No idea. Just thought I'd hang on to some of his trash. Might prove helpful later. At least we'll have his DNA. There were some notes and letters. Might not even be his. And I did get the vehicle's registration, too. Probably a stolen car. But you never know."

Sheriff Miller had just disconnected from a call he'd placed to Captain Spencer, Kate's boss. And just as she had warned, the call went to the precinct's switchboard, so all the sheriff could do was to leave a message requesting a callback.

He was anticipating a call from New York when his phone rang. He checked. It was his own dispatch.

"We just got a call from a resident on Short Street," said the female voice on the other end of the call. "According to my map, that's out there where you are right now."

"Yeah. I know where it is. What happened on Short Street?"

"Apparently there was a two-vehicle accident. They came together, and one of the vehicles crashed head-on into a large pine tree. Caller reported damage to the car, and to the tree."

"You've got a car en route yet? I can send one of my deputies from here if you don't. We're just wrapping this up."

"I do have a car on the way. Just thought I'd let you know that the resident, a Mrs. Rachel Clearey, said that she witnessed one of the occupants of the second vehicle, the one causing the accident, she said a female from that second vehicle was brandishing a pistol. ... That witness was Rachel C-l-e-a-r-e-y."

"Firearms?" the sheriff barked. "Drawn or holstered?"

"Brandishing was *my* word. But that's how Ms. Clearey described it. She said that the female passenger had a pistol drawn and pointed at the other car."

"Any shots fired?"

"No. She did not report any shots fired."

"Did she describe the persons with the gun?"

"Only that it was a man and a woman, and only the woman had a gun, as far as she knew. She described the man as tall and well built. And the woman as tall, and well dressed. She did not get a good look at their faces, but thought they appeared to be in their thirties or early forties. She said the woman was thin."

"I'm on my way. Are the vehicles still there?"

"The vehicle that hit the tree is still there. But the other one, and the couple with the gun, they drove off right after they had examined the car that had struck the tree. She said they appeared to have been in a hurry to leave."

"I'll just bet they were," Sheriff Miller said. "What else did she say?"

"She told me that after the couple drove off, she went out to check on the other driver, but his car was empty. The driver was gone."

"Where is this witness now? Do you have an address?"

"I have her address. She lives on Short Street. But she said she would wait at the scene until we got there. I sent Deputy Black."

"Has he arrived on the scene yet?"

"He is still on his way. If you're headed there, shall I call him off?"

"No. Just let me know when he reports in."

"10-4. Will do."

* * *

"Are you able to get an ID off of anything?" Henry asked.

"Actually, yes," Kate answered. "According to the registration the car was owned by Mildred Pruit. For some reason, I don't think that Ms. Pruit was driving that car when you spun it."

"How about the other stuff? Anything there?"

"The tissues look like they've got lipstick on them. So my guess is that they belonged to the Pruit woman. Maybe *everything* does. Everything except for the Snickers wrappers. I think they most likely would have been left by the guy driving the car."

"If your dad were around we could have them analyzed," Henry said. "But I don't have anyone to do that."

"I can take a look at them for latent prints," Kate said. "I'll do that tonight. But, as far as DNA, we might not be so lucky. Odds are the tissues did not belong to the driver. And we really don't have much else to go on, as far as DNA is concerned. The half-eaten candy bar might offer a usable sample, but that's iffy at best. The FBI is actually able to extract DNA from postage stamps—and I'm not talking about the ones you lick. But I wouldn't have access to their lab for testing. I could FedEx them to New York, and request their assistance. If you think it would help."

"I'm thinking we might be able to find this guy just hanging out in the area. Maybe waiting on a ride. So, we might want to poke around here a little longer—as long as we can keep out of the sheriff's hair. I expect him to be showing up any time."

"I agree. Someone had to have reported that accident. Just

wondering. Did you happen to spot a trail of blood? I saw some on the dash, and on the wheel. Not a lot, though. The driver must have got himself cut up at least a little when he smashed into the windshield. And not just his hands."

"I saw the same thing," Henry said. "I did notice that there was a little blood smeared on the hood—just a smear. I'd say he was scratched up a bit, but nothing that would result in significant blood loss. He sure didn't waste any time getting outta there. My guess is that he would of headed back over the highway—to the southeast. Decent place to wait for a pickup."

"If that were the plan," Kate added, "then it's likely that right now he'd be waiting somewhere along 85. If he made it even a quarter mile east down 85, there's all those trees. They come right up to the edge of the highway. He could hunker down in the forest and wait for his ride. That would make sense to me. It's not likely that this guy's a pro. So he's likely to seek out the most obvious. And those trees seem to me to be the most obvious."

"How do we monitor it?" Henry asked. "In your opinion. We have to watch out for the sheriff, too."

"Find a place where we can go off road. Park so we have a reasonably good vantage point. And just wait it out. Have to be careful that we're not too obvious. So get into the forest far enough so that we can't be easily spotted."

"Like here," Henry said, shooting off the road and through a small wood fence. He pushed on along a guardrail until he found an opening, veered into a patch of larger trees, and then smashed into one of them.

"Wow!" Kate said. "That was fun. Let me guess—you wanted to cover up the damage you did when you hit that Chevy. Right?"

"It's an insurance claim any way you slice it. At least now it appears that the damage was done when I struck that tree. Whatcha think? We ought to be able to keep an eye down the road. If that's where he's hiding."

"As good as it could be. Probably only an outside chance of success, but one worth attempting. Got to keep an eye out for the sheriff, too."

The stretch of highway Henry had selected lay on Highway 85 just south and east of Short Street. Well within a comfortable distance for even an injured man to run, Henry concluded. *As long as he had two good legs under him.*

It didn't take long. Within five minutes Kate and Henry spotted a patrol car south down 85.

"Betcha he's headed over to check out the Chevy," Henry said as a deputy passed them.

"I'm sure you're right," Kate said. "At least he didn't spot us. I'm a little surprised we haven't seen the sheriff drive by. And you can be pretty certain he'd be looking for us."

"Not yet," Henry said. "I'd bet, though, that he'll be along here anytime. Good chance he won't find us, though. I might have knocked that fence over, but I didn't leave any skid marks. I'd say we can hold out here a little longer. What do you think? Is this guy's ride gonna be coming from the north or the south?"

"I'd guess north," Kate answered. "But, odds are he will pass our guy and come on through to see if someone's watching for him. And then turn around, and pick him up on his way back."

"Makes sense," Henry replied. "So, we should keep an eye on everyone—coming and going."

"I'd say so," Kate said. "I still find it intriguing that this fellow was following us. Why do you suppose that would happen?"

"It might have to do with the dead guy—Roger Hornsboro."

"Do you think that he might be the killer?"

"Possibly," Henry answered. "Or maybe he works for the killer. At least somehow associated with those behind the killing. What do you think? Did that shooting look professional to you?"

"Could be. The fact that he used a revolver lends itself to that assumption. But anyone who's read a decent novel would know enough about how to pull off a hit to get most of it right. But the way he gave himself up by following us around. That was amateur-hour stuff. No one—"

"*Amateur hour?*" Henry repeated through a large laughing smile. "The only person I've heard say that was your dad."

"Shut up," Kate said, laughing at herself. "Dad does say that, doesn't he? Well, that's still probably the best term I could use to describe the tail that guy put on us. Very amateur."

"Yeah. I suppose it fits. Anyway, I'm sure that would be the term Jack would use to depict our friend. He sure as hell didn't know what he was doing. Especially if he *is* the killer. That's why I don't think he's the one who dropped the hammer on Hornsboro. If that was a professional hit, or even a half professional, the killer would not have stuck around. He'd be long gone. At least that's how it would seem to me."

"Keep in mind," Kate said. "Killers are usually pretty stupid people. And they are also often careless. Especially if they are motivated by emotion. Just like in most areas of life—it takes all kinds."

Another few moments passed while both considered Kate's words. Finally, they both spotted a late model Ford heading south down 85.

"Does it seem to you like that car is going a little slower than we might expect?" Henry observed.

"Sure does," Kate replied. "He's got two cars right on his tail. They think he's going too slow as well."

Henry reached across and pulled out a Canon Point-and-Shoot camera from the glove-box.

"Maybe I can get a shot of him as he goes past us."

He zoomed in as much as he could and began clicking off images of the driver.

"It's a female behind the wheel," he said.

And when the car grew closer Henry removed the camera from in front of his face, stared naked-eyed at the driver as the car passed, and then blurted out, "Damn, I *know* that woman!"

Chapter 40

Waiting behind the wheel of the Sprinter was a well-built man wearing a dark gray suit with a white shirt and blue tie.

"Gentlemen," Col. French said, "I'd like to introduce you to your driver."

"We do have a driver after all," Roger said to Jack as they stepped up to get in.

"Jack Handler," Col. French said, "This is Special Agent Benjamin Cross. He will be your driver for this mission."

Col. French then finished his introduction by informing the special agent that he would be serving the needs of Jack and Roger, whether it would be driving the van, loading and unloading the equipment, or any other task required of him.

Special Agent Cross greeted Jack and Roger in a friendly but professional manner, and told them that he would be at their service until the end of the mission.

"What, exactly, do you know about the mission?" Jack asked.

"Only that it involves the security for the President of the United States while he is in Singapore. That, and the fact that you were in charge of this detail, that's all I was told."

"Perfect," Jack said. "That's exactly right."

Once the introductions were completed, Col. French excused

himself and left the area.

"Do you get the feeling that the colonel was a bit eager to get the hell out of here?" Roger asked.

Jack sneered at the comment.

"Special Agent Cross," Jack said. "Would you please begin offloading the Sprinter? Everything needs to be out and transferred to the tower observation cabin. I think everything's on wheels. Right?"

"Yes, sir, it is. I'll take care of it."

"You bring it in," Jack said. "Any order. Roger and I will unpack and deploy it."

"Yes, sir."

Jack and Roger then positioned themselves inside the cabin and began distributing the weaponry on the deck as seemed appropriate.

"There seems to be at least two of every piece of ordnance," Jack noted. "That's great, I suppose, but it feels a little like overkill."

"Perhaps," Roger replied. "But there are two of us. And, who's to say that there might not be a defective piece of equipment. Like something jamming up. This way we will always have a backup."

"Right. I'm not complaining. Just observing out loud."

Once all of the smaller equipment had been unpacked and distributed around the deck, Jack and Roger began to consider how they might best prepare the MANPADS, acronym for *Man-Portable Air-Defense System*, for use. The special agent had wheeled in those two units last, largely because they were bigger and less maneuverable than the rest of the weaponry.

"What do you think, Jack?" Roger queried. "Position one on the east side of the cabin, and one on the south? Does that sound reasonable to you? Most likely the attack will come in from the sea. Of course, we don't know. But it seems likely."

"Hell," Jack said. "Sounds okay to me. We have no idea where the attack is going to originate from. *No* idea. So, it makes sense to think that a sea attack is more likely. So, let's stage one on the east, and one on the west. Then we'll have all contingencies covered. They're light enough, we can easily move them when we need to.

"Besides, we're going to hang on to Mr. Cross, here. He can move the munitions when needed. Right, Mr. Cross?"

"Please call me Ben. That's what everyone calls me. And, yes, I'd be honored to help out up here. But, maybe you could fill me in on what it is we're looking for? This looks like one hell of an arsenal. I've never even heard of much it before. Didn't know some of it even existed. Like these MANPADS. I've heard that these long-range portables were in the pipeline. But I did not know they'd been deployed yet."

"They haven't been deployed," Jack responded. "At least not officially. In fact, this is probably their first significant field test. As far as what we're looking for—we can't really talk about that. Because we don't actually know ourselves. For the most part, we're going to be improvising. Hell, we might not even have to use any of this shit."

"But, if you do, what is it exactly I should be looking for?"

Jack thought about it for a moment and then said, "If you keep your eye on Roger. If he's drinking a cup of coffee, or holding a can of beer and a cigar, then all is well. But, if he starts moving rapidly, cussing and swearing. Or, if he begins pissing his pants, then you will know that something's wrong, and at that point we will tell you what we need you to do. But, if nothing like that ever happens, then you should thank your lucky stars and start loading this shit back in the van."

"And by the way," Jack said as he pointed to an identical Mercedes Sprinter that was parked about fifty yards to the east. "What's the story behind that other van?"

"You know," Ben Cross said, "it arrived right after I did. After he'd parked, the driver handed me that briefcase. The one sitting on the floor over by the .308s. He told me that I should make sure you'd received the briefcase, and that you'd figure out what to do with the contents. But that's all he said. And right after that, a car came and picked him up."

"Really?" Jack replied as he walked over and picked up the case. "He said I'd know what to do with it, huh!"

Jack set the case down on a bench, triggered the latch release, and opened it up. Inside was a single folded sheet of paper lying on a permanently-affixed remote control. He opened the sheet and silently read the instructions: "The purpose of this remote is self-explanatory. Do not let it out of your possession. Use it only if *absolutely* necessary. Under no circumstance should you attempt to physically access Van II. And be sure to destroy it when mission is complete. If you do not survive this mission, Van II will be remotely destroyed by operatives working directly under Robert Fulbright."

Jack held the instruction sheet in his left hand, reading the operating instructions as he studied the buttons on the remote. After a few long contemplative moments, he mumbled, "Well, I'll be damned. I didn't know this technology even existed."

"Hey, Roger. Come over here and take a look at this. I've never seen anything like it. I'm serious. Get your ass over here and take a look. See what you think."

Roger was busy unpacking and checking out the array of firearms Bob had provided for them, and he knew that Jack was fully aware that he was quite busy. So, when Jack called to him, Roger initially thought he was just joking with him.

But, when Jack sternly repeated the request, Roger acquiesced.

"Whatcha got there, Jack?" Roger inquired.

"Take a look," Jack said, handing the note to his friend. "… But I recommend that you don't touch."

Jack then picked up the case and held it so Roger could read the labels beneath each of the control buttons.

"H-o-l-y s-h-i-t!" Roger slowly said. "Do you think that stuff's for real? How could it be? I've read about some of it. But I didn't think the technology to make it operational was ready. It's not even supposed to exist. Not yet. Do you think it even works?"

"Hell, yes!" Jack said. "Bob would not have given it to us if it didn't."

"Colonel French didn't say anything about this when he led us through his little *show-and-tell* on the plane."

"You're right," Jack agreed. "He never mentioned it."

"Maybe he's not even aware that we've got it. And do we? Do we have it? I sure as hell haven't seen anything like it in what I've unpacked."

"Over there," Jack said, pointing at the second Mercedes Sprinter. "See that van over there? Our buddy here, Ben Cross. He told me that someone drove that van up right after him, and parked it over there. And then the driver gave him this case, and told him to deliver it to us—that we'd know what to do with it."

"So, this remote somehow activates some specialized electronic shit in that van? Is that the idea?"

"That's obviously the case."

"And you think this remote will actually do what these instructions say it will do? I would sure as hell hate to think that we could be counting on something to work, and then be disappointed. You know what I mean?"

Jack smiled.

"*Disappointed?*" Jack said. "If it came down to our actually employing that van, and it didn't work as advertised, we wouldn't be disappointed. We'd be dead!"

"That's what I'm saying."

"All I know is that Bob would not let us down. If he sent that van as our last ditch tool, then he knows that it will work. He would not screw around with us, or our mission. The thing is, we must not trigger that monster unless we absolutely have to—that is, we'll use it only if and when we have no other options. Agreed?"

"Absolutely."

"Because, as soon as we employ it, every bad actor in the world will then know that this technology exists, and actually works, and they will do everything in their power to steal it."

"Exactly."

"Some of that equipment requires line-of-sight access to target," Jack said. "So, we have to assume that once called upon, AI will take Van II wherever it has to go until it acquires the geography it needs."

"That's the only way it could work," Roger added. "I don't see any controls on this remote indicating that we need to direct it. It has to be self-driving through AI. Wouldn't it be interesting to play around with it after this mission is over? Just kidding, of course. But you know what I mean."

"Right!" Jack said. "And if we did, it's probably smart enough to know what we were up to, and it would take *us* out."

Roger, laughing out loud, turned to face Van II and shouted, "Just kidding. I don't mean any of it. And, we're very glad to have you aboard on this mission. Semper Fi!"

Special Agent Ben Cross heard Roger's last comments. He stared out at the second van for a moment, and then said, "Who are you talking to? Did that driver come back? He warned me not to mess with Van II. If I did, he said something real bad would happen. He didn't spell it out, but the tone of his voice was ominous."

Neither Jack nor Roger responded.

Finally, he turned back to face Jack and asked, "Is there anything else you'd like me to do?"

"Yes," Jack said. "Take these binoculars and station yourself on the west side of the tower. Keep an eye out for the President's motorcade. Let me know when it arrives at the hotel. I think it's due about now. And keep your eyes peeled for any suspicious boats, or ships of any type or size, that appear to be moving extraordinarily slow. Or stationary. We're here to protect the President, and a vessel behaving in that fashion might be a harbinger of something—a bad omen."

"Yes, sir. I'll get right to it."

As soon as the special agent moved out of earshot, Jack removed a fire extinguisher from the wall of the cabin and replaced it with the small briefcase that housed the remote.

"Okay," he said to Roger. "There it is. Remove and use at your own risk."

"Jack," Roger announced. "POTUS is approaching at eleven o'clock. He's just crossing the Sentosa Gateway Bridge. It has to be him. Too early for Chairman Kim. Too damn bad we have to operate in the dark on this. There must be some members of the Service Bob can trust!"

"There are, my friend," Jack said. "And we're it! Apparently, no one knows for certain just who is in on the assassination attempt. Bob thinks it works its way to the top of the Intelligence Community—and throughout it. It has taken years for it to corrupt itself to this level, but now it's like a parasite sucking the life out of our government. But, you're right—it is too damn bad. As for now, we're going to have to make do with what we've got."

"And what, exactly, would that be?" Roger asked, straining to verify what he was viewing through his binoculars. "All we've got is our own two eyes. And Special Agent Cross."

"Don't forget our good buddy, Colonel French," Jack added. "And, by the way, where is he now? He sure as hell got out of here as quickly as he could."

"I don't think he was too happy about the way you roughed him up."

"That's too bad. He didn't strike me as much of a warrior anyway. More of a career ass-kisser, if you know what I mean."

"It is POTUS. Right on time. What time are the NoKos supposed to arrive?"

"Not officially announced. They like to be secretive—unpredictable. Especially since POTUS took out their nuke facility."

"Would you describe it as a love/hate relationship?" Roger asked as he followed POTUS's motorcade.

"Not so much love involved," Jack chuckled. "More like fear/

hate. Once POTUS settles in, we can expect Kim and his people will be driving up. He wants to stage his arrival to take place after the Americans. His notion of a power play, I suppose. It's good for us—not to have them exposed on the same street at the same time."

"They're scheduled for two meetings?" Roger asked. "Right? One late this afternoon, four o'clock Singapore time, I believe. And one tomorrow. Isn't that right?"

"Exactly as I understand it."

"But," Roger went on. "Do you have any doubts about when the anticipated hit will occur? I think it has to be at the earlier event—today. Because anything can happen when we're dealing with two volatile personalities. Like these guys have exhibited in the past. If someone fails to smile in a certain way, the whole summit could get cancelled."

Just then Jack's phone vibrated.

"Yes, Bob. Jack here."

"You're all set up, I assume?"

"Aren't you watching us?"

"Actually, I'm not," Bob replied. "I didn't want to draw unwanted attention to your location. So, I've limited my satellite surveillance to the Miami Beach Hotel. And I am keeping an eye on a number of ships at sea. Just what we would typically do in such situations. But your location, and your activities, they are staying off my radar. No one should know about you except for Colonel French and Special Agent Cross."

"How about the second van? We never had a chance to meet the driver. Is he still in the vicinity? And who might he be?"

"He's Mossad. And that's all I can tell you. No one knows much about that second van except for you two, my Mossad buddy, and me. No one inside our own services. I've known this Israeli agent as long as I've known you. He's very deep in Mossad. Have you talked to him?"

"No. He dropped the control remote off with our driver—Special Agent Cross. With instructions that no one should approach Van II, and that we should employ it only if absolutely necessary."

"Perfect," Bob said. "That's exactly right. And you are aware that it is to be destroyed after this mission is completed? No matter the outcome. You blow it up, or we do."

"Yes. We got the word."

"The time of the first meeting between POTUS and the Chairman is set at four P.M.

"Chairman Kim is not scheduled to arrive at the hotel until one P.M.—again your time. I understand POTUS is presently nearing the hotel. Are you observing him?"

"As we speak. Roger's got his eye on the motorcade."

"The plan is that he will settle in, have some lunch, and then meet with Chairman Kim at four.

"Kim will arrive sometime around one. He will also have lunch, and then the two of them will conduct their first meeting in the Executive Conference Suite at four. The Executive Conference Suite is located on the southeast corner of the hotel."

"That might suggest that any attack would likely originate east of the hotel. If so, it should present us with a very good view."

"*View of the damage*, that is. If it gets through. You and I both know that even if you knew exactly where it was coming from, and the flight path, it could still present a monstrous challenge. Even an older Tomahawk with a conventional warhead. It could be launched from the west, and then circle around and come in from the north. Or even from the east. It is going to be one helluva challenge. I'll help all I can from here, but you need to know that the odds are stacked against your mission. POTUS has brought this on himself—with his macho insistence on doing this summit. He's thinking that someone might take a shot at him with a .50 Cal. Something that the Secret Service would easily be able to defend against. He doesn't appreciate just what kind of damage a Tomahawk can do."

"So, have we nailed it down that we're dealing with an older model Tomahawk with a conventional payload?"

"You're mostly right. At least that's what we think. Except there are likely to be more than one Tomahawk."

"Do you know how many?"

"We seem to have *misplaced* a few of them."

"*Misplaced* a few?" Jack fired back. "A *few*? Exactly what could we be dealing with?"

"That's unknown."

"No it isn't. Somebody has to know."

"No. We actually do not know," Bob replied. "We've had a catastrophic server failure at a secret munitions depot. Just last week. We do not even know how many Tomahawks went missing. Or, even if any went missing."

"Sabotage?"

"Looks like it. It appears as though a whole rack of missiles was removed. And it also appears that the inventory was changed to cover it up. *Appears* is the operative word."

"How many on a rack?"

"Six."

"Six?" Jack blurted out. "You mean to tell me we might be dealing with six incoming missiles?"

"That's about it."

Roger, overhearing Jack's end of the conversation, turned and threw a middle finger at the phone. He was wearing his black mock turtleneck with a leather shoulder holster for his Glock. He also had one strapped around his ankle.

"We can't possibly deal with that. One's bound to get through. Hell, all six just might make it past us. What the hell are we supposed to do? Shoot them down with our handguns?"

"You've got some serious MANPADS with you," Bob countered. "I'll try to give you a heads up if we see any flashes coming from the ships we're monitoring.

"Keep in mind, the missiles you've got at your disposal only have to be fired in the general vicinity of the incoming missile. Granted, the range is *somewhat* limited. But if we catch the flash at launch, and that's what we'd like to do, if our satellite picks up the launch, we can follow it and let you know when to fire. And then we can direct it in to the target."

"Are the older Tomahawks capable of countermeasures?" Jack asked.

"Not typically. The ones that came up missing are not. It's possible, of course, that they have been modified. But highly unlikely. Once we have acquired the target, and have you fire, we can use a combination of control systems to steer the missile to the kill. Radar, infrared, and optical are at our disposal, plus the classified system that's currently residing on that second van—that we won't even discuss. So, even if the target were capable of employing some countermeasures, we will still kill it—with the help of that second van."

"And then you'll fire on the launch site?" Jack inquired. "Once you have confirmed it as such—you'll hit it?"

"Killing the target *left of launch*—that's what it is called. When you hit the target before launch. In this case, we'd be hitting it before the second launch. If they have all six of the missing Tomahawks onboard a single ship, that approach might be very effective. But we cannot count on that. The would-be assassins are not stupid or inexperienced. We think that it's likely that they will launch from multiple floating platforms. And they can be virtually anywhere, as long as they are located within a thousand miles or so."

Both men remained silent for a couple moments.

"If they do have six Tomahawks," Jack finally said. "And if they fire them from a few different platforms. Then, the limited number of MANPADS would not be sufficient. Right?"

"Well, that's what the second van is for, wouldn't you say?" Bob asked rhetorically.

"And you're pretty confident that the interceptors you have provided in the second van, you believe they will do the trick?"

"Jack, my man," Bob said. "If you need to use the second van, keep in mind that the term must be singular. There is a single interceptor located within it. Once it is used, that van will self-destruct. Now, keep in mind, I would rather you not put it to work. Not unless absolutely necessary. If you do, then we can be sure that a large number of negative characters will start researching it to see if they can duplicate it. Right now, it's unique. But not once it is utilized."

Finally, Jack spoke: "All I can tell you is that we will give it our best. Can't guarantee outcomes. But we'll sure as hell give it our best shot."

"I trust you will. If I would have had any doubts about that, I would have tasked this mission to someone else."

"Please, Bob. You know damn well that there isn't anyone else in the world who would sign on for this."

"Yeah. I know. You're probably right."

"By the way, what's in it for us?'

"You mean, besides the satisfaction of doing me a favor? And, of course, saving a lot of important lives?"

"Right. Roger and I need to look forward to something. What would that be?"

"Well," Bob said. "I was thinking about this. In fact, I did a *lot* of thinking about it. And this is what I decided to offer you. When you get back to the States, I'll have a box of primo Cubans for you."

"How about a whole shipping container?"

Bob laughed out loud and said, "Lifetime supply—for each of you. *Lifetime.*"

"That works," Jack said. "That's all I need—"

"Hey!" Jack interrupted himself. "Why are we headed down? Roger. What's this all about?"

What Jack was alluding to was the sudden jerking sensation caused by the mechanical device that lowered the donut-shaped cabin.

"I didn't do anything," Roger said. "It just started dropping."

Jack bolted over to the edge and peered down.

"I don't see *anyone* down there. But someone must have triggered it."

"Hope you don't mind my taking the cabin down," Ben Cross

said. "I left my lunch in the car. I thought I could just quickly run back and get it."

Jack was furious.

"Hell yes, I care!" he barked. "Stop it right here and take it back up. What the hell were you thinking?"

"Sure," Cross said. "I'm sorry. I didn't think you'd mind. It's been a long day already, and I'm getting hungry."

But, instead of turning toward the control closet, Cross put his right hand in his jacket pocket and began walking toward Roger.

"Stop right there!" Jack shouted.

By that point Cross was standing only a few feet from where Roger was working.

Jack knew something was up.

"Roger!" Jack shouted to his friend. "Drop!"

But it was too late.

While Jack saw Cross fall as a result of the three rounds he fired at him, he quickly made his way to the fallen Secret Service agent and fired an additional slug into the dead man's heart just to be sure. He then headed over to where Roger was crouching.

"Rog! Rog! Where're you hit? Is it bad?"

Roger looked up at Jack and smiled.

"Nothin' much," he said. "A couple of scratches. That's it. I can take care of myself. You'd better run this thing back up the tower. We need to be as elevated as possible."

"Let me see your wounds first," Jack barked. "Show them to me."

"Oh, hell. Okay. He skinned my left arm here."

Roger then produced a bloody through-and-through wound in his bicep, and anoth through his left shoulder.

From Deadwood to Deep State

Jack's Oft-Derailed Journey Back to Newberry

Part 2

Chapter 41

Millie stepped on the gas. Neither Angel nor the boys could accurately report on the number of occupants that were in the car that had been following them—only that there was a very tough looking driver, and that he was wearing a suit.

The boys agreed with Angel's assessment. "If there had been passengers in the car," they said, "by the time Angel had chucked the second bottle of grape juice, everyone in the car would have been kissing the floorboard."

Millie rapidly made her way back to West Main Street.

"Anyone following us?" she asked.

"No," Angel said. "I don't see anyone behind us."

"It would have been impossible for anyone to drive that car," Robby said, "With the windshield smashed up like that. Besides, the way it looked to me, she hit the driver's side so hard, he would have had a whole face full of glass. Would probably of gotten in his eyes. He couldn't have driven it like that."

"I thought car windows didn't break into sharp pieces. Like the glass in my shower door. When it shattered, it broke into little pieces, but stayed in the doorframe. Aren't car windows like that?"

Robby looked to Red for the explanation. Red was writing. When he was finished he handed it to Robby.

Robby read it to himself, and then commented, "Right. I knew that. Back and side windows are made of tempered glass. They break into popcorn. But windshields are made of two pieces of glass, with a center layer of vinyl. Usually only the outside glass breaks. But Angel's fury broke both layers with her bottle, showering the driver with little sharp pieces of glass. They are not going to follow us now."

"I'm still going to take an indirect route back to the Childresses," she said. "Not going to take chances."

Millie had left the Childresses at a small bar/restaurant located on Otsego Avenue near the center of town.

"Now we've got all their stuff," Angel said. "What are they gonna do? They're gonna have to go back to their house—wherever *that* is. We don't even know where their home is. Can't stay in Gaylord—too many people remember them around here. And Jessie still needs that surgery. Right? What are they gonna do? And what can we do to help? I think all they need is money. Can't we give them some?"

Millie paid close attention to what her daughter was saying. While she sympathized with her daughter's anguish over the plight of their newfound friends, she was not totally convinced.

It was a fact that Millie had adequate funds. She had inherited millions from the estate of her deceased father—lumber baron Michael Patrick O'Malley. But she questioned the rationale behind giving money away indiscriminately. "What would Mom do?" she frequently asked herself. Her mother, Amy Breeze, drummed into her daughter that it is not always kind to give people money. "Just because someone needs something you have does not dictate that you give it to them. In fact, giving people money might not be doing them a favor at all." And then she would add, "You give a friend a fish, he eats for one day. And then he's hungry again. And he's back at your door begging for food. But, you teach that friend to fish, and he will begin to feed himself. And he won't be showing up at your door crying and begging for help. Which approach, my darling daughter, was the proper way to deal with that friend?

Which was truly the kinder thing to do? Remember how Jesus dealt with the needy. Even though he was a skilled carpenter, he never made crutches or hospital beds. Instead, he healed the sick, and made whole the crippled."

So, that was the prism through which Millie viewed life. Even though she clearly understood the situation the Childresses were in, and she did desire to help, she feared that merely throwing money at their problems could do more harm than good. *We might solve their immediate problems,* she reasoned. *But, what about next week? Or next month? What should make me think that the same or a similar situation might not arise, and then, I won't be around to solve it for them? I need to know more about them before I jump in and try to fix everything.*

Angel and the boys kept their eyes open all the way back to the restaurant where Ellen, Rod, and Jessie were waiting. On Red's suggestion, they had also left Buddy with the Childresses. "If the characters who are hunting for Jessie and her parents come back," Red wrote, "Buddy should be there to protect them."

When they got to the restaurant they had a surprise waiting for them. Parked near the front entrance sat the dark-blue Malibu with a severely smashed-in rear bumper exactly like the one used in the abduction of Ellen and Rod.

"Check that out," Robby said. "Does that look familiar?"

"Damn!" Millie blurted out. She was not often given to profanity, especially around the children, but this time she was not able to control her tongue. "I'd hoped those guys had given up, or maybe were the ones driving the Mercedes. What do we do now?"

Everyone in the car understood that Millie's question was more rhetorical than literal.

Instead of pulling into the restaurant's parking lot, she drove on down South Otsego Avenue nearly a full block, and then pulled into a small strip mall. She sought out a parking place that provided a clear view of the front entrance of the restaurant, as well as the Malibu.

"They know all of us," Robby said. "None of us could sneak up on them now."

"You're right," Millie agreed. "But we do have one last trick up our sleeve. They don't know my voice. Angel, let me see that burner cell for a minute."

Millie then proceeded to dial the restaurant's "take-out" number as it was posted on a sign by the street.

"Hello," she said when the female voice at the restaurant answered, "this is FBI Special Agent Pam O'Malley. I'm calling you from Langley, Virginia. I believe you have a customer in your restaurant—a Mr. Rodney Childress. Would you please ask him to come to this phone? It is imperative that I talk to him immediately. His life could be in danger."

"This is the reservation and take-out line," the woman said. "We're not allowed to use this line for anything else—no personal calls. Sorry."

"Ma'am. What's your name?"

"My boss told us never to give out personal names. For our own safety."

"Ma'am. I asked you a question. What is your name?"

"Gracie."

"Look, Gracie. You do whatever it is you think you must do, but I am *ordering* you to page Mr. Rodney Childress and to put him on this phone right now. I'm not asking you—I'm telling you to do it. Right now!"

"Oh. All right. But, if I get in trouble. Never mind. I'm just gonna go get my manager and let you explain what you want to him."

"Gracie, you listen to me. Do you know what obstruction of justice is? Unless you want to find out what the inside of a federal prison looks like, you go get Mr. Childress this minute, and put him on this phone. Do you understand me?"

"You better not be shittin' me, lady. If I lose my job I'm gonna be suing you and the FBI. Hang on, I'll page him. What did you say his name was?"

"Mr. Rodney Childress."

Gracie set the phone down and keyed the PA microphone. And then she immediately walked back to the phone.

"Ma'am," Gracie said. "Is it okay if I tell him that you're with the FBI, and that his life could depend on his taking your call?"

"No! You may not tell him his life depends on it. Just tell him he has an emergency call and that he should come to this phone."

"Okay," Gracie responded. And then she set down the phone. A few seconds passed before Millie heard her voice come over the PA system: "If there is a Mr. Rodney Childless in the restaurant, would you please come to the wait station in the rear of the dining area. You have an important call. Mr. Childless. Please come to the wait station in the rear of the dining area. Thank you."

A little over a minute passed before Millie heard Gracie explaining to Rod Childress that the FBI was on the line, and directing him to the phone.

"Hello."

"Rodney Childress?" Millie inquired.

"Yes. This is Rod Childress. Who the hell is this?"

"This is FBI Special Agent Pam O'Malley. I'm calling you from Langley, Virginia. Are you alone? Can you talk?"

"Whathahell are you sayin'! FBI? What the hell! FBI? Really? Yes. I can talk. I've got a friend with me. But I can talk."

Millie knew immediately that one or both of the two men, Baldy Robinson or James Richards—the men who had originally abducted Rod and his wife—were listening in on the conversation.

"I have a car outside waiting for you. To escort you back to Portland. I need you to exit the restaurant immediately. With your wife and daughter. And, I understand you have a dog. Bring the dog out with you. There are two special agents here with me in the car. Do *not* keep them waiting. They can get very cranky. Do you understand? We have a second car stationed at the rear of the restaurant, with another two special agents. They are back there should you try to skip on us. Do you understand?"

"Yes. I'll get my family, pay the bill and meet your agents out front."

"If you have not surrendered into their custody in two minutes, they will come in and take you by force. If that happens it will effectively end your Witness Protection Program, and somebody is likely to get hurt. Do you completely understand me?"

"Yes. Of course. I will take care of my bill and be out front in two minutes. Or about two minutes. I have to pay the bill. I'll be out as soon as I can. Please don't come in and arrest me. I *promise* I will surrender peacefully. Please."

"As you say," Millie said. "Bring Ellen, Jessie and Buddy, but leave whoever else you might be chatting with—leave them inside. Got it?"

"Yes," Millie heard Rod say as she started to back out of her parking place. She checked her phone to be sure she had disconnected.

"Here," she said to Angel. "Make certain that I hung up."

Both Red and Robby sat silently in the back seat. They had just heard Millie swear—that was a totally new experience for them. Even though neither of them opened their mouths, Millie knew something was up when she spotted impish smiles paralyzing their faces.

"Okay, spill it," she ordered. "What's up with you guys? Didn't you know that I could fake an identity as well as your Uncle Jack?"

Robby glanced over at Red, and Red nodded his approval.

"We always figured you were pretty sly, Aunt Millie. We knew you had it in you. And, good job pulling that off, by the way."

Millie adjusted her interior mirror down so she could check the boys out.

"You're still smiling. What's *really* up?"

Robby looked over at Red again. But this time Red didn't react.

"Red wants to know," Robby said, "what FBI Special Agent Pam O'Malley was doing in *Langley* when FBI Headquarters is located in *Quantico*, Virginia. The *CIA* is based in Langley."

"Darn!" Millie moaned. "I think you're right. Good thing crooks are stupid."

Angel chuckled out loud at Robby's comment. "Good thing Buddy didn't hear you, Mom," she said, "he would have caught it and barked."

By that time Millie was actively engaging in the collective mirth.

Just as she was pulling into the restaurant's parking lot, Rod

Childress and his family rushed out through the front doors—Buddy leading the way.

"Boys," Millie commanded, "jump in the back with the luggage. Make room for them."

Buddy was the first one in. With his tail wagging wildly, he jumped into the back seat, and then all the way to where the boys were jammed in with the suitcases.

As soon as Rod shut the door, Millie sped off.

"How'd you know those guys were with us?" he asked.

"We saw their car in the parking lot," Millie replied. "It was easy to spot, with the rear end all smushed in like that.

"Actually," Millie continued. "It caught me by surprise that they were able to find you so quickly. And that they were willing to let you go. I take it that one of them was listening in to our conversation. Right?"

"Yes," Rod replied. "Baldy Robinson was standing over my shoulder. I recognized your voice. But he didn't. He knew that we were in Witness Protection, and so he bought your FBI story. He wanted nothing to do with the FBI. So he let us go."

"Do you think he might follow us?" Millie asked.

"He made James hide out in the restroom as soon as you hung up. He really did not want to deal with the FBI."

His comment made Millie smile.

Nothing was said for the next minute. Millie was deep in thought.

"I was wondering," she finally said. "I was wondering how in the world did they find you? I dropped you off less than an hour ago. And somehow they managed to find you that quickly. Doesn't make sense to me."

Rod took a deep breath and unzipped the Michigan hoodie he was wearing. He was still a bit stressed, yet relieved to be in what he thought to be a safe place with Millie and the kids. While he was putting on his seatbelt in the banged up vehicle, he explained: "Like I said before, we lived in this town for years. A lot of people know us. Someone must have recognized us and called these guys. I don't know how else it could of happened."

"Yeah," Millie said, glancing back at him for a minute in the rearview mirror; even with her sunglasses on she could see and sense the three-member family in her second row of seats were anxious to escape their situation. "That makes sense, I suppose. At least it makes more sense than anything else I can think of. What did they want from you? They managed to get their hands on the loot you had hidden away. What else was there for them to do? Except maybe to extract revenge for testifying against them?"

"That's the thing," Rod said. "I didn't exactly rat out Baldy and James. They were higher up the chain. The guys that went up—the ones I testified against—they didn't even know about Baldy and his buddies. I knew better than to name Baldy. He would have taken me apart piece by piece if I had done that. I was pretty high up in the organization, truth be told. And even the guys I testified against—they weren't exactly schmucks. Otherwise the Feds wouldn't of let me skate. They got the guys they were after. I just didn't spill the beans on the big boys. That's why they let me live."

"But, you did steal their money," Millie said. "Right?"

Rod cleared his throat and looked down at his feet—an unconscious admission of guilt showing through with his answer.

"Yeah, sure, I did that. But that's just business. There was more where that came from. I knew it. And they knew it. Of course, they weren't very happy about losing all that cash. But I didn't rat them out. That's what was really important to them. In the end, anyway. I kept their sorry asses out of prison, and now they let me live. Fair trade off, *they* think. But, I have to tell you, I was counting on that cash. I don't make shit with what I'm doin' now. We can't live on it. I wanted that money. It's only right. I worked hard for it. I deserve it. They've replaced it a hundred times since I went into the program. It was no skin off of their nose. But, no, they want it all. It's just a damn shame my family has to go through this."

Millie again remained silent for a long moment. She was replaying in her mind all that had just gone down before her. *Well*, she thought. *I've just seen a side of Mr. Childress I didn't know existed. Surprise. Surprise.*

After another minute she said, "What now? Where do we go from here?"

"We've got to get back to our home."

"Back into Witness Protection?"

"Exactly," he said. "It would be very bad for me to have the Feds find out that I've been colluding with known felons. I could end up in prison myself. Hell, I would get locked up. I didn't skate—I had to plead. One of the stipulations was that I could not associate with guys like these. I need to get back in the program. I need to go back right now."

"I suppose you can't tell me where home is," Millie said. "Can you?"

"No. I can't do that."

Millie remembered from earlier that the Childresses' car had Virginia plates, but she said nothing about it. *Might not even mean anything,* she reasoned. *He could have put Virginia plates on the car just to throw people off. No point offering to drive them someplace. They obviously are secretive about where they are living. The car might even have been a rental.*

"What are you going to drive back to—to wherever it is you live?" Millie asked.

"If you could drive us back to where you left my car. We can drive it. Hope it still has wheels under it. Do some of those suitcases in the back belong to us? A couple of them look familiar."

"Yes," Millie replied. "Angel went back to the hotel and gathered up your stuff, as well as ours. I'm not sure if she got it all, but she picked up everything that she could find."

"Well, Angel, that was sweet of you," Ellen said. "Thank you."

Ellen had not said much to this point. She was sitting behind Millie wearing a blue baseball cap with sunglasses—mostly to keep her face covered—and a matching blue tee-shirt, cropped jeans and sandals.

"No problem," Angel said. "Actually, I thought it was kind of exciting."

Robby feigned a snarl at her comment. "You would think that, wouldn't you?"

"If I drop you off at your car, do you think you'll be safe? Those two guys did quite a number on you and Ellen. I don't want you to get yourselves hurt again."

"We'll be fine. I'll keep my eyes open, and if anything looks wrong, I'll circle around and head back to Gaylord."

"What route are you going to take?" Millie asked.

"Not I-75," Rod answered. "I'll cut over to US-131 South. At least until I'm convinced I'm not being followed."

"Good plan," Millie said.

She thought about what Rod had just told her. *If his first choice would be to head south on 75, that would suggest that Witness Protection has him living south and east of Michigan. At least that's what it would seem. So, Virginia might actually be correct. But, FBI headquarters is located in Virginia. If they provided a car and plates for him, then that fact might not be a clue at all. I guess I don't need to figure this out. I just hope they make it to wherever they're going.*

Red rapped Robby on the arm and pointed down a side street.

"Red wants you to turn here," Robby blurted out as rapidly as he could. "He says the car is parked on this street. Or off of this street."

Red reached in his pocket and removed the key to the car. He tapped Rod on the shoulder and handed it to him.

"Thanks, kid," Rod said as he took the key.

Angel noticed that Jessie had not said a word since she left the restaurant.

She reached back and laid her hand on Jessie's. "You going to be okay?" she asked.

Jessie nodded her head and smiled, but she did not say anything. When their eyes met, Angel could see that she had been crying.

Angel removed a pen and a small piece of paper from her bag and wrote on it. She then reached back and tucked the note into Jessie's hand.

Jessie did not look at her new friend. She just gripped the piece of paper tightly and nodded slowly. Tears were now running down both sides of Jessie's face.

Rod was the first one out of the Suburban. He sprinted over to his car and cranked the engine. When it started right up he smiled and motioned for his family to join him.

Red and Robby jumped out and unloaded the Childresses' luggage. Rod helped them load it in the trunk of the Chevy.

Millie, who was now alone in the Suburban, opened her bag and removed five crisp one-hundred-dollar bills. She folded them up and handed them to Ellen.

"Here's a little gas money to get back home," she said.

"That's really big of you," Ellen said, trying to give the money back. "But we don't need your charity."

"This isn't charity," Millie said, refusing her effort. "I know you don't need it. I would just feel better if you'd keep it. You're not going to be able to use credit cards or write checks. They're too easy to trace. Having some cash would be a good thing—until you get home. Consider it a loan."

"No," she responded in protest. "I don't want your money."

"For God's sake, Ellen. Take the money. She's right. We do not dare leave any sort of trail. We'll need cash. Take it!"

Ellen turned abruptly and walked over to her husband.

"Here," she said to him. "You take it. I am not accepting money from anyone."

Rod accepted the money and slid it into his pants pocket.

"I'm sorry about that," he said to Millie. "My wife is exhausted. This whole thing has been very hard for her. She hates where we live. She hates our house. Our lives. Everything. She is very unhappy. And I don't blame her. She really was counting on that money. We both were. Now, we're gonna have to re-evaluate this whole Witness Protection thing. It's not as easy as you might think. You have to give up a lot. I'm not sure at this point that she considers it worth it. I'm not even sure what I think.

"Thanks for the money. If I can, I'll pay you back. Not sure when that will be, but someday, maybe, we'll get back on our feet. But, you're exactly right about cash. Gonna have to use cash until we get back to the program. I appreciate it."

Jessie had slid into the back seat of the car, grabbed her pillow and throw, and shut the door.

Angel wanted to say one last goodbye, so she opened a rear door and got in beside her.

"Jessie. My address and phone number are on that note I gave you. If you ever need to talk, just call me. Maybe later things will change. And you will be able to reach out. If that happens, call me. Okay?"

Jessie looked down at her hands and nodded her head. She was sobbing. Her hands were shaking.

Angel laid a small pack of tissues on Jessie's lap, and then leaned over and gave her a hug.

"Call me," she said one last time as she got back out of the car.

Their eyes did not meet, but Jessie had listened intently.

Red and Robby turned to watch and wave out of the rear window as Millie pulled away.

"What are they gonna do?" Red asked, turning back to face Millie. "Do you suppose they're going back to—to wherever it is that they came from? We don't even know where they came from, do we?"

"No. We don't know," Millie answered. "But I do think that's where they're going to end up. At least that's where they said they were headed. I don't know what else they *could* do. In the first place, the Federal Witness Protection Program is *very* hard to get into. The U.S. Attorney General's Office must have been pretty sure that their lives were in serious danger to have allowed them to enter the program."

"Red and I were wondering," Robby said, "what would happen if the FBI were to learn that they were hanging around with big-time crooks? 'Cuz that's exactly what they were doing."

"Yeah," Millie said. "You're right. They really had no business taking chances like that. They should have known better. If the U.S. Marshall's Service, they're the ones who oversee the program, if they were to find out that the Childresses had left their home and came here, and that they were hanging around with these very unsavory characters, no doubt they would be in serious trouble. I just hope that they are able to get back in one piece. Even though they are unhappy there, at least they're safe. Jessie deserves a safe place to grow up."

"Right," Robby agreed. "Too bad they don't live closer. Like on Sugar Island."

"Really?" Angel said, turning back toward the boys and flashing her signature smile. "Why's that?"

"Red thinks she's cute," Robby replied. "I think he wants to date her."

Red didn't hesitate. He delivered a powerful blow to Robby's upper arm.

"Ow!" Robby moaned. "Damn it! Red—that really hurt!"

"Boys!" Millie shouted as she slammed on the brakes. She then turned around and laid down the law.

"I know we've just had a very difficult couple of days. And we are all a little frazzled at the seams. But, that is no excuse to use bad words. I want you to understand that there will be no more cursing, and no more hitting. For as long as this trip lasts—that's the *last* of it. Got it?"

The boys both felt guilty for what they had done but they just sat silently looking down at their hands, which they had folded across their laps.

"I want an answer," Millie said. "We're not moving until we get this straightened out. No more hitting, and no more swearing. Got it?"

"Yes, ma'am," Robby said, now sheepishly looking at her. Red looked up and nodded in agreement.

Buddy reacted as well. At first he was conflicted by Red's punch. He did not know how to react. He recognized that Robby was in pain and unhappy, but he was not about to take sides. So, just before Millie intervened, Buddy registered his displeasure by leaning over the back of the rear seats and delivering a single sharp, well-articulated bark.

"Ruff!"

Angel took the bark as her signal to turn around and face forward. She did not like trouble. She was disappointed that Red had struck Robby so hard, and she was equally displeased with Robby's reaction to the blow. While she would have liked to side with the boys vis-à-vis her mother's harsh words, she knew better than to intervene.

Finally, she spoke up.

"I really like Jessie too," she said. "She's got it pretty rough—not having a regular home and everything. Especially being a teenager in high school. How could you explain your past life to your friends? They're going to ask questions about your old school, your old friends, and you'd have nothing to say. I would just hate it."

"It would be difficult," Millie agreed. "But, even so, she seems to be a fairly well-adjusted teenage girl. Given all the circumstances."

"Seems like," Angel added. "She seems well-adjusted and all. But I think that it is tearing her apart. She couldn't stop crying. When I said goodbye to her in the car, she just sat there crying her eyes out. Her hands were shaking like crazy. She couldn't even look me in the eye. Or say goodbye. I just wished there was something we could do to help her. You can be sure her parents aren't going to give her any support."

"What do you mean by that?" Millie asked. She was a little confused by her daughter's comment. "I think they are doing the best they can, given the circumstances. They really don't have many options. There's a good chance that they would have been killed by those two men, had we not come along. I know, it would have been a lot less complicated if her father had not gotten involved with the gang in the first place. He's obviously a very bright guy. He could have made a good living legally. He didn't have to work for those criminals. But, at this point, he's stuck. He made a few mistakes, and now he has to make the best of it. Or, at least he's trying to."

"They can't ever leave their secret house," Angel said. "Can they? Jessie's stuck there forever. Sort of forever. I mean, where can she go? If she goes to college, or gets a job, can't she be traced back? DNA, or something?"

"She has a real new name," Robby said. "Childress. That's not the name she had before they went into the program. She has a new total identity. Right? Childress is her new name. Or was that their old name?"

"They were registered at the hotel as Childress," Angel said.

"So that must be the new name. If that's the case, it's pretty scary. Those guys who her dad used to work for, they knew the secret name. So, they could probably find him in his new city. That's scary."

The next two hours found Millie and her crew shooting south on I-75. The boys were playing their Nintendo Switch, and Angel—playing her music on with her earbuds—was riding shotgun with her mom. Just before they entered Flint, Millie pulled off to get gas.

"Mom," Angel said as she stood beside her mother with a bag of white cheddar popcorn she had just purchased. "I was thinking. Why weren't they scared to be with those two guys in the restaurant—the ones who had made them give back the money? And how was it that they—those really bad guys—how was it that they found them there in the first place? In that restaurant? Jessie's father must have called them. Don't you think?"

"I've been wondering about that, too," Millie said. "It just doesn't make sense, does it?"

Chapter 42

There was a long moment of silence as Millie and the kids mulled over Angel's dilemma.

"What do you think, Red?" Millie finally asked.

Red had just walked up with his own bag full of M&Ms, red licorice and a Blue Raspberry Powerade. Having not yet fully adjusted to functioning without a cell phone, he quickly wrote out his response: "Something's up. Those guys shouldn't have been there. And why did they let Mr. Childress leave without a fight?"

By that time Robby with his own snacks had joined the group. Red showed him his note.

"Right," he said. "We were talking about that. Something is just not right."

Millie continued pumping gas until the tank was full. As she hung the hose onto the pump, Angel took her mother's hand until Millie looked her in the eye.

"Mom," Angel said. "We need to do something. You know we do. Right?"

"Get in the car."

Robby, who had been cleaning the bugs from the windshield, dropped the squeegee into the bucket. The rest of the group immediately complied as well.

However, instead of pulling out of the gas station, Millie pulled into a marked parking place and turned off the ignition.

"Okay, guys," she said. "I can see that we've all got some concerns. But, we have to be logical. Practical. We can't be acting like the Lone Ranger here. Jack sent us out of town because he wanted us to be safe. From what, I have no idea. But I'm sure he must have had his reasons."

Red nodded his head and feigned using a cell phone.

"You're suggesting we call your uncle?" Millie asked.

Red nodded.

"Uhh," Millie said. "I'm not so sure about that. Jack was very specific. He said *he* would call us on the burner when it was safe and appropriate. If we were to have an emergency, I would definitely pre-empt his call. But, for us, this is not an emergency. Do you agree?"

They all nodded, including Red.

"Is there anything we can do?" Angel asked. "I think we would all feel better if we did something. Is there some specific time when we have to be someplace?"

"Are you suggesting something?" Millie asked.

"I don't know," Angel said. "I just don't feel right walking away from this situation. I don't have a good feeling about Jessie. It's kind of like we're abandoning her. When I left her in the car, like I said, she was bawling her eyes out. But it wasn't like she was crying because she was going to miss us. She was scared to death about something. I don't know what, but there was something really bothering her."

"We don't even know where they were headed," Millie said. "Do we? Does any of us really know where they might be? Right now?"

Red started writing: "No. But Gaylord's not a very big town.

And we know what their vehicle looks like."

"Yeah," Angel agreed. "We could make a sweep through the city. Hit all the main streets. And if we don't turn anything up, then we can head back south. I know we'd all feel better about it. Right?"

"I suppose," Millie said. "I think we all want to do something. If for nothing else than just to make us feel better."

"And I gave Jessie the number of our burner cell," Angel said. "I told her that if she needed to talk to me about anything, she could call it. Maybe we'll hear from her on our way back. It could happen."

"All right," Millie acquiesced. "We'll give it a shot and see what happens. Do we all agree?"

Millie was not looking for their approval. Nor was she seeking a democratic solution. Rather, she was leaving the path open for one of them to air out a strong objection. But nothing of the sort happened or appeared forthcoming.

"Then let's get going. It's about two hours back, and considering the speed limit here is now 75, I will turn on my radar detector and drive 80. If we don't turn up anything, I'd still like to spend the night south of Toledo. Let's go."

The spirit of the group had risen precipitously. Even Buddy seemed happier. He had been walked, watered and had a rawhide bone to keep him busy. The two boys were paying greater attention to everything around them. They began checking out vehicles in the southbound lanes in their quest to locate Jessie's car. Finally, as they got closer to Gaylord, Millie even found herself scrutinizing oncoming traffic.

And then it happened.

Just north of where Marlette Road crosses I-75 they noticed a number of State Police and County Sheriff patrol cars stopping traffic in the southbound lanes.

Millie saw it first.

"What is going on over there?" she said as she inadvertently began to slow down.

"It looks like a roadblock," Robby said. "I wonder what that could be about."

Red sat upright in order to get a better look as they drove past the roadblock. He then reached forward to touch Angel's shoulder. Once he had her attention, he pointed at the radio. Angel understood his gesture, and turned on the radio.

"What's the news station around here?" she asked. "Red thinks we might be able to learn what this is all about."

"WTCM," Robby spoke out. "News Talk 480. It's not based in Gaylord, but close. It's located just west of here in Traverse City."

Red nodded his approval.

Angel quickly tuned into the male voice on AM 480. "Is that Rush Limbaugh?" she asked. "I don't think it sounds like him. Is it?"

"Too late for Rush," Robby declared.

"They'll probably have local news at the hour," Angel said. "It's five to, right now."

"There must have been a robbery, or something," Robby said. "You don't see roadblocks every day."

"You live on Sugar Island!" Angel giggled. "Where could there be a roadblock on Sugar Island?"

"Yeah. Right. How many roadblocks have you ever seen? In the big city of Sault Ste. Marie? Tell me—"

"Listen!" Millie interrupted. "They're saying something right now."

"This is Jeff Conners reporting from the scene of what appears to have been a deadly robbery attempt at First National Bank in Gaylord. According to eyewitnesses, one of the robbers was shot on the street just outside the bank. An eyewitness tells us that the driver of a *Protect One* armored truck shot a man who was allegedly attempting to rob the truck. Unfortunately, we cannot get in any closer. But, if I look past the police barriers, I can see what looks like a body lying in the street. Obviously, I cannot tell for sure what I am looking at. It must be ninety yards away. Perhaps even more. But it appears as though the police have covered it up with a tarp. So, it figures it might be a body. But I am just speculating.

"Here is what we do know. According to Sergeant Malcolm Snyder, Michigan State Police spokesperson, at around four-fifteen P.M. this afternoon, two people, a man and a woman, drove up behind an armored truck that was parked in front of the First National Bank here in Gaylord. When the truck's security personnel began on loading several bags of currency, the man and the woman in the car got out of their vehicle, produced handguns, and confronted the truck's personnel.

"And then, again according Sergeant Snyder, as the woman was loading bags from the armored truck into the car, the driver of the truck suddenly confronted the alleged robbers, shooting the male, and shooting at the woman as she retreated to the car. She reportedly backed rapidly away from the scene, leaving her male counterpart wounded on the street.

"Sergeant Snyder then stated that the wounded male perpetrator has since passed away from his injuries.

"A manhunt is now underway for the female.

"This is Jeff Conners, News Talk 480, reporting from the scene of a deadly robbery of an armored vehicle in front of First National Bank in downtown Gaylord, Michigan. I'll send you back to the News Talk 480 studio."

"So," Robby said, "there has been a robbery in Gaylord. And that roadblock—that would have been set up to catch the woman. Right?"

"I'd say that was what must have happened," Millie said.

"Wait," Angel said. "There's more on the radio about it. Listen."

"We have just been informed by the Michigan State Police that the State Police and the Otsego County Sheriff are looking for an older brown Chevy Impala, 2012 or 2013. With a cracked windshield. It is driven by a woman. She might have been shot, but that is unknown.

"Anyone encountering such a vehicle should immediately contact the State Police, but should not attempt to confront anyone in the car. The driver might be armed and should be considered dangerous."

"Oh my God!" Millie muttered. "What sort of car were the Childresses driving? Wasn't it an older brown Chevy Impala?"

"With a broken front window," added Robby. "Do you think it could be them?"

Red was nodding his head.

"Red thinks it is them," Angel said. "If it is them, where do you suppose Jessie is? They didn't mention anything about a girl with them. They must have left her *someplace*. We've got to find her."

Red snatched a piece of paper from his jacket and began to

write.

"The theater," he wrote. "Check the movie theater."

"That's right!" Robby said. "Red says we need to go to the Gaylord movie theater. Sounds like a place Jessie would like. That might be where they would drop her off. If it was them—that could be where she would be hangin' out."

"I'll head there first," Millie said. "It's worth a shot. How many are there—theaters in Gaylord?"

"I don't know," Angel said. "The only one I saw was on West Main Street. Do you guys know if there's more than one?"

Red was slowly shaking his head.

"That's the only one we know about."

"Then that's where we'll start," Millie said. "I think I remember driving past one earlier."

"Oh," Angel breathed softly. "I just hope she's there. If that was her mother doing that robbery, maybe she stopped and picked her up. Or maybe she was hiding in the car all along. Maybe."

"Could be," Millie said. "But I think the movie theater's our best chance. She could hide out there for hours, if she had to."

"And eat stale popcorn and Skittles," Robby added. "Yum."

"I like Skittles," Angel countered.

It took eighteen minutes for Millie and the kids to reach the Main Street exit, and then to cover the mile and a quarter to Cinema One's parking lot.

"Well," Millie said, taking a deep breath. "Spot any movies you'd like to watch?"

Angel looked over at her mother with a "what-are-you-talking-about" scowl.

"We're going to have to buy tickets to see something. We can't just barge in. Here's some money. You three buy tickets and see if you can find her. Check every seat in every theater. She could be sleeping."

"Or hiding," Angel added. "She must know something is going on that isn't good. She might be slouched down in the front row. We're going to have to look hard."

Red wrote a short note and handed it to Angel.

"Be sure to check toilets," it said.

"Right," Angel said, "I'll check the bathrooms. Mom, aren't you coming in with us?"

"I'll wait out here in the car. Just in case she spots you and tries to make a run for it. One more thing. It looks like there are five screens. You're going to have to check them all. Even if there's not a movie playing in one of them. Here, I have only one flashlight. Take it. And if a theater is dark, you'll still be able to see if she's in it."

Robby was closest, so he took the flashlight.

As they walked up to buy tickets, Robby asked Red, with a sarcastic tone, "Which show are you going to see? Looks like there's only one *chick flick*."

"I say we all just get tickets to whatever," Angel said, "and then we can move from theater to theater until we find her."

Red nodded his approval.

"I'll get two tickets for the same show," Angel said. "One for me, and one for Red. And then we can split up once we're in."

Red did not respond, but Angel read his silence as agreeing with her offer.

As soon as the three kids disappeared into the theater complex, a news bulletin came over the radio:

"This is Jeff Conners reporting on scene of the armored vehicle robbery that occurred earlier today in front of the downtown branch of First National Bank in Gaylord. I have just learned that the car used in this robbery has been located. Sergeant Malcolm Snyder, Michigan State Police Spokesperson, has informed this reporter that the getaway car has crashed on I-75 just south of Gaylord. It is not known for certain, but it is thought that the female driver died in the crash. Sergeant Snyder said that she might have been wounded by gunfire during the robbery, but that could not be confirmed at this time. He also said that he believed that all the cash stolen in the robbery was recovered at the crash scene. Although, that could not be confirmed at this time. But, as I understand it, the State Police are no longer looking for any additional individuals with regard to this crime. He also said that the roadblocks that had been set up on all the major routes out of Gaylord have now been removed. This is Jeff Conners, reporting at the scene of today's armored truck robbery here in front of First National Bank in downtown Gaylord. I will now return you to the regularly-scheduled broadcast at News/Talk 480."

"Oh my God!" Millie moaned out loud. "How do I break this to Jessie? How totally awful."

Millie realized that she was not able to monitor all the doors that exited the theater, so she pulled out and relocated closer to Main Street. She kept the engine running. This allowed for the running lights to stay on so the kids would be better able to spot her after the movie.

"Any luck?" Robby asked Red. They had each just emerged from different theaters.

Red shook his head.

"Me neither. Have you seen Angel? Wonder how she's doing."

Red shook his head again.

"Looks like that one's empty," Robby said, handing the flashlight over to Red. "I peeked in already. But it isn't dark. So I won't need a flashlight. I'm going in to check it out. You wanna check out the other empty theater? Here, take the flashlight."

Red nodded and received it.

Angel had already checked out one of the theaters, and was busy going through the women's restroom. When she had finished, she stood and waited for the boys to come out so she could find out what remained to be searched.

Robby first appeared.

"What has to be done yet?" she asked.

"Red's going through *Theater 5*. I think that's the last one. That is, as long as you did the bathroom and *Theater 1*."

"I have. Too bad—Jessie must not be here. It was a gamble, anyway. We all thought that, I'm sure."

"Yeah. It was a long shot at best. I'm gonna run into '5' and see how Red's doing."

"Okay. I'll take one last look in the women's restroom, and then head out to the car."

"Right. See you there."

Red was nearly finished. All that remained was the far end of the front row of *Theater 5*. He thought that if a person wanted to hide, he could crouch down at the end of a row and not be seen. And, he was right. Just as he neared the end of the front row, Jessie quickly grabbed a small fabric roller bag and jumped up. She ran out of the rear exit door, which was located near the front of the theater.

Red let out a loud screeching shout, but Jessie did not respond with anything but her feet.

She slammed the door behind her, and looked around quickly. Lying on its side near the door was a wooden sawhorse. She picked it up and jammed it in endwise between the door handle and the gravel walkway. And then she ran. When Red tried to open the door, the force of his effort drove the end of the sawhorse into the gravel, effectively locking the door closed.

Millie could barely digest what she had just heard. "Oh my God!" she muttered. "*Both* of her parents—dead. That poor, poor child."

It was right then when she spotted Jessie running from the rear of the theater complex.

"There she is!" Millie blurted out.

Buddy spotted Jessie at the same time and let out a single piercing bark.

Millie slid the shifter into drive and sped off toward Jessie to head her off.

Red and Robby, realizing that they would not be able to get past the blocked exit door, bolted out of the theater and headed toward the front entrance.

As Millie approached Jessie, the girl spotted her and abruptly changed direction. Now she was running as quickly as she could toward Main Street. Red and Robby emerged from the complex just as Jessie ran by. They shouted for her to stop, but she continued on, pulling the suitcase behind her.

Red reached her first. Just before she had made it to the street, Red caught up.

"What are you doing?" she scolded him. "Leave me alone or

I'll call the cops. You aren't the boss of me. You can't make me go with you."

By then Robby had reached them, with Angel right on his heels.

When Jessie saw them coming, she just shrugged her shoulders and slammed the handle of the suitcase on the pavement.

"Leave me alone! Just go away and leave me be. You can't be stalking me. There are laws. I'll have all of you arrested. My parents will be here any minute. And they are going to be real mad at you for bothering me like this. Just leave me alone!"

"Jessie," Millie said through an open window as she drove up, "hop in for a minute. I need to talk to you. Please."

Jessie hesitated for a long moment, and then got in the front seat, dragging a bag in with her and stashing it on her lap. It was a small suitcase that her mom had given her.

"Hey, kids," Millie said. "Would you run back into the theater for a bit? I need some time alone with Jessie. I'll come in and get you in a few minutes. Okay?"

"I know you mean well," Jessie said. "And you guys have already helped me out a lot. I appreciate it very much. But, it's time to back off. I'm fine. My parents are fine. And you and your posse, you all need to back off and leave us alone. Okay? I would really appreciate it. Okay? We all thought you were on your way to wherever you're going. New York, or someplace like that. My parents think you should be long gone by now."

"Darlin'," Millie said. "That's the thing. Your parents are not coming back for you."

"You don't know that! They *are* coming back. I just know it. And they should be here anytime now. I'm leavin'."

Jessie opened the car door and started to get out.

"Jessie, your parents are not coming back. They have been killed in a horrible accident."

"What! What are you talking about? You crazy bitch. You don't know shit! They *are* coming back to pick me up. They told me they would. They don't lie to me. That's why I have my bag packed and ready. They should be here anytime now. What's this lie you're telling me about an accident? Mom called me forty minutes ago and told me to be ready—that she would pull into this parking lot and pick me up. They aren't dead. You're lying!"

"Jessie, I'm not lying. I'm telling you the truth. Do you know where they went when they dropped you off earlier?"

"Yes, I do. Mom said that they had a business deal going down, and that they had some loose ends they needed to tie up. And then, like I said, Mom just called and told me that they would be here anytime to pick me up."

"The business deal they were talking about was the robbery of an armored truck in downtown Gaylord. It just happened, and your father. ... It pains me to tell you this, but your father was shot and killed during the robbery."

"No!" Jessie blurted out as she slammed the door behind her. "That just couldn't be!"

"I'm so sorry, Jessie. But, we saw the roadblock that was set up on I-75 earlier. And they just said on the radio that both your mother and father were killed. She was shot during the robbery as well. And she passed away driving from the scene—probably on her way over here to pick you up. I am so very sorry, darling, but they are both gone. Please, get back in the car and let's figure out what we're going to do next. We need a plan. We have to figure out what our possibilities are."

Slowly Jessie got back in with Millie, but sat staring out of the front window for a full minute. Neither spoke. Finally tears began flowing from her eyes. They ran down her cheeks and dripped off her chin. Millie ripped several tissues from a box in the center console. She tucked them in Jessie's hands, which she had folded on her suitcase. She wiped the tears from her cheeks with a wad of tissues, and gracefully blotted the moisture from her nose. She then took a deep breath, turned her eyes toward Millie and leaned over to hug her.

After a lengthy embrace, Jessie sat back upright in her seat and began to speak.

"Are you sure? What do I do now?" she said, trying hard not to begin crying again. "… Are you absolutely positive my parents are dead? Can you help me find out for certain? I need to know."

"Of course," Millie answered. "We have to find out for certain. We *have* to do that before we can plan our next move."

Millie had not intended to commit to helping Jessie extricate herself from Gaylord. But she heard her own words: "*Our* next move." There it was—an iron-clad commitment. Technically, her word slip could be interpreted in a number of ways. The *next move* she was contemplating might be to simply boot the girl out of her Suburban with an insincere smile and an officious goodbye. But that was not the way Jessie interpreted it, nor was it what Millie intended. *That was a true Freudian slip,* Millie was thinking. *Jessie is not by any measure my problem, but it must be that my subconscious mind thinks otherwise.*

Jessie didn't miss it either. Even though she did not visibly react to Millie's choice of words, they definitely registered. *Our next move*, she said to herself. *That could dramatically alter my game plan. My game plan. Like I even had one. Well, at least I can count on Millie and the kids to help me out of this mess.*

"First, we need to find out exactly what happened," Millie said. "I heard on the radio news that they both had been fatally injured. But, we need to know for certain."

At those words Jessie's head sank and tears again began to flow.

Chapter 43

Millie found herself torn between reason and emotion. Even though Jessie had been forced to deal with the danger implicit in her family's situation, she still remained emotionally vulnerable when confronted with its reality.

"I am *so* sorry, Jessie. This is terrible. It's even worse than that. But we have to face up to what is likely to be the outcome. I'll try to see what I can find out. And you can stick around with Angel and the boys. Okay?"

Millie then slid the Suburban in gear and pulled up close to the front of the theater. All three kids were standing inside checking out what Millie and Jessie were up to. Millie parked and motioned for the three kids to come out to the Suburban. But Millie did not wait for them to reach her. Instead she jumped out, telling Jessie that she needed to talk to her daughter, and that she'd be right back.

Jessie did not react.

Millie closed the door behind her and met up with the group about twenty yards from the Suburban.

"Here's the scoop," she said. "I heard on the news that there were two robbers involved in the armored truck heist—a man and a woman. We have to assume they were Jessie's parents. The woman had been shot at the scene of the robbery, as was the man. However, her wounds were such that she was able to make an escape in their car. But she apparently succumbed to her injuries several blocks from the bank. Both are now reported as dead."

"Are we sure that they, the dead man and woman, are we absolutely convinced that they are Jessie's parents?" Angel asked.

"I think that is the case. There have been no names released on the radio, but it's pretty likely that they are the ones. The car matches. And they have a criminal history. We don't know for certain right now, but that's what I am thinking."

"How do we find out for sure?" Robby asked. "Can we just call the cops and ask them?"

"We have to be very careful how we go about this. We don't have any idea as to how much they might know about Jessie. As far as we know right now, Jessie might not even exist, in their eyes."

"Where do we start?" Angel asked.

"I want you guys to come wait in the truck with Jessie. While I call around."

Red immediately started writing a note: "Why not have us wait in the theater? Be easier to keep her occupied in there?"

When he had finished writing he handed the note to Robby for him to read aloud.

"That's a good idea," Angel said. "They even have a small sit-down area in there where we could get some snacks when the movie's finished."

"Are they sick of seeing you guys run around in there?" Millie asked.

"Probably," Angel chuckled. "But, if we buy more tickets, they'll be okay with it, I think."

"Sounds good. I'll get Jessie. You guys go get in line for tickets."

Millie started back to the Suburban as the three kids entered the theater.

"Jessie," she said upon opening the driver's door. "The kids are going to see a show. I'd like to have you go with them while I make a few phone calls. I'll come back for you as soon as I know something definitive."

Jessie looked up but didn't say anything. She opened the door and got out, dragging her suitcase with her.

"You should leave it in the truck," Millie advised. "No need to take it into the theater with you. It'll be okay."

"I need to have it with me. My mom said to keep it with me for when she came to pick me up. I'm gonna take it."

"Fine," Millie said. "But please stick with the other three so when I come back I can pick all of you up together. Okay?"

Jessie did not respond. Instead she just turned abruptly and began walking toward the theater entrance, dragging her suitcase behind her.

By the time she reached the door, the other three kids were coming back out.

"Is Mom still here?" Angel said in a bit of a panic. "We need money for tickets."

She scoured the parking lot for her mother but could not locate the Suburban.

"I think she's gone," Robby said. "We're gonna need some cash to buy tickets. Do you know where she's headed?"

Jessie shook her head. "But don't worry," she said, looking over at Robby and then Red. "I've got some money in my suitcase. How much do we need?"

Robby shrugged his shoulders and reached into his pocket to see how much cash he still had.

"Here, just take this this," Jesse said handing each of them a very crisp twenty-dollar bill. "I think that'll cover the price of a ticket. Whaddya think we should see?"

The two boys were standing slightly behind and to the left of Jessie when she zipped open the bag, and even though she attempted to block their view with her body, Red still got a good look at the contents.

"Great," Angel said. "That's really great. Mom will pay you back later."

"It's okay. She doesn't have to pay me back. You guys—all of you—you have done so much for me. It's the least I can do."

"Sweet," Angel said. "We appreciate it. About what show we should go to. I don't know. Do you guys have a preference?"

Red shrugged his shoulders and looked over at Robby.

Robby then said, "Do you think we should all go to the same movie? Or could Red and I see that *Godzilla* flick? Then you girls could go to something else if you wanted. What do you think? Or, would you like to catch *Endgame* with the Avenger Rocket Raccoon rappelling into a fire? What would you like to see?"

"I think as long as we all know where the rest of us are," Angel said. "... Does that make sense? You know what I mean. When Mom comes back, she's not gonna want to be looking around for us. So, as long as we can find each other quickly, we should be fine. I think Jessie and I might prefer something else. Right, Jessie?"

"I think so," Jessie replied. "I'd really like to see that Lily James flick. Have you seen it yet?"

"Sounds good," Angel said. "We'll see that Lily James movie, and you boys watch your *bro show*. Okay."

"Our *bro show*?" Robby said. Both boys were laughing. "Is that what you call a good *action movie*—a *bro show*?"

"My mom calls them *prick flicks*," Jessie countered.

As soon as she had said those words in reference to her mother, Jessie was reminded that her mother was dead, and that she would never talk to her again.

Angel caught her friend's suddenly sullen countenance and spoke up: "Great. Let's do it that way. We'll do the *chick flick* and you *men* can see the *bro show*. Let's go, Jes, our movie starts in ten. I want to grab some popcorn and a soda first."

"Do you want a snack?" Robby asked Red. "I think our movie already started, or is just about ready to start. Shall we get our seats and then decide?"

Red nodded and headed for the theater.

"Number two," Robby said to Angel as the boys walked away. "We'll be in Theater Number 2."

Angel turned and smiled as she and Jessie headed for the concession counter.

"How do you like your popcorn?" Jessie asked.

"Salt. Lots of salt. And I like butter. Do you?"

"Yeah. How about a drink? Coke?"

"Perfect," Angel said. "Can we share?"

"Sounds good."

"Could you get it?" Angel asked. "I really need to run into the Ladies. Okay?"

"Yup. I'll get it. I think we buy the ticket here too. I'll see. I'll meet you right here and you can help me carry it. Salt *and* butter. That's how I like it too."

"Great. And the Coke sounds good. See ya in a few."

After a few minutes Angel re-emerged and began looking for her friend.

"Do you know where my friend is?" she asked the concession clerk. "She was ordering a buttered popcorn and a large Coke. Did she say where she was going?"

"That's her purchase right there," the clerk said, pointing toward a popcorn and a soda. "Her father and another man came in and left with her."

"What? Her *father* was here?"

"I thought it must have been her father. But I don't know that for sure. He walked right up to her and told her that her mother had asked him to bring the girl to her. I just assumed that it was her father. He made her leave her cell phone here too. That's it beside the popcorn."

"Did she take her bag with her? She had a pull-along bag—a small suitcase. Did she take it?"

"Yes. Well, *she* didn't actually take it. Her dad grabbed it and carried it for her. They seemed to be in a hurry."

"How long ago?"

"Not long. Just a minute or so. In fact, that's them right there," he said, taking a couple steps to his right and pointing toward the parking lot. "You can still see them."

Angel spun around, peered out through the front glass and said, "I see them. Thanks."

Jessie and the two men had just stepped off the sidewalk and were heading toward a white Mercedes SUV.

Initially Angel was tempted to run out of the theater complex and try to stop them. But then she thought better of it. Instead she tore off toward Theater 2. As soon as she burst through the sound-insulated doors she shouted as loud as she could, "Red. Robby. Jessie needs help."

The boys, who were sitting near the front, exploded out of their seats and leapt over to the empty row in front of them and shot down it until they reached the aisle, and then ran out through the door.

Angle had already broke into a full run and was headed toward the outside door.

"This way!" she shouted as she pointed at the white Mercedes. "Two men. They've taken Jessie. Hurry!"

Red was the quickest. He sprinted past Angel and bolted toward the two men and Jessie. Robby was on his heels. Just as they reached the Mercedes, it shot backward, and tore off toward Main Street. For a couple of seconds the boys allowed panic and frustration to flood their emotions. Robby threw a look of anguish back at Angel. She had stopped dead in her tracks. "No catching them now," she said to herself.

Red, however, was not willing to give up. Instead he allowed his eyes to scour his surroundings in search of some workable solution to the problem. And then he spotted it.

Parked less than twenty yards away was a brand new Chevy Traverse. The driver's side door was wide open and it looked to Red like it was still running. So he grabbed Robby's arm and pointed toward it. The boys quick-stepped in its direction. As they neared it they observed that the engine was indeed running, and that the driver was standing behind an opened rear hatch.

Just as they reached the Traverse, the vehicle's owner, a middle-aged man, slammed the hatch closed. By that time Red had jumped behind the steering wheel, and Robby was getting in on the opposite side.

"Hold it!" the owner said loudly. "What's going on here?" Just as Robby slammed his door, Red threw the shifter into drive, which locked all of the doors. The owner of the Traverse tried the two doors on the driver's side, but to no avail. Since there was no vehicle in the parking slot directly in front of the Traverse, Red was able to shoot forward from his parking place and tear off toward the street, leaving the owner standing alone, hands on hips, in utter disbelief.

"They turned left!" Robby shouted. "I saw them. They turned left. In fact, there they go. I can still see the Mercedes. They're definitely headed west. I don't think they know we're chasing 'em. So maybe we can catch up. Do you think?"

Of course Red could not articulate his response, but Robby's familiarity with Red's style of communication allowed him to interpret his friend's response as an affirmative.

Red hit the gas. He took a look back in the rearview mirror to be sure the driver he was leaving behind was not somehow pursuing them. He spotted a disgruntled middle-aged woman standing where the Traverse had been parked. She appeared to be highly agitated. *I hope she's not calling the police,* Red complained to himself. *We'd better make this as quick as we can.* He kept his foot on the accelerator, backing off only when necessary.

As they approached the traffic signal in front of the Meijer store just west of Gaylord, they observed the Mercedes hurrying through an amber light.

"Dang!" Robby groaned, "we'll never catch them now."

There were three vehicles stopped at the red signal ahead of the boys. Red thought about it for less than a second. He cranked the Traverse to the right and shot through the red light using the right turn lane. Luckily all the drivers affected by Red's maneuver were able to avoid running into the Traverse, and the boys were able to slide back into the traffic lane heading west.

"I don't see them anymore," Robby announced. "Do you?"

Red scrutinized the road ahead and issued a grunt connoting a negative. So he hit the gas.

"Maybe they spotted us," Robby said.

Red did not respond audibly. Instead, he just continued to gradually accelerate.

Two miles up there was a major split in the road—a sharp left led to a small town to the southwest called Alba. A gradual right led northwest toward another small town—Elmira. Red had hoped to reach the divide before the Mercedes had disappeared, but it didn't happen.

"I didn't see which way they went," Robby declared. "Did you?"

Again, Red did not respond with anything but his right foot. He sped around the long curve leading toward Elmira. He had recalled a bit of advice his father had shared with him as a small child: "When in total doubt, do something. Always a fifty-percent chance you'll be right—that's much better odds than the Babe had every time he went to the plate. And he's a legend."

Robby didn't comment on Red's decision. He just leaned forward trying to get a better look at what lay ahead.

I'm pretty sure there are no vehicles between us, Red reasoned. *Not as fast as I've been driving. So, if they went this way, I should be catching up to them before long. If they went this way.*

Red had his eyes fixed on the road ahead of him. And then he glanced down at the speedometer. "Darn," he grumbled to himself. "Eighty miles per hour. I'm driving way too fast. This is crazy. Uncle Jack would be furious."

But he didn't let up.

"There!" Robby shouted. "We drove past them. They turned

right on Huxtable. We gotta go back. I'm sure that was them."

Huxtable was a less-traveled side road leading east off of the Elmira road. Red slammed the brakes on, finally coming to a stop three hundred feet past the intersection. Fortunately, he had been going so fast that there were no vehicles close behind, so he was able to reverse the Traverse to the shoulder and back to Huxtable Road.

"I still don't think they know we're back here," Robby said. "I can see them. It looks like they're stopping. Their brake lights are on."

Red backed past the intersection far enough to turn the Traverse east down Huxtable Road.

"Now their back-up lights are on," Robby said. "Must have driven past where they wanted to go."

Red hit the gas again and sped down the narrow road.

Just as the boys approached the Mercedes, it stopped going backwards and began making a left turn into a driveway.

Red slowed dramatically, but he did not attempt to pass the vehicle. Instead, he caught it firmly on the left rear quarter-panel, spinning it around and into some pine trees on the north side of the road. The tires caught in the loose dirt and the vehicle flipped over onto its side, and then slowly it rolled again, ending up on its top and resting against the pine trees.

Almost before the vehicle had stopped moving, Jessie clambered out of the broken door glass, dragging her suitcase behind her. She crawled directly away from the Mercedes.

As soon as she had cleared the danger zone, Red cranked the Traverse in tightly against the side of the overturned vehicle, successfully blocking the men's escape. Robby then shouted for Jessie to get in the Traverse.

Once she had slammed the door behind her, Red shoved the shifter into reverse and sped backward. Robby ducked down behind the back of the seat and ordered Jessie to, "hit the deck."

Red continued to race in reverse for over fifty yards, not slowing to turn around until he was safely out of pistol range. Jack had told both boys that the effective range and accuracy of a round fired from a pistol is substantially less than that distance. The boys knew that they were under fire. Not only could they hear the shots being fired, one of the rounds hit the windshield on the driver's side. While it did not strike the laminated safety glass directly enough to penetrate it, it did serve as a clear warning that the men from the Mercedes meant business.

Both Robby and Jessie felt their vehicle slowing and they sat up.

"Was that close or what?" Robby asked as he reached over to feel the spot on the windshield where the bullet had struck.

"Lucky for you that didn't come all the way through," he said as he shoved a stiff finger into Red's upper chest. "That would have hit you right about here."

Looking much like Floyd Mayweather Junior, Red reached rapidly across his body with his left hand, snatching Robby's finger before he was able to pull it back.

"Ow!" Robby protested loudly. "Okay. Okay. You've made your point. You're *hurting* my finger."

"Would you boys stop it?" Jessie barked. "Just knock it off for a minute. I almost got killed. *We* almost got killed. Those men had their minds made up to kill me. I know they did. And they would have killed you too. They were very bad men."

Red and Robby exchanged glances.

"So, what was that all about?" Robby asked. "What did they want with you?"

Jessie was hesitant to answer.

"What makes you think they were going to kill you? Did they *say* that?"

"Not exactly. They didn't come out and tell me that. But I'm sure that's what they had in mind. That house where they were taking me. It's empty. No one lives there. I'm sure that they were planning to kill me and bury me on that property. No one would ever find me. I'm sure that was their plan."

"But why? Why did they want you dead?"

Jessie hesitated again.

"Do you know why they wanted to kill you?"

"Yes. Because I knew too much. I knew what they were up to. I heard them talking with my parents about robbing the armored truck today. In front of the bank. They planned the whole thing."

"Then," Robby began, "that was your parents who were involved in that shootout downtown?"

"Yes," she said in a quivering voice. She was not able to control her emotions. "They were both—they both died. They were shot."

"Oh! No," Robby said. "We are so sorry. The guy selling popcorn at the theater told us that one of the men said that he was going to take you to see your mother. That wasn't true, then? Are you sure she's … she's dead?"

"Yeah. I'm sure they're both dead. Those guys set the whole robbery up. They had the times and all the information. Mom and Dad were supposed to hold them up—the men in the armored truck. They were going to get the moneybags and turn them over to them, and they would give Mom fifty thousand dollars. That was what they were going to pay Mom."

"Your mom? How about your dad? Wasn't he involved?"

"This was all Mom's doing. Her idea. She was sick of being so poor. She was going to take the fifty thousand and start a new life. With me. Leave Dad in the program. He didn't want to leave the program. He was scared to leave. But Mom couldn't handle it anymore.

"We would both take her mother's maiden name, and start over. That's what the fifty thousand was for. And this suitcase. It has another fifteen thousand in it. She thought that with the sixty-five thousand dollars, we could move to Texas, that's where her parents were from. We could move to Texas and start fresh. That's what she thought."

"So why did they bring you all the way out here?"

"I don't know. Maybe so that they could make sure nobody could find my body. I guess. So that I would just disappear with no trace. If anyone found my body, and if I was identified, then this whole thing might be traced back to them. Maybe that was what they were thinking. I don't know.

"I do know that they wanted the money I had with me. That I know. They talked about it. They were really disappointed that my parents weren't successful with the robbery. They didn't get a penny of that money. I guess what Millie had said about Mom getting wounded and then crashing the car—I guess that was what did happen. And she had the moneybags with her. So the cops ended up with it. That's why they came after me."

Finally, Robby turned around to talk to Jessie, as Red drove off.

"Whose money is that, then?" Robby asked. "The money in

your suitcase. Where did it come from?"

Jessie did not like the question. *What business is it of his?* she asked herself. *It's my money now. My mother gave it to me to hold for her. And now she's dead.*

"It's *my* money," she finally managed to say. "Mom gave it to me."

Red and Robby exchanged an incredulous glance.

"But, where'd it originally come from?" Robby asked.

"Why all the questions?" Jessie asked defensively. "It's my money. That's all you haave to know. End of story."

Neither of the boys were satisfied with her response, but they knew better than to pursue it further. At least not at this time.

"Don't we have to hook up with your mom at some point?" Jessie queried, partly in an effort to put an end to what she viewed as an inquisition.

"Actually, yes. Sort of," Robby replied. "We do need to somehow meet up with Millie, but she's Angel's mom, not ours. But, you are right about finding a way to get hold of her. And Angel. The cops are going to be swarming around here. Someone had to have heard that gunfire. And spotted the crashed Mercedes."

"Don't forget the carjacking from the parking lot. You boys are in huge trouble if you get caught."

Red offered his best sardonic smile and nodded.

"We're in trouble any way you slice it. If the cops don't catch us, Millie will. And then there's Uncle Jack. It's gonna be ugly no matter what happens."

Red stopped when he reached the main road and took a careful look in the rearview mirror. *No one coming*, he said to himself. He then turned right. This took him toward the little town of Elmira instead of back to Gaylord.

"Not heading back to find Millie?" Robby asked.

Red shook his head slowly.

"Cops?" Robby said.

Red did not respond this time.

"How are we gonna get hold of Millie?"

"I have an idea," Jessie offered, leaning over the back of the front seats. "What if we head back to the theater and park across the street? We could watch for Millie from there and—"

"Cops are gonna be all over," Robby interrupted. "We stole this car and wrecked it. We're in a lot of trouble, any way you want to look at it. We could sure use Uncle Jack about now."

Red nodded in agreement.

"Then, we can't go back to Gaylord?" Jessie asked in totally unaffected disgruntle.

"Not if we want to remain free."

"Then, can you just drop me off?" Jessie asked. "You saved my life. But I can take it from here. I can take care of myself."

Red shook his head in a prolonged fashion.

"I think we want to get back with Millie and Angel. We've got some big decisions to make, and *they* need to have their say as well."

"Then, if we can't go back to Gaylord, and we can't call her, just exactly how do you plan to hook up with them?"

Robby looked over at Red. His friend's confident expression convinced Robby that there was a plan in the hatching.

"Red's got it all worked out," he said. "I'm not exactly sure what he has in mind, but we'll find a way to contact Angel and her mom."

Jessie abruptly threw herself back into her seat.

Red back-handed Robby to get his attention. He then touched his seatbelt latch and then pointed at Robby's seatbelt, followed by a thumb signal directed at Jessie.

"Red wants us to click our belts," he said.

As soon as he had latched his, he waited to hear Jessie's snap together.

"Click."

"That usually means we could be in for a rough ride," Robby told her, "so get ready."

Chapter 44

And Robby was dead-on correct.

Seconds after Red heard Jessie's belt snap together, he cranked the car to the right and onto a two-track that seemed to both Robby and Jessie as though it led to nothing significant. The road appeared to be a seldom-used service road. It served as the means to get to an agricultural plot that lay behind a sizable field of pig corn. But Red had his sights on a large patch of forest that encompassed the back boundary of the farthest field. Robby saw the tall stand of trees and immediately understood what his friend had in mind.

But, even though the trail was fraught with large divots and troublesome rocks, Red did not slow. Instead, he accelerated. Robby leaned over to get a closer look at the speedometer.

"Fifty miles per hour!" he said.

And then turning back to announce it to Jessie, he said, "We're going over fifty. You'd better hang on tight!"

Just after Red had sped past the cornfield, he bottomed out on a particularly large rock. As soon as he hit it, the car began sounding like a dragster at the county fairgrounds.

"That must have been our muffler."

Jessie snapped her head around.

"Yeah. I see it," she announced. "I think we should slow down. You're gonna get us all killed."

Red wasn't fazed by her advice.

But, as soon as they had entered the woods, he backed off the gas pedal and slowed down. And once far enough into the trees that he was confident that no one would spot the car from the road, he pulled into a small stand of scrub pines and stopped.

"Wow!" Robby said. "Was that exciting or what?"

"Right," Jessie said. "We're back here in the woods. But what now? How do we get out? We can't just walk down the road."

"Relax," Robby advised. "Didn't I tell you, Red always has a plan? Well, let's just see what he has in mind."

Robby then turned to address his friend.

"So, Red, what's the plan?" he asked.

Red turned to Robby and smiled broadly, and then held his hands out, palms up, and shrugged his shoulders.

"There," Jessie said. "See, he doesn't have any idea how we're going to get out of this mess. He's as lost as we are. His so-called plan is a bunch of BS."

Red smiled again at Robby and then began writing on his notepad.

"Hear that?" Jessie said. "Those are cop cars. Sounds like a whole parade of cop cars. They're most certainly headed over to where you guys flipped that Mercedes. It's only a matter of time until they discover us back here. We don't stand a chance. No chance at all."

Red handed Robby the note he had written. It read: "I'll check trunk. You search inside."

Just as Red started to get out, Robby grabbed his arm. Red turned toward him with a smile and raised eyebrows.

"What exactly are we looking for?" Robby asked.

Red returned his query with a shrug and his typical "I don't know" gesture.

"Okay," Robby replied. "Fair enough."

He then turned toward Jessie and said, "Check out *everything* back there and see what you can turn up. I'm not sure what Red has in mind, but let's inventory everything—just like he said."

"All I have back here is a box of tissues and a broken window scraper. There's some plastic bags and stuff in the way back. Do you want me to reach it?"

"No, Red will check that stuff out."

Just then Red popped open the rear hatch and began rummaging through the bags of groceries. Suddenly, he let out a monstrous growl. It shocked Jessie—she snapped up in her seat and shoved her body back against the rear of the front seat. Robby, however, knew exactly how to interpret Red's articulation. He jumped out of the door and ran around to where Red was standing. In his hand was a cell phone.

Red shook the phone and pointed to the purse, indicating that someone had left a purse in the rear of the Traverse.

While he was making that clear to Robby, he was at the same time texting Millie:

"Need help now!! Elmira Road up 2 miles? from Alba Road. Pick us up ASAP."

And then, as quickly as his trembling fingers could work, Red opened the cell phone and removed its battery.

Jessie, who was watching all of this, protested, "Why'd he pull the battery? I need to talk to Millie. She was going to find out about my mom. Give it to me. I need to make a call."

But Red did not heed her request. Instead, he reared back

like a centerfielder throwing to the plate, and hurled the phone as deeply into the woods as he could.

"No!" Jessie shouted. "I said I need that phone to call Millie. I don't understand why you'd do that. Are you crazy? Has Red totally lost it?"

Red went back, snatched up some tissues from the back seat, and then began wiping the Traverse down.

Robby rushed over and grabbed Jessie before she could get past the corner of the vehicle.

"No," he said. "Leave it. The cops could use that cell phone to find us. They could trace it. That's why Red removed the battery. Keep away from the car, too. Red's wiping it down for prints, so they can't identify us. This is now a stolen vehicle. The longer it is before we can be identified, the greater our head start. Red will get your suitcase for you. But you must let him do his job. It will protect us."

"Over here," Robby said to Red, as he pointed to the rear of the Traverse. "Jessie just touched the back of the fender. Hand me some tissues and I'll wipe it down. Did you get the back of the seats, and the dash?"

Red tossed Robby a thumbs-up, and then signaled that they needed to get going.

"Right," Robby agreed. "We don't want Millie to miss us. And it's quite a hike over there anyway. At least half a mile."

Red pointed upward, indicating that it was more than a half-mile away.

Initially, Red retraced the path he had used when he drove the Traverse into the woods. But once he had led the group out of the forest, rather expose them to scrutiny by walking down the two-track, he led them to the drainage ditch just off the trail opposite the farmland.

As the distance between Red and the other two grew, Robby said, "Red is in a hurry. I think he's afraid Millie is going to beat us to the main road, and drive right past us. So, let's get a move on."

The farther along they managed to scramble through the difficult terrain, the greater the distance grew between Red and the other two. "Here," Robby finally said, reaching out to offer Jessie his hand. "Let me help you a little. And let me carry that suitcase. We really need to get moving a little more quickly."

Jessie was hesitant to hand the bag over, but she relented. She did, however, very willingly allow Robby to take her in tow.

"I know you are very capable of pulling your own weight," he said in a consoling fashion. "It's just that your shoes are not exactly what you want when hiking through a ditch. Next time you can help me."

Next time? Jessie said to herself. *This boy's dreaming. There will never be a next time. Not if I can ever help it. Me and this money are going to start a new life. I wonder how much I've got here. Mom never did say. I think it's all twenties and hundreds. That is a lot of cash. Probably not a million. But a lot. Maybe fifty thousand. I don't know. All I know is it's a lot. I can start my new life. That is, if Mom's no longer around. I don't wish her ill. I'll miss her a lot. But, if she is dead, then I'm totally on my own, and I have a whole pile of money to start my new life.*

Red took a look back and growled. And when he saw that he had their attention, he frantically motioned for them to catch up. This led Robby to tug harder on Jessie's hand, which led her to delve all the more deeply into her fantasy world of wealth and freedom.

Even though Red was not pleased with their pace, he was beginning to recognize that his encouragement was not having the desired effect. However, all of that changed as they approached the halfway point.

Suddenly Red not only turned toward the other two, but this time he ran full-speed to them and dragged them to the ground. At first Robby and Jessie did not understand the reason for Red's drastic action, and they started to protest. Red countered their reaction by placing his hand over Jessie's mouth to silence her.

Robby knew Red well enough to realize that his friend must have had a good reason for tackling them, so he just lay silently on his face as he waited for more information. And it came.

Rumbling along the bumpy two-track beside them bounced a patrol car—headlights and emergency flashing, but no siren. The sight of the cop car threw Jessie's body into paralysis. After it had passed, Red placed a hand on the backs of his friends as he raised himself up to survey the situation. Once satisfied that the patrol car was safely past them, he grabbed the arms of the other two and tugged them fiercely into the adjacent field, and then on toward the road. Now they were running at full speed.

As they approached the road, Red spotted what appeared to be a white Suburban progressing slowly in their direction, but he wasn't sure it was Millie. He pointed at the vehicle, while turning to his friends and encouraging them to pick up speed.

Red was still fifty yards from the road when the white vehicle drew even with him, while the other two were slightly farther back. He feared committing too soon, given the possibility that it was not Millie's Suburban. It was at precisely that moment Red spotted something extremely familiar to him—Buddy's gold and brown snout sticking slightly out of the Suburban window. Millie had cracked the rear passenger-side window just enough for Buddy to squeeze his muzzle through. But it was enough.

Buddy had captured Red's scent and had withdrawn his nose far enough to announce clearly what he had found. He had found Red, and he let Millie know about his discovery. Immediately she pulled to the side of the road.

Red opened the rear door and held it while Jessie and Robby made a mad dash out of the field. As soon as Red had pulled himself in and slammed the door behind him, he grabbed Buddy around the neck and planted a big kiss on the dog's nose—an act that Buddy did not approve of as it caused him to sneeze three times in rapid succession.

The whole process was amazingly quick. From the time Millie's tires ceased rolling until she was back on the road at full speed was only a matter of ten to twelve seconds. Fortunately, there were no vehicles immediately behind her. That was probably because she had already slowed to under twenty-five miles per hour, causing the pickup that had been behind her to pass.

Red grabbed his tablet and wrote: "Got to get out of area fast!"

When he showed it to Millie she said, "Red says we have to get going. We have to get away. And I agree. We'll head south down 131 after we get to Elmira, and then cut over to I-75 farther south—maybe by Grand Rapids.

"And, by the way, just how much of what just went down do I want to know about?"

Red threw a glance over at Jessie and Robby, shaking his head as he stared them down.

"We've got nothing to say," Robby told her. "All is well with us now. Maybe we can talk more about it later? Is that okay?"

"Then, for right now, there's nothing more that I really need to know?" Millie asked.

Red looked at Robby and shook his head.

"No," Robby said, "We think we're good—for now."

"Okay," Millie said.

Angel thought a little levity might be in order, so she added, "Then I suppose we can assume that you've left no one dead or dying. Right?"

"Exactly," Robby said.

"Does bleeding from the nose count?" Jessie said, wanting to get in on the conversation. "I think one of those guys got—"

"Jessie!" Robby interrupted. "Where's your suitcase?"

She rapidly searched the vehicle with her eyes, and then screamed, "You left it in the field—when that cop car went by. You were carrying it and you left it there!"

"Cop!" Mille interjected. "Why are the cops involved?"

"I think that's part of the 'we'll talk about it later' that Robby was getting at," Angel said through a snicker.

"My suitcase!" Jessie persisted. "We've got to go back and get it."

Red growled and shook his head forcefully, and then growled a second time for emphasis.

"Can't go back," Robby said. "Sorry about your suitcase, but it'd be much too dangerous to go back for it. The cops have certainly found the Traverse by now, and might even be interviewing those two guys in the Mercedes if they stuck around. We just can't take a chance on going back."

"Don't worry, Jessie," Millie said trying to console her. "We can buy you more clothes, if the boys think it would be a bad idea to go back for it. We'll go shopping in Grand Rapids. Or, if you want to go to New York with us, there are lots of great shops there."

"I don't think it's the clothes she's worried about, Mom," Angel said. "I think it's the other stuff she had in her bag."

"What *other stuff* are you talking about? Oh my God! You don't use drugs, do you?"

Jessie just snarled in her anger and sank down into the seat.

"No, Mom, Jessie wasn't carrying drugs. She had some money in her bag."

"She didn't just have *some* money," Robby offered. "Her whole suitcase was *full* of cash."

"The whole bag was full of money?" Millie repeated. "And where did that come from?"

Jessie refused to answer, so Millie asked her again: "The money—where'd it come from?"

Still Jessie wouldn't respond. She just slouched even more deeply into her seat as though she thought she might be able to disappear.

"She told us that her mom gave it to her to hold," Robby said.

"Oh," Millie said. "I see."

But she didn't say anything else on that subject—at least not at that time.

And as she sat behind the wheel thinking about what next to say to Jessie, the burner cell that Jack had sent with her rang.

"Millie," the voice said. "This is Jack. What's your 10-20?"

Chapter 45

Henry and Kate remained hidden off-road as the Ford continued past them on US-85 toward the southwest until it was out of sight.

"You said that you know who that woman is?" Kate asked.

"I sure do. That was Claire Mansfield—the one who originally hired us. She's the one from up in the UP. She's the reason we're here right now."

"You've got to be kidding. That was her? But I thought she was back in Michigan. What's she doing *here*?"

"Now that's a good question."

Henry started the car.

"Hang on," Kate said. "Let's wait here to see if she comes back. I still think our guy might be around here just waiting for a ride. Maybe he'll show himself."

"Yeah," Henry agreed, leaving the engine idling, but turning the running lights off. "You keep your eye upstream, and I'll watch downstream."

They only had to wait a few minutes before that same Ford reappeared.

"Here she comes back," he said as he focused the car in on a pair of binoculars.

"Still only one person as far as I can tell. Anything going on up ahead?"

"I don't see anything yet," Kate said. "And she doesn't seem to be pulling over, either."

"If our guy doesn't pop outta the woods soon," Henry said, "I'm going to pull out. He still might be in the car, just ducking out of sight."

Henry and Kate remained hidden off the side of the road as Claire Mansfield passed.

"Damn!" Henry growled. "She's still going slow. Too slow. If she'd already picked the guy up, and he was hiding in her car, it seems like she'd be in a hurry to get the hell outta here."

"Yeah," Kate said. "Sure seems likely. Let's hang in here for another minute, until she crests that hill. And then, if nothing happens, drive like hell until we catch up. She won't be able to see us coming until we get over that hill too."

Just before the Ford reached the top of the hill Kate announced, "There! She's braking! I see her brake lights."

"And she's pulling over," Henry said. "Let's go after 'em."

Henry slammed the car in reverse and retraced his tracks back through the fence and onto the road.

"What do you have in mind when we catch up?" Kate asked.

"I dunno. Should we shoot 'em? What do you think?"

"Not until we question them," Kate laughed. "We need to find out what this Mansfield woman is doing in Deadwood. And what, if anything, she might have had to do with killing Hornsboro."

"Okay. If you insist. Anyway, I'd like to find out who that guy was that was following us. Just what his involvement might be."

"Keep your eye out for the sheriff. He's going to be poking around too. And I don't think he likes us very much."

"I hope to hell he doesn't pull us over before we round up Claire and her friend," Henry said.

But just as he shoved the shifter into drive, the flashing of reds and blues began bouncing around the interior of the Taurus.

"Shit!" Henry barked loudly, slapping the steering wheel three times in rapid succession.

"Pull over," Kate ordered. "Don't make this guy madder than he already is. And be as nice as you can. Trust me on this one, Henry. We do not want to antagonize this man."

"Right. Right. I do know how to be good. It's just a damn shame that we have to let Claire and this guy get away like this—Claire and her friend, whoever he is. I would really like to ask them some questions."

So Henry did pull over just as he had promised Kate. And when he did, the patrol car he thought was trying to stop him accelerated dramatically and sped past them.

"Wow!" Kate said through a tight smile of amazement. "This must be your lucky day."

"I just hope to hell he's not chasing the same car we are. Now *that* would be a bummer."

Henry gave the patrol car a little time to create some space and then he pulled back onto the pavement.

"If he's after your Claire and her friend," Kate said, "it'd be for a different reason. Like maybe she made an illegal U-turn back there."

"I hope you're right. I guess we'll soon find out."

As Henry crested the hill they spotted the patrol car's flashing lights off to the side of the road only a few hundred yards ahead.

"Looks like he's got his man," Henry said.

"Or his woman. Pretty sure that's your Claire lady he's got pulled over."

"Sure is. And it looks like he's called for some backup. Got another strobe coming up from behind. Think I'll find a cozy spot up ahead. Where we can park and keep an eye on what's going down.

Could be interesting."

"Good idea," Kate agreed. "And maybe when the law's done with them, we can take a turn. What's that right there on the left? Looks like apartments. That'd work. We ought to be able to park in there for a few."

"Yeah. That works. I can slide around and get in here so that we've got a good clear line of sight."

Henry maneuvered his car right into a group of several residents' vehicles and pointed it facing the traffic stop.

"Perfect," Kate said. "We can see everything from here."

By the time Henry got parked the second patrol car had pulled in behind the first. Between them, there were a total of three sheriff's deputies surrounding Claire's Ford. They appeared to be ready for action, but all still had their firearms holstered.

"That look right to you?" Henry asked. "For a routine traffic stop."

"It's been a very long time since I was on the road," Kate said. "But I'd have to say that they've got more on their minds than an illegal U-turn. By the way the two deputies have positioned themselves, front and rear, it looks to me like we might be here for a while."

"I think you're right," Henry said. "That looks like a third car might be joining them. He's slowing down. We'll see if he stops."

The third patrol car clicked on his emergency lights and pulled in ahead of Claire's Ford.

"I think that's the sheriff himself," Kate announced as the tall trim frame of Lawrence County Sheriff William Miller slowly emerged from the third patrol car.

"I feel like a mouse trying to figure out where all the cats are hiding," Henry said. "At least we now know where a whole bunch of them are."

"I'd say that the sheriff showing up answers our question about whether or not this is a standard run-of-the-mill traffic stop," Kate said. "Wouldn't be surprised to see them slapping some cuffs on them."

"I'd sure like to hear what they're talking about," Henry said. "How about you taking a stroll down there and asking Billy Boy what it's all about? I think he kinda likes you."

"Great idea," Kate said, responding to Henry's attempt at humor. "I'll have to give that one some thought."

Both Kate and Henry grew silent for a minute as they carefully scrutinized the scene taking place before them.

"Did you see that?" Kate said, breaking the silence. "The sheriff just inspected the front of their car."

"He's looking for damage that might have been caused by our dust up over on Short Street. Damn. We're gonna want to sneak out of here before he expands his search."

"We do need to get out of here," Kate agreed. "But before we leave it'd be nice to get a picture of those two. Do you have any type of telephoto lens on that point-and-shoot? Maybe you could get a snapshot of Claire and her friend before we go. I'm pretty sure they're going to take them out of the Ford so they can search it. Maybe you can get some shots then."

Henry liked that idea. The Canon camera he was using had a motorized telephoto lens, and so he extended it to its maximum, and prepared to snap some shots when and if the situation presented. And it soon did.

Only seconds later one of the deputies opened the driver's side door and requested that Claire step out of the vehicle. At the same time a second deputy opened the passenger door and helped the man out of the car.

Henry had clicked off several shots of Claire as she emerged, and he did the same for her passenger.

"Here come the cuffs," Kate declared. "I wondered when they'd get to that."

"Looks like the passenger might have a little blood on his shirt," Henry said. "That sure does make him look like our guy."

"*Our guy* meaning what?" Kate queried.

"Our guy that we crashed."

"That would most likely be right," Kate agreed. "He does fit the bill for that. But we can't tie him to anything else. We've no evidence that he is in any way involved with the Hornsboro killing."

"That's right," Henry said. "I totally agree. I hope you don't think that's what I was suggesting."

"I know. I was just thinking out loud. I wonder if we could do anything with facial recognition. My lab back in New York might be able to run him. We should try to run them both, actually. After all, we really don't know if this babe is who she says she is. Does your camera have Wi-Fi?"

"It does."

"Then we can transfer your images to my iPhone, and ship them on to New York. They just might be able to help us identify who we're dealing with."

After that exchange Kate and Henry slunk out of the parking lot and headed back toward Deadwood.

"Tonight," Henry said to Kate, "I'd like to introduce you to a couple friends of mine."

"You've got friends in Deadwood? How do you know them?"

"Drinking buddies, of course, from down at the saloon."

"Ahh. Right. You're referring to those old-timers you and Dad looked up. The ones who knew some of the people who might have helpful recollections, or photographs, relating to the folks you've been checking up on."

"Yup. Those are the ones I want you to meet."

"How do you know how to reach them? Do you have phone numbers? Have you already called them about tonight?"

"I do have a number. But I don't think I need to call it. Odds are one or more of them will be drinking down at Seven Stallions."

"Is that the name of the bar— Seven Stallions? Or are we going to have to tip a few at half a dozen other establishments first?"

"That's the name of the bar. But I like your spirit. I'm not even sure that there are seven bars in Deadwood. But, we could do a little survey if you like."

"Maybe tomorrow night. We can meet with your friends tonight, but I want to be at my best in the morning when we have to deal with the sheriff."

"Yeah. If you're naughty, Sheriff Miller might tell your boss about it and get you in trouble."

"No chance. Captain Spencer will *never* call him back. He just doesn't return calls. Period. Not unless he knows you. Then he will. I could call him right now and he'd pick up, or ring me back. But all numbers *not* on his list just bounce over to the precinct, and they never put anything through."

Henry and Kate continued chatting on their way to the rental car office, where Henry switched out the 2019 white Taurus with an identical vehicle—except for the smashed up front end.

Kate freshened up, added some lip gloss, and pulled the scrunchie from her ponytail, while pulling out a small travel brush to run through her long caramel-colored hair.

"What exactly are we hoping to learn tonight?" Kate asked. "You and Dad have already talked to these old guys. Right? Was there something else you think they might know? Something that might help?"

"The last guy we talked to that night—Jimmy Jackson. I would like to talk to him again. His aunt, or great-aunt, was the main clerk in the post office back in the 1920s. She had a wanted poster that fit the description of the brothers we were looking for. Except, the name they were using was *Smith*, not *Pierce*.

"I found a lot of Smiths in the historic cemetery. I wrote them down—at least the ones that dated to that era. I'd like to see if that Jimmy guy can tell us anything about those people.

"I did find a couple Pierces, too. But not as many as I would have liked—that is if there were a strong contingent of Pierces in Deadwood at that time."

"Did you check the county recorder's office?" Kate asked. "To see if there were any properties owned by your guys?"

"Let's do that right now," Henry suggested. "Do we have time?"

"Better shoot for it tomorrow," Kate said. "Right after we meet with the sheriff in the morning."

"Sounds good," Henry said. "Maybe we can get to the bottom of that business with Claire Mansfield yet today."

"What do you have in mind?" Kate asked. "They might be in custody by now."

"Let's find out," Henry said as he dialed her number.

"Claire. This is Henry. Any further word on the Roger Hornsboro death? I haven't heard anything. Thought you might have."

"Henry. I'm so glad you called. I don't know anything else about it. I have talked to the sheriff, but he didn't tell me a thing. He actually stopped me and my brother and asked us questions about it. I'm not sure if I told you, but I'm staying in Deadwood for a few days—my brother and I. The sheriff stopped us, put us in cuffs and everything. And questioned us about the murder. But then he let us go."

"So, are you saying that you are here in Deadwood right now?"

"Yes."

"I didn't know that. I thought you were still back in Michigan."

"After that lawyer reminded me that the deadline was drawing near—after that conversation I decided that I needed to get more hands-on. You know what I mean? It's not that I don't have all the confidence in the world in what you and Jack Handler are doing, but I just felt that it wouldn't hurt if I learned a little bit about the whole situation. And, maybe, I might be of some help along the way. That's the only reason we drove out here. By *we*, I mean my brother and me.

"And then that business about Roger Hornsboro—that just tops it all off. First he calls and says he has some information. And the next thing we know is that he's dead. Murdered, I think. Even though it probably has nothing to do with the inheritance, it still seems very strange to me. That he'd just up and get murdered like that. That sort of stuff just doesn't happen every day—not in my world. Time is running out, you know. And, I guess Jack, your partner, is not working on this right now. So we thought we'd see if there was anything we could do to expedite the investigation."

"Well, did you have any luck?" Henry asked.

"Aside from attracting the ire of the sheriff, no. But, I don't think he's very happy about *you*, either. You and that New York detective you've got with you: Jack's daughter—Kate. He sounded a little pissed about having to deal with her, too."

Kate could hear the conversation and smiled at that comment. She was, while Henry was conversing with Claire, checking up on the images she had earlier sent in for her forensics to perform a facial recognition search in their database.

"You said that they cuffed you and took you in for questioning?" Henry asked.

"They did cuff us and had us sit in a patrol car, but only for a few minutes. As soon as they had finished searching our car—for who knows what—they removed the cuffs and released us. The sheriff himself showed up at the scene. He said you had dropped my name at the Hornsboro house. That was okay. I understand why you would do that, after all it was me who told you to talk to the man. Who knew he'd get himself murdered before any of us could talk to him.

"So, I suppose you didn't have any luck finding out what it was that he knew, did you?"

"No, he was dead by the time we got there. And the sheriff wouldn't let us set foot in his camper."

"Camper? You mean one of those things that fit on the back of a pickup truck? Is that what he was living in?"

"That's right."

"Oh my God! Didn't he live in a house? A regular house, I mean?"

"I'm not sure what his permanent address was. But, as far as I know, around here, that's where he called home."

"Then, he's not actually from this area?"

"I don't know where he really lived," Henry said. "All I know is that when we called his phone number, the sheriff answered and directed us to this camper. It was a well-cared-for camper, but that's exactly what it was. An older camper, at that."

Kate wrote this note to Henry while he was still talking to Claire: "Facial recognition—nothing in database on female. Male has a record—drug bust and car theft. The name on the RAP sheet: Franklin James Mansfield."

"What did you say your brother's name was?" Henry asked.

"Frank, Frank Mansfield. He's not actually my brother. He's my husband's brother—my brother-in-law. My husband, John, is not a healthy man. And he didn't want me to come out here to Deadwood by myself. So he sent Frank with me."

Kate cringed when she heard Claire's comment, her face assuming a bewildered expression.

Henry glanced over at her, shrugged his shoulders and smiled.

"So where are you staying?" Henry asked.

"We're staying at the Marriott in Deadwood. How about you?"

"That's where we're staying too. Funny I haven't seen you there. It's not a huge hotel."

"We just checked in last night."

"How long will you be in town?"

"The sheriff didn't tell us we had to stay in the area, so we are planning on leaving today. People are dying around here. Granted, about this Hornsboro guy. No one thinks that he got murdered because of my investigation. But, it's still striking too close to home. And then there was this incident involving Frank. Today a car ran him off the road and then pushed him into a tree. He got pretty banged up. Wrecked the car."

"Oh, no! That's terrible," Henry said, struggling to restrain from laughing. "So what are you driving now? You did say it wrecked your car."

"It did, but Frank had borrowed the car. It wasn't mine. So we can get back to Michigan okay. But we just think that there's really nothing we can accomplish here. You and Jack can see what you can turn up. And we'll let it go at that. Where is Jack, by the way? The sheriff didn't say anything at all about Jack. Only his daughter. Is she still here in Deadwood?"

"That's right. Jack did get called away for a day or two. But he'll be right back at it. He asked me to run down some leads. And Kate. He sent Kate in to help out as well. We should be winding it up soon. What did you say that attorney's name was? The one who is in charge of this whole thing?"

"You're probably referring to Craig Conklin. He's not actually in charge, though. He's the attorney I retained to protect my interests. There is another attorney, however. His name is Sidney Schaffer. His office is in Grand Rapids. Initially he worked for my parents, and before that his firm represented my mother's family. The Schaffer firm is the one who is serving as the executor of the whole estate—has been for decades. I know, it does get very complicated. I think that's where this Roger Hornsboro comes in. He was, I believe, hired by my attorney to delve into the financial end of the whole matter—to see just how much money that was actually involved. That's why when he called me directly, instead of going through my lawyer, I took it so seriously. If what he was saying was true, that he had some information that could dramatically affect the whole situation—he called it earthshaking. He said he wouldn't tell me what it was over the phone—rather, he wanted to sell it to me. That's when I figured that whatever he had could really be important."

"Oh my God!" Henry said. "I should think that you could have brought us up to speed immediately—when your attorney first mentioned it. We could have worked together and got more done."

"Well," Claire said, "I think you *were* working together, it's just that you weren't aware of the partnership."

"What are you suggesting? I've never even heard anything about this Hornsboro fellow until you called me and asked me to meet with him. And that's when he got killed. How could I have been working with somebody I've never even talked to?"

"Apparently you have one source in common—someone named James Jackson. Or Jimmy, as most people refer to him."

"Jimmy Jackson? He has talked to Jimmy? Jimmy Jackson never said anything about having met with a Roger Hornsboro. I think he would have told me about it if he had."

"I think he was in the bar—the Seven Stallions —the other night at the same time you were in there. But after you left. He saw you leave and he went over and struck up a conversation with the Jimmy guy, and someone else—a guy named Walt. He even said that you bought him some beers. Does any of this sound familiar?"

"I suppose. I was talking with guys named Jimmy and Walt. So, I guess he could have met with them after I left. Did he say that these guys actually gave him some information that was earthshaking? I talked to them for a couple of hours. They had a lot to say, but nothing definitive—certainly nothing I would consider earthshaking."

"Well, that's the word he used—earthshaking. That was—"

"Okay," Henry interrupted. "Didn't you say earlier that the new evidence Mr. Hornsboro was offering was in the form of a letter—a correspondence of some sort?"

"That's what he said. A letter."

"Okay," Henry said again. "Now we're cooking. I'm going to be talking to Jimmy Jackson tonight. I'll see what he has to say about it. I should be able to find out just which of his letters he handed off to your guy."

"I'm headed back to Munising as soon as I can get my stuff together," Claire said. "I would love to stay in the area and see what you come up with, but I'm not comfortable about hanging around here with the sheriff sniffing at our heels. Especially Frank. That sheriff seems to want to hang that Hornsboro murder on him—at least that's what *he* thinks."

"I suppose that if the sheriff did not specifically order you and your brother-in-law to stick around, then you might be wise to go back home. Michigan would not extradite without solid evidence. So I'd say you'd be better off creating some distance between yourselves and Deadwood law enforcement. I'll follow up with those guys at the bar and see what I can come up with. Please, give me a call if you hear anything else. Time is becoming an issue, and any information might make the difference."

After Henry had disconnected the call he sat silently thinking for nearly a full minute.

Chapter 46

"Okay," Kate finally said, interrupting his contemplation. "So what's piqued your attention? You've grown awfully quiet all of a sudden."

"Jimmy," Henry said. "I can't see Jimmy handing over any of his material to a stranger. He might have allowed Hornsboro to snap some shots with his camera, but he would not have let anyone walk out of that bar with the actual artifact. He just would not have allowed it."

"Oh," Kate said. "I get it. You're thinking that this Hornsboro fellow did not have a piece of paper in his possession, just an image on his phone. Is that what you're suggesting?"

"Absolutely! Positively!"

"Then we've got to get back to this friend of yours and take a look at the letter. Do you think you can get him to come out to the bar tonight? To meet us there?"

"I sure as hell hope so," Henry replied as he checked his list of phone numbers. "I do have both their numbers—Walt's and Jimmy's. I should be able to reach one of them.

"I'll give Jimmy a try first."

The phone rang the customary number of times and then went to voicemail. Henry waited for the tone and said, "Jimmy, this is Henry, Jack's friend from the bar the other night. He and I talked to you at length about all the great pictures and letters you had dating back to the 1920s. You were so helpful. We really appreciate it. I'm hoping we can talk again today, or tonight, at the same place. Like I said, I would really appreciate it. Give me a call, or just meet us there in the evening. Thanks."

"A lot of people won't pick up," Kate said. "Especially if the call isn't from someone on their contact list. You said you had the other guy's number as well?"

"Walt. Yes, I have his number too."

Walt's phone rang three times when he picked up.

"Yes," he said, not recognizing Henry's number. "This is Walt. What can I do for you?"

"Walt. Thanks for answering. This is Henry. From the other night in the bar— Seven Stallions. Do you recall talking to my associate and me? Jack Handler. We were asking you and your friend James Jackson a number of questions about a man named William Lawrence Owens, and two brothers, Edward and Isaac Pierce. Do you remember that conversation?"

"Yes, of course."

"I was hoping I could get together with you and Jimmy again today, or this evening, and—"

"Oh hell! You haven't heard the news? It's all over the TV and the radio? About Jimmy. You haven't heard?"

"I haven't had the TV on. What's up?"

"Even if you'd had the TV on, it wouldn't have mattered. They didn't give his name. Just said that an elderly man was struck and killed while crossing Main Street. Right here in Deadwood, just down the street from the saloon. Ran a stop sign at Wall Street. Hit-and-run, I heard. They didn't give his name, but all us locals knew it was Jimmy. Strangest thing in the world. People who saw it said it didn't make sense to them at all."

"I just can't believe this," Henry said. "Are you telling me that Jimmy Jackson is dead? The guy I was just talking to in the bar the other night—he's dead?"

"Yup. The very same. And, like I was saying, it was very strange. The way it all happened. Awful damn strange—if you ask me."

"Shit!" Henry moaned. "That's horrible. What do you mean that it was *strange*? How was it so strange?"

"Look," Walt said impatiently. "I gotta go. I will be at the saloon later. We can talk then, if you want."

"No. Wait. Tell me how it was so strange. I will meet you tonight. But quickly explain what it is you're talking about."

"He was hit by a brand new black SUV—a Cadillac SUV. What are they? Eighty thousand or so? The people who saw it say the Caddy did not even slow down. And it swerved over toward the sidewalk as though it was intentionally trying to hit Jimmy. And then it just kept going—heading east out of town.

"It sent Jimmy flying right into the front of the hotel. And then it dragged his roller suitcase almost a block along Main Street, strewing pictures and letters all along the street. And then, while everyone was checking up on Jimmy—he was still alive and talking that whole time—while the ambulance was coming, someone picked up all of Jimmy's stuff and disappeared. Along with the Caddy. They both totally disappeared. All his pictures and papers—everything. It all got picked up and never heard from again. The cops are investigating it. But I gotta go now. Really. Gotta go. Meeting with Jimmy's friends at the funeral home. I'll be at the bar later this evening, if you want to talk. But gotta go right now."

Henry had pulled over to the shoulder when he first heard about Jimmy getting killed.

"Did you catch that?" he asked Kate.

"Most of it," she said. "Enough to know that your friend Jimmy got hit by an SUV and was killed. And all his stuff is now missing—the info he had with him when he got hit. Sounds very suspicious to me. What do you make of it?"

"Hell. I don't know what to think. First we have this Hornsboro getting murdered. And now Jimmy—the same guy who had produced the letter, or letters, that Hornsboro was bragging about. Both men dead—killed, actually. One shot inside his camper, the other done in by a hit-and-run driver. Does not feel like a coincidence to me. It just smells very bad—like someone doesn't want this info getting out—the stuff that Jimmy had found. Whoever it is that killed Hornsboro, he is probably going to be the same person who got to Jimmy."

"And," Kate added, "it sure seems likely that there were at least two of them. One person was driving the SUV that ran your friend Jimmy down, and someone else gathered up the materials from the man's suitcase. So, we are talking about at least two people. That makes it a conspiracy."

"But why?" Henry asked. "Okay. So we've got two people murdered now. One of them—Hornsboro—because he had some information that he was hoping to sell to Claire. Seemingly. A letter. The other victim, Jimmy Jackson, he was probably killed by the same person. Or at least someone representing the interests of that same person. All I can say is that somebody has a very strong interest in quashing our investigation."

"And now that person's motivation has just been magnified," Kate said.

"Because of the murders?"

"Exactly," Kate said. "Most likely the initial motive for both murders would have been money. I'm not sure about how much money is at stake here, but I think you suggested it was a million dollars plus. Right? Well, other people have killed for a lot less. But, now, money is not the only incentive. In fact, it's not even the major factor. Now, the killer has to be concerned with covering up his subsequent crimes—the killings. Especially now that we know that more than one person is involved. That increases the killer's exposure—exponentially. Now there is a second person, maybe more than one, who, if reached, can turn state's evidence on the killer. Especially if it is a single perp in both killings. If that is the case, then the killer has a lot to worry about."

"Think about this," Henry said. "There has to be a reason the killer went after Jimmy the way he did."

Henry was trying to pull together this puzzle. He wished he could have been visiting Deadwood as a simple tourist. *Seems like a fun town without all of this drama*, he was thinking. But now, as he sat there with Kate, he cranked up the AC, and concentrated on the case at hand.

"What are you getting at?"

"If, if the killer was already in possession of the letter—the one Walt says Jimmy showed Hornsboro. If the guy who killed Hornsboro in his camper, if he was in the *physical* possession of that letter, he wouldn't need to go after Jimmy. But he did. It looks like he somehow lured Jimmy out of his apartment with all his stuff, ran him over, and then had an associate gather up the goods from off the street."

"So, we can now probably deduce that the killer has the letter," Kate said. "But that he didn't have it before. Right? Is that what you're suggesting? If it is, you could be right. But, that would mean that what Hornsboro really had was a *photocopy* of the actual letter, and that your friend Jimmy remained in possession of the original."

"Exactly right," Henry agreed. "Besides, I can't see Jimmy handing over the physical letter to anyone. When Jack and I talked to him, he did not seem the least bit interested in letting any of his artifacts out of his possession. I think it's safe to say that Jimmy allowed Hornsboro to take a picture of the letter, just like he let Jack do when we met with him."

"You need to talk to the other fellow again—your buddy, Walt. I think you called him Walt. Right? The fellow you were just talking to—that was Walt?"

"Yeah, Walt," Henry said. "You're right. Good chance he was with Jimmy at the bar when Hornsboro met with him."

Henry immediately redialed Walt's number, but there was no answer.

"He's not picking up," Henry declared and he clicked off his attempt. "If I can't reach him yet today, we'll have to catch him at the bar tonight. Hopefully."

"I'll tell you what I think we should do right now," Kate said. "I say we head over to the bar and find him there. What was that? Seven Stallions. Right? What if we go there right now and poke around. I think that it's the chief watering hole in Deadwood. Even if Walt isn't there right now, you could call him—keep calling him—until you get hold of him.

"And, just maybe, someone else at the bar might have some information. Whaddya think?"

"Makes sense. The bartender there might be able to help us. Mikey. He seemed like a pretty savvy guy. I hope he's working today."

"And the other night—when Jimmy met with Hornsboro.

Hope he was around that night as well."

"Yeah. Well, someone was sure as hell working then, and whoever's on right now would know who that'd be. Let's go find out."

They were still several miles out of Deadwood at the time Henry had been talking to Walt. So by the time they reached Main Street in Deadwood it was pushing five in the evening.

"Not too early to start drinking, is it?" Kate asked, half concealing her smile.

"Who the hell cares what time it is?" Henry retorted. "It's what we do best. I should add that. Drinking is what I do best. Besides, this is Deadwood. Most everyone here is drinking and gambling—or serving those who are so occupied. It's that kind of a town."

Ten minutes later they were approaching downtown Deadwood.

"Would you look at that?" Kate asked rhetorically, sitting up in her seat and leaning forward to get a better look. "They've still got part of the street blocked off like it was a crime scene."

What Kate was alluding to was the yellow plastic tape that read, "Police Line Do Not Cross." It blocked off entrance to all the buildings on the north side of Main Street along the stretch where Jimmy had been struck. Not only did it cordon off the sidewalk in front of those buildings, all of which were commercial enterprises, but it also blocked off half of westbound Main Street.

"They obviously regard Jimmy's death as a crime," Henry said.

"Yeah," Kate agreed. "It would be interesting to know what they suspected—if they're investigating it as a homicide, or a hit-and-run. We'll have to ask around about that as well."

Once Henry got parked, he and Kate made their way into the saloon and walked directly up to the bar.

"Grady," Henry said, reading the bartender's name tag. "I guess Mikey isn't working today."

"Not right now," Grady answered. "He should be in shortly, though. What can I get ya?"

"Two Coors Lights would be great," Henry said, finding two seats directly in front of the tap. "Would prefer it on tap, if you got it."

"I'm famished," Kate interjected. "Can you make us each a BLT?"

Grady nodded and smiled. And just moments later brought over an amazing tall stack of homemade bread, toasted, six thick bacon slices, fresh tomatoes layered with deep green rich lettuce, and a side of fries with the skins on. All were served in a black wire basket lined with a commercial restaurant paper showing "daily news" from the last century.

"You know Mikey pretty well?" Grady asked as he continued setting the first two mugs of cold Coors down on the bar right in front of them. He then grabbed two more mugs and started to fill them.

"Met him once," Henry said. "The other night. My friend Jack and I were in here for nearly two hours. We were lifting a few with two of your regulars—Walt Silverman and James Jackson. I suppose you know those two pretty well. Right?"

The mention of James Jackson and Walt Silverman stopped the bartender cold. He turned and walked back to Henry.

"You heard about Jimmy. Right?" he asked softly, leaning in toward Henry so as not to be heard by others. "You heard about his accident?"

"Yes, I just learned that he got hit by a car. Was it serious?"

"Hell yes! The poor bastard's dead."

"No shit! How'd that happen?"

"Not sure. The sheriff's still investigating. Hit-and-run."

"Oh my God! And they don't have any idea what happened—that is, who hit him?"

"All I've heard is that there was this big, black SUV—quite new. It ran a stop sign right here on Main Street, crossed over the centerline, and creamed poor Jimmy as he was crossing. He was headed here! Poor guy. Messed him up real bad. Never hit the brakes, either. Mikey was working at the time. He didn't hear a thing. Not until people started screaming."

"Do they have any idea who did this? Deadwood is not a huge city, after all. Can't be that many new black SUVs."

"There's a few, but none of them turned out to be the culprit. They're still looking. That's why the street and sidewalk are still taped off."

"Any video?" Henry asked. "As many businesses as you've got along here, someone must have caught it on CCTV."

"Yeah. *We* did."

"You captured it?"

"We did. The cops were here, uh," Grady said, glancing down at his watch, "about an hour and a half ago. They picked up a thumb drive with the video of the accident. If you can call it an accident. Looked to me like the SUV picked up speed and swerved right into Jimmy. He didn't stand a chance. You could see his tracks, earlier, the driver either hit Jimmy on purpose, or else he was really high or delusional. You know, crazy, or somethin'. You know what I mean? Like maybe he was hearing voices. I don't know."

"Can we take a look at that video?" Henry asked. "Jimmy and I were working together on a project, and we had grown quite fond of him."

"I don't know about that. We've never done anything like that before—not for regular civilians. I could check with my boss when he comes in later. Actually, he won't be in until tomorrow. But I can check with him then."

"My friend here, Kate, she's a police lieutenant—homicide. We'd really like to take a look right now, while it's still fresh. Do you suppose you could make an exception?

"You're cops?"

"Kate's in homicide, and I work for a private investigator. I do the footwork. If you've got an extra thumb drive laying around, we'd pay you for it."

Henry peeled off a hundred-dollar bill and laid it down in front of the bartender.

Grady's eyes followed Henry's hand the second he initiated the motion of reaching down to his belt.

"I'll see if I have another thumb drive," Grady said as he snatched up the *Franklin* and hid it in the palm of his hand. "Be right back."

"Okay if I come back with you?" Henry asked.

"Hell, no. The boss doesn't let anyone back in the office. Security, you know."

"Even cops?"

Grady took a look at the crisp one-hundred-dollar bill, and then slid it into his pants pockets.

"Cops? Sure. You can come with me. Just don't touch a thing."

Before he left his station Grady gently touched the side of Christie, his attractive bartending partner. "Cover for me. Okay?"

he said when she turned and smiled. "I'll be right back."

She did not answer—her wink and smile conveyed her response.

Henry and Kate followed Grady to the bar's office.

Chapter 47

Once they had entered the security office, Grady closed the door behind them.

"Okay," Grady said. "Let's make this quick. I probably shouldn't be doing this.

"The sheriff had me run off the entire incident. A single camera. Nearly an hour. Ten minutes before Jimmy got hit, to twenty minutes after the ambulance picked him up. He was already dead by then. From what people told me, he died only a few minutes after the vehicle struck him. I guess it knocked him up in the air, and that when he came down, the SUV ran right over him. He didn't stand a chance."

"Can you give me the same as you gave the sheriff?"

"Yeah, sure. It's amazing how much compressed video you can put on a little thumb drive these days. I guess that's because the thumb drives are so much bigger now—not in physical size, but in capacity. And the video recorders compress the data, so it doesn't use—"

"If you've got room on that drive," Kate interrupted, "could you give us thirty minutes before the incident, and one hour after the ambulance picked Jimmy up? That would be very helpful. If you can do it."

"Should be no problem. This will only take a minute or two no matter how much we put on it."

"Did I hear you say you have only one camera covering the street?" Kate asked.

"Right," Grady answered. "That is, there's only one camera

covering that part of the street. We have two cameras mounted right side by side—one's pointed east up Main Street. That's the one that recorded the accident. The other camera is pointed west. Actually it's northeast and southwest. And then there's a camera just inside the front door."

"Could you fit all the video from that time frame onto that drive?" Kate asked. "All three cameras?"

"Yeah," Grady moaned.

It was clear to Henry that the helpful bartender was growing a little impatient with Kate's demands.

"Thanks a lot, Grady," Henry said, placing his massive right hand on the bartender's shoulder to get his attention. And with his left hand he held out a second one-hundred-dollar bill.

"The first one more than covers this," Grady said.

"We insist," Henry said. "You've been more than helpful here."

Henry did not wait for Grady to accept the money, as he tucked the bill into the front pocket of the bartender's shirt.

"We really appreciate what you're doing," Henry said. "Not so much for us, but for your friend Jimmy. I promise you that we will do everything we can to bring whoever did this to him, to bring them to justice."

"Thanks," Grady said. "But you didn't have to do that. You've already been more than generous."

"You're gonna send flowers for the funeral. Right?" Henry asked.

"Then just put 'Your Many Friends' on the card. That would be perfect. Will you do that for us?"

"Sure. Happy to. And, here's your thumb drive—it has all three cameras on it. You'll be able, I'm sure, to tell which file is from which camera. The numbers are ten, eleven, and six—the one at the door is six. But you'll know which is which, I'm sure."

"Won't be a problem," Henry said. "Kate here can handle anything. She is the big shot homicide detective, you know."

The two men laughed. Kate smiled.

"Do you work for Bill Miller, the sheriff?" Grady asked as they were leaving the office.

"No," Kate answered. "I work directly under Captain Spencer."

"Never heard of him. Is he with the Sheriff's Department?"

"No. My boss works for the New York City Police Department, Homicide Division."

"No kidding!" Grady said as he turned toward her. "New York City. What the hell does New York want here in Deadwood? Could I see some ID? Like your badge."

"Certainly," she said, opening her bag and flipping open her badge.

"Well, I'll be damned. Looks totally legit to me. Wait till I tell Jim—he's my boss—about you guys."

"What's Jim's last name?" Henry asked, seeking to deflect Grady's attention.

"Jim K. That's what we all call him. I can't pronounce his last name, we all call him Jim K. He's the only Jim K. who works here. I've really got to get back to the bar. We're gonna start getting busy about now. Especially with Jimmy getting killed and all. All the locals are gonna be in here asking questions and shit. It'll likely be a real pain in the ass. But whatcha gonna do? Everybody knew and liked Jimmy. They're gonna want to hear more about it. Hope Christie hasn't tossed your beers."

Henry and Kate clearly heard Grady's comment, but they were

not in the least concerned about losing their Coors. They had video recordings of the crime taking place, and that was all they could have hoped for.

As they walked back to the bar, Henry asked, "Grady. Were you working the last time Jimmy was in the bar?"

"Yeah, actually I was."

"Great. Then, you'd remember who was sitting at Jimmy's table. Right?"

"Not really."

At first Henry wondered if Grady was intentionally being vague in order to solicit more money from him. But then the bartender clarified his comment.

"Walt, you know Walt. Walt was at the table with Jimmy. And then there was another one of our regulars. A friend of both Walt and Jimmy—Hector. He's another old-timer. Must be in his eighties. He was there. And then there was another man. Younger. I'd never seen him before. I remember him coming in a little earlier and asking about Jimmy. I think they had set up a little meeting at the bar, and Jimmy was running a little late."

"Do you remember his name?" Kate asked.

"No—not his last name. I'm not very good with last names. His first name was Roger. That I remember. I call everyone by their first names here. So does everyone else. I doubt that any of our regulars could tell you my last name. To all of them I'm just Grady. And everyone knows who they're talking about when they mention the name *Grady*."

"Can you describe this Roger fellow?" Henry asked.

"Not really. The sheriff asked me that question too. All I can tell you for sure is that the Roger guy was not the man driving the big SUV. Different man altogether."

"And you're quite sure about that?" Henry asked.

"Positive. This Roger was very tall. Muscular build. Had long blond hair. Maybe light brown would be more accurate. But he was fairly young—maybe thirtyish. Something like that. But, the driver of the SUV—the one that hit Jimmy. He was much older. Bald, in fact. And he looked like he was overweight. You'll see what I mean when you view the video. You can probably blow it up on your computer. You'll see that the driver was at least middle-aged, and was quite heavy. At least his face looked fat. Totally unlike this Roger."

"You wouldn't have some video of Roger, would you?"

"We don't video our customers. At least we don't target them with the cameras. The cameras are placed at the doors and over the cash registers. But none look directly at where the customers are sitting. That's how management wants it. Initially, when we first had the cameras installed, they did video some of the customers. And they were as angry as hell. So the owner eliminated some of the cameras, and redirected or moved most of the others—especially the ones they complained about. Now everyone's happy, but that means that I don't have any images of this Roger."

"How about when he walked in?" Henry asked. "You said you had a camera at the doors."

"That's right. We do. But I can't get the video for you. Privacy concerns by management. I wouldn't even produce that video for the sheriff, if he were to ask for it. But he didn't. He would need a warrant to get that.

"But, there was one time a few years ago. When we got robbed. The cops wanted the video for facial recognition. We caught the guy at the main cash register, and at the front door, and we also had him getting in his car. He didn't get far. But, I can't give you what you are asking for without special permission from the owner, or my manager. Sorry."

"That's cool," Henry said. "You've given us a very good description of the guy. We appreciate that."

"Well, I appreciate the cash," Grady said as he dumped out their two beers and poured them fresh ones. "I'll be sure to send some nice flowers to the funeral home. Not sure when that funeral's gonna be—at least not yet. My guess is that the bar's gonna be pickin' up the tab for it, because Jimmy doesn't have any money—*didn't* have any money, I should say. God, it's hard to imagine that Jimmy's no longer with us. It's just sad. That's what it is. Sad."

"Thanks for the fresh ones," Henry said. "I think we're going to grab a table and see if we can get Walt over here to join us. You wouldn't have Hector's phone number, would you?"

"I can't give any phone numbers out. Sorry. But, I have a hunch that Walt will be stopping by later—he usually does. And he has Hector's number. What is this all about? The sheriff didn't even ask me that many questions about that Roger guy, or Hector. Hornblower. That was his name. It just came to me. That Roger's last name was Hornblower, or something like that."

"How about Hornsboro? Does that sound familiar?" Kate asked.

"That definitely could be. It was something like that. Hornsboro. *Very* unusual name, don't you think? That could be it. Walt would probably know better. But then, Walt's getting old. He might not know who this guy was. But Hornsblower, or Hornblower—that sounds pretty close to me."

"Well, Grady, we thank you for all your help," Henry said, as he stood and turned toward the table he'd shared with Walt and Jimmy earlier. "We're gonna grab that table now—while we still can. Before you get too busy."

"Pleasure was all mine," the bartender replied, flashing a smile as he placed his hand over his shirt pocket. "Maybe we can *talk* again down the road. Fee free."

Henry turned back to make momentary eye contact, he then smiled back and headed over to the empty table. Kate led the way.

No sooner had they taken a seat than Walt walked through the door. Henry immediately stood to his feet and motioned the old man over.

"Walt," Henry said, "I want you to meet my good friend Kate Handler. Kate, this is the man I've been talking about. This is Walter Silverman, the undisputed king of local historians."

"Kate Handler," Walt said after shaking hands with Henry, and touching the brim of his red Rapid City Rush sports cap. "Very pleased to meet you, Kate. With a last name like Handler, would that make you the wife or daughter of Jack Handler? Or is that name purely coincidental?"

Both Kate and Henry chuckled.

"You've met my dad, Henry tells me. Jack Handler is my father. But, I can assure you that he'd get a kick out of your comment about my being his wife. I don't recall that ever happening before. I'll be sure and share that with him next time I talk to him."

"So," Walt said, after he was comfortably seated. "I take it that Jack won't be joining us tonight?"

"That's right," Henry said. "Jack got called away on business—a bit of an emergency."

"So, he brought his daughter in to take his place?"

"Not exactly," Henry said. "It just turned out that way—Kate had a little time off, and she decided to spend it with you and me. We should be honored—I know I am. Kate is a very accomplished professional police detective. She is a lieutenant in the New York City Police Department, Homicide Division."

"Really?" Walt said. "That is impressive. Maybe you can solve our latest crime here in Deadwood. I'm sure Henry told you about Jimmy, my good friend. He was struck down right outside this bar. In broad daylight. Hit-and-run, it was."

"Have the police declared that to be a homicide?" Henry asked. "I know it looks suspicious, but is it official yet?"

"I don't know about the official part," Walt replied. "But, what else could it be? Right after the truck hit Jimmy, you could see the tracks. The driver crossed over both lanes of traffic, and ran a stop sign, all just to hit Jimmy. Even if alcohol or drugs played a part, I can't see something like that happening unless it was *totally* intentional. And then, the driver was alert enough to pull back over in his own lane and avoid hitting opposing traffic. But, he never stopped—he just kept going. What do you think, Henry? Don't you think that sounds like it was on purpose?"

Henry hesitated to respond immediately. He sensed that whatever he might say would eventually get back to the sheriff. He tried to weigh his words carefully.

"For sure the sheriff has got a challenge here," Henry finally said.

Walt leaned forward toward Henry, awaiting his next words. Kate was silent as well.

"We do understand that Jimmy and you had met right here at

the bar just the other evening. Just like you and he shared drinks and conversation with me. Isn't that right?"

"Yeah. We did."

"And who else was with you?" Henry asked. "I understand that another man joined the two of you, and then that the *three* of you spent some time talking—over an hour. Right?"

"We did," Walt admitted. "And we had company. Hector Cruz joined us. And a man—an out-of-towner—Roger. I forget his last name."

"Could it have been Roger Hornsboro?"

"Could have been," Walt said. "Sounds about right. He'd stopped in the bar and Grady introduced us. He had questions about the same shit you asked us about. Going back to the 1920s. This Roger guy was very excited about one of the letters Jimmy found after he talked to you. Later that night, he went back through his stuff and he found a letter that had somehow been saved by his aunt, or his mother. The one who worked in the local post office. I forget if it was his aunt or his mom. Anyway, Jimmy found this letter that had never been delivered, for whatever reason. It ended up in the papers that Jimmy found and saved. It never meant much to him until you brought all this stuff up."

"A letter?" Henry asked. "What sort of letter? Did he actually have a copy of it with him the other night?"

"Better than that. He had the *original* letter—intact, just like it was when it was originally opened back in 1924, I think."

"What was in it?" Henry asked. "The letter, I mean. Do you recall what it said? Even in general terms."

"It was a long letter. I don't remember much, except it was long and sad."

"Sad?"

"Yeah," Walt said. "It was very sad. I think it was from the wife or ex-wife of someone named Isaac. Could have been your Isaac Pierce, I suppose. Could have been. And she was leaving town, and taking her two young sons with her, and moving back to a place called Newberry. I think it was in Michigan. It was very, very heart-wrenching. Almost like this woman, Marie. I think her name was Marie, or maybe Maria. It was like this woman was trying to patch things up with her husband, or boyfriend, Isaac. Like she really wanted to stay in Deadwood, but that she felt he didn't want her to. That's how it sounded.

"I really think that it could have related to one of the brothers you were talking about. Can you recall their names, now? But there was a brother, an older brother to Isaac that was mentioned in the letter. I think his name was Edward, just like the one you mentioned. I think. And it was almost like this Marie was trying to win this Edward guy over—like she almost needed, or thought she needed, his permission to stay in Deadwood. And she felt like Edward wanted her gone. That's how it sounded, and it was very sad."

"Did she mention a kid?" Henry asked.

"You know," Walt said. "I had too many beers that night. You guys had bought them for us. We both—Jimmy and me—wanted to thank you. Mikey was on that night. And he just kept bringing us fresh beers. I had way too many. So did Jimmy. But there was a kid mentioned. This Maria did have a son. But I don't recall that his name was Billy. I thought at the time that it could have been the kid you were talking about: William could be Billy. But, I don't know that for sure. Could have been. Was the mother named Marie? Jimmy and I didn't remember for sure if that was it. Was it?"

"It was Maria," Henry assured him. "Do you know where that letter is now? Did he hand it over to this Roger Hornsboro?"

"No. Not the letter itself. However, he did let this Roger snap a picture of the letter. It was two pages long. With writing on one side."

"And, did Jimmy then take the letter itself with him when he left the bar?" Henry asked.

"As far as I know. I'm pretty sure he did. It would not have been like him to just hand any of his info over to anybody. He would allow people to take pictures, make copies—stuff like that. But the actual letter, he would not have let it out of his sight. At least, that's always been his way. He's very proud of the stuff he's accumulated through the years, and that's just the way he is. Or, rather, the way he was. God, I just can't get used to having him gone. Damn!"

Walt paused for a moment and looked down at his hands folded on the table. It was almost as though he were about to cry. And then a man whom Henry had never met walked up and touched him on the shoulder.

"How ya doin'?" he said to Walt as he leaned down to get a good look at him. "Are the arrangements all set? Anything I can do to help?"

"Oh, hi, Hector," Walt replied. "I stopped over at the funeral home earlier. I just had to get outta there. It was getting to me. I needed a beer."

"Pull up a chair, Hect. Let me introduce you to my friends. This is Henry—sorry, Henry, but I forgot your last name. Anyway, this is Henry and this beautiful young lady is his friend, Kate Handler. I do remember *your* last name.

"And this is my old friend Hector Cruz. He was also a good friend of Jimmy's. I've known Hector since I went to high school here in Deadwood. That's been a very long time ago."

Henry stood to greet Hector.

"Mr. Cruz," Henry said, "it's a real pleasure to meet you."

"Call me Hector, or, like Walt here, you can call me Hect. I think he's the only person I know who calls me by that—Hect. But, I answer to it. It's just that *nobody* I know calls me Mr. Cruz."

Hector was decked out in his Sunday best, which consisted of a handsome top-grain leather cowboy hat made of lambskin and cowhide with a reptile texture crown. His jacket had long fringes, and was decorated with beading and bones. But his boots—they were a different story—they looked like they had been handed down from earlier generations. They looked well-worn and genuine.

"You got it!" Henry said as he sat down. "Then, Hector, I understand that you were here with Walt and Jimmy the other night when Jimmy was showing off a letter he had from the 1920s. Do you remember that?"

"I do," Hector said. "But are you some kind of cop? I like to know who I'm talking to."

"Actually, I'm not a cop, but I do work for a private investigator—Jack Handler. And this lady to my left, Kate Handler, she is Jack Handler's daughter. And, she is a cop—an off-duty police officer from New York City."

"Then is this some kind of official business? Like an investigation?"

"Nothing official at all," Henry said. "We're just trying to piece together some information about one of my relatives who passed away, trying to find out if my cousin stands to inherit some money. Jimmy was helpful to us earlier this week, when we were at this same bar—sitting at this very table, I think. And please, Hector, sit down and join us."

"Whoever or whatever," Hector said. "That whole thing has certainly got people around here all worked up. That other guy—Roger something. The one who was asking all the questions the other night. And snapping pictures with his phone. I don't remember his last name. That fellow seemed to be taking a lot of interest in some of the same sort of stuff. He was trying to find out about a woman—someone named Maria. That was my mother's name—God rest her soul. That's how I can remember that name. I don't remember the last name. But it was very sad about this Maria woman. Very sad. I think she was moving back to Michigan, but she didn't really want to. Had a baby through a man that wasn't her husband. At least, that was my take on it. Named the boy William. I remember that too because that was my father's name. Guillermo, that was actually my father's name. That's Mexican for William."

"Do you remember any of the last names?" Henry asked. "Either William's last name or Maria's last name?"

"Pierce. That was one of the last names. I think hers. And her husband's. But he wasn't the biological father. Isaac Pierce and Maria Pierce. And the baby's name was William. But I forgot if he had a different last name. Might have. Can't say. Had too many beers. They were free that night. Somebody had bought them for us."

"And you're lookin' at him," Walt told his friend. "Henry, here, he's the guy I told you about. One of them. The other one was named Jack Handler. And Kate here is Jack Handler's daughter.

Jack and Henry paid for the beers we were drinking the other night."

"Really? Thanks!" Hector said as he reached out to shake Henry's hand for the second time. "That was mighty damn nice of you. I sure did take advantage of it. That's why my memory might be a little blurry. I don't remember how many bottles I had. Maybe five. I usually don't drink more than three. Three's generally my limit—so I might have overdone it—free beers and all. You know what I mean. Thanks again."

"Totally welcome," Henry said. "Happy to do it. In fact, the beers are on me tonight—that is, if no one objects."

Henry threw up his hand and bellowed, "Hey, Grady, got a minute?"

The bartender, hearing Henry's beckon, glanced up at him and nodded. A minute later he wiped his hands on his apron and bolted off toward their table with a huge bowl of seasoned pretzels.

"Henry, what can I do for you?"

"Here," Henry said, handing Grady yet another Franklin, "this should cover our drinks over here for the evening. But I'll check in with you before I take off. We can square up then, in case we get really thirsty over here."

"Terrific. I'll let your waitress know about our arrangement."

"Thanks, Grady. And you can send her over here now. I think my new friend Hector could use a beer. What's her name, by the way?"

"Liz. Liz is taking care of you tonight."

"Thanks."

Grady immediately found Liz and intercepted her on the way back to the bar.

"My friends over at that table," he said to her as he pointed out where Henry was sitting. "Henry and friends. They need your attention. And they are all paid up for the evening. Just keep a tab on what they order."

"Then I don't have to turn over anything at the bar?"

"Right. Whatever they give you is yours."

"Got it. Thanks." Liz then spun around and headed over to where Henry and the gang were sitting.

"Okay, Henry," Liz said leaning over so she could lay her order pad on the table, while at the same time providing Henry and the others a very sizable view of her equally sizable cleavage. "What can I get you?"

"What are you drinking tonight?" Henry asked Hector.

There were 10 top beers listed on a chalkboard above the bar. Henry pointed out the list, and Hector studied it carefully. He read each brew out loud—mispronouncing most: "Oatmeal Stout – Miner Brewing Co. (Hill City, SD); Farmhouse Ale – Wooden Legs Brewing Co. (Brookings, SD); Grace Anne Stout – Bitter Esters Brewhouse (Custer, SD); Naughty Redhead Imperial Red Ale – Sick N Twisted Brewing Co. (Hill City, SD); Wickedly Charming Chili Ale – Crow Peak Brewing (Spearfish, SD); Hot Mam – Sick N Twisted Brewing Co. (Hill City, SD); Mjolnir (Thor's Hammer) – Crow Peak Brewing (Spearfish, SD); Pile O' Dirt Porter – Crow Peak Brewing (Spearfish, SD); Buffalo Bitter – Firehouse Brewing Co. (Rapid City, SD); and Chukkar English Pale Ale – Firehouse Brewing Co. (Rapid City, SD)."

When he had finished, he announced that, "I think Coors Light would be great—on tap."

Henry was more than a little surprised at Hector's choice.

"Then Coors all around," he said, "if that works for Walt."

"That'd be fine," Walt said.

"Then, easy enough. Just bring us a couple of pitchers and some glasses, or mugs—whatever you like to use. And we'll take care of serving it up."

"You got it."

Liz made a beeline to the bar and ordered two pitchers and four frosty mugs. When she set the mugs down on the table she began filling them. When she was finished she distributed them around the table and prepared to leave.

"Hang on," Henry said as he reached out with a twenty-dollar bill. "This is for you. We've already taken care of the tab with Grady."

"Thanks, Henry," she said as she headed to another table.

After they all had taken a couple swigs of their cold Coors, and began to munch on the salty snacks in front of them, Henry ventured a question: "Hector, what do you remember about the other night? When you were here with Walt and Jimmy, and the other gentleman. Do you recall the name of the third fellow?"

"Roger. His first name was Roger."

"Yeah, that's what Walt was thinking, too," Henry agreed. "What can you recall about the gist of the conversation? I think he was mostly talking to Jimmy, is that right?"

"*He* was doing most of the talking. Asking questions, mostly."

"About what?" Henry asked. "This Roger was asking questions about what sort of things?"

"His father was from these parts, he said. And his grandparents. I don't remember the names, exactly, maybe Walt could do better with that."

"I've already talked to Walt about it. I'm most interested in how you remember the evening—what were Jimmy and Roger talking about. And anything else, of course."

"Okay," Hector said. "You must realize, I was in it for the free beers. And, by the way, thanks again. Anyways, Jimmy had brung his roller cart—the one with all the pictures and other shit in. He's so damn proud of that. Anyways, Jimmy was tossing out picture after picture, trying to find one that this stranger would recognize. Jimmy really likes to please."

"Damn it," Hector said, catching himself mid-tear, "it's hard to think about—Jimmy being gone and everything. All he ever wanted to do was have people like him. To show off his stuf, and be appreciated."

Hector took off his hat out of respect for his dead friend. It exposed his white head of hair, which he had pulled back in a short ponytail. His leathery skin and deep wrinkles were illuminated by the tiny mason jar candle in the center of the table. He was deeply saddened this day by the sorrowful loss of his friend.

"That's what most everybody wants out of life," Kate interjected. "His ability to share his pictures, and his knowledge of the past, that's what made him feel relevant. It gave value to his life. And all you guys, his friends, you all added to it for him. You were all good friends, and he knew it."

"It's just a damn shame that someone did that to him," Hector said after blowing his nose. "Some people are saying that the guy that hit him, that he did it on purpose. That it wasn't an accident at all. Do you think that could be true? That somebody murdered Jimmy?"

"Well," Walt said, "that's sure as hell how it looks to me. Did you see those tracks? When they were fresh? I don't know—"

"It's terrible that your friend had to die like that," Henry interrupted, "but now it's the job of law enforcement to get to the bottom of it and—"

"Kate," Walt came back, "you're a cop, a real big city detective, how do you see it?"

"I don't have enough information to draw any conclusions. The sheriff will get to the bottom of it. It's his job. He's got the necessary resources to investigate it the proper way. He'll get it all figured out, and if the evidence dictates that someone intentionally singled out your friend for harm, the sheriff will figure out who it was, and issue a warrant. But right now, I would not be able to reach any conclusions. None."

"And I think that's how it has to go," Henry added. "But what I'm interested in finding out tonight is why Roger found the materials Jimmy was showing him was so interesting. How about it, Hector, what do you remember about that?"

Hector wanted to help them get to the bottom of this quest for truth—basically, to not let Jimmy's death be in vain.

"This guy, Roger, he looked at probably a hundred or more old, smelly pictures—all from the 1920s, I think. At least most of them were from the twenties. Right, Walt?"

Walt kept his silence, but did nod affirmatively.

"But then," Hector said, "then Jimmy suddenly remembered that he had a whole file of letters. I think that up to that time he had basically forgotten about the letters. He had just been showing Roger his pictures. Pictures *are* more interesting. You know what they say: 'A picture is worth a thousand words.'"

Hector hesitated after his quote as though awaiting an agreeing comment by Henry, but when he saw that none was forthcoming, he continued.

"After he had showed Roger a dozen or so letters, Jimmy pulled one out of the file and glanced through it himself. And then it was as if a light came on inside Jimmy's brain. He said something like, 'Oh my God!' after he'd read it.

"I don't think he'd ever read it before—not really. I'm not sure exactly what it said, because he did not show it to Walt and me, but this guy, Roger, it had the same effect on him as it did on Jimmy. Even more."

"What did Roger say when he read it?" Henry asked.

"I don't remember exactly, but he was excited. Right, Walt?"

"Yeah. He sure was. He said something like, 'Where did *this* come from?' And Jimmy explained that his relative—his aunt or mother—was the postmistress at the time, and this letter was dropped off, but it did not have a stamp, and instead of sending it out postage due, she just hung on to it. And it stayed there—never actually being posted."

"That's how I remember it too," Hector agreed.

"Can you recall what was in the letter?" Henry asked.

"Like I said, Walt and I didn't read it. We just heard what Jimmy and this guy were saying about it. By the way, this Roger guy was new in town. None of us had ever met him before. His family was from this area, I guess, or so he said. But he was from somewhere out-of-state. Do you think he might have had something to do with Jimmy's death?"

Kate again jumped in at that comment.

"That would be speculation. I'm sure the sheriff will pursue every angle until he figures out who was responsible for Jimmy's death. And if a crime was actually committed, then it will be up to his department to investigate it. I'm sure he'll check out this Roger Hornsboro to find out if he might be connected to your friend's death in any way. But we really should avoid uninformed speculation. It can be most unproductive, and almost always proves to be inaccurate. Rest assured, the sheriff will figure it all out."

Kate sat back in her chair, and with her view of the entire bar, she sensed that this group of four should be safe from any threats, at least for the moment. However, as was always the case, her confidence was bolstered by the knowledge that *Mr. Glock* was at her disposal.

"As far as the letter is concerned," Henry repeated as he poured Hector another mug, "from what Jimmy and Roger were saying, what do you remember about the letter's content? Like, who it was from, who it was to, and just what was it that the writer was trying to say?"

Chapter 48

Hector took a long swig on his brew, and said, "It was written by a lady named Maria, I think. Pretty sure her name was Maria. It was very sad. She had just given birth. A boy. She named him William. I remember that name. Now I come to think of it, I'm pretty sure that the name Owens was also in there. I'm not sure if that was her name, or someone else's. Don't know that. I didn't read the letter. And Pierce. That name was also in the letter. Right, Walt?"

This time Walt did not respond.

"I'm pretty sure about those four names: Maria wrote the letter. And William was mentioned. I'm sure about that. And the names Owens, and of course, Pierce. Those names—the four of them—I believe were all in that letter."

"What else do you recall?"

"Thanks for the beer," Hector said as he prepared to continue.

"Like I said, the whole tone of the letter was very sad. The woman, Maria, was telling someone that she had decided to move back to Michigan. To some small town I'd never heard of—Mayberry, or something like that."

"Could it have been *Newberry*?" Henry asked.

"That sounds right, but I don't know. I think *berry* was part of it. Could have been *Newberry*. I just don't know."

"Okay," Henry said. "That's good enough. Just go on and remember what you can."

"She was sad. Sounded almost desperate. She basically pleaded to whoever she was writing this letter to, she wanted him—pretty sure it was sent to a man—to forgive her and take her back. Don't know because I didn't actually read the actual letter, but my guess is that she was begging the husband to somehow forgive her. That she really still loved him and wanted him to raise the baby. William could have been the baby's name. I think it was."

"But you don't know that for a fact, do you?" Henry asked.

"No, but I think that's what this Roger was saying when he was talking to Jimmy, that this Maria was going to move back to Michigan if things couldn't be worked out with her husband. That's how it sounded. And, like I said, that was about the time I was drinking that fifth beer. And, you got to remember, I made at least three trips to the john during that time as well. So I would have missed a lot of what went on.

"In fact, that last time I went—takin' a leak—when I got back, this Roger guy was already gone."

"So, you really don't know if he took that letter with him, or if he left it with Jimmy, do you?" Henry asked.

"I didn't see how it ended between Jimmy and this guy. But Walt here, he was at the table when the man left. Right, Walt?"

"Yeah, I was there when he left. He offered to buy the letter from Jimmy. Offered him a hundred dollars—five crisp twenties. But Jimmy wouldn't give up the letter. So the guy, Roger, asked if he could snap a picture of the letter—it was two pages. Actually, it was two pages, but on one sheet of stationery. Anyway, Jimmy said it was fine with him if he took a picture with his cell phone. And, so he did. He shot a few, in fact, until he got what he wanted.

"And then he excused himself and left. But, as he stood up to leave, he slid the five twenties over to Jimmy saying, 'Here, take the money. I really appreciate your help.'

"Jimmy refused to take it, but the man insisted. It was just pride on Jimmy's part. I know damn well that he could use the cash. Hell, all of us old guys could use some extra cash. He's on social security just like the rest of us. An extra hundred would help any of us. So, Jimmy did not put up too much of an argument. Just enough to save face. But right after the fellow left, Jimmy scooped it up and stuck it in his pocket.

"And as he did," Walt continued his story with a chuckle in his voice, "Jimmy made some stupid comment about how rude it was to try to buy him off like that, that he was happy to help, and that it was insulting to him that this stranger automatically assumed that he—Jimmy that is—needed the money. So, I don't get what he was beefing about. Hell, somebody offer me a hundred bucks, for virtually nothin' at all, I'm gonna take the cash and not complain. Jimmy's just proud. He couldn't help bein' that way, I suppose."

At that point Walt got this far-away look in his eyes, and he began to tear up.

"That's just the way Jimmy was. *Very* proud. But he'd give you anything he had. No matter. Jimmy was one damn good friend. And he was generous to a fault."

"Exactly right," Hector chimed in. "Never really discussed it before, but my gut would have told me that Jimmy would not be willing to sell any of his treasures. But he'd be okay with someone taking pictures of them. So that doesn't surprise me none. That's just Jimmy."

"Yeah," Kate said, looking directly at Hector with her big beautiful brown eyes. "That's exactly how I've come to see your friend. Even though I never physically met Jimmy, I feel like I know him a little. And I like him as such. You are both very blessed to have had a good friend like Jimmy Jackson."

And then Kate looked directly at Walt and said, "There's just no doubt about that.

"But, on a little different note," she continued, "I have another question. Actually, it is really along the same lines. The letter that Jimmy showed to this guy, Roger Hornsboro, where do you think it ended up? I think you are saying that Roger left here with an image of that letter on his phone—"

"He had a couple images," Walt interrupted. "Several, in fact. I'd guess he shot it maybe ten or more times."

"Right," Kate responded. "He obviously did not leave empty-handed. He had what he'd come after, it seems. But, do we know what happened to the original letter? Jimmy left with it. Right?"

"That's right," Walt said.

"What do we know about what happened to it after he left?"

"We don't know anything. All we could assume is that he had it in his apartment, with the rest of his collection."

"But, what about this morning? When he got hit out front. He was pulling that suitcase, and all the pictures and whatever else that was in it, it got strewn about the street and sidewalk. Right?"

"I guess it did."

"Do you think that the letter from that Maria might have been in it at that time?"

"Don't know about that," Walt said. "Probably a good chance it was."

"Why do you suppose Jimmy was still pulling that suitcase around the next morning?" Kate queried. "Doesn't that sound a little curious to you fellows? On any given day, would not your friend have left his collection at home? I mean, if he was going out for breakfast, would it not have been his custom to leave all that stuff back in his apartment? Why would he have had it back out the next day?"

"I really don't know," Walt said. "It does sound a little strange. Maybe this guy, this Roger, maybe he wanted to get another look at it, or something. Or, it could be that he wanted to go through Jimmy's stuff some more, looking for other objects that he found interesting. I didn't talk to Jimmy between the time he left the bar, and when he got himself kilt out front. So I don't know what he was up to. But, if this Roger had called him to set up another meeting to go through his shit, he would have jumped at the chance. Hell yes. He would have thought that there was more money in it for him, and he would have been very eager to show it to him again."

"Or, to someone else," Kate said. "Right? As far as you know, had someone else called him, he would have been willing to show his pictures and letters to another interested party. So, perhaps that is what was happening. Is that possible?"

"Hadn't thought of it like that," Walt said. "But, that would explain why he was carting that stuff around again—this Roger guy, or someone else, might have called him up to meet with him again."

"Did Roger Hornsboro ask for Jimmy's phone number? As far as you know."

"Absolutely," Walt responded immediately.

"He's right," Hector agreed. "As soon as this guy read that one letter, he immediately asked for Jimmy's phone number, and he gave it to him. I heard all that."

"So, for whatever reason that your friend had his collection out the next morning," Kate asked, "can we assume that it is quite likely that the letter we're talking about, that it was in the case at the time he got hit?"

"That'd be my guess," Walt said.

"Mine too," Hector agreed.

"Then," Henry said, "it is even likely that that very same letter might have been strewn out on the street, or on the sidewalk, when Jimmy got hit."

"Probably was," Walt replied. "It would seem likely, I mean."

"Okay, then," Kate said. "Who then ended up with it? Do we know?"

"I don't know. Somebody did pick all the shit up and stuck it back in the suitcase. I was out there pretty quickly. People were screaming. I saw this guy picking it all up. The suitcase appeared messed up, but he was poking it all back in it even so. The wind was not making it easy. Could have been the 25mph gusts that frequently roll through that area. He had to chase down some of it. But we were all interested mostly in Jimmy. It was clear that he was seriously hurt, but he was still alive at that time, and talking to us. He was in shock. I don't think he knew how badly he was messed up. But, we could see that he was real bad hurt. His guts were actually hanging outside. You could see them. And he was bleeding badly. His legs were broken—both of them. The bones were poking through his skin. Anyone who saw him knew he was dying. But he didn't know that. His only worry was for someone to pick up his shit. I told him someone was taking care of it, and that he shouldn't worry about it. It was all being taken care of.

"It was then that he started to die. You could see it. He started slurring his words badly, and going in and out.

"When this was happening, I didn't pay any attention to his stuff. I don't recall the man who was picking it all up, and I don't remember him bringing it over when he was done. And when I saw Jimmy was dying, I forgot all about it. I don't know what finally happened to it. Do you know where it went, Hector?"

"I don't know nothin' about the whole thing. I didn't see anything. I was sleepin' off a hangover. I'm not used to drinking that much."

"I think we're just about done here," Henry said. "I just have a couple more questions, if it's okay with you fellows."

"Sure, it's okay with me," Hector said.

"How about you, Walt. Can you give us a few more minutes?"

"Sure. Jimmy was my good friend. Anything to help."

"Great," Henry said. "Just a little more and we can wind this up. I know it's been difficult for both of you."

Neither Walt nor Hector responded. They were both eager to wind up the meeting and get on with their mourning of their good friend.

"As far as the fellow who gathered up all of the stuff that belonged to Jimmy," Henry said, "was he at all familiar to either one of you? That is, had either of you ever seen this man before?"

"I didn't know him," Walt answered quickly.

"Neither did I," Hector said. "In fact, I don't think I even saw him at all. I got there after Jimmy had passed. All that stuff had occurred before I got there."

"In fact," Walt immediately followed, "he wasn't dressed like a local. I'd say he was from someplace else."

"What do you mean by that?" Kate asked.

"He was wearing a black turtleneck sweater," Walt said. "And a knit hat, I think. He had some sort of hat on. And it wasn't a baseball cap. I think it was a knit hat. Not something I'd expect to see very often around here. Especially with the black sweater. I dunno. It just felt out of place to me, now I think about it."

"How about the driver of the vehicle that struck Jimmy," Henry asked. "Do you remember him at all?"

"I didn't see him," Walt said. "I got there pretty quickly, but the vehicle that hit him had long gone. I did see the tracks, and it didn't look to me like there were any signs of the car braking. Not even after impact. It just kept going after it hit him. Just awful, it was."

"Yes," Kate said as she began gathering herself up to go. "I know that this whole thing has to be very hard for both of you. I want you both to know how much Henry and I appreciate your patience and your help."

As she stood to her feet she addressed Henry.

"I would say that were finished here, right, Henry?"

"Right," Henry agreed. "I believe we are finished here for now. If anything else comes to mind—anything we might have missed that either of you think might be useful, or if there is something new that you learn, would you please give us a call? And, Hector, I don't think we have a phone number to reach you if we need to. We do for Walt, but not for you. Would you mind giving Kate your phone number in case we need to reach out? Would that be okay?"

"Sure," Hector said as he wrote his number on a piece of napkin that he'd torn in two. "No problem."

"You guys should feel free to stick around after we leave," Henry said. "I'll make sure your tab is covered for the evening. And I'll say it again, if you think of anything, give one of us a call. I'm leaving a couple of my cards on the table. Kate's number is written on it as well. Thanks again for all the help."

Henry smiled and nodded his final goodbye, and then he and Kate headed up toward the bar in order to make provisions with Grady to keep serving the two men at the table.

As they reached the bar Grady motioned for them to slide down away from the seated patrons.

"Is it true?" he asked in a whisper. "I just heard from a deputy that the guy they found murdered just west of town, in Lead, that it was the same fellow who was in here last night—the guy who spent a long time talking to Hector and Walt. And Jimmy, of course—God rest his soul. Was it the same guy?"

"That's right," Henry said. "Roger Hornsboro—the man who met with your friends. Same guy."

"Did you know that when you came in here?"

"Not exactly," Henry said. "We knew that there was a shooting west of here, but we didn't know that it was the same fellow who was in here last night—not until Walt explained it to us. Pretty radical revelation, wouldn't you say?"

"Hell, yes!" Grady agreed. "Insane. He spent over an hour in here last night talking to Jimmy. And then, the next day, they're both dead. One of them, the guy that was shot, apparently was murdered. Is that what you heard? That's what Deputy Corker thought. I went to high school with him—Deputy Corker, that is. But he couldn't come out and say it was murder. Not until there's an official autopsy. What do *you* know about it? Was he murdered? Have you heard anything?"

"I don't want to get out in front of this," Henry said. "But, I do wonder what brought your buddy in here, Deputy Corker. Did he know that the victim had been in here last night? Or was he here for something else?"

"Oh, he knew the guy had been here all right. He took a book of our matches off him. So damn sick—the matches were covered in blood, he said. But there were some phone numbers written inside the book of matches. One of the numbers had a 'JJ' written, along with Jimmy's phone number. That's why Corker was here. He was asking about whether that guy was in here or not, and if he was meeting with anyone. He's over there talking to Walt right now. This is just too damn weird to be believable. Don't you think? Ain't it just too damn crazy weird?"

As soon as Grady announced that the deputy was talking to Walt, Henry turned to Kate and said, "We gotta be movin' along," but he never looked over in Walt's direction.

"Here's another Franklin, my friend. This should keep the boys in beers for the rest of the evening. Whatever's left over, split it up between yourself and our waitress. Okay?"

"You ain't leavin' now, are you?"

"We've gotta be goin'. Got some errands to run yet tonight. We'll be back in before we head out of town. Appreciate all the fine attention. You run a great place here."

"I'll bet Deputy Corker would like to talk to you. Hang in a minute, I'll call him over."

"No!" Henry barked in his most demonstrative whisper. "Like I said, we've got some business to attend to. We'll be meeting with the sheriff in the morning. We'll answer all his questions at that time. Gotta go. Catch you around the bend. Nice meeting you, Grady."

"Okay," Grady said. "Cool. If the deputy asks I'll tell him you had to shove off, but that you'll be talking to the sheriff tomorrow."

Kate and Henry had walked only a couple steps toward the door when Grady shouted out to them, "Hey, Henry, hold on a second. I think you might want to take a look at this." He was holding out a thick Manila envelope.

Chapter 49

When Kate and Henry heard Grady's words, they both stopped in their tracks, looked at each other, and turned back in Grady's direction.

"Maybe I should be talking to Walt about this instead of you," he said. "But, since you're here, I'll give it to you."

"Whatcha got?" Henry asked, taking a couple steps back toward Grady.

"Last night," Grady said, "after Jimmy met with that other guy, when Mikey was working. He told me about it later. While they were cleaning up they found this under the table where those guys had been sitting. I forgot it until just now. But, since you're here, I'll give it to you. Okay?"

"Sure," Henry said, reaching out to receive the very old and tattered nine-by-twelve age-stained envelope.

"I think Mikey said it had some pictures or posters in it. I don't remember. He just said that it must have slid down on one of the chairs that weren't bein' used, and when they picked them up to clean the floor, it fell under the table. You take it, and I'll be sure to let Mikey know that I gave it to you. If you have any questions about it, you can talk to him—he'll be back in for work tomorrow. Come back then if you want, and you can find out if there was anything else he knows about it, or about Jimmy. I just assume that he meant for you to have it, since you were there. And now that Jimmy is no longer among us."

"Thanks a bunch," Henry said as he quickly tucked it into his belt beneath his jacket and made his way toward the front entry.

Kate shared his desire to leave the bar expeditiously and without attracting additional attention. But it wasn't to be.

"Hey! Hey!" exploded the deputy's voice, seeming to bounce off of every hard object nearby. "Henry! Hold up, I need to ask you some questions."

Kate and Henry had made it as far as the door they were aiming for, but not through it.

"Deputy," Henry said as he turned to greet his eager beckoner. He was surprised to discover that the uniformed deputy was still nearly thirty feet away, but closing fast. Henry recognized him from the crime scene earlier that day.

"Henry. Kate. I remember seeing both of you out at the Hornsboro site."

"Yes. Of course. I believe you were the deputy who ran our licenses. Right?"

"Yup," said the deputy as he glanced around looking for an appropriate spot to conduct a mini interview. "That was me all right. Deputy Craig Corker. I realize that both of you are meeting with the sheriff in the morning. But, I do have a few questions I'd like to ask you before that. Would that be okay with you two? We could do it here, or I could take you back to our office."

"Sure, whatever you want."

"Great," the deputy said. "I'll round us up a table and we can get this over with quickly."

"Ma'am," he said as he flagged down a waitress. "Could you find us a table where we could talk? And maybe bring us over a few cups of coffee."

He then turned to Henry and said, "Coffee okay? I'd buy you a pitcher but my boss frowns on my drinking on the job. Besides, it wouldn't look very good to be drinking in uniform."

"Coffee's fine," Henry said.

The waitress looked over at the host to get his permission.

"Fourteen's open," he said. "You can seat them there."

"Follow me," she said. "Table fourteen is not in my section tonight. Your waitress will be Cheryl. I'll pass your order on to her. Right this way."

As they slid their chairs out to sit down, she said, "Three regular coffees. Will that do it?"

All three nodded their approval.

"I'm hoping this will not take long," Henry said. "We've still got some errands to run, and it's getting late. Are you sure this can't wait until the morning?"

"It'll only take me a few minutes. I'm sure, since we're all here right now, that the sheriff would want me to ask you about Jimmy Jackson. When you talked to him earlier today, he was not aware that you had met Mr. Jackson. Your friends over at that other table—Walter Silverman and Hector Cruz—just told me that you had met with Mr. Jackson at this very place the other night. They pointed you out to me when you were standing at the bar. And then I called my boss and told him. He was surprised too. I just got off the phone with the sheriff, and he suggested that I talk briefly to the two of you. So, even though you are meeting with him in the morning, he wants me to ask you a few questions tonight. Is that okay with you folks?"

"Sure," Henry said. "We want to be as helpful as we can."

"Thanks for your cooperation. I will make this as brief as I can."

"Hello," the new waitress said as she set three mugs of freshly brewed hot coffee onto the table and slid one over to each of them.

"My name is Cheryl. I'll be your server tonight. Chris said you just wanted coffee for right now. I'll check back later to take your order. Or, you can just get my attention by waving or something. Does this work for now?"

"That's just wonderful, Cheryl. If we need anything else I'll flag you down. Thank you."

"Like I said, my name is Deputy Craig Corker, and you two are?"

"Chuchip Kalyesveh. But people call me Henry. As you already know."

"And my name is Kate Handler. Lieutenant Kate Handler, New York City Police Department, Homicide Division."

"Right," the deputy said. "I recall *that* when I ran your license. Not often do we get New York homicide detectives in our county. What brings you here?"

"My father is a licensed private investigator. Henry works with him, and they are running down some leads. I just arrived. I thought I'd spend some time with my dad. But, he got called out of town on other business, so I'm just running around with Henry for a day or two. My trip is totally unofficial. It has nothing whatsoever to do with my work."

"So, Henry, you're working on a case with her father. What brings you to our county?"

"One of the principals in the investigation may have lived in Deadwood for a short time—as a child. I'm just running down some leads on him."

"And what was his name? The person you're investigating?"

"Well, that's the thing. We're not totally sure about that. We think his last name would have been Pierce, or Owens. He would have been the son of William Lawrence Owens. But we're not sure if the son ever actually turned up here, or even if the son ever existed, period. That's the nature of the investigation."

"I don't get it," the deputy said. "What would be so difficult about tracking something like that down? It's not a huge community."

"This whole matter dates back to 1924. And the possible father, that William Lawrence Owens, he was murdered before the child was even born. We are tracking the leads down to determine if there are any legitimate heirs to Mr. Owens."

"And, as Mr. Walter Silverman informed me, you met with him, and Mr. Jackson, two nights ago. What was that all about?"

"We had heard that—"

"And who exactly would that 'we' be? You and Lieutenant Handler?"

"No, Kate just got in town. Her father, Jack Handler, and I had heard that there were some old sages who frequented this bar—Walt being one of them. And Jimmy Jackson. We decided that we should sit down with these gentlemen and see what they could tell us about the subject of our inquiry. About whether or not there was a baby born to one of the women we're checking into, and if that baby—if there even was one—might have been fathered by William Lawrence Owens."

"So, did you learn anything that helped?"

"Not sure about that. Not yet. Mr. Jackson did have some information that might have been helpful. I did some checking up on that at the old cemetery the next morning. Didn't turn up anything definitive. These things can take a little time. But I'm sure you know all about that."

"Tomorrow you'll be talking to a detective—the sheriff. His background isn't *actually* as a detective. But he did take and pass the test a few years before he ran. And he officially did become a detective. But, for most of his early career with the department, he was in charge of dispatch. And now he's sheriff. He never really did detective work. But, don't get me wrong. I don't mean any disrespect. The whole department really likes this sheriff."

"I understand," Henry said. "We really liked him as well. Looking forward to meeting with him in the morning."

"Then," Deputy Corker said, "Am I to understand that, before yesterday, you had never before even met Mr. Jackson?"

"That's correct. Walt—Mr. Silverman—had suggested that we talk to Mr. Jackson. So he called him up and asked him to join us. We met with him for a while, and then Mr. Jackson decided that we should see some of his papers—very old papers, like letters, old wanted posters, old pictures, that sort of stuff. And Walt convinced his friend to bring some of it over to the bar for us to look at. And that's what he did."

"Did you find anything of interest?"

"We thought we might have. So, Jack used his camera to snap some shots of a particular wanted poster, and some various images—those that were of particular interest to Jack."

"Do you have those images tonight? I'd like to take a look at them if you do."

"Jimmy would not give us permission to keep any of his original artifacts, and all the images shot that evening were on Jack's phone. So that's where we're at on that score."

"And how can I get hold of Mr. Handler?"

"He's not taking calls right now. At least as far as I know. How about you, Kate? Has he called you in the last day or so?"

"No. Last I heard he was headed to New York on business."

"Same here."

Henry then turned back to the deputy and said, "That's all we know. I can give you his cell number, but he's not picking up."

"Does he do that often? Disappear off the face of the earth?"

"He hasn't disappeared. He's just working on a different case. And we don't happen to know anything about it. When he's ready he'll check back in with us. And when he does, we'll tell him that you'd like to talk to him. Beyond that, as far as Jack Handler's concerned, right now we can't help you."

"I'm sure the sheriff will follow up on this tomorrow. But, back to Mr. Jackson, are you telling me that Mr. Jackson did not give you any material when you met with him two nights ago? Is that what you are saying?"

"That's correct. Neither Walt nor Jimmy gave us any physical objects. We had a couple beers, looked at some of the pictures and letters that he had brought, and took some pictures of a few of them. Jack might have taken some notes, too. I can't say for sure about that. And as far as the images on his phone, I do not have any of them. I did not shoot any pictures of anything. That's exactly how it stands right now. Maybe I'll hear from Jack tonight, and if so, I'll have him send me the pictures he took, and I'll get them to the sheriff in the morning."

"Okay. Sounds fair enough. Then, the sheriff will talk to you tomorrow. I think I'm finished with this interview. You're welcome to stay and finish your coffee. I've got the check and the tip. Thanks for your help. I'll make sure and let the sheriff know that you were very cooperative."

The meeting between the three of them ended at that point. Henry and Kate excused themselves and headed again toward the door.

Once in their vehicle, Kate said, "Well, at least you were honest. As far as I could tell. Can't lie to these fellows. They don't seem very forgiving to me."

"I'm just damn glad I didn't open that envelope Grady gave me. Because right now I can honestly say that I do not know what is in it. We need to go somewhere so that I can take images of everything we've got here, and then we can hand it all over to the sheriff in the morning. Wouldn't surprise me if our deputy goes right in and talks to Grady, and then tries to chase us down. Where do you say we go to shoot it?"

"Drop me off with it at the first public restroom that you see," Kate said. "And then drive around for fifteen minutes. If he comes after you, he'll not stop us before we get it copied. Right there. What's that?"

Kate had spotted a casino/bar just up Main Street from Seven Stallions.

Henry quickly pulled in and stopped.

"Let me check my charge," Kate said as she scrutinized the status of her battery.

"It's been a long day, but it should be fine. Don't see our deputy buddy around, do you?"

"No, but you're probably right. He'll be out looking for us as soon as he talks to Grady."

Kate gathered up the Manila envelope and stepped out of the car.

"This feels pretty hefty," she said. "Better give me half an hour.

Or, better yet, I'll call you when I'm finished."

"Right. Call me when you've finished. If I don't hear from you I'll come back in half an hour."

After that brief exchange, Kate shut the door and headed for the casino entrance.

Henry, instead of pulling directly back onto Main Street, took Wall Street over to Broadway, and turned left.

Must be a coffee shop, or eatery of some sort, with a big dark parking lot, he thought. *Someplace where I can hang out until Kate gets done.* He soon found what he was looking for and proceeded to tuck his rental into a remote parking space reserved for employees. And, because the car he had rented was registered in Indiana, it did not require a front license plate—so he backed into the parking slot. *It should take my deputy at least half an hour to find my car back here,* he reasoned as he entered the diner. But, he was wrong.

He had been seated less than ten minutes when he observed Deputy Corker slowly pull up in front of his car and activate his emergency lights.

"Damn it all!" Henry muttered. "That guy is just too damn efficient. Can't believe he's found me that quickly."

Just as Henry stood to his feet his waitress walked up with his coffee.

"Hey, thanks, Traci," he said reading her name tag. "I'm gonna use the restroom. I'll be right back. I'll bet you've got some very good pies. Right? What's your most popular?"

"Oh, they're all *so* good. The sorghum buttermilk is great. But my personal favorite would be our chokecherry. That's just *my* favorite."

"Good enough for me. I'll have your chokecherry. Maybe with a scoop of vanilla ice cream. Can you do that?"

"Sure. I'll be right back with it."

As Henry walked toward the restroom he caught a glimpse of the deputy checking out his plate number.

"Damn …"

Chapter 50

Kate selected the handicap stall so she would have more room to work. She sat down and opened the unsealed envelope. She set its end on her lap and peered into the opening. "This is absolutely incredible," she said to herself. "There must be forty, fifty, maybe even sixty different objects in here. I could easily be here for forty-five minutes. If I do the job right. Maybe longer."

She then carefully tipped the envelope over and poured its contents into her hand and onto her lap. She made sure the floor beside her was clean, and then placed the empty envelope there. After adjusting her phone's camera, she briefly examined each object, and then shot it front and rear. Even if the back side of a document was blank and unmarked, she took a picture of it nonetheless. She did so because she reasoned that each piece of information, whether it be a letter, photograph, or some other sort of record, needed to have its contents, or lack thereof, thoroughly documented in order to properly support any research for which it might be called upon in the future. *Just good police work,* she told herself—Criminal Justice 101.

She was only about a dozen pieces of camera shots into her project when one particular handwritten letter caught her eye. It was not particularly long—front and back of a single sheet of stationery.

At first it caught her eye because of the handwriting itself. All of the lines were equally spaced and straight. *This is obviously the product of a woman's hand,* she reasoned. And, she was right. It was signed *Maria Pierce.*

The second she saw the name she began reading the content of the letter.

"Oh my God," she said out loud. "This is it. This is the letter that Henry was talking about. The one that got those two men killed. This is absolutely it!"

For a moment Kate had the urge to scoop everything up and deliver it all back to Henry. *This letter is much too significant to turn over to the sheriff,* she was thinking. But almost immediately her innate common sense took back over. *No, got to finish this job. And we do have to turn this over to the sheriff—tomorrow at the latest.*

And even though she had the sense that she had already captured the image of the Magna Carta, she still needed to finish the project in a professional manner.

Snap. Snap. Snap. Snap. Snap. Snap.

On and on the shooting continued. After each image was captured, Kate would stop long enough to examine the end product on her phone, and then move on to the next.

Finally, after shooting her fifty-second image, she was struck by a series of wanted posters.

"I don't believe this," she mumbled lowly. "These are the real things. These are *real* wanted posters. They've actually got the holes in where they've been tacked to the wall."

After shooting a half dozen posters, she began a cursory reading of what was printed on them. It was the last one in the group that attracted her attention the most. It read that there was a reward offered for two brothers, Edward and Isaac Smith. And the charge for which they were wanted was bootlegging.

That sounded familiar to her, so she then carefully examined the poster:

Notice

Reward of $500
Is offered by the city of Deadwood
for the capture of
Edward Smith and his younger brother
Isaac Smith.
Wanted for bootlegging
And attempted murder.
And they are suspected in other murders.
Edward is 6 feet tall, and Isaac
Is 5 feet 10 inches.
Edward is known for carrying
A long-barreled six-shooter.
He sometimes carries it in a holster sewn to his vest.
Although he is right handed, he wears
It on his left side, and cross draws
In John Wesley Hardin fashion
They have been known to work as lumberjacks.
Both men should be approached with great caution.

"That sounds a lot like how Henry described those Pierce brothers," she said to herself as she verified the image she had just taken of the poster. "A whole lot like them."

But it was when she turned the poster over to snap a picture of its underside that she nearly fell off the toilet. It read: "I've heard that these brothers have also been called by the last name of *Pierce*.

This should be checked out."

She then verified the quality of that last picture, and tucked all of the documents back into the envelope.

Before I leave here, she determined, *I'm going to send these images to Henry. Can't take any chances of them getting lost.*

Chapter 51

"Looks like your ice cream's getting melted," the officer said to Henry.

Deputy Corker had waited for Henry to dry his hands, and then he walked him back to his table. Henry did not respond to the deputy's comment. Instead, he just stoically began eating his chokecherry pie à la mode.

Finally, Deputy Corker asked the question: "Well. Are you going to tell me where Kate is? She's obviously not with you here at the diner. So, where is she?"

Henry continued to chew his pie.

And then his phone rang.

"Kate. Everything okay?"

Deputy Corker could hear the other side of the conversation only well enough to tell that Henry was talking to a woman. So, he correctly assumed who the woman was.

"Is that Kate Handler?" he asked.

Henry did not answer verbally, but he did look the deputy in the eye, smile and nod.

"Where is she?"

Again Henry did not answer. Instead he held up his index finger indicating that Deputy Corker should hang on for a minute.

The deputy was growing impatient.

"Okay, Henry. I've had it with you two. Tell me where she is, and how long it's going to take her to get over here, or I'm gonna run you in and you can spend the night in lock up. I'm not playing around with you guys anymore."

Henry then looked up at the deputy and smiled. "Just give me a couple seconds and I will let you know where she is and when she will be here. One second."

Henry then checked his inbox to be sure that he had received the images Kate had sent. And then he said to her, "All's fine here. Deputy Corker wants to see you again. When can you get over here to the diner?"

Kate responded but only Henry could hear what she said.

"Absolutely," Henry replied to her. "The deputy and I will come over immediately. We can be there in five minutes, give or take. Does that work?"

Again Kate responded.

"I'll check with the deputy," Henry said.

"Deputy Corker, Kate wants to know if we will join her over at the casino. She is without a car and would like you or me to pick her up. Can we do that?"

"Which casino?"

"I don't know the name. It's right over there on Wall Street. Only five minutes away. Can I tell her that we'll be right over?"

"Sure. You can ride with me, or drive yourself. I just don't want you to get lost. If you know what I mean."

"Terrific," Henry replied to the deputy's offer, as he got in the back of the patrol car.

"Kate," Henry said in the phone. "The deputy and I will meet you at the front entrance. Okay?"

"One more thing before you hang up," Deputy Corker said to Henry. "Grady, over at Seven Stallions, he told me that he gave an envelope to you guys. It contained some letters and pictures, and who knows what else. Do either of you have that on your person right now? If so, I would like you to hand it over."

"I don't have anything like that," Henry answered. "I could check in the car. Maybe it's in the car. Or, maybe Kate's got it. I'll ask her."

"Kate. The deputy is asking about an envelope—I guess with some pictures in it. And other stuff. Grady, from over at the saloon, he's supposed to have given it to us. Have you seen anything like that?"

"Yeah. I've got it with me," Kate answered.

"Oh, that's just great," Henry said. "The deputy will be very happy to hear that. You can give it to him when we come over. See you in about five."

Henry then turned to the deputy and said, "She's got the envelope with her, and she's just around the corner. Do you want to pick it up from her now? Or should we just hand it over to the sheriff in the morning? Your call."

"I'll take it right now. It's evidence. Or, at least it *could* be evidence. When you see the sheriff tomorrow you might ask him about it. He will probably have checked it out by then. He might just hand it back to you."

It did take Henry only a few minutes to find Kate. As they drove up to the main entrance of the casino she was already standing out front with the brown Manila envelope in her hand. Henry powered down the window and motioned for Kate to hand the envelope over the deputy—which she did.

"Get in," the deputy said to Kate. "I'll drop the two of you off back at your car."

* * *

"Well," Henry announced as she sat down beside him, while at the same time waving a goodbye at the deputy, "that should get the law off our asses for the night. I skimmed through the pictures you sent. There was a lot more information in that envelope than I had ever imagined."

"I'll say. What did I shoot? I think over a hundred images. I snapped everything—front and back. I'll catalog them later for future reference. Some of them might prove useful. Not *might*, actually. I know some of them are significant."

"Really? Did you take the time to study them?"

"No. Most of them were text documents. I didn't read them all. But, I did see the wanted poster we had discussed. That was in there. And the letter Walt and Hector talked about. It was there."

"No shit!" Henry snorted. "The letter that Maria wrote to her husband begging him to take her back? Are you sure about that?"

"Sure am. It was in that envelope with the others. I'm positive. I sent you a picture of it."

"Damn. You know, two men were murdered because of it. Apparently that letter was the main reason for the killings. And all the time, it was safely tucked away under the bar at Seven Stallions. What a waste. What a damn waste."

"It'll be very interesting to see what else we find among those documents."

"Right. Exactly. And, you know what else? The missing cell phone—the one belonging to that Hornsboro fellow. That's why his phone turned up missing. The boys said that he had snapped some images as well. Remember?"

"I would like to have some prints made of these images. So we can study them. There must be something very significant revealed in them. They must have an important story to tell."

"Yeah, right. Enough to get two men killed."

"Do you have a theory?" Kate asked.

"Theory about what?"

"Do you have an idea as to why someone would feel the need to kill other people because of something revealed by those documents?"

"Well," Henry said. "As far as motives. I think we can rule out some of them. But, *I'm* not the detective. You are. I'm sure my perspective will be a little different from yours."

"Not necessarily. Think like this. Put yourself in Walt's shoes for a minute. One of his best friends gets run down and killed. And the day before his friend is murdered, the guy he was drinking with the night before is shot and killed. Who would you suspect?"

"What are the biggies, anyway?" Henry asked. "Most common motives. I think they are: money, sex, and revenge. I'm sure there's many more, and variations. But, if there is a motive involved in this case, I'd say that it would be likely to fall under one of those headings. What do you think?"

"I would agree. Generally, that would cover it. There are others, such as greed, politics, hate, power and protection. But the ones you mentioned, they generally make the most sense."

"I'm not sure how sex would play a part here," Henry said. "But I've heard it often does."

"Another possible factor might be reputation," Kate said. "Sometimes pride is a factor. If a person fears that some news might emerge that would prove immensely embarrassing, sometimes he feels the need to kill in order to protect his reputation."

"Is that how you see it here?" Henry asked.

"I'm like you. I do not detect a clear motive. Not yet. I have found in dealing with murders, that often there are a number of people with strong motives, and that sometimes these different people have different incentives—different motivating factors. A lot of the time the people with the strongest driving reasons are also the ones with the most powerful character, and the staunchest self-control. But, while reason must always be considered, it's not necessarily the driving factor."

"So," Henry said, "we really don't know much about who has done this or that, or why."

"I'm not even so sure that we must be overly concerned about that aspect, either—at least not initially. After all, it's not our job to solve this crime, unless in doing so we are able to determine the rightful heir that you and Dad were hired to find. There is one rather important fact that has occurred to me. And that is something that you should be concerned about."

"And what is that?"

"Two of the people involved in your investigation have turned up dead—Jimmy Jackson, and Roger Hornsboro. Both of them spent a considerable amount of time sitting in the Seven Stallions bar, and both of them ended up dead."

"Are you suggesting that Walt and I, and your dad, are vulnerable as well?"

"Not that so much, but there does seem to be something that certain parties are loath to have you investigate. And, it wouldn't surprise me, if the answer to this mystery resided in those images I sent you earlier. Perhaps not the whole solution, but at least part of it. I'm looking forward to hitting them with a vengeance—perhaps even later tonight."

"Before we meet with the sheriff?"

"Possibly. I'd like to."

"Hey! Shit!" Henry said, quickly darting off to the side of the street and pulling a rapid U-turn. "Kate, did you get a good look at that car?"

Kate, who had earlier used her cell to copy most of the images from the envelope, had been fingering through the shots and so missed even seeing the car Henry was talking about.

"No! What's up?" she said.

"It wasn't the car so much. But the driver sure as hell looked familiar from that security video. The one where James Jackson was hit. Maybe it was my imagination, but it looked like that same old shit driving it."

"What are you going to do?" Kate asked. "You going to try to catch them?"

"No. Got no cause. But, if I can see where they're headed. Maybe find out who they know. It might help us to figure out who they are."

"They're probably headed home for the night. Or maybe to meet up with someone. Which car is it?"

"The Escalade. Two up."

Just then police car emergency lights flashed into Henry's rear window.

Chapter 52

"Damn it!" Henry barked. "That's Corker. He must have taken exception to my U-turn. Damn, I don't want to pull over and explain this."

"Pull over," Kate snapped. "We don't need *him* for an enemy. Or his boss tomorrow."

"Yeah. I know. …You didn't catch that plate number, did you?"

"No," Kate said. "It was a South Dakota tag. And it had seven characters. I couldn't identify them all. Only that it started with two zeros, or two Oscars, and ended with a seven. I'm pretty sure about that. You'd better pull over for the deputy. No point—"

"Yes," Henry said as he jerked the wheel to the side and stopped. "Deputy, what can I do for you?"

"Mr. Kal-yes-veh. Henry. What's your rush?"

"Sorry, deputy. I thought I spotted a friend up there. And, I thought I might catch up with him. Sorry about that."

"Oh really? Which car are you talking about?"

"The white Escalade. At least I think it was an Escalade. I couldn't really tell, though. Too far away. It was an Escalade or a fancy Tahoe."

"You can't identify the vehicle, but you think you knew the driver? That doesn't add up."

"Yeah, I know it don't make sense. It's just that he did look a little familiar to the fellow I tipped a couple beers with the other night. In the bar. It was when we were getting in our cars afterward that I saw him behind the wheel. Something about the way he hung out the window when he drove. Reminds me of this guy tonight. Did you see him? Do you know his name? I never did learn his last name?"

"Not sure. I did catch someone I recognized out of the corner of my eye. It could have been a white Escalade. If it's the same guy I'm talking about, I think his name might be *Jim*, or something."

"That could be," Henry said. "In fact that sounds like it could be right. We weren't formally introduced, but I did hear others mention his name. *Jimbo* comes to mind. But I'm not sure. Do you remember his last name, by any chance?"

"That's not what I pulled you over for. As long as you're gonna be driving in our county, I want you to obey the laws. And it's against the law to pull a U-turn like that inside the town of Deadwood. In fact it's against the law to do that wherever it's unsafe."

"Yes, deputy, I am truly sorry. I won't do it again. I promise. Not in your county. But, you're sure you don't remember that guy's last name?"

"Look, I'm feeling generous. I'm not gonna give you a ticket tonight. Not as long as you can promise me you will pay more attention to your driving—to your *driving*. Can you do that?"

"Absolutely, deputy. I promise I will do a better job. Promise."

"Okay, then you can be on your way. By the way, what time are you meeting with the sheriff tomorrow? Is it first thing in the morning?"

"Ten, I believe," Henry replied. "Isn't that right, Kate?"

"Ten in Sheriff Miller's office. That's right."

"Don't be late," the deputy said. "Just a friendly warning. The sheriff does not have much patience with *any* of that *being late shit*."

"We'll be on time," Henry said through a smile. "Thanks for the heads up. Then, are you finished with me for tonight?"

"You tell me," Deputy Corker said, "Am I?"

Henry smiled and replied, "I'll do my best, deputy."

"Have a good night, folks," Deputy Corker said, tipping his hat. "And, by the way, I don't think that Jim guy was the one you were talking to at the bar. If it's the fellow I'm thinking about. That Jim guy is rich. And I don't think that he hangs out drinking at the local bars."

"Oh? Really? I could be wrong, then. What is he, some kind of doctor or lawyer?"

"No. I think that Jim is some kind of a stockbroker. Maybe not a broker. But he deals in money, somehow. And he has a lot of it himself. But he doesn't hang out at any of the local bars as far as I know. I've never seen him drinking. He goes to my church. I don't think he even drinks."

"But you don't remember his last name?"

"I thought you said you had *mistaken* him. He wouldn't have been drinking with you, I said. So, just drop it and don't get yourself in any more trouble."

Henry watched the deputy walk back to his car.

"Damn," Henry said, "that was weird. Don't you think?"

"It was," Kate replied. "It was almost like he was trying to protect that fellow. At least, that's how it felt to me. But, there's really nothing unusual about that. He could have been a friend of the deputy—going to the same church and all."

"He was sure that the guy went to his church," Henry said.

"Which means he must have seen him there on a regular basis. That would be why he wanted me to drop it. Of course, I could even be wrong about the guy. It could have been someone else altogether. All I did is spot a guy in that Escalade that resembled the fellow in the car that ran Jimmy down. And, from that closed circuit camera, the driver tonight resembled the driver of that hit-and-run. While I didn't get a good look at either, all I can say is that my guy tonight carried a similar build, and sat in a similar fashion. I'll just have to take a closer look at that video."

Henry and Kate drove around the neighborhood for nearly half an hour but never again saw the white Escalade.

Finally Kate spoke up: "Let's head to the hotel. I'm getting tired, and I really do not expect to spot your buddy again. I'd say he's vacated the area. What do you think?"

"I agree," Henry replied. "I'm ready, too."

When he got back to the hotel Henry pulled up the video on his computer and viewed it at least a dozen times. But, when he had finished, he remained even less sure about the identity of the man shown hitting Jimmy. Just before he turned in, Kate called him and asked him what he thought about the video now.

"Can't say that it helped," he said. "All the video shows is that the driver who ran Jimmy down was a big, forty-five-ish, red-haired gent. That's about it. Definitely not enough info to warrant my checking further into the driver I saw tonight, at least not right now."

"I don't think you said anything about that driver tonight being a redhead. Was he?"

"I don't think he was. But wigs are cheap. I think what made me think that it might have been the same guy was the way he sat.

Both of them poured themselves behind the wheel in much the same manner. And they were both about the same size. I think that was what might have made me see the similarity. I don't know. I just know I need some rest."

Before they turned in, Kate and Henry discussed briefly their plans for the next day. Their intention was to sleep in until seven-thirty, and then to go down to the hotel restaurant for breakfast. They would then meet with the sheriff at ten, and hopefully pick his brain regarding some of the loose ends that remained—they could discuss the details over breakfast. And then after their meeting with the sheriff, they would chase down some of the answers that remained.

However, it did not all go exactly as planned.

At exactly six A.M. two of the sheriff's deputies—Deputy Corker being in the lead—pounded loudly on Henry's door.

"Henry Kal-yes-veh!" Deputy Corker shouted. "This is Deputy Corker from the Lawrence County Sheriff's Department. I need to talk to you right now. Please open the door. Right now!"

The loud knocking awakened Henry from a sound sleep. Not only did it wake Henry up, it was so loud that it also awakened Kate in the room next door.

"Yeah, yeah, yeah," Henry growled. "I'll be right there. Hang on a second."

That little delay was more than Deputy Corker was willing to tolerate.

"Go ahead and open the door," he ordered the desk clerk, whom he had brought with him.

So, before Henry had been able to slip on his trousers, the door opened until it was suddenly halted by the safety chain.

"Remove this chain and open the door!" the deputy barked. "Do it now!"

Henry drew his belt snug and approached the door. He could see through the small opening that Deputy Corker had drawn his sidearm.

"Dammit all!" Henry muttered loud enough for the deputy to hear. "This is just simply ridiculous."

He closed the door and unlatched the safety chain, and then opened the door fully.

"There you go, deputy," he said. "Come on in."

"We'll take it from here," the deputy said, excusing the desk clerk. He then stepped fully into the room with his partner following. The desk clerk remained in the corridor.

"Where's the girl—Kate?" Deputy Corker said. "I need to see her too."

"She's in a different room," Henry said. "What the hell is this all about? We're not supposed to meet with the sheriff until much later—ten o'clock. We haven't even had breakfast yet. What the hell are you doing here *now*? It's only six o'clock!"

"Some new stuff came up," the deputy said as he slid his Glock back into his holster. "There's been a change of plans. The sheriff wants to see you two in his office now."

"Shit. You mean it can't wait until ten? What the hell's going on here?"

"Look, Kal-yes-veh," Deputy Corker said, slowly placing his hand back on his Glock. "If you want to do this the hard way, we can do it the hard way. Or we can be friendly and do it the easy way. Which will it be?"

"Oh, I'll go with you. I don't want any trouble. Just let me take a piss and put my shoes on. Do you want to come in here with me? Or can I take a piss by myself?"

"Go ahead and do your thing," the deputy said. "Where's your friend? The woman?"

"Lieutenant Kate Handler?" Henry said through a cold stare. "You're talking about Detective Kate Handler? Like I said, she's in another room. I'll get her as soon as I finish. Is that okay?"

"*Detective* Kate Handler," the deputy repeated. "Did you call her detective? What kind of a detective is she? Where does she work?"

"Lieutenant Handler is a homicide detective in the New York City homicide department. Now, are you going to let me take that piss, or do I need to go get her right now? What's it gonna be?"

After the second deputy had walked into the hotel room the door had automatically closed behind him, but did not latch. And right then Kate walked up to the door and knocked: "Hello. Henry. This is Kate. Can I come in?"

"Yeah," Henry spoke out. "Sure. Kate. Come on in. I've got some company here and they want to see you too."

"Yeah, Detective Handler," Deputy Corker said. "Step in."

Immediately after Deputy Corker issued his invitation to Kate, Deputy Griffin, the young officer who accompanied Corker, stepped back to the door and opened it for Kate, and then stood back.

"Come on in," he said.

"Yes," Deputy Corker said, "by all means. Henry is using the restroom. He'll be right out. I did not know that you were a bona fide homicide detective. And in New York City, of all places. Are you here on official business? If I might ask."

"Nothing official. I'd hoped to see my father here in Deadwood, but he got called away. So I'm just spending a little time reconnecting with my good friend, Henry. So, what's this early morning meeting all about? Is something up?"

"No, not really. Neither of you are in trouble, or anything like that. The sheriff just had some additional questions for you. About your car. I don't know exactly what his concern was, but he asked me to round you two up and bring you in a little early. Do you think it'll be a problem?"

"No. No problem. Does the sheriff really need to see *both* of us?"

"Yeah. I'm pretty sure he asked me to bring you both in."

"That'll be fine. Give me a minute and I'll brush my teeth and comb my hair."

"Sure," Deputy Corker said. "That'd be fine. You do what you have to do. And, by the way, is the sheriff aware that you are a homicide detective?"

"I would imagine he is," Kate turned and said. "I put him in touch with my boss out at the crime scene. I suspect he's been in touch with the captain by now. With your permission, then, I'll be right back."

Kate took another step toward the door, and then turned again.

"Deputy Corker," she said. "Do you know what this is all about? Why the sheriff needs to see us so early?"

"No, actually he didn't spell it all out to me. I just know that he heard from the place you rented your car from, and it upset him. I guess he has some more questions for you, but I don't know what they are. The sheriff is a quirky kinda guy. If he has a question about anything, he wants an answer immediately—and directly from the source. Don't get me wrong. He's a great boss. Very fair. He just can be a little demanding. Don't worry about it. If we get you in there immediately, you'll get out early. That'll free up the rest of your day to do your stuff."

"Thanks," she said with a smile. "I'll be right back."

Henry emerged from the bathroom at virtually the same time as Kate entered his room.

"You're both all set to head to the office with us?" Deputy Corker asked. It was obvious to Henry that the tone of the deputy's voice had mellowed. *Must be the deputy's discovery about Kate's being a big city homicide detective helped him calm down a bit,* he reasoned. *That's good news, because the dude was beginning to grate on my nerves.*

"Do you want us to ride with you, or shall I drive?" Henry asked.

"I think the sheriff would like his people to examine your rental," Deputy Corker replied. "The 2019 Ford Taurus. That's what you're still driving—right?"

"Yup," Henry said.

"Then you two drive that down to the office, and we'll follow. Just try not to run into anything on the way. You can manage that, can't you?"

"I'll do my best," Henry answered. "Even though I haven't had my morning coffee."

"Don't worry about the coffee," Deputy Corker said. "Deputy Griffin made some this morning. You're welcome to as much as you like. The sheriff thinks he mixes it with battery acid—so I'm sure there'll be plenty left."

Henry and Kate both feigned a chuckle at the deputy's humor

as they made their way to their vehicle.

Just before he reached the Taurus, Henry made the suggestion that Deputy Corker lead the way because he was not really sure about how to find the sheriff's office. "Just take it slow so I don't lose you," he said after the deputy agreed to go first.

"What do you suppose the concern is all about?" Henry asked Kate as they pulled in behind the deputy's car. "Sounds like they discovered the damage we did to the first Taurus. That would likely be it, wouldn't it?"

"They haven't had enough time to match paint on the front of the Taurus with that of the Chevy we ran off the road and into that tree. But, the sheriff undoubtedly has a pretty good idea about what happened. So I'd be careful about what we tell him. Maybe you could blame him for the crash. The driver we ran off is already on the sheriff's troublemaker list, so he'd probably buy that version of the story. Maybe take fifty-fifty credit for the accident. I don't know. What do you think?"

"Wouldn't be wise to deny the whole thing, I don't think," Henry suggested. "Eventually the lab is going to match up that paint."

"When the sheriff gets you in front of him, most likely he will not let on what he knows. He'll have you tell your whole story to him, and he will then determine if you are lying or telling the truth. That's what I'd do. Relax and be honest. It's okay to slant the story in your direction, but you have to get the facts straight, and keep your motives plausible."

During the remainder of the trip to the sheriff's office Kate and Henry ran over their versions of the story in order to make it sound the same.

"I really don't know what to expect from this guy," Kate said. "I think his biggest concern about us is really about you—he doesn't know what to expect from you. About me, I don't think he is so much concerned. I'm a cop with a lot to lose. But you, he's going to find out that you have a record, and he immediately is going to get suspicious. Especially since it has to feel to him like he is not making any headway on the murder cases."

"That's what I was thinking, too. It always works out that way for me," Henry agreed. "First of all, no one can pronounce my Native American name the first try. And then, my prison record. That never sits well with law enforcement. How do you think this turns out?"

"No idea," Kate said as they got out of the car. "I guess we'll soon find out."

And did they ever.

Chapter 53

The next three hours passed more strangely than either Kate or Henry could have anticipated. As they were about to enter Sheriff Miller's office they were separated—Henry was ushered into Interrogation One, and Kate into Interrogation Three.

"See you later, Henry," Kate said as she was led away from him by Det. Walter Weaver. The sheriff himself accompanied Henry.

"Yeah," Henry said with a broad smile, "don't forget to take the dog for a walk."

Kate returned the smile and replied, "Don't worry, I've got it covered."

While they had never shared that line before, she knew what Henry was intending to convey. Given that there was no dog in play on this trip, his directive was code to mean "I have absolutely no idea about what is about to take place. So, make the best of it."

"Well, Mr. Kalyesveh," Sheriff Miller said through his sneer, "looks to me like you've been a very busy fellow, if you know what I mean."

Henry did not respond.

"I'm talking about all your trips to jails and prisons. Looks to me like you've spent most of your life behind bars, of one type or another. And when you weren't behind bars, you were in some sort of prison camp. Which, in my opinion, amounts to just about the same thing. Wouldn't you agree?"

Henry responded, "Whatever you say."

"Apparently, Henry, you like to fight. In fact, you like to fight so much, that you have seriously injured some of the people you have fought with. Is that correct."

"I never start a fight. Someone always picks the fights with me."

"You might not start the fight, but it looks like you always end it. And, sometimes my friend, you end the fight by killing the person you're fighting with. That is sure one hell of a way to end a fight. Final in the ultimate sense, I'll have to say. I believe you were sent to prison for killing two men by literally punching their lights out. Is that correct?"

"Like I said, I never wanted to hurt anyone. They would hit me first, and when I struck back, they were not able to defend adequately. But, I think you'll find that I served my time. In every case, I paid my price to the system. My freedom was gained legitimately before all the courts."

"Well, that is how it appears to be," the sheriff agreed. "But, I still say that I don't get men with your record through my county very often."

Henry looked down at his hands and did not respond.

"But," the sheriff picked up again, "Mr. Kalyesveh, that doesn't answer all the questions. The mere fact that you have served your time doesn't answer the question about the Chevy you ran off the road out there by that murder scene—the Hornsboro murder scene. You know, into that big pine tree. Do you recall that? That car was driven by one Franklin James Mansfield. Is all that familiar to you at all?"

"I don't know anyone named Franklin Mansfield," Henry said. "I did accidently run into a car out by where that fellow got shot. But I don't know his name."

"*Accidently?* Are you saying that you accidently ran into that other car? The one that was driven by someone who you did not know. Is that what you're telling me right now?"

"He hit me. I hit him. All I know is that our cars accidently came together out there. I'm really sorry it happened. I explained it all to Ajax Car Rental. They told me that I should have gotten an accident report. I didn't know that. So I am planning on filing a report today, here at your offices. That's the best I can do now. Is that how you want me to handle it?"

"When you crash into a car, you're supposed to call the proper authority and file a report at the scene. South Dakota Codified Laws 32-34-6. This is a misdemeanor punishable by up to a year in jail. This is especially important when there is an injury. When someone gets injured at an accident, and if you don't file a report in a timely fashion, it becomes a felony. I'm sorry to have to tell you this, Mr. Kalyesveh, but you, my friend, are in big trouble."

"He didn't stick around so we could," Henry said. "I looked in the glove box for some identification, and on the seat and in the center consul, and all I found were some old candy wrappers, a paperback book that was set in Michigan's Upper Peninsula, and some papers that said that the car was owned by some woman named *Mildred Pruit.*

"Now, I'm no expert on these things, but I got a good enough look at the driver that ran into us to see that it was a man. And I doubt that he would have gone by the name of Mildred. And, besides, why the hell did he take off through the broken windshield? Kate and I are convinced that he crawled out through the space where the windshield had been. Strange behavior, unless, the car was stolen. Do you suppose that could have been the case—that the car was stolen, and then crashed into us? We wondered about that, so we went out looking for the driver. Our intentions always were to report the accident after we found the other driver. I'm real sorry about my mistake. I should have reported it sooner."

"Sooner?" the sheriff barked. "*Sooner?* Look here, asshole. It wasn't a matter of sooner or later. You didn't bother to report the accident—if it even was an *accident*—you never reported it at all."

"You're right. I explained it to the rental company so I could turn it into my insurance, and I gave them the name that was on the registration, and they said they would take care of the rest. You said something about there being an injury? I'm sorry to hear that. Is he in the hospital? And, what was his name by the way? I'd like to have a record of whoever it was that ran into me. If you don't mind? And, by the way, did *he* file an accident report?"

"So, you're the ones who ended up with the paperwork on that car. He, the driver you ran off the road, told us the car belonged to him, but that he'd misplaced the registration. Do you still have it?"

"Not with me. It's probably at our hotel. I could go back and look for it. And then I could bring it in to you. I'd be happy to do that if you want me to."

Sheriff Miller did not immediately respond. Instead he stood to his feet and studied Henry's reflection in the two-way mirror. Finally he spoke.

"This Kate Handler. Your friend. What exactly is the connection between you two? If you don't mind my asking. As I understand it she is a New York City homicide detective. A lieutenant, in fact. Are you somehow related to this lady? Or just good friends? What's the connection?"

"I am a good friend of her father—Jack Handler. That's it. In a lot of ways, Kate is like a sister to me. And, you could say that we are good friends. That's it."

"Interesting. Very interesting. And just what is it you do for Mr. Handler? I understand that he is a private investigator? Is that what you do too? Are you a private investigator?"

"Me? No. Jack is a licensed private investigator. I'm just a good friend. With my criminal record, I could never qualify for a license. I'm just his friend."

"But, didn't you say you *worked* for him? In what capacity are you employed by him?"

"I serve him and Kate as their chief maintenance officer at their resort on Sugar Island, in Michigan's Upper Peninsula."

The sheriff turned and faced Henry. It was obvious that his mind was racing.

"Sugar Island, you say. In Michigan's Upper Peninsula. Right?"

"That's right. I live at the resort, as does Jack. Obviously, Kate lives and works in New York. She is on the title as the owner of the resort, but Jack actually runs it. And I help maintain it."

"And didn't you say that the book you found in that Chevy that you ran off the road, didn't you say that it was called *Sugar Island*? And that it was set in Michigan's Upper Peninsula?"

"The title was *Murder on Sugar Island*. And it's the same Sugar Island. The book—I've read it. It was set on the same Sugar Island."

"Same place. Right?"

"Yes."

"Isn't that a little strange? That a book written about the place where you live would be found in a car driven by the driver of the car that collides with yours? How do you suppose that came about?"

"I have no idea. Kate and I thought it a little strange as well. But we don't know how it happened."

"Was the driver from Sugar Island too?"

"We don't know anything about that. Do you? Do you know if he was from Michigan?"

"Tell me exactly what you are doing in Deadwood? Surely you can't be doing maintenance all the way out here in South Dakota? Are you on some sort of resort business? Or are you by any chance assisting your boss—Jack Handler—in his private investigator business?"

"Of course not. It would not be legal for me to be assisting Jack in his business. Sometimes he has me drive him around. He's not as young as he used to be, so sometimes he has me help him like that. Kind of like a chauffeur. But not as an assistant investigator, or anything official."

"And Kate. Is she working for him as an investigator? And, by the way, did you tell me where Mr. Handler is right now? Is he in Deadwood? I understand he was here up until a day or two ago. Where, exactly, is he right now?"

"I'm sure I didn't tell you where Jack is, because I don't know where he is. But, you're right—he was in Deadwood earlier this week. We had a drink in a local bar. Apparently he got called out of town unexpectedly on one of his cases. But he didn't tell me where he was headed. And Kate—I'm really not sure why she's here. I guess she came out to see her dad, but he was gone when she got here. So she decided to stomp around Deadwood with me for a day or two, and then fly back to New York. She's never been to this area before, and she thought it might be fun. But you'll have to ask her. I'm just guessing on her motives."

"So, your visit out to the Hornsboro murder scene yesterday— that was just part of your sightseeing adventure? And your meeting with Walter Silverman and his buddy, James Jackson—our aging Deadwood antiquarians—*that* wasn't business related?"

"Like I said, Jack was suddenly called out of town. He was right in the middle of his work here, and so I helped him out by taking some of his calls while he was gone. And this Hornsboro fellow—I had never heard of him before. But when one of Jack's clients called and asked me to meet with him about something—maybe pick something up from him—I don't really know. Kate and I discussed it briefly, and she and I thought it would be a good idea to run out there and see him. We didn't know anything about his misfortune until we talked to you. Too bad about that."

"So, when we're done here, you're prepared to drop back into the same hole you crawled out of? That is, provided I don't just lock you up? If you walk out of here today, what are you going to do?"

"We've got a couple of loose ends we need to tie up. And then we'll be driving back to Sugar Island."

"Really? What's this about—your asking around about one of Deadwood's most prominent figures—Jeffry Speelman? Deputy Corker said something about you trying to follow Mr. Speelman's Escalade around town last night. Is that true, or was my deputy lying to me?"

Whoa! Henry said to himself. *Jeffry Speelman. That had to have been a slip of the tongue. So that has to be that dude's name. And why, pray tell, was that such a big deal to the sheriff and his deputy? I'd better not make too big of a deal out of this.*

"I just thought he looked like someone I ran into at the bar the other night. Kate and I just wondered if he would be interested in having a drink with us. Very interesting fellow, that Speelman guy.

He's some kind of an investment broker, or something like that. Right?"

The sheriff immediately realized that he had misspoken.

"Not real sure exactly what it is that he does. But I do know that he is a prominent member of our community. And a very beloved and generous contributor at most every charitable event. I'm sure you can understand that it makes us all very uncomfortable to have a stranger to our city, and a convict to boot, following around after one of our favorite sons. Right? You can appreciate that, can't you?"

"I meant no harm. I merely thought that the guy in the Escalade resembled someone that I had enjoyed tipping a few beers with the other night. That's it. Your Deputy Corker told me that this Speelman fellow could *not* have been the man I met in the bar, because he doesn't frequent establishments like that. So, I have to assume that he wasn't the man I thought he was. My interest starts and stops with that."

"I think Corker's right," the sheriff said. "I sometimes have a beer myself, and I've never run into Jeff in a bar. What did you discuss with Jeff that made you think that he was so interesting?"

"Like I said, I'm now sure that these were two different guys. The fellow I talked to apparently could not have been this Speelman guy. The man I found interesting knew all about golf. And that, right now, is what I'm thinking about all the time. Jack and I are beginning to play a lot of golf, and I like getting pointers from people who know the game. And the guy I met the other night—he knew the game inside and out. That's what piqued my interest—golf. Is Speelman a golfer too?"

"Not that I know about," the sheriff replied. He was beginning to lose interest in talking further with Henry.

"Look, my Michigan friend. If I let you walk out of here in the next hour, what will be your plans? Will you pack up and head back to Sugar Island soon? Or do you have other intentions? What are *these loose* ends that you referred to?"

Henry hesitated. *If I say too much here*, he said to himself, *I could end up in the sheriff's jail. And he could probably drum something up to send me before an unfriendly judge. I get the feeling that he just wants me out of his hair. If I make getting on the road my principal goal, he just might open up the door and kick my ass outta here.*

"Once I square my rental car away, I intend to hit the road. I can't really head back before I take care of that business. Thanks to that crazy driver, I owe the rental place some money—or more correctly, my insurance company owes them some money. Can't run away from that, or I could be in trouble. But, that's all I have left to do here in South Dakota. I'm sure you can appreciate that."

The sheriff turned his back on Henry while he contemplated his next move. Finally, after nearly a minute of silence, he turned around and said, "Henry, Mr. Kalyesveh, you hang in here for a bit. I need to see how the interview is going with the Handler woman. Okay? Can you just chill for a while?"

"I'm fine," Henry replied.

"Good enough," the sheriff said.

He then swiped his prox card in front of the reader, causing the door strike to click loudly. He opened the door and left. As the door closed, the door strike clicked again, locking behind him.

"Hey, Corkey," the sheriff said upon entering the room where Deputy Corker was interviewing Kate. "How's it going over here?

Learn anything new?"

"Miss Handler has been very cooperative," Deputy Corker said. "But I don't think we've really learned anything new."

"May I take a look at your notes?" the sheriff asked.

"Sure. Help yourself. But, like I said. Miss Handler didn't actually provide any new information."

Sheriff Miller picked up Deputy Corker's clipboard. It had a single sheet of paper attached to it containing about ten lines of barely legible scribbling. The sheriff scowled as he tried to decipher what was written. He was drawn to the fourth line, but he didn't address the matter immediately. Instead, he sent Deputy Corker over to the interrogation room where Henry was being held.

"Miss Handler," the sheriff said after Deputy Corker had left. "It says here that you and Henry were requested to pay a visit to Mr. Hornsboro by your father—Jack Handler. Is that correct?"

Kate had to think that through before responding.

"Henry was the one who was first introduced to the existence of Roger Hornsboro. The actual request for us to interview the man came from a woman named Claire Mansfield. She, as I understand it, was the client my dad was working for. Since my dad was unavailable, I agreed to talk to Hornsboro myself. Henry then proceeded to drive me over there. And that's when I ran into you, and the very dead Roger Hornsboro. That's a more thorough explanation of how that whole thing actually transpired. Does that answer your question?"

"Almost. Just one more thing about that. Am I to assume from your statement that you and Henry Kalyesveh were working on behalf of your father the licensed private investigator?"

Again Kate hesitated. *He's trying to get me to admit that we were working as private investigators*, Kate said to herself. *And Henry, as an ex-convict, could be in considerable jeopardy were he to do that.*

"No," she said to the sheriff, "that's not how I would describe it. Had Mr. Hornsboro not been dead when we arrived, we would have identified ourselves to him as associates of Mrs. Mansfield—not as agents acting on behalf of a private investigator. I would have let him know that Mrs. Mansfield has authorized us to pick up whatever he had for her, and if he wanted to verify that fact, he could call her and check on it. But we would not have identified ourselves as private investigators. I guess you could say that those two rounds nullified that possibility. By the way, have you determined who it was that shot Mr. Hornsboro? Have there been any arrests made?"

The sheriff allowed his eyes to lock onto Kate's. He smiled but did not respond to her question.

"Those dents and scratches on Henry's rental," he said, after allowing sufficient time to pass to permit the introduction of a different topic of conversation. "They were all on the front of that Buick Henry was driving. What was it that he ran into? Was it that car we found wrapped around that tree? It had dents and scratches too, but they were all on the rear quarter-panel. Henry must have run into that Chevy. Right? How did that happen? What did he seek to accomplish? Was he trying to run him off the road and into that tree? Or was it an accident? It didn't look to me like an accident. If I'm objective about it, I'd say Henry was attempting a PIT Maneuver—you surely know what that means. PIT is the acronym for *Precision Immobilization Technique*. That's what it looked like to me—a well performed PIT Maneuver. What do you say?"

"I think we're getting something confused here. Henry was driving a 2019 Taurus, not a Buick. And, as for the scratches, I wasn't looking when it happened. It was so fast. I do know that the Chevy was also in motion. But I'm just not sure how it was they came together. Henry's a great driver. I understand that it was an accident—but that's just what I heard. And I can't believe that it was Henry's fault. I think you're going to have to get that information from him. I just didn't see it happen."

The sheriff had not expected Kate to answer that question any differently from the way she did. *They've obviously rehearsed their stories*, he said to himself. *Not likely that they will entangle one another in any meaningful way. Besides, she's an active homicide detective—a lieutenant, no less. I don't think I want to pick an unnecessary dustup with the New York City Police Department. And I think I can be sure that neither of these two are responsible for either of these two murders. So, what the hell …*

"What, Kate, are your immediate plans?" he asked. "When you walk out of here?"

His principal goal is to get us on our way out of town, she said to herself. *I should encourage him along that line, at least a little.*

"I'm not completely sure what Henry has in mind. But I do know I'd like to see where Hickok was murdered—shot in the back of the head by Jack McCall. I think it was in Saloon #10. I would hate to tell my friends that I visited Deadwood but did not see that famous chair. But, as far as I'm concerned, I'm ready to head back to Sugar Island. Depends, of course, on Henry's plans. He's driving, and I'm not really sure about what he has in mind."

"You do realize that none of that stuff you mentioned are the originals. Right? All the real artifacts were destroyed in one of our great fires. But, I'm sure you're already aware of that."

"Yes. I've read about the city's history. Still, if you visit Deadwood, you're expected to check out the Hickok shooting. Just something you have to do."

"Of course. I understand. But, beyond that, is there anything else keeping you two in town? Or can I expect you to move along?"

Wonder what he's so concerned about? Kate asked herself. *Surely he doesn't think we are somehow involved in these killings he's dealing with. But, there is something about our being here that bothers him. What could that be? I wonder.*

"Aside from what I just told you, there's nothing I want to do here," she finally said to the sheriff.

"That's pretty much the same story Henry tells me," the sheriff said. "He says that the only thing holding him in Deadwood is dealing with the car rental company, with regard to the accident. Otherwise, he says he's ready to move on. Can I assume that's how you see it?"

"Yeah, I'd say so," Kate replied. "But I do have a question."

"And what would that be?"

"Is there something we've done that troubles you? Like somehow sets us apart from any of the other Deadwood tourists?"

"That's just it," the sheriff said, "you and your friend, Henry, are not the *typical* tourists. First of all, you were poking your noses around the Hornsboro camper, and he ends up getting shot just before you get there. And then Henry spends the evening with Jimmy Jackson, and *he* then gets run down in the street. Murdered. *Murdered!* I *hav*e to conclude that Jimmy was murdered. I'm not a believer in coincidence. Not in the least.

"Now, don't take this like I suspect that you two had anything *directly* to do with these fellows getting murdered—like you are responsible for their murders. That's not at all the case. But, it seems to me that being around you two tends to shorten a man's life. And now, Henry is poking his nose into the life of one of my deputy's good friends—Jeffry Speelman. A *new* friend—I should say. But this shit has to end. Just what is it about you two?"

"I don't think I know what you are talking about. I'm sorry, but I don't recall ever having heard that name before—Speelman."

"Jeffry Speelman. You've never heard Speelman?"

"No, I don't think so."

"How about last night? The man who Henry was about to chase down. Before Deputy Corker stopped him. The man driving that Escalade. You don't remember him?"

"That man was the Jeffry Speelman who you're talking about? Is that what you're saying?"

"You've never heard of him?"

"No. And I didn't really see who it was that Henry had thought he spotted. I couldn't even swear that it was an Escalade. I'm sorry, but I don't think I can help you at all in this regard. Who is this Speelman character, anyway? Is he a friend of yours too?"

"I'm the elected sheriff of Lawrence County. Everybody who lives here is my friend. James Jackson was my friend. But, he still got himself murdered. Jeffry Speelman doesn't actually live in Deadwood. He's a visitor, kinda like you two are. From Grand Rapids, I think Corker said. And he has been hanging around with my deputy lately. Now, I'm not sure what *you* guys are doing here, but I don't want to see any more of my friends or visitors get murdered. I fear that if I don't get to the bottom of this pretty damn soon, someone else is going to get hurt. It's got to stop!

"Kate Handler, you're a detective. A big city *homicide* detective, even. What do you think about this? What's going on? Why did these two men get murdered? And how is it that you guys knew them *both*?"

"Actually, I never met either one of them—at least not while they were still alive."

"But both of them somehow worked into your friend Henry's life. He spent much of that evening questioning Jimmy Jackson about that Michigan horseshit. I don't even know what that was all about, but I think it had something to do with a man getting murdered over there in Michigan nearly a hundred years ago. Right? Now, it would be foolish to think that whoever killed that Upper Peninsula fellow, that he would still be alive. Took place much too long ago. So, how in the bloody hell could a case that old be sparking the sort of interest that this one appears to be sparking? What is there about this ancient case that could make *anyone* this angry? Or scared? You're a homicide detective, *Homicide Detective* Kate Handler. This should be right up your alley. What does your gut tell you? Any ideas?"

"I honestly don't know, sheriff," Kate said. "I'll admit, I was taken aback when we drove up to Hornsboro's camper, and it was lit up by a street full of patrol cars and ambulances. Of course, I was just arriving from New York. I didn't know what to expect. But, to answer your question about what I thought about your case—I don't have any idea how it does, or might, relate to what my father is working on. I haven't discussed this case with him. And, as you know, he was called away by other pressing business.

"Now, that might tell me something—the fact that Dad left

Deadwood to pursue another matter altogether. That could mean that he didn't think what he's found here, in Deadwood, that it just might not be significant. Or, at least not *sufficiently* significant. Not knowing much at all about the Deadwood matter, but knowing my father very well, I could easily come to that conclusion. However, that would be reaching a conclusion through assumption—and we both know how dangerous that can be. So, I'd rather leave the matter totally open. At least until I can run everything past my father. Does that all make sense to you?"

Again, the sheriff did not respond to her question. Instead, he merely stared at her face, his eyes unfocused. After a long pause, he spoke.

"What do you know about this Speelman fellow?" he asked. "Please humor me and tell me again."

Wow! Kate said to herself. *The sheriff must have some serious concerns about this guy.*

"I know absolutely nothing about a person named Jeffry Speelman. Nothing whatsoever. And, to my knowledge, Henry doesn't know anything either. We've never discussed the matter.

"Now, that is not to say that Deputy Corker might not have been describing Speelman when he shared some information with Henry and me. That would have been when he pulled us over last night. If that was Speelman that the deputy was talking about, he did mention something about how he knew the man from his church. And he had some good things to say about him. But he didn't mention the Speelman name. So the man he was talking about might not have been the fellow you're talking about. That's it. That's all I know. Rather, that's my only thoughts on the matter."

"Are you making another assumption?" the sheriff asked.

"I suppose you could say that. But, I'm trying to be as candid as possible. You are the sheriff of the county. I feel I owe it to you to lay it all out there—even my best guesses."

"How is it that the subject of this stranger," the sheriff asked, "whether Speelman, or some other friend of Deputy Corker—how did it come up in the first place?"

"Apparently Henry thought he saw someone who looked familiar to him. The man was driving an Escalade in the opposite direction. And Henry made a U-turn to follow him. Deputy Corker saw what Henry had done, and he might have assumed that he had made the U-turn in order to check out the man in the Escalade. So, that's why he stopped us. It could have been like that."

"Really? That was the *only* reason he pulled you two over? Because he observed that Henry took some inordinate interest in the man driving the Escalade? Is that about right?"

"I think that could be the case. You could ask your deputy about it. But, as I recall, by the way he talked about the man when he stopped, it seems as though that might be the case. And when he spotted Henry taking the illegal U-turn, he may have put two and two together, and felt the need to intervene. But, I can't swear that's what he was thinking."

"Very interesting," the sheriff noted. And then he turned toward the two-way mirror as though signaling to someone on the other side of it. But that wasn't the case. He was merely thinking about what Kate had just said. After a moment, he turned back toward her and said, "If I were to release you right now—you and your friend, Henry—when did you say you'd be headed out of the county?"

"Well, I would like to check out your little town a bit more—like a regular tourist."

"And Henry? Would he be willing to go along with that plan?"

"I can't speak for Henry," Kate replied. "But he hasn't suggested that he needed to stick around Deadwood. You should ask him. See what his plans are."

"I did," the sheriff said. "And he was just about as evasive as you were. What say we do this? I let you both go. You do your touristy stuff today. While Henry squares away his business with the rental vehicle. And, with the sunrise, you two check out of your hotel and get on the road headed east. How does that sound? Can you do that?"

"Works for me. And now that you remind me, Henry did say he had some insurance things he had to arrange with the damage on the Taurus. Yeah. I'd say that would work. Is that how you want to handle it?"

"Why don't you walk down the hall and we'll check with Henry. If he goes along with this plan, then the two of you are free to go. I can tell you this. You'd *damn well better* accept the offer, and carry through with it, before I change my mind and toss you both into lockup."

Kate believed that the sheriff wasn't bluffing. *Small town law enforcement, and county sheriffs*, she said to herself, *they operate under a different set of rules. I'm sure my boss would spring me immediately. But Henry—he's a different story. His criminal record could pose a real problem for him. Even my captain might not be able to get Henry out. So—I hope Henry uses his head and doesn't irritate the sheriff any more than he already has.*

"Sheriff," Kate said as they walked toward Henry's interrogation room. "Could you give me a minute or two with Henry first, and let me explain the situation? Could we do it that way?"

"Sure. We can do it your way. I'll send my deputy on his way, and then you go in. I'll give you five minutes. See what you two can come up with. Remember, it's nothing personal. I just want the both of you out of my hair ASAP. You understand?"

Kate turned toward the sheriff and smiled, as he broke off and escorted Deputy Corker back to his office.

"No offense," she said. "Henry and I will do our best to accommodate."

"Five minutes," the sheriff added as he walked away. "I'll be back in five to get your update."

"What's up?" Henry asked. "Where's the sheriff going? What's this five minute update crap? What did he mean by that?"

Chapter 54

As soon as the sheriff had left their company, and Kate was certain that no one else could monitor their conversation, she said to Henry, "He really wants us to get out of South Dakota in the morning. If we aren't, I think he'll find some reason to lock you up. Do you think we can get done what we need to today?"

"That's pretty much how he left it with me too. I think if we can get out of here soon, I could get done what I have to, and that we could head out in the morning. How about you?"

"I don't think he wants to hassle me too much, and have to deal with my boss. But you, I think you intimidate him a little. And with Dad out of the picture right now, he just might toss you in his little pokey. If that happens, you never know what it could turn into. I'd like to move on in the morning, if you do."

"Let's go for it."

"He's going to be monitoring you. Maybe me too. But you for sure. He's expecting you to be dealing with the rental. If you make a list, I'll check out everything else you want done. And if he or his deputy questions me about what I'm up to, I can deal with it."

"Time's up," the sheriff said as he popped open the door. "What's it gonna be? Can you be on the road in the morning?"

"That works for us," Henry said, making every effort to appear cooperative. "Like I said, I have a little business to take care of with the rental company, and Kate would like to do a little sightseeing. But we can be on our way in the morning."

"Fine, then," the sheriff said. "Grab your jackets and I'll show you to the door. All will be fine if you keep your word. But, if you're still around tomorrow, and we see you, it's not gonna go well for you. Understand?"

"We're good with that, sheriff," Henry said as they followed the sheriff out of the door.

Once outside, the sheriff turned and walked back into the building.

"Did you notice Corker?" Kate asked as they walked toward the Taurus.

"Yeah, I saw him. He's not gonna let us out of his sight until we cross the county line."

"He can't follow both of us," Kate said. "My guess is that when you head out to the car rental, he'll follow you, not me. So let's go back to the hotel and talk this over. I don't know what you're thinking, but it seems to me like we need to find out just what role Jeffry Speelman is playing in this whole matter."

"Exactly," Henry agreed. "I'm a little surprised that the sheriff dropped that name on us. He must have some questions about the dude himself. What did he say to you about him?"

"Nothing, really. Only that Speelman was from Michigan, and that he had become friends with Deputy Corker. It was the part about the Michigan connection that got my attention. What was he doing here? On some sort of extended stay. We need to get to the bottom of that. Any ideas?"

"Shit. Can that be some sort of coincidence? What part of Michigan is Speelman from? And what does he do for a living? And what could he have been doing here? Very strange, I'd say."

Kate didn't waste any time in dialing her office.

"This is Lieutenant Kate Handler. Who is this?"

"Sergeant Gambino. Lieutenant Handler. How are you doin'? I

heard you had taken a little trip. Where'd you go, anyway? I heard you went to Montana, or one of the Dakotas. Where are you?"

"I'm in South Dakota," she replied. "Deadwood, to be more precise. Sergeant Gambino. I need you to run a name for me. See what you can find. The party I want you to check out is a male named Jeffry Speelman. I believe the name is spelled J-E-F-F-R-Y S-P-E-E-L-M-A-N. I don't have a specific address, but I understand he works in Grand Rapids, Michigan. So, I would think that he lives in the Greater Grand Rapids area.

"I would like you to find out as much as you can—occupation, marital status, sexual preference, hobbies, criminal record, of course. And health records, if they're available."

"Are you working a case for the department?"

"No. But I did run into a couple murders out here in Deadwood. And, this Jeffry Speelman is a person of interest in one of my father's cases. I'm taking a look at it for him while I'm here. Can you help us out a little? I'll owe you one if you do—a big one."

"How old, about, would you say your subject might be?" Sgt. Gambino asked.

"I don't know," she said. "I'll find out."

She then covered her phone with her hand and asked Henry, "Henry—how old would you say Speelman was?"

"Forties. Maybe late thirties. Very big guy—hard to gauge a big guy's age."

Kate then forwarded that information on to Sgt. Gambino.

"We think Speelman is in his late thirties to mid-forties. Looks to be six three, or maybe even taller. Big guy. Not so much fat—just a big man. Anything else you need? I'd like you to see what you can turn up in the next hour or so. Can you get right on it?"

"I'm plugging it in as we speak. I should have something shortly. Want to stay on with me, or call me back? Or I could call you. What do you want it to be?"

"I'll let you get on with it. If I haven't called you back by the time you get it together, call me."

"Will do."

Henry looked over at Kate and remarked, "*Gambino?* Really? I thought that name stood for something entirely different."

"Antonio Gambino. That's his real name. His first name is Antonio. Everyone calls him Tony. Who do you know from Grand Rapids?"

"No one, actually," Henry said. "Jack has contacts there, but I don't."

"Yeah. Dad knows someone in every Midwest community. This thing with the rental company. Do you really have to pay them a visit? Or was all that just a way to bargain for more time?"

"I really do have to get with them. We have to negotiate the costs of repair. If I can avoid making an insurance claim I will. They said they would have their shop take a look and see what it's gonna cost."

"That's good," Kate said. "That'll give me some time to poke around here—legitimately. Will be interesting to see what Tony comes up with. It does seem all too curious that this guy from Grand Rapids comes to Deadwood. And then people start dying. Weird, to say the least."

Just as those words passed between Kate's lips, a call from New York came in.

"Kate here."

"Lieutenant. Got some interesting news about this Jeffry Speelman. I don't have the whole story yet, but it looked curious enough to warrant a preliminary call. Hope I'm not interrupting anything. Are you ready for it?"

"Yeah. Great. Tell me what you found out."

"I only found one Jeffry Speelman from that area—at least only one that fit your general description. I really think I got the right guy. You tell me. The Jeffry Speelman I found is a white male. Forty years of age. He lives in Ada, Michigan. Ada is an upscale neighborhood located north and east of Grand Rapids.

"Mr. Speelman played basketball at MSU—Michigan State University. He was a power forward, which means he would be a large, powerful man.

"He earned a degree in business administration there, and then received a degree in law at Cooley Law School."

"So our guy was a big college basketball player," Kate said aloud for Henry's benefit. "And he has a law degree."

"That's right," Sgt. Gambino said, "but there's a lot more. Shall I go on?"

"Yeah. What else you got?"

"This is where it gets very interesting. After passing the Michigan Bar, Mr. Speelman took a job with a small law firm in Grand Rapids—Chris, Chris, and Sparks. They specialized in trusts and estates."

"He practices law in Grand Rapids," Kate repeated, "for a firm specializing in trusts and estates. How about a criminal record? Has he got a sheet?"

"Not exactly. That's where it gets interesting. He's not been arrested, but the Michigan State Bar suspended him for a year for unethical practices. That was two years ago. Surprisingly, he was not fired by his firm. That suggests that he might have been some kind of *rainmaker*—that's someone who has a knack for bringing business into their firm. That's just a supposition. It might be that he has developed some special relationship with one of the partners. I can dig into that deeper."

"That won't be necessary," Kate replied. "We've got to get this done. Just pick the low-hanging fruit. We don't have much time. Do you have any information as to what it was that got our guy suspended?"

"Mr. Speelman was alleged to have engaged heavily in a Bitcoin investment scheme to the tune of nearly a hundred million dollars. Apparently the IRS did not believe his filings were up to par, and proceeded to initiate an action against him. This resulted in the suspension."

"Bitcoin," Kate parroted. "Speelman is a speculator."

"You could say that," Sgt. Gambino said. "Some would call him a crazy gambler. But he did somehow finagle his way out of his legal troubles, and last year the suspension was rescinded. Don't show a resolution to his IRS problems however. At least not yet, as far as I can tell. That's all I've got for now. Shall I continue to dig?"

"You've already dug up a lot, Tony. But, would you see if you can—"

"I've got something for him to look into," Henry interrupted.

Kate then said to Sgt. Gambino, "Hold on, Tony. Henry, my associate, has something for you to look into. I'm giving you to him."

"Sergeant Gambino. My name is Henry Kalyesveh. I'm a good friend and associate of Lieutenant Handler. … I have one more thing you could check out for us. If you would be so kind, could you find out if Speelman has any association with Craig Conklin, Claire Mansfield, or Franklin James Mansfield? If you would check that out, it could help us get to the bottom of this whole matter. Could you do that?"

"Give me back to Kate," Sgt. Gambino said without responding to Henry's request.

"Yes, Tony," Kate said. "If you could, when you get a chance, just see if there is any connections between Speelman and the parties Henry mentioned. It could be instrumental in this matter."

"Lieutenant Handler," Tony said, clearly bothered. "You know I want to help you all I can. But I'm a busy guy too. Just tell me something. Does any of this involve some case that you are working on here? If the captain busts my chops for an explanation, what can I tell him? You understand what I'm saying?"

"Totally, Tony. You've already been a huge help. And I deeply appreciate it. If this is something that you're not comfortable with spending any more time, then, by all means, just forget it. I know that Captain Spencer can be a hard ass about stuff like this. I totally get it. But if somehow you can squeeze this in, or maybe have Julie take a minute to follow up on it, then I'd be very appreciative. But, if she's tied up with other matters, then just pass on it. You've already been a huge help."

Julie was a rookie officer in the department and she had been assigned to help Sgt. Gambino out with clerical work. She ended up with a temporary desk job while her ankle healed after her partner crashed their patrol car into a parked car while he was trying to eat a Big Mac while driving.

"Give me those names again," Sgt. Gambino said. "I'll see what I can do. I've got a bunch of other shit on my plate, so I won't be able to get around to it until later. But I'll see what I can do."

"Terrific!" Kate said. And then she had Henry repeat the names for him.

When Henry handed the phone back to Kate, she had one more question for Sgt. Gambino: "As far as marital status—did your probe turn up anything?"

"Single. Sorry, I didn't give you that. Mr. Speelman is not a married man. And, as far as I could dig up, he has no children."

"Fantastic. You've been a huge help. Talk to you later. Oh! Hang on. Are you still there?"

"Yeah. Is there something else I can help you with?"

"There is. Could you see if you can dig up a recent picture of Mr. Speelman? There might be something floating around out there, if he had a run-in with the court system. See what you or Julie can find. Would you? And, Tony, I'll be deeply in your debt for all this help. Count on it."

"Yes," Sgt. Gambino agreed, "You will be. But, you know me, I'm always eager to help you when I can. Goodbye, lieutenant."

"So," Henry said, "Speelman's a lawyer who gambles. He's not married—or, most likely not married. He just got off of suspension. What the hell's he doin' in Deadwood? That's the big question I have."

"Do you really think that you have to drive all the way out to that rental place?" Kate asked. "How important is that?"

"Got to. I told the sheriff that I had to settle my account with them. And it's true. It's an insurance thing. And I don't want to give Miller an excuse to haul me back in. Gotta do this."

"That's fine," Kate said. "Think you should run out there right after you drop me off at the hotel?"

"That's what I was thinking. And you could get done anything you need to while I'm gone. When I get back, we can go out for dinner, and discuss what we need to do before we haul ass outta here."

"That works," Kate said. "I can take care of everything I need to do over the phone."

When Kate got back to the hotel, her first call went to the offices of Chris, Chris, and Sparks:

"My name is Darlene Green. Could I speak to Jeff Speelman, please?"

Chapter 55

"I'm sorry," an officious female at Chris, Chris, and Sparks replied to Kate. "Jeffry is not in today. May I help you?"

"I was in Jeff's class at MSU—we called him Jeff back then," Kate said. "I haven't talked to him in years. I married and moved to New York."

Kate knew that her cell would register on caller ID with a New York area code.

"I'm going to be in Grand Rapids for a few days and I was hoping that we could get together and talk about old times. Will he be in later today? Or, even tomorrow?"

"Actually, Jeffry will not be in this entire week. But, he does call in for his messages. I'd be happy to give him a message."

"You could tell him that Darlene, his friend from college—the girl with the red sweaters. Tell him that I'm going to be in town, and I'd like to buy him dinner. But, if he's not going to be in Grand Rapids for a week, then I'll miss him. Just tell him that. By the way, where is he? If it's not too far, maybe I could drive over and see him. How far is it?"

"I don't think you're going to feel like driving to where he is. It's over a thousand miles."

"Oh my God! Really? Where's Jeff at? Does he have clients that far away?"

"I can't be more specific. But he's not serving one of our clients. He's taking some personal time."

"I understand. Being a lawyer can be very stressful. I'm a lawyer too. That's what broke up my marriage. Maybe you can put me in touch with his wife. Lora. I think her name was Lora. Can you connect me with her? She was a good friend, too."

"Lora? We don't know of any friend of Jeffry's named Lora. And, as far as we know Jeffry is not now married, nor ever has been. At least as far as we know. Are you sure we're talking about the same guy?"

"I think so. The Jeff I'm talking about is a big, handsome fellow. Very popular at MSU. Played basketball. Does that sound like your Jeffry?"

"The big and handsome fits, but I've never known him to date women."

"Oh, don't tell me that Jeff goes the other way. Is he gay?"

"I'm sorry, ma'am, but I can't discuss this with you any further. I will let him know you called—when he calls in for his messages. I'll tell him Darlene Green, that's your name, right? I'll tell him that you were a friend back in his college days, and that you would have liked to get together with him. Does that about do it?"

"That would be wonderful. Thanks so much. Maybe next time. But, there is one more thing. Would you please tell him that one of our other old friends, Claire Mansfield, would like to hear from him as well. She's also living in the Grand Rapids area. Would you please add that to the message?"

The operator hesitated for a moment. And then she said in a clearly irritated tone, "I will pass your messages on to Jeffry. Would there be anything else?"

She did not give Kate any time to reply.

"Goodbye, Ms. Green," she said. And then she hung up the phone.

Kate leaned back in her chair, and smiled slyly.

"Damn!" she mouthed out loud. "I wish I could be in the room with Jeffry when he gets that message. It's going to scare the living shit out of him. He's going to strain his brain thinking back, trying to remember someone from college named *Darlene Green*, and then he'll wonder how in the hell I knew about Mrs. Mansfield. He'll be scared to death—looking for a hole to climb into."

Kate sat there for nearly a minute contemplating her next move.

"I wonder how Henry's doing," she said to herself. "If all's going well, he could be winding it up about now. Maybe I should give him a call."

"Kate," he said when he picked up her call. "How's it goin' in Deadwood? Learn anything new?"

"Yes, as a matter of fact, I have come across some very interesting information about our Jeffry Speelman. The reason Sergeant Gambino did not provide us with any details about Mrs. Speelman is because there is no Mrs. Speelman. I called his office and talked to the secretary, and that's what she told me. And she said it in such a way so as to lead me to think that Speelman might be gay. She didn't come right out and say it, but she certainly intimated that he was … that he was gay. She also said that Speelman would be out of the office for an unspecified amount of time. A thousand miles removed from Grand Rapids. So, there is every reason to think that Speelman—the Grand Rapids lawyer—is actually *our* Speelman, our person of interest.

"What's happening at your end? Are you about to head back?"

"I hope so. I sure as hell wish they'd hurry up and get this figured out. Sheriff's Department has already paid them a visit just before I got here. Asking questions about the damaged front bumper. They told the rental place to save all the parts they remove for them to inspect. I guess they want to run them through their lab. I requested that they be repaired rather than replaced, but that won't be possible for everything. They're beginning to wonder what's up. What I did or might have done. I'll tell you one thing: we won't be gettin' out of town fast enough to please me. I just wish your dad were here. No offense intended. It's just that Jack has a way of working through situations like this. People don't like to mess with him.

"But me, it's a different story. I might be able to kick their asses, but I don't pack the same psychological punch as your dad."

"No one does," Kate said. "He just knows how to intimidate people. And get his way. Hey, we should be able to get out of Dodge first thing in the morning. Even if they get those parts to their lab, it'll take a day or more to run the forensics. We should be okay. So, how long before you can get back here? I've got some ideas, but I'm going to need you to pull them off."

"Ideas? What sort of ideas? What have you got in mind?"

"It might be taking us a little out on a limb. I don't know. But, it seemed to me, if we could tail our guy around, for what time we have left, we might be able to find out who he's hanging around with. We might learn something from that—like, who his significant other might be. Could have something to do with your case. I don't know, but I think it's worth a try."

"Yeah, I think it could be. But I really have to stick this out until they're satisfied. Otherwise I could end up having a warrant issued for me. That's exactly how the sheriff would like it go down. See what you can do on your own, and I will call you when I'm on my way. Maybe we could meet up someplace. Just try not to hurt anybody. Okay?"

"Right, Henry," Kate chuckled.

Just then she observed a text coming into her cell.

"Damn! How's that for good timing?" she said to herself.

There on her screen were three images of Jeffry Speelman.

"Tony Gambino, my friend. You've outdone yourself today."

She immediately ran a comb through her hair and put on some fresh red lipstick.

"Okay, Jeffry, here I come. Ready or not."

But, as she approached the double main doors she caught a glimpse of one of the sheriff's patrol cars parked directly across the street from the hotel.

"Well, hello there, sheriff," she said to herself. "I'd bet you are waiting for me. Hate to disappoint you, but I think I'll sneak out the back door."

The first three restaurants and bars that she visited could not help her. The fourth door she entered, however, was a different story. It led into what she suspected was one of the better restaurants in Deadwood. At least, it appeared to serve a higher-end clientele. She walked directly up to the hostess and showed her the picture on her cell.

"This is my brother, Jeffry. He said he would meet me here this afternoon, I'm just not sure I got the right place. He said he eats at this particular restaurant often. Please, take a close look and see if you recognize him. Have you seen him here before?"

"Oh, yes. We know him. He eats here almost every evening. He's your brother? I don't think I've seen you here before."

"I just got in town. I'm from New York, my brother's from

Michigan—Grand Rapids. We just happened to be visiting your town at the same time, so we decided to have dinner together. Except, he didn't say what time I should meet him. When does he usually eat? I'm guessing five-thirty—that's when we usually had dinner when we were kids. Do you remember when he typically comes in?"

"Not five-thirty by a long shot. More like seven-thirty or eight."

"Well, I guess time changes people. I'll plan on seven-thirty, then. Thank you so much."

"Don't you have his cell number to verify? Can't you just call him?"

"He must have been in meetings. Or maybe it's been my carrier. Anyway, you've been very helpful. I'll plan on seven-thirty. Thanks for all your help."

As she approached her hotel she spotted Deputy Corker and his partner—in the same non-parking place as they were before. She smiled brightly and waved as she passed them. They did not respond to her, but the two officers did exchange a lengthy glower between them.

Fifteen minutes after Kate walked in her room, Henry was knocking on her door.

"Well," she greeted him, "it's good to see you're not in cuffs. Not sure my key would fit the sheriff's brand of shackles."

"Tell me about it," he said with a chuckle.

"Any further run-ins with the law?" she asked. "And, did you notice Deputy Corker and his partner parked across the street? Or didn't you come in the front entrance?"

"I came in from the garage," he answered. "But, when I stopped to check for messages, I did step outside for a moment to see if anything was going on. I didn't see any cop cars."

"They must have left after I came in," she said. "Probably irritated with me because I had spotted them before I left the hotel, and so I slid out of the back. Oh well."

"So, what did you learn? Anything interesting?"

"I figured out where we're going to have dinner tonight. And what time."

"Really. What does that mean?"

"The Cottage Restaurant. I checked out their menu. And while it's very expensive, I understand that it boasts a very noteworthy clientele."

"Noteworthy clientele. How's that?"

"Almost every evening, a tall, muscular man dines there—Jeffry Something-or-other."

"Oh. That's interesting, all right. You think he'll be there tonight?"

"Worth a shot, don't you think? I should think that after my conversation with his secretary earlier that his teeth ought to be on edge tonight. … I'm sure that she would have called him by now. Hopefully I didn't scare him away from the restaurant. … I think he'll still be there."

"We'll give the restaurant a shot tonight, regardless," Henry said. "We've got to eat, you know."

That evening Henry and Kate entered the Cottage Restaurant at seven P.M. sharp. They asked to be seated by a window on the other side of the dining area. That way they could keep an eye on the table Jeffry was said to prefer, but still not be on top of it. They ordered water. Kate asked for a glass of Zinfandel, and Henry ordered a six-ounce glass of their house Merlot. And they waited.

At precisely seven-thirty, a very big man entered the restaurant, accompanied by, of all people, Deputy Corker. The hostess led them over to Jeffry's favorite table, and pulled out the seat for the man they thought must be Jeffry Speelman.

"There's our guy!" Henry mouthed quietly.

"And look who's with him. Your favorite person west of Lake Michigan."

"*Favorite* my ass. That jerk *hates* my guts."

"Maybe so," Kate said through a huge smile. "But we're still glad to see them. Right?"

"You could say that. I wonder if he will recognize us."

"If he doesn't, I'm sure his dinner guest will. As soon as Corker spots you, he'll point you out to Jeffry. It will be very interesting to see his reaction. Or, maybe we'll find out what sort of self-control he possesses."

Kate had a much better view of the pair's table than Henry did. When Henry was looking at Kate, Speelman's table would be to his left and slightly behind him.

Kate, however, could look directly into Henry's eyes, and still be able to monitor their two subjects.

"You're drinking that Merlot much slower than usual," Kate observed. "Going to make it last in case we're here for a while? That your plan?"

"I think I'm ready to order," Henry finally said. "How about you? Know what you want?"

"I think so," she replied. "I think I'll have their six ounce filet, and cold water lobster tail. That'd be for the main course. I'll have a small Caesar salad to start with, and maybe some roasted spring vegetables. That all sounds good to me. What are you going to have?"

"That does sound good. But I think I'll pass on the salad. I think I'll have their sixteen-ounce ribeye, with garlic mashed pota—"

"Who's that?" Kate interrupted.

"Who are you talking about?" Henry said as he turned toward the two men. "What are you looking at?"

"Over there," she said. "The little guy who just walked in. The hostess talked to him just a minute ago, but he didn't let her seat him. He's just standing there staring at our two buddies. He looks mad."

Henry turned totally around so that he could see the front entrance.

"Yeah, I see what you're talking about. He does look a little troubled. No doubt about that."

"Okay," Kate said. "He's walking toward their table. But they haven't noticed him. Must be he wants to talk to one of them."

As the little man approached the table, he reached under his jacket and pulled out a shiny, long-barreled pistol—it looked to be a .45 caliber, or a 44 mag. revolver. Deputy Corker spotted the gun and immediately tried to react. He stood to his feet and backed up two steps, all the while unsnapping and drawing his Glock 10mm.

But he was too late. The little man was able to fire off a single shot before Deputy Corker could pump four fast rounds into his crumpling body.

It was enough. Both men lay dead. The single large slug that entered Jeffry Speelman's head through the back of his upper neck, passed through his brain. After it blew his right eye out, the deformed bullet passed over the heads of a dozen or more seated patrons and shattered the window directly behind Kate and Henry. The deadly missile's departure was followed by an enormous spray of blood and flesh, along with an ample amount of shattered skull and brain matter.

Chapter 56

While Jack saw Cross fall as a result of the three rounds he fired at him, he quickly made his way to the fallen Secret Service agent and fired an additional slug into the man's dead heart just to be sure.

He then headed over to where Roger was crouching.

"Rog! Rog! Where're you hit? Is it bad?"

Roger looked up at Jack and smiled.

"Nothin' much," he said. "A couple of scratches. That's it. I can take care of myself. You'd better run this thing back up the tower. We need to be as elevated as possible."

"Let me see your wounds first," Jack barked. "Show them to me."

"Oh, hell. Okay. He skinned my left arm here."

Roger then produced through-and-through bloody wounds in his bicep just above the elbow.

"It's nothin.'"

"Let me see you make a fist with that left hand. Do it! Make a fist!"

Roger struggled to lift his arm but he could not. Blood was dripping profusely from his dangling fingers.

"Close it," Jack said. "Let me see you make a fist."

Roger tried, but he could not move his fingers.

"Where'd the other round hit you?"

"It hit me in the shoulder. Same side. I didn't feel either of them. I wouldn't know I even got hit, but I saw the blood."

Jack peeled Roger's collar open and examined his shoulder.

"That could be your problem—why you can't use your hand.

Looks like it might have taken some ligaments and tendons out. You're bleeding like that because of the hole in your arm. Must have hit an artery. We can tie that one off. But there's nothing we can do about the shoulder wound. Not right now. It looks like it went straight through. The exit wound is relatively small, so it probably didn't hit any bones. And it's not bleeding too bad, so most likely that one didn't hit a major blood vessel.

"Let's get something around that arm to slow up the blood flow. Otherwise you're going to fall asleep on me."

Jack ripped the shirt off of Roger and fashioned a crude but effective tourniquet.

"Are you going to get this carriage back up the tower?" Roger protested. "We need to be up to the top. We need to get it back up as soon as possible. That's what we're here for, you know."

Jack looked around for something to use for a windlass rod. Not seeing anything appropriate, he pulled his reading glasses out of his shirt pocket and inserted them into the makeshift medical device. He carefully twisted the tourniquet tighter until he observed the blood stop pouring out of the wound.

"Here," Jack said. "Hold this firmly, but don't break the glasses. Keep the blood flow to a minimum. I'll get this thing back to the top, and then see if I can find a better way to deal with your arm."

"Take care of business," Roger barked. "I can handle this from here."

"Right," Jack said. "I'll get this headed in the right direction, and then I'll come right back."

"Damn it all, Jack. Would you stop worrying about me! We've got a mission here—to prevent an assassination. I swear to God, I can take care of myself. You need to figure out how we are going to stop those cruise missiles."

"See if you can find something better than a pair of cheap reading glasses," Jack ordered. "I'm afraid they're going to break and you'll start bleeding out. Got it?"

"I'm fine. Just do your job."

Jack ran over to the control room and reversed the motion of the observation deck.

"Jack!" Roger shouted. "Kim is about to arrive. His motorcade is just getting off the Gateway Bridge."

Jack heard him but could not make out much of what he said. He left the control room and ran over to where Roger was standing.

"What's up, buddy?" Jack asked.

Roger observed Jack approaching and pointed out through the hole facing north.

"His motorcade's just crossing the channel. Kim's. He'll be at the hotel within a few minutes."

"Kim was very late getting here," Jack commented. "I suppose we can expect the fireworks to start any time after he arrives."

"I thought we agreed that it would most likely occur at the four o'clock meeting—when the two men are sure to be in the same room," Roger said. "I just looked at my watch. I took it off to keep my juices from wrecking it. It's two-ten now. Anyway, at three they're scheduled to move into their respective meeting rooms, which are adjacent to the formal conference room—that's where the summit will actually take place. They will meet briefly with the press, and then they will move into the big room for their talks. Logically, that's when the attack will occur."

"True," Jack agreed. "But I've grown a little troubled about the logistics. Let me run this by you. These guys might be using antiquated munitions to pull this off. However, some of the best minds in the world are orchestrating the hit. Remember, we're dealing with the Deep State."

"So," Roger countered, "how is the plan to hit the two men when they are together sitting on opposite sides of the same table—how is that plan not sophisticated?"

"It makes sense—I would agree. But both of these personalities are just a little warped. Either one of them is fully capable of getting up from the negotiating table at any minute—that is particularly true of POTUS. Very unpredictable.

"And then there's the breaks they take for consultation—when they sense the need to remove themselves for a short period to discuss specific points with their aides. If the missile hits at one of those minutes, it would be only marginally effective. And I think it's more likely to be POTUS who would be the one consulting away from the table. In that case, he might very well survive the attack, and Kim would be killed."

"I see your point," Roger said. "While the odds are pretty good that if they fired on the summit once it starts, they'd catch the men at the table. But, what you say is very possible. Do you see a better way to attack the meeting—with a better chance of hitting POTUS?"

"Perhaps," Jack said. "What if the missiles were intended to force the two leaders to vacate the meeting? That could be the plan—to force the men down into the emergency bunker. I've read up on this hotel a little bit. While it is a fact that the whole building is constructed to withstand almost any hostile attack, even these older cruise missiles would penetrate the outside walls—to one degree or another."

"That's pretty much a given," Roger said. "So, how does that change things? Wouldn't it make sense to hit the men while they were in the same room?"

"Sure," Jack said. "But, if there is any chance that POTUS would not be in that selected room at the chosen time, the whole mission could easily fail. Got to have them together—both have to die in the attack. Or, if only POTUS is killed, it would look like a targeted assassination.

"What I'm getting at is this: if the missile is fired from some platform at sea, it will take from five to fifty minutes for it to reach the hotel—depending on how far away it is when fired. During even a one-minute period, either one of the men might sense the need to leave the room. Were that to happen, any attempt, even the most elaborate, would fall flat. Remember all the failed attempts to assassinate Hitler?"

"Are you suggesting that there might be a better way?"

"Possibly," Jack said.

"And what might that be?"

"What if the cruise missile attack was designed to be a diversion?"

"Okay," Roger replied. "A diversion to do what, exactly?"

"What if the plan was to emulate Bush's tactic in the Iraq War—remember Shock and Awe?"

"How would that be implemented? And why?"

"The *why* is easy—self-explanatory. Covered that already. The necessity of having the two men together. And to kill them both at the same time using relatively antiquated conventional weapons.

"The *how* is what would necessitate careful planning. What

got me thinking about it is when we learned that there were five or six cruise missiles stolen. Made me ask myself, *why so many?* Any precise, deep-state plan should require only a single missile. That is, if POTUS and Chairman Kim were *certain* to be at the same table, at the same time—one missile carrying a standard explosive package would easily do the trick.

"But the planners are well aware that both of these principals are complicated characters—unpredictable."

"But," Roger said in a challenging tone, "once the first missile hits the hotel, everyone's headed for cover—all the additional cruise missiles in their arsenal won't make a difference."

"You're right, as far as *killing* Chairman Kim or POTUS. But the Deep State plotters are thinking beyond the obvious—so must we. They are totally aware of the fact that once the first missile strikes the hotel, the element of surprise is gone. So, why would they have stolen multiple cruise missiles? Knowing that only the first one could possibly accomplish their goal?"

"Dammit! Jack! You're suggesting that the purpose of the missiles is primarily to funnel the targets down into the bunkers. Right? And you think that is where the real bad-ass shit's gonna go down. Is that about it? You think that they have managed to place some sort of hairy explosive device, and that is what will take them out."

"Something like that could very well be what they have in mind. Odds are that they will target and time the missiles to be as effective as possible. The one we have to fear the most will be the first one. Most likely our original thinking was sound—they will wait until the summit talks have begun—and then they will fire the first missile. If that manages to get through us, it will do the job—their mission will be accomplished.

"But, they will have no way of knowing for sure that they were successful—not for hours after the first blast. So, they will most likely follow through with the remaining missiles."

"And all the subsequent explosions will be as you suggested—merely designed to force them to the bunker."

"I think that makes the most sense," Jack agreed. "After all, they already know that we're here trying to defend against the missile attack. How else would they have known to send our very special, Special Agent Benjamin Cross? They are totally aware of our being here, and our mission. Yet, they don't seem particularly concerned. They had to have known that Cross would not be able to take us both out. And they weren't that worried about us.

"That means that they have a bigger plan. Bigger and more deadly than cruise missiles."

"So, how do you intend to counter it? If you're right."

"You stay here and ward off the cruise missiles. And I will go to the hotel and sniff out whatever they've got in mind for the executive bunker. How's your arm? Think you can handle things here? With one good arm?"

"You're damn right I can handle this. But you've got an impossible task to accomplish over there. You're going to need my help, don't you think?"

"If they don't see an attempt to take down the missiles, they are going to know something's up. They will assume that we took out Agent Cross, and they will know for sure that we're here. If it all goes as I think it will, the only missile that can hurt us is the first one. They will do everything they possibly can to get that one through. That will be your big challenge. If you are successful, the remaining four or five will be as I suggested. Not intended to kill the targets—merely to drive them underground.

"Now, it is entirely possible that they will not wait until the summit starts. They might just start firing early. Possibly all of them at once, knowing that some are likely to get through. All they really have to do is hit the building with one missile. That's it."

"Then you'd better get going. I've got it under control here."

"Yeah. Right," Jack agreed.

"Yeah. Right," Roger looked him in the eyes and said. "You say that like there is something else. Spill it. What's bugging you?"

"We're dealing with Deep State here," Jack said. "So, we have to assume that they are able to monitor all radio signals."

"Which means that we cannot communicate with each other once you leave. Is that what you're saying?"

"Yup."

"Damn. You have a point. Even though our equipment is fully encrypted, they're Deep State—they undoubtedly have the ability to eavesdrop."

"We cannot take a chance on it. So, you just do the best job you can. Communicate with Bob as much as necessary. But don't try to get me. I'll get with you once I know the principals are safe."

"How many missiles do you think they have?"

"We have to believe they have six. Might be five. But we have to prepare ourselves for six and one might have your name on it."

"Yeah—I thought about that. You taking the donut down to the ground?"

"Can't. I'm sure they've got a visual on us too. I'll grab Cross's jacket and see if I can slip out through the tower."

Jack was thinking all the way over to Agent Cross's body:

Damn. I hope that jacket isn't saturated in blood. Both rounds were headshots. And the last one to the heart—he'd already stopped bleeding. So it might not be too bad.

He was pleased to find that the only blood was around the collar, and he was able to wipe most of it off.

Jack made sure Cross's picture ID was intact and pinned to his jacket. He left it there. He then removed Cross's holster and magazine pouch from his belt, and strapped them on. He picked up the agent's Glock 19 and slid in a fresh magazine.

Turning the body over, he removed Cross's wallet, sunglasses, and the van keys. He shoved them all into his pocket.

Jack took a couple steps toward the tower, and then he had another thought: *one of us is likely not to make it through this.* So, he turned and walked back to where Roger was standing. He put his hand on the back of Roger's neck, careful to avoid the wound to his shoulder.

"Rog, old buddy. I'm taking off now. Want you to know that it has been a real treat working with you through the years. Couldn't have asked for a better friend."

"You bet your ass, Handler. We've had some fun. And we ain't done yet. But, you know what. The really sad thing about this whole mess is that once we're done, and back in the States, we'll never be able to talk about it—except to each other. So, you'd damn well better survive this, or else I'm going to have to go to my grave never having had the chance to brag about it to anyone. You'd better be prepared to dodge some bullets. Got it?"

"We've got to pull this off," Jack said. "We always do, don't we?"

"We're still alive, so I guess you're right."

"Give me your credentials—all of them," Jack said reaching

out to Roger. "I'm now Special Agent Benjamin Cross. Jack Handler's dead—at least for the time being. You need to disappear too. Better to be an utter nobody, than the infamous Roger Minsk … at least for now."

Roger removed his wallet and handed it to Jack.

"So, how you getting over to the hotel?" Roger asked. "You going to drive yourself or take a taxi?"

"I have Cross's keys. I'll drive the van. Think I can pass for the special agent? We're about the same size, wouldn't you say?"

"Sure. Why not?" Roger said. "… And maybe you should wear a hat, or grow some hair. Just be prepared to shoot a few doubters. How'd that blood get on your collar, Agent Cross?

"Here, let me help you with that," Roger continued, pulling a red shop cloth out of his pocket. He poured some water on it from a bottle he had sitting beside him, and used it to clean most of the remaining blood from Cross's jacket.

"That should do it," he said, tossing the rag on the floor. "Take care, my friend."

"You bet," Jack replied. "Join me for a couple Cubans at Timber Charlies? Two weeks from today? Actually, we won't light the cigars until after Timber Charlies. See you there?"

"Sounds good to me. I think we're going to feel like celebrating after this mess is settled. Timber Charlies would be perfect. Call me when we get back."

Jack smiled and nodded.

"See you there," he said as he walked off.

Jack opened the entrance to the tower and embarked on the long trip down. "Damn!" he muttered. "I'm sure as hell glad I'm not climbing these damn things."

Not sure at all what he might encounter on exit, he lifted Cross's Glock up in the holster slightly to ensure the ease of the draw should he be suddenly challenged on egress. Thankfully that did not happen. At least not then.

Before he opened the door to leave the tower, he pulled out Cross's sunglasses and slipped them on.

"I'm no longer Jack Handler," he said to himself. "My name is now Benjamin Cross—Special Agent Benjamin Cross. Gotta locate that damn executive security bunker, and see what the hell awaits those unsuspecting world leaders."

He took a look at his watch.

"Damn! I have no good idea about how much time I have left. I gotta make a beeline to that bunker. No matter how many unsuspecting souls I have to eliminate. How the hell am I gonna pull this off? Shit! I hope I brought enough rounds."

Jack was careful not to give his apprehension away. *I'm sure someone's watching me*, he was thinking. *Must be careful not to look unsure of myself. Agent Cross would have prided himself in killing Roger and me. He would have bounce in his step. That was his mission, and he must look the part of the successful special agent.*

The Miami Beach Hotel was not far—less than a kilometer and a half west of the tower. Jack was prepared to walk it, if he had any trouble starting the van. *There might be some sort of ignition code. Or it might require a prox card. If I cannot fire it up, I will feign looking for something. I will then start muttering profanities, jump out of the van, slam the door, and head toward the hotel—looking as angry as possible.*

He inserted the key in the ignition and turned it. The engine turned over twice, and then it fired.

"Great!" he said loudly. "The damn thing started right up."

Jack let the motor warm up for fifteen seconds, which was his standard practice.

"Shit!" he muttered lowly.

That was Jack Handler starting this van, he reasoned. *Probably not the way Special Agent Benjamin Cross would do it. I've got to be more careful.*

Cross was not the brightest man in the world, Jack believed. *He would probably leave some rubber behind.*

So, Jack checked his mirror, and nailed the accelerator. But only for a brief moment. Just enough to elicit a short-lived screeching sound.

Jack knew that Siloso Road, the only way to get to the hotel, passed directly by the tower. *So, the trek to the hotel should be a breeze,* he reasoned. But reality was about to come crashing down on him with a vengeance.

Chapter 57

After leaving a small patch of rubber, Jack adjusted his driving back to a more judicious manner. He had progressed only a few hundred yards down Imbiah Road, which is what Siloso was called once it approached the tower, when he observed a patrol car pull out from the curb. Even though the patrol car did not activate its flashing emergency lights or siren, he knew that he was about to be stopped.

And so it happened.

The car pulled right up on his rear bumper and began flashing its headlights.

Jack immediately pulled toward the side of the road. But he didn't stop. Instead he flipped on his four-ways and proceeded slowly until he spotted the entrance road into Megazip Adventure Park. He figured that *if this goes sideways, at least our vehicles will not be abandoned on a major road.*

He pulled into the park far enough so that they would not be easily visible to Imbiah traffic. Carefully, he slid his Smith and Wesson .357 out from under his belt and rested it on his lap—still mindful that it remained covered by his jacket. He preferred a revolver in situations like this because it could be more effectively affixed with a suppressor than his Glock—and it was. Plus, it didn't spew spent cartridges.

He watched as a uniformed officer pulled up behind him, but did not immediately exit his vehicle. *Looks like he's on his radio,* Jack reasoned. *Must be checking my plates. I'm not sure what standard procedure dictates in Singapore, but I'd guess he was reporting on his location and what he was doing here. Can't let that stand.*

Eventually the officer exited his patrol car and headed up to

Jack's side of the van.

His Glock is still holstered, Jack observed. *That's a good sign.*

Jack watched his every move.

As the officer approached Jack's door, he unsnapped his holster and rested his hand on his firearm. *I wonder if this guy is just cautious, or suspicious,* Jack thought to himself.

Jack lowered his window, but still kept a close eye on the officer's gun-hand.

"You speak English?" he asked.

"Yes."

"Are you attached to the American Embassy?"

"No," Jack responded. "I am United States Secret Service Special Agent Benjamin Cross. Would you like to see my ID?"

"Yes, please."

"May I remove it from my pocket?" he asked.

"Yes. Go ahead."

Jack leaned forward as though preparing to reach for his billfold. But, instead of producing his badge and card, he reached out with his left hand, grabbed the officer's shirt just below his chin and pulled his face into the barrel of his .357.

"Lift both hands and lock your fingers behind your head!" he barked.

The officer did as commanded.

Jack then reached down with his left hand, pulled the officer's Glock 19 out of its holster and slid it into his jacket pocket.

"Now, keep your hands where they are and take two steps backward," Jack firmly directed.

Again, the officer did as told.

Jack slowly opened his door and yanked the officer's radio

from its belt pouch.

"Any more firearms?" Jack asked.

The officer shook his head.

"Pull up your trouser legs and let me see what you've got down there. Now! Do it!"

Slowly the officer pulled up his pant legs. There, strapped to his right calf was a Glock 42 .380.

"Don't touch it!" Jack yelled. "You lyin' sack of shit. Touch it and you're dead. Lock your fingers behind your head again. I should just shoot you for lyin'. Sit your ass down on the ground. Keep your hands behind your head and sit down."

As soon as the officer's butt hit the ground Jack snatched the Glock 42 from his calf.

Jack then ripped the officer's cuffs from his belt and told him to stand up.

"Lean forward and place your hands on the van," Jack said.

Jack pulled the officer's right hand behind his back and locked the cuffs on his wrist. He then yanked his right elbow back, causing the officer to smash face-first into the van door. Jack locked the cuffs on that wrist as well.

"Where's your cell phone?" he asked as he led the officer around and helped him into the van's passenger seat.

"My cell's back in the car. I left it in the car."

"You shittin' me again?"

"No sir. I'm telling you the truth. My cell phone's in the car. I don't have any more guns or cell phones on me. Promise."

"You better not. Not if you want to live.

"What does your office know about this?" Jack asked. "What did you tell them before you got out of your car?"

"I gave them your plate number. That's all I had. They were going to run it through to see what we had on the van. That's it."

Jack pulled a pair of his own handcuffs out of the center console and locked one end of them to a safety grab bar, and the other to the chain of the officer's cuffs.

"There you go, my friend," Jack said as he patted the officer on the shoulder. "All you have to do to survive is to just sit there quietly. Do you hear what I'm saying?"

The officer nodded his head.

"Great. Glad to see we're on the same page here," Jack said. "You have to understand. I'd hate like hell to have to clean your blood off the seat. So, just behave yourself, and you'll save me a lot of work. Okay?"

Again, the officer nodded.

"Just hang on here, I'll be right back."

Jack trotted back to the patrol car and briefly surveyed the contents. He then briskly walked back to the van.

"Take your clothes off," Jack said as he unlocked the handcuffs from the officer's wrists. "And don't make me wait. Do it quickly."

"What?" the officer asked.

"Strip!" Jack barked. "Right down to your panties. I want your shoes, trousers and your shirt. Chop! Chop! Hurry up."

After Jack had helped him pull his shirt off, he took his jacket and shirt off and put on the officer's shirt.

"Now your shoes and pants. And be quick about it."

Before the officer could react, Jack had already pulled the man's shoes off.

"I'll let you take your own pants off," Jack said with a chuckle as he unbuckled his belt, slipped his shoes off, emptied his pockets, and then took his own pants off.

"Here," Jack said, snatching the officer's pants. "Give me those. And you put mine on."

"I'm keeping my own shoes," Jack said. "My feet are too big for yours. So you can put your own shoes back on."

As soon as the officer had tied his shoes, Jack quickly slid the cuffs back on.

He went through Roger's billfold and removed everything that had his picture on it, and then stuffed it back into the officer's left rear pocket.

"There," Jack said as he started the van. "You need to be behind the wheel."

Jack unlocked the cuffs again and led the officer around to the driver's side. He sat him down in the seat and then cuffed him tightly to the top of the steering wheel, making sure that even were he able to turn the wheel, he would not be able to reach the ignition key or the shifter on the center console.

"You just going to leave me here in this running van?" the officer asked. "The fumes could kill me. This is not right."

"You know what?" Jack replied. "You've got a point."

The officer turned his hand as much as possible in order to make the key slot accessible for Jack. But Jack did not remove the cuffs. Instead he delivered a short, but powerfully effective left hook to the left side of the officer's upper cheek. The punch knocked him instantly unconscious. Jack then reached in and fastened the seatbelt, put the van in drive, turned the steering wheel slightly to the right, and stepped back. The van jumped the curb on the opposite side of the road and rolled quickly over a patch of lawn, and then disappeared into a small but thick group of trees.

Jack did not wait around to watch what happened to the van. He quickly made his way back to the patrol car, shoved it into reverse, and made a quick U-turn—which took him momentarily off the road. And then swung around and back to Sentosa Road toward the Miami Beach Hotel.

If I'm going to have to explain myself to U.S. Secret Service, he reasoned, *I'd rather do it as a Singapore cop, not another Secret Service special agent. ... But, if I'm to be scrutinized by a local, I'd prefer to fall back on the original plan. At any rate, this poor Roger Minsk will be trying to explain himself to whoever it is that finds him up against some tree in the middle of the woods. Might be hours before he's found. ... Hopefully, the confusion will give us at least enough time for us to get our job done.*

"I wonder what sort of cop this fellow was?" Jack asked himself.

He pulled the officer's wallet out from his right pocket and took a closer look at it. He read aloud what it said, "Sergeant Ryan Hin Tan. His name was Ryan Tan. And let's see. Oh my God! What's this? *Special Tactics and Rescue.* He was not your everyday cop. He was a STAR. A real special dude, he is. These guys are authorized to carry all sorts of specialized gear. Especially in the firepower department.

"Wonder what he's got here," Jack continued, turning to check out what was in the back seat.

"Nothing back there. Maybe in the trunk? What do you think, Jack? Maybe he's got the serious shit in the trunk. Have to check that out when I get a chance."

Jack listened to his own words, and he went silent. His mind had become fixed on what he might have given up by relinquishing the remaining armament that might have been in the van. *But it was the right thing to do,* he reasoned. *Any way you slice it. It was the right move. Good old Ryan Hin Tan—Sergeant Ryan Hin Tan —he's going to have one hell of a sweet time trying to explain away all the crap that's going to be associated with that van. I'm sure that at least some of it is going to go beyond what he is authorized to have in his possession. Gun laws in Singapore are as strict as they are anywhere. He can't possibly come up with a story that they'll buy—at least not right away. That's all I really need—a little time. And a lot of luck.*

Jack knew that he had to put some distance between himself and Sgt. Tan. He was confident that he had bought himself *some* time, but he had no idea how much. The first cruise missile could be fired at any minute, so he had no time to waste.

I'll wait until I make it back to the hotel before I inspect the trunk, he reasoned. *Got to get away from here.*

Just then Jack recalled spotting a device in the van that especially sparked his interest. It was a new portable MS device—MS standing for *mobility spectrometry*; which is a complicated term for a machine designed to detect explosives. He'd heard rumblings about it but had heard that it was still under development in Israel and the U.S.

"If good old Benjamin left it in the van," Jack said aloud, "then it will soon fall into the hands of the Singapore police. I sure as hell could have used it in the bunker. Oh well. That mistake is on me—failure to anticipate. I should have grabbed it."

Jack and Roger had used an earlier model of a similar device, but had left it with the head of security as a courtesy.

"Cinch there's nothing like that in the trunk of this car."

Jack discovered a roadblock across Siloso Road just before the hotel. While it did make his heart beat fast, it was nothing he had not anticipated. "What's going to get me through this the quickest?" he asked himself. "Those manning it are *not* locals. I should have more luck with my using Sergeant Ryan Hin Tan's STAR jacket—especially since I'm driving a Singapore cop's car."

Quickly he altered the picture of Sgt. Tan with a permanent marker, and then he tossed Special Agent Benjamin Cross's jacket onto the floor of the patrol car in behind the passenger seat and approached the roadblock at a virtual crawl.

"Sergeant Ryan Hin Tan," he announced confidently to Sgt. William Crank, the Secret Service agent assigned to check IDs. POTUS, via an executive order, had authorized the unit of the USSSUD—United States Secret Service Uniformed Division—assigned to protect the White House to accompany him to the summit.

"Sergeant Tan," Agent Crank said, reading from ID pinned on the jacket. "Your last name is *Tan*? And you're a member of STAR. What does STAR stand for?"

"STAR is the *Special Tactical and Rescue* unit of the Singapore police. I am a sergeant in that unit."

"You don't sound or look like any of the Singaporeans I've ever met. Do you have a picture ID?"

"I was born in Philadelphia," Jack said as he handed Sgt. Tan's photo ID to the officer. "I was adopted as a baby by the Tans. My adoptive father was an ambassador at that time."

"What the hell happened to this picture?" Agent Crank said in disbelief. "It doesn't look anything like you."

"I know," Jack replied, feigning a corny demeanor. "My daughter told me last night that I didn't smile enough. So she gave me a big smiley face, and those ugly sunglasses. I haven't had the time to pick up my new ID. Because of the big meeting. My captain had me assigned to the detail that would monitor activity in the hotel, probably because I look so American."

"Okay," the agent said. "What's your captain's name? I'll see if I can get hold of him."

"His name is Captain Lim Tan."

"His last name is the same as yours? How's that?"

"Captain Tan's my uncle—my father's brother."

"Do you have a number for him? So I can give him a call."

"The number is on top. Just call that number and ask for Captain Tan."

The agent pulled out his cell phone and dialed the number on the card, but all he got was a busy signal. He tried it again, and the same thing happened. He tried it a third time, but to no avail.

He was about to dial the number a fourth time when Lt. Ralph Campbell, the Secret Service agent in charge, stepped up to see if he could help.

"What seems to be the problem here?" Lt. Campbell asked.

"Sergeant Tan here seems to have a damaged picture ID. And I was trying to get hold of his supervisor to verify his identity."

Lt. Campbell took a glance at the line of vehicles that was building behind Jack's *borrowed* patrol car and said, "Let me take a look at it—this suspicious ID."

Sgt. Crank handed him the card.

"Holy shit, Sergeant Tan," he said laughing out loud. "What the hell happened to your ID? Looks like your girlfriend got mad at you, or something. Care to explain what this is?"

"My twelve-year-old daughter. She said I was too serious all the time. So she gave me a smile, moustache and sunglasses. It happened last night. I've got my request in to get it replaced, but we're all too busy right now with this meeting. I apologize. But I really need to get into the hotel. The captain has requested me. I'm sorry, but he's going to be mad as hell if I don't get my ass in the hotel right now."

Lt. Campbell took another look at the cars lined up behind Jack's. He handed the ID back to Jack and begrudgingly waved him through.

"Thanks," Jack said as he took his foot off of the brake and eased ahead.

"Shit," Jack muttered to himself. "That was close. Can't believe they let me through so easily."

He drove slowly in front of the hotel. "Damn," he complained out loud. "There sure as hell are a lot of cop cars here. I think I might do better in back."

He pulled around to the west side of the huge building. The entrance there was much smaller, and thus was manned by a single pair of Singapore officers.

"That might work better for me," Jack said. "Actually, I think it's about time for Special Agent Benjamin Cross to make his move."

Jack pulled his patrol car around the corner of the building so as to not be viewed by the officers guarding the door he intended to enter. He switched on his emergency lights and jumped the right wheels of the patrol car up onto the curb. He then grabbed Agent Cross's jacket and put it on.

"I wonder what surprises Officer Tan's got for me in the back of this car," he said, as he slipped on the sunglasses he found in

Agent Cross's jacket pocket and walked to the back of the patrol car. He inserted the key into the lock and opened the trunk. He was impressed with what he found.

Nothing was labeled, but each item had its own place in a carved out foam bed.

I wonder what I might need in there, he was thinking. *Let's see, what all do we have here?*

Jack's eyes first did an inventory. While he ceased speaking to himself out loud, he mouthed the name of each item as he identified it: Glock 19. SCAR-L—Special Operations Forces Combat Assault Rifle.

"That could come in handy," he said out loud, as he removed it and its reserve magazine.

He skipped over several of the other pieces, one of which was a SAR 21.

"That seems a bit redundant," he muttered.

And then his eyes landed on a well-formed large protective case off to the side. The lid was covered with Chinese writing.

"I wonder what the hell that is," he said. "Not shaped like a gun case. Maybe it's an explosive material detector."

He released the three latches that secured it and opened the lid.

"Shit!" he grumbled. "I don't know what the hell you are. Doesn't look like anything *I've* ever seen."

He snatched what looked to be an operating manual and fumbled through it. The language of choice was, of course, Chinese. But that was followed by instructions in French, German, and finally in English.

"Here we go," he said with a slight smile, "This ought to tell me something."

He turned back to the first page of the English text and read the heading: "Explosive Detector."

"Yes. This should do the trick," he said. "Or maybe. It looks like an older technology. At least, older than the one Bob sent with us. Better than nothin', I suppose."

When he pulled the case out to set it on the pavement, he spotted a second, far larger protective case beneath it.

"Holy shit!" he said. "Looks like Sergeant Tan came pretty well equipped. This is *huge*. What do we have here—some sort of rocket launcher?"

After he slid the case containing the SAR-21 over, he looked closely at the instructions on the cover of his new discovery. Again, the first language used was Chinese. But, this time, directly beneath the Chinese script, were the instructions in English. He read the writing out loud: "This device is designed to detect airborne hazards. Open only in a clean environment, and when ready to use."

"Oh, what the hell!" he said as he popped a whole series of spring-loaded latches, and lifted the environmentally sealed cover.

"Damn!" he said in surprise. "This looks like some pretty serious equipment."

He quickly studied the English section of the operating instructions. And then he had an idea.

This shit ought to get me past security in a snap. They'll be more interested in inspecting these cases for bombs than in over scrutinizing my papers.

It was with a big smile on his face that he snatched up the two cases.

"But, I sure as hell better be wearing the right shirt," he muttered to hmself, half serious and half in jest. He slipped off Cross' jacket and tossed it in the trunk. As he headed for the hotel entrance he was a little surprised to see that the men stationed at the door were members of USSSUD.

"Sergeant Ryan Hin Tan, STAR. My captain sent me here to do a secondary inspection of the executive bunker for explosives. Not sure why. He just felt it was in order. Could be purely precautionary. Don't really know. It was requested by the Secret Service."

"What the hell do you have there?" the agent in charge asked. "Set them up here on the desk and let me have a closer look. And hand over your weapons. I'm talking knives, guns, clubs—anything sharp, pointed, heavy or loud. In other words, *any* item that could be considered a weapon.

"You say you are a *STAR*. What does that mean?"

"STAR is the *Special Tactical and Rescue* unit of the Singapore police. I am a sergeant in that unit."

"What's in these cases?" the interrogating agent asked. "Are they going to blow up when I open them? Or is a poisonous gas going to be released? What the hell are they? Tell me. Twenty words or less."

"Sensing devices. That's all they are. I'm supposed to look for any explosive devices, and to do a brief inspection of air quality—to see if there are any hazardous gases drifting in or around the bunker. It'll take me only a few minutes. You could send one of your men with me if you want. Just someone who has keys and codes to access the bunker and adjacent rooms."

"What rooms are you talking about?" the agent asked. "And why do you have to see in them?"

"Any room that shares a common wall could be a problem. This equipment is fast and effective. If they turn up nothing, I'll tie your man up for less than a half hour. In and out, basically."

The agent examined the explosive sensor and said, "I don't know what good this is gonna do. How the hell old is it? We've already been through the whole hotel with the best equipment in the world. And it turned up nothing. I think this is a total waste of time. And if there was a poison gas problem, we'd all be dead by now. I don't think there's any point to any of this. But, I'll check with my captain and see what he thinks. Who'd you say authorized this shit? You got a name for me?"

"His name is Captain Lim Tan. Same last name as mine. Tan. He's my uncle. My father's brother."

"Really? And can I get hold of him?"

"Sure," Jack said. "His number is right here on my ID. You can call him. But I do say that time is critical. We really should get this done. It'll only take a few minutes. Your guy can hold his firearm on me. I don't care. I just need to get this done, or my uncle's going to go nuts on me."

"What the hell kind of scribbling you got on your ID? Looks like a kid made it."

"My daughter drew the smile on it. And the sunglasses were also her idea. For a joke. I haven't had time to get it replaced yet. And I'm the only one in our unit that is certified on this equipment. Hell. Send *two* of your men down to keep their eye on me. Just let's get this done right away. There's no one important down there now, so it shouldn't be a problem. Right?"

Just as the agent picked up his phone to get the inspection authorized, it rang. He received the call.

Chapter 58

"Yes, sir," the agent said as he answered his phone. And then he listened for a lengthy amount of time. After nearly a minute, he replied, "Yes, sir." And then he disconnected. He summoned one of the guards he had stationed at the door, Sgt. William Crosby, and told him to go with Jack for the inspection.

"Does your man have the necessary keys and codes to access all the rooms we need to check out?"

"Don't worry, he's got what you need," the agent in charge abruptly snorted. "Just be quick about it. We've got a lot of work to do around here. You should be aware, I just learned that …," the agent paused to look at his watch, "that five minutes ago the Tiger Tower was blown to hell. My captain says that it's flat on the ground. What's left is burning."

"No shit!" Jack said. "But nothing here. Right?"

"Not yet."

"What caused the explosion? Do you know? Was it a gas leak? Or an attack of some sort?"

"Don't know. Won't know for sure until forensics moves in. You'd better get busy and check us out here. The captain says that they're moving on full speed ahead here with the summit. Our fearless president is one stubborn son-of-a-bitch. Or else crazy as hell. But he won't be deterred by anything. I swear, this hotel could be on fire, and if he thought he could strike a deal with the NoKos, he'd be walking around with a fire extinguisher.

"Sergeant Tan. Either you take Sergeant Crosby and get on with your inspection right now, or get the hell outta here. You're beginning to get on my nerves."

Jack immediately turned away from the desk and said to Sgt. Crosby, "You lead the way, sergeant, and I'll follow."

The two men headed toward the elevator. All Jack could think about was Roger. At first he tried to conceive of scenarios whereby his friend would have survived. *If he escaped using the emergency stairway, it would have taken too long,* he reasoned. *The same with the elevator—it would have been too slow—I cut the power to it, and he would have had to locate the control room, and reactivate it. Besides, Roger's not the type to abandon his post. Roger's gone.*

Many other thoughts crossed his mind as he rode down to the sub-basement. *What do I do now to stop the missiles? Without Roger, there's likely to be five or six more strikes. They knew we were there. That asshole Ben passed the word up the line. That's how they knew to hit the tower first. Damn it all! It's only a matter of time before security begins moving the principals down to the bunker. And they're not going to think much of me poking around when they start. I have minutes at the most.*

"This is it, partner," Sgt. Crosby said as he swiped his card and entered a code on the keypad. He then opened the door and declared without making eye contact with Jack, "Have at it. I'd say you have five minutes. Ten at the most. You'd better get busy. There's only one door to the bunker. I'll be waiting right here."

He then unsnapped his holster and slipped a Glock semi-auto out. He held it at his side.

"If you try anything. Anything at all. I'll kill you where you stand. Do you understand me?"

Jack made eye contact with him, but said nothing.

"Then get your ass in there and get busy."

Jack still did not verbally respond. He entered the vault, set the two instruments down on a table, and opened the case housing the explosion sensor.

He discovered, as he thought, an older version of the device that he had left behind in the van with the real Sgt. Tan. It was a basic ion mobility spectrometer technology (IMS). While it was good in its day, which was about twenty years ago, it was currently not as effective as the newer mass spectrometry system.

"Whatever," Jack muttered to himself. "I'll use what I got."

And he then began testing for any evidence of explosive material.

As he worked his way through the bunker complex, he was satisfied that the equipment he was using had not found any sign of trapping the rooms with explosives.

And then, at the rear of the main sitting room, he came upon two louvered openings—one at ceiling level, and the other six inches off the floor.

"Ventilation ducts," he silently said to himself. "Must be where the fresh air is piped in. This would be a great place to hide an explosive device. Anything exploding right here would send a wall of fire throughout the whole area. It would kill any living thing around."

So he spent an inordinate amount of time inspecting the two vents for explosives. But, he found nothing.

"That's a good sign, I suppose," he muttered. "No indication of a bomb in this area." He put the detector back into its protective case and prepared to move into the room that housed the ventilation system.

When he reached down to pick up the air-testing device, he had second thoughts.

"Hell," he said out loud. "I'm here, and it's here. Why not?"

So he opened the large case and did a quick study of the operating instructions.

"That's not too complicated," he said. "Might as well get on with it."

He removed the tester from its case and turned it on. "Let's see," he said to himself, "all it's got is a simple on/off switch. No adjustments or anything. This thing was designed to be operated by very average men. Thank God for that. All I need is for Sergeant Crosby to come in here and find me reading the instruction manual. If he mouths off to me again, or sticks that Glock in my nose, I'm going to take it away from him and blow his teeth to the back of his brain."

Jack was almost finished testing the air. And, just as when he used the explosive testing device, he intended to wind up his effort in the bunker at the ventilation louvers.

First he tested the lower vent. *If there were to be any sign of bad air*, he reasoned, *this is where it would show up.*

The needle on the sensor did not move, and the warning signal remained silent.

He moved the device from side to side to see if it found anything. Still, it did not signal anything.

And then he held it up to the upper vent. Still nothing.

Noticing that the slats on the upper louver were closed, he used the sensing device as a tool and placed the receiving port on the unit under the middle louver and applied pressure. It gave way, forcing all the louvers to open nearly an inch. When it did, it freed up about half a gram of dust that had been trapped by the closed slats of the louver.

And then it happened.

The low-volume sounder on the device sounded three times, and a red warning LED light started flashing a *level-one* alert. And then it stopped.

"What the hell did that mean?" he grumbled. "Did I break this foreign-made piece of shit?"

He took a close look at the device. It was now silent and the light had ceased flashing. "I'd better see what all this means," he said to himself as he walked back to the case to again study the instructions.

He read this part out loud: "When sounder is activated, even at level-one, and momentarily, poisoned air has been detected, anyone in the vicinity should immediately put on portable ventilation system. This is especially true for the person operating this sensing device. DO NOT CONTINUE TO TEST UNPROTECTED. TO DO SO COULD RESULT IN INJURY OR DEATH."

"Damn!" Jack barked sternly yet quietly. "I don't have anything like that with me. Must be a bad read."

Thinking that the sensor could be defective—that he might even have damaged it when he shoved the louver open by using the device as a tool—he decided to reset it and start over. It took about forty-five seconds to power it down, and then to restart it. When it became operational, he again made his rounds throughout the three rooms that made up the bunker area. Nothing happened—the sensor remained silent. Jack was relieved.

But then he returned to the louvered vents. First, he tested the lower duct—nothing. However, as soon as he passed the device's intake in front of the upper vent, it registered "Hazard," and the warning tone sounded—just like before.

"Okay," he muttered, "I'm going to have to inspect the source of this damn problem."

"Hey, sergeant!" he yelled loudly, as he turned toward the bunker's door. "I'm coming out. Don't shoot. I got a question for you."

"You done in there?" Sgt. Crosby said, looking down at his watch. "I think you've been at it long enough. I got to get back to my post."

"One more thing I need to check out. There's a ventilation system I need to have a look at. I need you to take me in there, wherever it is, so I can run some tests in there."

"We just got the whole thing replaced—courtesy of the U.S. Government. Last week—week before last. When they announced that they were holding the summit talks at this hotel. I was here while they did it. I'm not taking you anywhere near it. They told me that once they closed and locked the door, I wasn't to let anyone else into the room. 'Top-secret shit,' they said. So, you're just gonna have to wind it up so we can get the hell outta here. Savvy?"

"Yeah," Jack replied. "I'm just about ready. Show me the entry door, and I will test it. Then I can cross it off my list. You know—keep my boss happy. How do we get to it?"

"I don't believe this crap! Didn't I just tell you that it was our guys—the Secret Service—that put the system in? And I know for a fact that no one has been near that room since they were here two weeks ago. Pack it up, buddy. We're gonna get the hell outta here. Now!"

"Yeah," Jack said. "I totally agree. Just give me one minute outside that room, and then we can head up. One minute."

"Come on," Sgt. Crosby begrudgingly acquiesced. "Get your fancy vacuum cleaner ready, and I'll show you the door. And you'd better make it quick. Or, after I show you the door, I'll show you my boot up your sorry ass. You've got one minute."

Jack was quickly growing irritated with having to put up with Sgt. Crosby's mouth. *This won't last much longer*, he said to himself. *I don't find anything out of the ordinary at the door, I just pack it up. Had to have been a bad reading. This foreign shit machine.*

"Here you are," Sgt. Crosby said. "Have a go at it. Just remember—you have sixty seconds." After his final words, he raised his Glock in a threatening fashion.

"You bet," Jack said, as he set the explosion sensing device down beside the door. "Too bad you don't have the key to this room. Seems like they'd trust you with it."

"Oh, I've got all the keys. They just don't want idiots like you poking around in there. Now get to it, or get the hell outta here. I've got real work to do."

"Help me out here," Jack said, lifting the air-testing device up toward Sgt. Crosby with his left hand. "Take a look at this piece of Chinese shit and tell me what you think. I'm not sure I'm doing this right. See what you think."

As soon as Jack saw Sgt. Crosby's eyes moving to the sensor, he delivered a short right to the sergeant's temple, instantly knocking him unconscious. As the man was falling down Jack snatched the Glock from his hand.

After he safely tucked the pistol into his belt, he unhooked the keychain from the sergeant's crumpled body, unlocked the mechanical room door, and dragged the body into the room.

Before he was able to close the door behind him, Jack felt the building shake. While it felt like an earthquake, Jack knew that it was not.

"That was an explosion!" he muttered. "The second Tomahawk, no doubt. They are now targeting the hotel. This place is going to be crawling with suits very soon."

Jack looked around. "This is one huge mechanical room," he said in near disbelief. "Larger than the bunker itself."

Jack then realized that he had left the explosion-testing device outside the door, so he opened it to make a retrieval. When he did, he was confronted by a camo-clad soldier carrying an M-16.

"What're you doin' down here?" the soldier demanded.

"Sergeant Crosby has me doing some emergency sensing to be sure all is safe down here in the bunker. I'll be finished in a flash."

"Where is the sergeant?" he asked.

"He got called upstairs. He gave me only a few minutes to finish up down here. So I'd better get busy."

"You're gonna have to leave. Now. This is the executive bunker. You're not authorized to be down here. In about two minutes this area will be populated with the members of both leadership groups. You might not be aware, but there has been an explosion on the roof of the hotel. The Secret Service has declared this an emergency, and we are evacuating the hotel. The leaders will be escorted to the executive bunker. It is adjacent to this room—whatever that room is. Anyway, you have to leave."

"Something very strange is going on in here," Jack said as he stepped into the room. "Come take a look."

"I don't have time for this," the soldier said. "Come on out, now. I'll escort you up."

When the soldier stepped forward, Jack grabbed the barrel of the M-16 with his right hand and pushed it away from him. At the same time he delivered a skull-crushing left to the bridge of the soldier's nose, knocking him out. He then reached out and grabbed the explosion sensor, slid it down on the floor of the mechanical room, and slammed the door closed.

Both men were still not moving, but Jack knew that it was only a matter of time. He removed the handcuffs from Sgt. Crosby's belt and attached them to the sergeant's right wrist. He then dragged him over to where the soldier was lying, wrapped the cuffs behind an exposed water pipe, and attached them to the soldier's wrist.

After he had removed the soldier's side arm and the M-16, Jack returned to his mission. The air-sensing device was still powered up, so he began testing for airborne poisons. As he approached the area where the ductwork was connected to bunker's louvered vent, the emergency sounder on the sensing device went off.

"Damn!" Jack grumbled. "Something's up here. Another *level-one* alert. There has to be a problem with the air. But why aren't we all dead? I wonder how high it goes. If this is a level-one problem—when does it really get dangerous?"

That was when Jack made a startling discovery. Attached on the side of the duct itself was a pressurized container about the size and design of a small propane tank. Located at the valve was what appeared to Jack to be a battery-powered wireless receiver.

"This is some crazy shit!" Jack barked. He immediately realized what he was dealing with. The workers who Sgt. Crosby described as Secret Service were actually members of the Deep State, and they had installed a remotely controlled system designed to pump poisoned air into the executive bunker.

Now they were launching the Tomahawk missiles into the upper floors of the hotel, knowing that in so doing, they would force security to bring POTUS and the North Korean leaders down into the executive bunker death chamber.

Once they force all the significant parties involved in this summit to the bunker, he concluded, *once that has been accomplished, they will activate the remote and release the gas—whatever that might be. But, I can imagine that they would not have made some provision to destroy the evidence. So, they must have secured a substantial quantity of explosive—probably a type of the same era as that of the Tomahawks; they would want to blow up this entire area. Primarily to destroy all evidence. I need gas masks if I'm going to get POTUS out of here alive. Immediately!*

Jack scrambled over to the two cuffed men. Sgt. Crosby had his eyes open, but his mouth shut.

"Sergeant Crosby!" Jack said, shaking him by the shoulder. "Can you understand me?"

The man did not respond, so Jack said again, "Sergeant Crosby. Do you hear me?"

"Yes," the man said slowly.

"Gas masks. Where are they?"

"Don't need gas masks. The bunkers are sealed off and oxygen is piped in."

"The oxygen is poisoned. I need masks. Now! Where are they?"

"How'd you get in here?"

"I used your keys."

"Damn. My head is spinning. What happened? Why am I cuffed to this man? I don't know him. What happened to him?"

"Look, you son-of-a-bitch, tell me where the masks are right now or I'm going to put a 10m round in your knee. Where the hell are they?"

"There in the bunker—the executive bunker. In the closet. There's thirty of them. That's the capacity, plus five. The bunker is rated for twenty-five."

"Is the closet locked?"

"No. The emergency closet is never locked."

"I'm going in there now. If I find it locked, I'll be back here to deal with you."

"It's not locked. It doesn't even have a lock on it."

"We'll see," Jack said as he headed for the door.

"Wait," Sgt. Crosby yelled. "Don't leave me in here. Wait!"

Jack did not stop or reply. He grabbed the M-16, bolted out of the door and ran into the executive bunker. And, just as Sgt. Crosby had said, the closet was unlocked, and the masks were hanging on numbered hooks on the wall.

Just as Jack was putting on one of the masks, he heard loud talking headed toward the bunker. *Must be POTUS, Chairman Kim, and their entourage,* he surmised. He pulled the closet door closed and waited until they had all entered the bunker and secured the door behind them.

Jack slid the mask up off his face, but left it covering the top of his head. And then he waited.

"Now, if you all will find a seat," a voice said loudly, "I will give you instructions for your time in the bunker."

As soon as he had finished speaking, the NoKo interpreter translated his directive.

The speaker is standing at two o'clock, Jack calculated, *and the interpreter at nine. I wonder how many weapons I have out there.*

"Oh! Hell!" he muttered quietly, "I don't have time to think about this."

Bam! He kicked the closet door open, and it smashed against the wall. He virtually flew out of the closet with the M-16 leading the way—safety off.

Chapter 59

"Hands up in the air!" Jack shouted. "Everyone! Now!"

"What the hell do you think you're doing?" POTUS barked, pointing his finger at Jack. "Who the hell are *you*?"

"Mr. President. This room is a death trap. It's booby-trapped to kill all of you. I've got to get you out of here. Now!"

"What the hell are you talking about?" POTUS said.

"Poison gas, and I believe explosives. The plan was to get all of you down here, and then to kill you. Chairman Kim as well. We don't have any time to talk about it."

"I don't know who you are, and—"

Just then the Secret Service agent who had been giving instructions interrupted, "We are safe in here. This room is explosion proof, and it has its own air supply and ventilation system. We are not going—"

"Shut up!" POTUS shouted him down. "I'm doing the talking here. You just shut your mouth."

And then POTUS turned toward Jack. "Now tell me. Who the hell are you? And how'd you get in here?"

"Bob Fulbright, the ex-President. You know him quite well I'm told. He sent me here to keep you alive. And that's what I'm doing. We've got to get you out of here, now."

"Fulbright?"

"Right," Jack said.

"His politics suck," POTUS said, "But he is a friend of mine. And he sent you? You wouldn't be Jack Handler, would you?"

"That's me."

"Holy shit," POTUS said. "He has a lot of confidence in you. And, he sent you here for this?"

"Right. Now, we've got to get going."

Then POTUS turned to the interpreter and told her, "Tell Chairman Kim that the man with the gun is a friend of mine, and that he is here to protect us."

Dutifully, the interpreter complied.

"He is going to lead us to a safe place," POTUS said. "Do you wish to go with us, or do you choose to remain here in this bunker?"

All the North Koreans turned to the interpreter as she translated.

And then Chairman Kim spoke.

His answer was short, and the translation equally as short: "Why do we have to leave here?"

"Stay or go with me?" POTUS abruptly asked. "There might be poison gas in here shortly. But you can do what you want to do."

The interpreter translated the question accurately, and Chairman Kim responded quickly.

"I trust you, Mr. President," the interpreter said. "We will go with you."

"Fine," Jack said. "All of you must put on gas masks."

Just as he said that the ventilation system kicked on.

"That's the problem!" Jack shouted. "Poison gas. Get the masks on now!"

He then stepped into the closet and began grabbing the masks two at a time with his left hand and tossing them to those standing with their hands lifted. He kept his right trigger finger ready.

After the third round of pitching the protection, Jack spotted the Secret Service agent attempt to key his radio.

"Stop it right there and get your hands up," Jack shouted at him.

POTUS bolted over to the agent and ripped the radio away from him, threw it on the floor and stomped on it. "Here, you piece of shit!" POTUS growled as he shoved his gas mask into the agent's gut. "Take this and put it on. Try anything like that again and I'll personally break your skinny neck."

Jack quickly tossed POTUS another mask and told him to put it on immediately. "That's poison air coming into the room right now! Get that damn mask on or you're dead!"

Two of Chairman Kim's entourage, who were standing next to the louvered vent, were too slow and were felled by the gas. The rest witnessed their demise and expedited the process. Even the lead agent became a believer at that time.

"Where're you gonna take us?" POTUS asked.

"Good question," Jack said. "I just know we've got to get out of this hotel as quickly as possible. Now, let's get the hell out of here."

"Do you have a vehicle outside?" POTUS asked.

"My partner was in Tiger Tower. He would have come for us."

"The missile hit the tower," POTUS said. "Right?"

"Right," Jack replied. "The tower's gone, and he was at the top of it. We'll figure out something. We got to get going. I suspect there's an explosive in here somewhere. It's gonna take this whole room out soon. Let's get our asses moving."

"Roger," POTUS said as they were leaving. "That partner you're talking about, that wasn't Roger Minsk. Was it?"

"Yeah. I'm afraid so. Do you know him?"

"I do. He's another friend of Bob's. Roger is one hell of a guy.

Did he … did he make it out safely?"

"You're right about that—Roger is one hell of a guy. But, we can't be distracted at this point. There'll be time for all that later. I've got to get you guys out of here as quickly as possible."

Just as Jack and POTUS's American contingent reached the bunker door, Jack turned to see if Chairman Kim was behind them. He was surprised to see the North Koreans huddled toward the rear of the bunker.

"Are you coming, or not?" Jack asked, looking directly at the interpreter. By that time they had all slipped on their gas masks.

As the interpreter began translating for Kim, Jack spoke again.

"Those gas masks will be useful in getting out of the building, but they will not save you in here. Either come with me now, or you will die here. Your choice."

The interpreter stopped translating while Jack was speaking. But, as soon as he had finished, she turned back and continued, but now with a greater expression of urgency capturing her face.

Chairman Kim heard her out, and then waited in place for another few seconds. And then he took one more look in Jack's direction, and bolted for the door.

"We've got to hurry," Jack said. "No time to waste."

Before the NoKo contingent even started toward the door, one more of them staggered and fell. Jack, remaining inside the door, witnessed the incident, but would not allow aid to be rendered. POTUS, who stood with him, had taken one step toward the fallen aide.

Jack grabbed him and said, "He's gone—probably breathed too much of the gas before he got his mask on. No saving him now. We got to get moving. Let's go!"

Before Jack opened the door, he removed his jacket and wrapped it around the Glock he had removed from one of the agents earlier. And, as anticipated, when he opened the door he was faced with two uniformed Secret Service agents. He wasted no time, shooting them both dead with the Glock. While the jacket did not totally silence the rounds being fired, it did the job pretty well.

"What the hell did you just do?" POTUS asked in shock.

"They have to be in on it," he said. "From here on out, we have to assume every player we run into wants you dead. And take them out first. Tough way to live, but we have to think that way."

Once all those able to walk had exited, Jack then closed the door. "Let's keep as much of that shit in there as we can."

"Stick as close to me as possible," Jack said to POTUS as he handed him the Glock. "You should have this, after all, you're the target of this whole Deep State mission. I lose you and they win."

"Deep State! They're behind this? Damn those bastards! They don't give up, do they? They've been trying to get me out of the White House ever since I was elected. They don't care who, or how many, they hurt. Are you sure they're the ones responsible?"

"That's what Bob tells me."

"Why did he give this task to you? You're one man. Couldn't he enlist the military?"

"He doesn't know who to trust."

"That's the whole damn problem. *I* don't know who to trust. We've got disloyals up and down every branch of the military too. It's not just a few, either. They're all over. When I decided to run for the office, I knew it was bad. But I never dreamed it was *this* bad."

Jack and POTUS had made their way to the front of the pack and were now jogging. Everyone else had fallen into place behind them.

"Can we take these gas masks off now?" the English interpreter asked. "Some of us are not in such good shape, and it's a little difficult to get enough air through these things."

"Leave them on for now," Jack ordered. "We don't know what else they might have in mind for us. If I don't make it, when you get outside you can take them off."

"You think there's more?" POTUS asked. "Like maybe they're gonna try something else?"

"Has to be a backup plan. At least I would think. But I'd have no idea what it might be. Might even be more than one. I'm sure we'll soon find out. Stick close to me and be ready for anything."

Jack spotted an exit sign with an arrow pointing down a hall.

"Let's give that a shot," he said. "The sooner we get out of this building the better. Who knows—they might have enough explosives hidden in the hotel to bring the whole damn structure down."

Just then the building shook again. But this time, the explosion appeared to be closer to them.

Chapter 60

"Tomahawk cruise missiles," Jack said to POTUS. "Stolen cruise missiles. That's what they're using. We think they have as many as six. And, counting the one they used to bring the tower down, I think I count four—three here, and one into the tower. That means they have one or two left. The next one, or ones, could take out the main level. Maybe even drop the whole building."

"That one sounded closer than the others," POTUS said. "Like they're striking the building on the lower floors. Is that what you think?"

"Exactly. They were trying to drive you into the bunker by hitting the upper floors first."

"Hold up!" Jack said, holding his hand up as they approached an intersection in the hallway. Slowly he peeked around the corner. When he pulled his head back he said to POTUS, "We've got two armed men at the door. They look agitated. Cinch they heard me shooting their buddies."

Jack thought for a moment, and then leaned the M-16 against the wall and said, "Mr. President. I need your help here. Use the pistol—with the jacket covering it. It'll hold down the decibels. When one or both of those fellows get close enough, shoot them. Got it?"

"You want me, the President of the United States of America, to shoot two Secret Service agents? They will impeach me for sure if I do that."

Jack thought about it for a few seconds, and then agreed. "Right," he agreed. "Could happen. Okay, you stumble out there.

Make sure they see you real good. When you're sure they've had a good look at you, fake a heart attack. Fall down on your face. Don't go out too far. If both of them come over to check you out, I'll try to get them to surrender without shooting. If not, then I'll do what I have to do. We don't have time to discuss this. Just do it."

"I hope I don't have to explain this shit to anyone," POTUS said. "Ever.

"I don't fall so good," he complained. "Gonna do this my own way, if you don't mind."

"Do it any way you like," Jack said. "Just get on with it. We've got to get our asses out of here, pronto."

With that admonition, POTUS shed his suit coat, and handed it to his translator. "Hold this for me," he said. "And take good care of it."

He then took his tie off and handed it to the translator.

"Do I dare take off this gas mask?" he asked Jack.

"Yeah, we all can," Jack said as he pulled his mask off. "The bunker must be virtually airtight. Those agents aren't wearing anything."

"Okay, Jack," he said as he ripped off his mask. "You ready for me to put on a show?"

"Go for it—I'm all set."

"Whaddya gonna do?" POTUS asked as he underwent his self-imposed transformation. "I mean, how are you gonna capture them once I coax them over here?"

"I'll do what needs to be done—as painless as possible. Just keep in mind, they are the ones who made their decision to follow after this crazed leadership. Nobody forced them to turn on legitimate leadership. Now, Mr. President, if you are not willing to help me pull this off, I'll find someone else. But, it seems to me, that you more than anyone else would know that this has to be done—in one way or another. It's your call. If you don't want to help me, just let me know."

POTUS frowned as he weighed Jack's words.

"Oh hell!" he grumbled. "I suppose you gotta do what you gotta do. I'm with ya."

While still out of the sight of the two sentries at the door, POTUS then removed his cufflinks, and rolled up his sleeves. He then messed up his hair, dropped to his hands and knees, and began crawling out into the hall.

"Oh!" he moaned loudly, "I'm sick. I need help. Oh, God, I'm sick."

He then acted as though he were trying to stand up, and as soon as he managed to place a foot beneath him, he topped over sideways and lay still.

The agents had spotted him immediately. "Hey, mister, what's wrong with you?" one of them yelled. "Are you drunk? Do you need help?"

POTUS did not acknowledge their questions. He did not respond in any fashion.

"Hey! Mister, what's wrong with you?"

Still no response.

POTUS then moaned loudly, rolled over on his side to the point that he could make eye contact with Jack, and he lay still.

Jack motioned for all the NoKos and the American aides to press up against the wall to remain out of sight.

"They're coming," POTUS mouthed. "Get ready."

Jack leaned against the wall and held up two fingers for PO-

TUS to see.

"Yes, both," he breathed so only Jack could hear.

He moaned loudly again and began trying to stand up. This was an attempt to garner all their attention so that they would not spot Jack until the perfect time.

Jack squeezed the jacket tightly around the Glock and prepared to pounce.

As soon as he caught the first glimpse of the two men, Jack leapt out from behind the corner of the wall and fired two rounds into each of them. The first struck the lead agent in the right side of his head, killing him instantly. The second round hit the trailing agent in the chest. It incapacitated him, and the third round struck him in the head, killing him. Jack then fired a fourth round into the chest of the first man. He did it as an insurance policy in case the headshot had merely stunned him.

"Let's go!" Jack whispered loudly at the NoKos, as he motioned for them to follow. He then reached down and helped POTUS to his feet.

"You too, Dustin, com'on, let me help you up. I'm sure there's an Academy Award hidden somewhere in that performance. But, it's time to get the hell out of here before it all blows up."

"You still think that? Why? Weren't they going to do poison gas? Why would they need to blow me up too?"

"They will want to bring the whole building down. That way it will be much harder to gather evidence. It will give them longer to shape the narrative. We've got minutes, if not less. Let's move."

Jack and POTUS headed in a brisk jog for the door the sentries had just vacated. Jack checked to be sure the whole group was ready to exit before he leaned on the egress bar.

"Hold up for a second," he said as he stuck his head out. "We need to know what we're getting into."

Given that the area that they occupied was two levels below grade, Jack was uncertain as to what he might find when he peered out. All he could see when he opened the door was an empty stairwell leading upward. He closed the door and took a look around the area where the sentries were positioned. On the desk was a CCTV monitor split up into nine segments, each displaying a different image. He studied it. One of them depicted the view he had when he first opened the door. The next one showed street level. The rest showed various views of the remainder of the sub-basement, as well as the front entry.

He clicked on the image of the street above, and it expanded to the full screen.

"There," he said. "This one shows what I need to know."

He studied that image for nearly a minute. He then switched to the front entrance and reviewed that image.

"Looks like they are evacuating the upper levels through the main entrance. I think we might be able to sneak out of here if we do it now."

Jack turned to address the whole group.

"It appears like a lot of people are evacuating from the upper levels," he reported to the group as he tried to hand POTUS one of the M-16s he had appropriated. "They are leaving through the main entrance. It looks pretty clear."

"Not me," POTUS objected when he saw the firearm, holding both hands up in a stand-off posture. "I will not engage these people with a firearm. Check with Andy and Larry. They are part of my security group. For some crazy reason they were not allowed to carry weapons into this hotel. But they're trained.

"Larry, Andy," POTUS said loudly enough to be heard by the whole group. "Fellows. Get up here. Jack needs your help."

The two men broke ranks and headed toward them without hesitation.

"Jack," POTUS said introducing them. "These are my friends, Andy Hotchkins and Larry Host. They are my excellent bodyguards. They will do whatever you require. Just tell them what to do. Absolutely great guys. Both of them. Great Americans."

When they approached Jack handed Andy, the first one to reach him, one of the M-16s.

"I trust you know how to use this," he said.

"Yes, sir," Andy said. "Nine years in the Marines—three in Iraq, and three in Afghanistan."

"And, Larry. How about you? M-16 or a Glock?"

"Whatever you say, sir," Larry said. "I was a Marine, too. I like the M-16, but I am happy with a Glock. You call it."

Jack handed him the other M-16, and stuck the Glock under his own belt with the other Glock.

"Do your best not to show your firearms," Jack ordered. "Stay in the middle of the group. I'll call you when I need you."

"Yes, sir," the ex-Marines said practically in unison.

"Let me take another look out there and see if it's still clear," Jack said, again reviewing the screens on the monitor. He spotted men wearing orange and red vests dragging a barricade across the street. "Get ready, guys. Looks like they're closing off Siloso, so we're going to have to hike a bit. Need to move quickly once we leave the hotel. If we're going to find a bus to hijack, we're going to have to expend some serious energy to find one. That means we stick together and move quickly."

Jack then looked over his group and said, "Are you all ready? Then let's go!"

After having witnessed Jack kill the two guards only moments before, his assemblage seemed more eager to comply with his wishes than before.

"Walk in front of me a bit," he said to POTUS. "Everyone recognizes you. Ought to draw them out more quickly."

As soon as we hit the street, Jack calculated, *it's a cinch that Deep State will be onto what we're doing and will make every effort to stop us.* He had not taken five steps above ground before he spotted imminent danger. Two uniformed Americans observed them and promptly keyed a radio. *Seeking orders from their supervisor,* Jack assumed. Covertly he pulled a Glock and held it behind his back. He was careful to select the one with a full magazine and affixed with a suppressor. To avoid surrendering his back, he steered POTUS directly at them and told him to pick up the pace.

"Eighty feet and closing," he said under his breath. "I need to get in closer before I engage."

The two uniforms did not know how to react. While they were both armed with M-16s, they knew it would be unsightly to open fire on Jack's group without provocation.

"Fifty feet," Jack said to himself.

Finding that he was pulling even with POTUS, Jack barked, "Pick it up a little, sir. Head directly at the uniforms, but do not make eye contact with them."

Jack also avoided eye contact.

Once they had reached a distance of thirty feet he then cast his gaze directly on his two potential adversaries.

"Fifteen feet," Jack muttered—now out loud.

The uniforms observed Jack's stare and it panicked them. Immediately they raised their rifles to engage. But, before they could get a round off, Jack fired. His first shot was to the head of the first man—his second grazed the head of the other uniform. POTUS slowed his pace allowing Jack to pass him. As he came to stand over the first downed man, Jack observed that his bullet had struck the man in the forehead just above the bridge of his nose and slightly to the left of center.

Dead, Jack concluded. *No point in overdoing this.*

The same was not the case with the second man. Jack observed that both men were, as he had thought, protected by bulletproof vests. So, he fired his third round into the temple of the second man.

"Don't slow down and don't stare at them," he commanded. "Keep moving!"

He then addressed POTUS: "I'm sure our every move is monitored. Our best chance at getting out of here alive is to push through until we find a vehicle large enough to accommodate all of us. I'm thinking a bus or a truck. Keep your eyes open, but let me move out ahead."

Because of the explosions at the hotel, the whole building was being evacuated. With throngs of panicked people walking fast down Siloso Road, Jack was able to melt into the crowd. They had walked nearly a full kilometer before they observed any suitable vehicle.

"This will do the trick," Jack said when he spotted a bus facing east. "Prepare to board."

As the group grew closer, Jack observed a small line of passengers still waiting to get off. "Those are all local police officers," he announced. "Andy, Larry, do *not* show your weapons."

When most of the passengers wishing to get off the bus were on the street, Jack made his move. He pulled out one of the pistols and held it at his side, while at the same time presenting his Sgt. Ryan Hin Tan picture ID for those waiting to get on the bus to see. It worked. All the would-be passengers stood aside and allowed Jack and his entourage to get on the bus.

Once inside, he shoved the ID in the faces of the remaining passengers attempting to de-bus, forcing them to retreat toward the rear. When he came face to face with the bus driver, he showed him his ID and asked him, "Do you speak English?"

"Yes," the driver said. "What the hell are you trying to do?"

"It's an emergency. The building is under siege. I need your bus."

"I know what's happening. That's why I'm here. And, who are *you*? Exactly. What gives you the right to—"

"Did you look at what I just tried to show you?" Jack barked, interrupting the driver mid-sentence. "Do you know what that 'STAR' on my ID signifies? In case you don't, it stands for 'Special Tactical and Rescue.' These people I have with me are guests of our government—they are world leaders. My job is to make sure nothing bad happens to them. And your job today is to make sure I succeed. If you object to me protecting our nation's guests, I will be happy to make your displeasure known to my boss. So, what'll it be? Do you help me, or do you choose to stand in my way? I need your answer right now. What is it?"

"Of course I will help you. That's why I'm here. General Benjamin Lim—do you know him? Anyway, he ordered me to bring my bus in as close to the hotel as I could. He has some people he needs to transport. I assume these are the ones he was concerned with. Right?"

"Absolutely," Jack answered. "How did he reach you—radio or cell phone?"

"He called me on my cell phone. We are in a radio blackout. For some reason, they do not want me to communicate on my radio. Not sure what that's all about."

"Give it to me!" Jack ordered.

"Excuse me," the driver said. "What are you asking me to do?"

"I'm not *asking* you anything, you sonofabitch!" Jack retorted. "I *told* you to give me your cell phone. You'd damn well do it right now or I'll shoot your nose off!"

"I can't do that. I have to be ready for my next order."

"This is it," Jack said, pushing the Glock against the side of the driver's nose. "Your only order is to hand over your cell phone to me. This second!"

Jack then lowered the Glock and rested the muzzle on the driver's chest. "Now! Hand it over."

"This whole thing is highly unusual," the driver complained as he removed his smartphone from his jacket pocket and delivered it to Jack. "I'm not at all sure about this."

"Write my name and number down," Jack said. "And, when this is all over, you can report me. But, I don't think you will. You will be too busy meeting with the Mayor of Singapore to receive the key to the city."

That was all Jack had to do to quiet the protests, as the prospect of receiving the key to the city captivated the driver's imagination and ushered him into a compliant mindset. "Where do you want me to take you?" he asked in a very pleasant tone of voice.

Jack thought about what the driver was asking, and he hesitated to say anything. *I'm not sure how many of those cruise missiles have been used,* he was thinking. *Hell, I'm not even sure how many Deep State had to start with. If they know where POTUS is, or where he's headed, they could just re-target and put an end to the whole thing.*

The bus was approaching a red traffic signal. While Jack was busy contemplating his next move, he was constantly assessing his surroundings. And then he spotted it.

"Holy shit!" he muttered. "Open the damn door and let me outta here!"

The driver was too slow to please Jack, so he manually operated the door opener. But, before he jumped out, he reached over and turned the ignition switch off, killing the engine. He put the bus key in his pocket and said, "Wait right here until I get back."

He then took one large step and was on the street. Immediately he dashed in front of the bus and, forcing all traffic to stop, darted diagonally across the intersection. Many blew their horns and cursed at him. But he remained undeterred.

His target, the Mercedes van, stopped at the light heading in the opposite direction. It was Roger. He had spotted Jack the moment he jumped out of the bus. By the time he reached the van, Roger had rolled the window down.

"How the hell did you get this running?" Jack asked. "It was supposed to blow up, or something, if anyone tried. Right?"

"Yeah, that's how it was programmed. After Deep State took out the tower, I received a communiqué from Bob. He had his people reprogram the van so I could drive it. Otherwise I would have died right there. This thing is built like an Abrams M1A2 Tank. They hit me with everything they had, and it didn't faze it."

"They hit you with a cruise missile?" Jack asked.

"No. Hardly. But they fired everything they had available. Didn't even dent it. But, I'm sure a Tomahawk would blow me up. And, I'm pretty sure they have one left. Bob still didn't know if they had a total of five or six. So, maybe not. They've fired five to this point. So they might have one more. Don't know. You got POTUS in the bus? How about Chairman Kim. You got him too?"

"Yes. Both of them."

"Where're you taking them?"

"Hell if I know. I just know I had to get them out of the hotel. The executive bunker turned out to be a gas chamber. That was their plan. Hit the building with missiles, until they could get the two leaders into the bunker, and then kill them with poison gas. I got them out just in time. But I don't know where's best to head. Definitely, we have to keep moving. What do you suggest?"

"I know what you *should* do," Roger said. "Head straight down this street. It becomes Artillery Avenue right here. Tell your driver that you want to go to Sentosa Golf Club. It's not that far. POTUS already has some of his people there. He's scheduled to shoot nine holes after the Summit, so it's about as safe a spot for him as any. You have the driver head that way. I'll do a U-turn and pull in behind you. It's not far."

"Anything in there we can use to communicate?" Jack asked.

"Here," Roger said. "Grab that device on the dash. It's encoded with the very latest. Nobody can crack it. Not even Deep State."

Jack reached in and took the radio Roger had pointed out.

"How's that arm?" Jack asked. "You doing okay?"

"Good enough for now."

"Are you ready?" Jack asked.

"Let's roll."

Jack headed back to the bus.

"Can you read me?" Jack said, testing the new radio.

"Sure can," Roger reported.

"I'm just going to leave this open so we can monitor each other," Jack said. "For now, anyway."

"Sounds good."

When Jack reached the bus he found the passenger door closed and latched. He pounded. Nothing happened. He looked in and did not see the driver. He pounded again—this time much harder.

Finally, the driver walked up from the rear of the bus and opened the door. Jack stepped in and said, "What's up? We got to get going."

"Better talk to your friends. They may have had a change of mind. Just check with them before we go."

Jack was not happy about the delay. When he glanced back at POTUS he thought he detected an uncomfortable return glance. And then there was the matter of the two armed guards standing directly behind their boss and Chairman Kim.

"What the hell!" he muttered as he quickly set about walking back to where this adventure was now playing out. "Looks like the natives are getting restless," he muttered to himself.

Chapter 61

"Gentlemen, what's going on?" Jack growled as he approached POTUS and the others in the back of the bus. "We should get going."

POTUS remained silent, but one of his guards said in a disturbing tone, "We need the bus keys, Handler."

"Really. What for?"

Roger did not hesitate. Observing what was underway He scrambled to enter a few numbers on the van's computer, and then hit the "Fire" button.

Not detectible from the bus, a small door opened on the roof of Roger's van. Seconds later four miniature drones—each barely three inches in length—lifted themselves through the small opening and set about their mission. Two of them were programmed for "battlefield preparation," and the other two set to "seek and destroy."

The first wave of attack saw the first two drones attach themselves onto the safety glass of the bus's windshield. They were as yet undetected. A few seconds later they each emitted a firm popping noise when they detonated a small self-destructive charge blowing two three-inch holes through the glass.

The other two drones, which had been lying in wait at a safe distance, then shot through the holes.

The two guards heard the first two drones blow up, but they did not know what was going on. And when the attack drones flew through the windshield, the guards then became aware that something extraordinary was taking place, and that whatever it was, it was not under their control.

"What the hell's goin' on?" Larry Hotchkins barked. "Andy. Check out what's goin' on up front."

Andy immediately looked over at Hotchkins, but he didn't move.

"Might be a sniper," Hotchkins said, "so you're gonna want to stay out of sight."

"Did you see that?" Andy asked.

"I saw *something*," Hotchkins said, "but I'll be damned if I know what it was. Like I said, keep your head down, and go up and check it out."

Andy was reluctant.

"I don't think it's anything to worry about," he said.

"Just get your ass up there and check it out. Now!"

Andy squeezed past Larry and Jack and grudgingly moved toward the front. He had proceeded no more than ten feet when it happened.

Splat.

One of the *seek and destroy* drones nailed itself to Andy's forehead. He swiped at it twice but he could not dislodge it.

And then, *bang*!

The force of the directed explosion projected a small capsule through the thick bone and into his brain. It passed through the soft tissue all the way to the back of his skull. And there it exploded with such force it nearly launched his eyeballs out of their sockets. Death was virtually instantaneous.

Larry saw it all.

"Andy," he shouted. "You okay?"

Larry, while he did witness it, did not catch sight of the attacking drone. He heard something that sounded to him like a humming bird, his eyes only saw his partner falling to the floor.

He stood still without mouthing another word for fifteen seconds. And then he shouted out another unheeded attempt to arouse his friend.

"Andy, what are you doing? Don't be shittin' around with me now! You hear me? You sonofabitch, you'd better get your stinkin' ass up off the floor right now! Damn you! You're starting to—"

That was all he got out when he heard the second *seek and destroy* drone fly from the front of the bus. It moved so quickly that again he could not see it. The attack was swift. Like a little bird, it whizzed past him. And then, turning abruptly, it smashed into his head from behind. Attaching itself to his hat, it immediately fired its load.

"Bang!"

"What the hell is happening?" POTUS said, his eyes wide with astonishment.

Jack first checked out the status of Larry Hotchkins. He touched the back of his head and felt a tiny spot of moisture on his cap, and then looked at his fingers.

"Blood, but not very damn much of it," he said, largely to himself.

He then proceeded to turn the body over so he could get a look at his face.

"Holy shit!" Jack exclaimed. "Just take a look at those eyes. It's a wonder they didn't pop out. I don't think this bastard lost more than a thimble-full of blood—yet he is as dead as a doornail. Pardon the cliché, but I've never seen anything like this before."

Just then Roger spoke up over the radio.

"That's thanks to some of that new shit Bob sent our way,"

Roger said. "I wasn't sure how it would work—or even *if* it would work. Definitely a new technology. Probably imported from Israel."

When POTUS heard Roger talking he suddenly sat up. "Is that who I think it is?" he said.

"That's Roger," Jack explained. "He's been monitoring the situation."

"Is ... is Larry dead?" POTUS asked.

"Very much so," Jack said, grabbing the bus driver by the collar and hoisting him to his feet. "I'd say we'd better get the hell out of here now while we still can."

Jack then turned to address POTUS: "So far, everything they've thrown at you has failed. They're no longer going to worry about who gets blamed for your death—all their fancy planning is scuttled as long as they get you. That means they'll be prepared to toss anything and everything in your direction—until you're dead. You should get ready to move quickly."

"And you," Jack said to the driver. "You come with me. You're going to help me drive this piece of shit outta here."

"Jack," Roger said. "Bob has managed to round up a squad of Marines he knows he can trust. They've taken position in a building that is still under construction. It's at the other end of the island—Cape Royale."

"I know where that is," POTUS announced. "That's just east of the golf course. On the ocean. Beautiful place."

"He's right," Roger replied through a big smile. "They've orders to escort POTUS to the airport, and then back to the U.S.. Do you think you can convince your driver to deliver his passengers there safely?"

Jack glanced over at the driver, who was devouring Roger's every word. He was nodding his approval of his new orders.

"Should be no problem," Jack replied. "But, what about the NoKos? What shall I do with them?"

"Hell," Roger said. "Let *them* decide. … Better yet—once POTUS and you are safe at the Cape, have the driver bring them back to the hotel—where the summit was supposed to take place. Or what's left of it. They'll be safe there. Singapore police will see to that."

"Because they're not the real target anyway. Right?"

"Exactly. But I'd get the hell out of there immediately. I think they've exhausted, or nearly exhausted, their Tomahawk arsenal—that is, if our intel is correct. But who knows what else they might have in mind? Now that they've exposed themselves and their intentions, it's hard to predict what might follow."

Jack pushed the driver in front of him and they both walked briskly up to the cockpit. POTUS, shocked by all the recent revelations, followed close behind.

"You heard what Roger told us to do, didn't you?" Jack asked the driver. "He wants you to take us to Cape Royale. You can get us there, right?"

"Yes, sir, I can."

Jack sat down on a first-row seat opposite the driver. His right hand gripped a Glock. POTUS slid in directly behind the driver.

"Who the hell is responsible for all this?" he asked Jack, wide-eyed and pale-faced.

"I would think that you should know by now," Jack looked him in the eye and said. "Most refer to them as Deep State. You've heard about them, haven't you?"

"Yeah. Of course I have. But aren't they just the disgruntled members of the opposing party? That's how I always regarded them. You know, the *swamp dwellers*."

"It's much more insidious than that," Jack replied.

"How so?"

"Members of the Deep State are career players. Some are in government. And some are not. Many have tenure at the top-flight universities. It's like a big club, in some respects."

"Where does the media come into this scenario?" POTUS asked. "Are they also *players*, as you refer to Deep State members?"

"Some are. But, for the most part, those in the media who sympathize most vociferously are really Deep State wannabes. The same holds true for those employed by the universities—those who teach the undergraduates, many of them are attracted by what they view as the success enjoyed by the professional scholars in the grad schools. And they would like to identify."

"Oh my God!" POTUS exclaimed. "This is far more pervasive than anything I ever imagined. How the hell can I overcome this cesspool? Do I stand a chance?"

Jack thought about it for a moment, and then said, "Well, you start by staying alive. That's why Bob had me fly over here with Roger. We've got to start somewhere. They want you dead, or at least in jail. My challenge is to accomplish the first part of it. It's up to you and your friends to keep you on the fresh-air side of the bars. Hell, I'll be lucky if they don't lock me up after this debacle."

Jack, who had been carefully listening to POTUS and monitoring his body language, took a glance toward the rear of the bus.

"Looks like they're getting a little antsy," he said, observing that the NoKo translators had been listening to everything he had just said, and were rapidly converting his words into Korean for Chairman Kim. "... Let me check something out with Roger."

Jack then spoke to Roger, who had been listening to his conversation with POTUS. "Roger. Do we actually need the NoKos at this point? They're not the target anyway. Actually, I think they might be better off on their own. What do you think?"

"Let me run it by Bob," Roger replied. "What you say makes sense, I think. I'll see if he can arrange a pickup for them. Give me a second."

Less than a minute later the bus was suddenly set upon by a group of what appeared to Jack to be a nearly innumerable ensemble of uniformed troops delivered by Chinese-made armored vehicles, and all of them sporting automatic weapons—AK-47s.

"What the hell is *that* all about?" POTUS snarled. "They're here to kill me, aren't they! I've just about had as much of this shit as I can stand. Give me a gun!"

Chapter 62

Two weeks had passed. Henry, sitting at the bar at Timber Charlies in downtown Newberry, was nursing his third Ore Dock (MQT) on draft. It was nine-fifty P.M. He'd spent the past hour or so eating chips and waiting for Kate. Her flight from New York arrived in Grand Rapids mid-afternoon. She had rented a Jeep there and was headed north. Originally the plans were for her to meet up with Henry at the bar around nine. She was running a little late.

While neither Henry nor Kate were aware of the nature of Jack's mission, they knew that it had to have been important— aka, extremely dangerous. Not only did they both understand the potential gravity of any situation involving Jack, Bob and Roger, they were doubly concerned because they had not heard from Jack since the moment he and Roger sent Henry back to Deadwood after Jack's plane had crashed. Both Kate and Henry had attempted to reach out to him, but Jack had not responded—a fact that, while it generated some worry, did not surprise either one of them. They had both assumed that Jack would be back to Sugar Island within two weeks. That was why they'd put off getting together at Timber Charlies until then.

Kate was the first to invite her father to join them for a beer. When Jack did not respond to her text, Henry followed up Kate's invitation with one of his own—still no word from him.

Just then Henry's phone started playing the first few bars of Sinatra's *New York, New York*: "The greatest city in the whole world. Start spreading the news …" That was Kate's ring tone.

"Henry," she said. "You haven't given up on me, have you?"

"No. But I am on my third round. If you want to talk to me while I still make sense, you should probably hurry up."

"You're going to get me stopped for speeding."

"You'd better slow down. We don't have many friends in Luce County Sheriff's Office. Have you heard from your father at all?"

"No. That's what I was going to ask you. He hasn't called you either?"

"That's right. Nothing."

"Whoa!" she said. "I'm just bouncing across the railroad tracks. I guess I'm closer than I thought. I should be walking through the door there in just a minute or two. Why don't you order one for me? Okay? I'm about to find a parking place right now."

"I could arrange that," Henry said. "What sounds good to you? They do have Ore Dock on tap. But they offer all the regulars as well. Whaddya think?"

"Sounds good to me. I think that's what I had when I was there before."

Henry caught the eye of the waitress and held up two fingers. She smiled and nodded.

Less than five minutes later Kate walked through the door.

"Still cold," Henry informed her. "Amber just set it down."

"Looks great. I can sure use it tonight. I tried calling Dad again on my way over here. I even ran over to the resort to check up on things first. Still no word from him. How about you? You heard from him at all?"

"Nothing. But, I think we will. Jack picked this date. Somehow, some way, he'll reach out to us. Unless, well, we don't need to go there."

"Unless he can't," Kate said, finishing his comment. "If he's still in the middle of something that prohibits him, then he will stay silent. You know him almost as well as I do. If it's possible for him to be here, he will. And, if he can't, then he will call us."

"And if he can't call us, then we'll just have to enjoy each other's company without him."

"Exactly," Kate agreed, taking a long sip of her drink.

"Yeah, this is the same one I had the last time we were here," she said as she set it down. "It's pretty good. What's the final word on that job we were working on in South Dakota? Did you get that all resolved to everyone's satisfaction?"

"Nothin' is ever perfect. We did get to the bottom of it—but not everyone is happy."

"Well, fill me in. I feel like I ran out on you, but I had to get back to my job. Was it pretty much like we thought when I left? Or, were we not over the target?"

"Let's see," Henry said. "When you went back to New York. That was right after that restaurant shooting where Jeffry Speelman, the big guy, got his brains blown out by his little friend. And then Deputy Corker dispatched Speelman's killer. What a wild time that was. Two dead within seconds of one another. Just amazing. And, your dad wasn't even involved. Even more amazing."

Kate feigned a disparaging smile, and then said, "Did you ever figure out what the connection was between Speelman and his killer? I know—or I think you told me—that you'd heard the little fellow was somehow sexually involved with Speelman. Did that actually turn out to be the case?"

"Lindsey Coffin. That was the name of Speelman's killer. And it appears that he was gay—that Coffin fellow. And he did hang around with Speelman most of the time. But, there were a couple different takes on the nature of their relationship. One is that it was not sexual, at least from Speelman's standpoint. Some think that he was leading the Coffin guy on, but that they were not actually involved—not in a sexual way."

"That's weird. Did the little guy live in Deadwood? Or was he from Grand Rapids too?"

"Lindsey Coffin was an attorney there in Deadwood. Part of a small two-man law office—Coffin and Schmidt. Apparently, he did some legal work for Speelman. That's how they met, I believe."

"That had something to do with Speelman's Bitcoin racket? Or was it something else?"

"Totally to do with that business—or so I've heard."

"Did you get your information from the sheriff?"

"Not exactly," Henry said with a snicker. "I stuck with the story we came up with after the shooting—that neither one of us saw anything. After you flew back to New York, I did stick around Deadwood for a couple days."

"I'm surprised the sheriff would let you do that. He'd seemed so adamant about both of us getting out of Dodge right away. He was okay with your hanging back for two full days? How'd that come about?"

"Not sure. I think he might not have believed us about not seeing a thing, and he wanted to see if I dropped any clues. I actually got to interview Deputy Corker about it the day after you left at his request. Actually, he was interviewing me. But I got to ask a few questions. Just had to be careful not to give myself away."

"What did you learn? And how did it affect the outcome of your case?"

"I learned quite a bit talking to him. He accidently dropped a clue while we were talking. He asked something like, 'Did your interest in him, Speelman, have anything to do with investments?' And, 'Did the people you were representing include any of Mr. Speelman's Bitcoin investors?'

"That got me to thinking that maybe this Speelman guy had gotten himself over-extended in speculating on Bitcoin. I know I've read that Bitcoin investments can fluctuate dramatically, even in the short term. And, because a Bitcoin investment involves cryptocurrency, which means it exists only on a computer, it is vulnerable to hackers."

"Did this little guy, Lindsey Coffin, the one who shot Speelman," Kate asked, "was he a disgruntled investor?"

"That's not the info I was fed," Henry replied. "I suppose that might have been the case, or a part of it, but the scuttlebutt I came up with was that Speelman used Coffin in order to tap the wealthy gay community. Apparently Coffin misinterpreted Speelman's intentions. And when it became clear to him that Speelman was not interested in him sexually, he blew his cork. And when some of Coffin's friends began expressing concern that many of their mutual acquaintances had been hoodwinked into buying Bitcoins, Coffin's view of his new friend soured. He loaded up his .44, and went looking for Speelman."

"Sounds like the old story of unrequited love," Kate said.

"Exactly," Henry replied. "But with an additional twist. Coffin knew Deputy Corker quite well. It would have come as no surprise to him that Corker was a cop, and that he would be armed."

"Suicide by cop—is that what you're suggesting?"

"I didn't come up with that scenario in a vacuum. While that's probably the conclusion I would have come to on my own, more than one or two of the people I talked to openly suggested that. In fact, Deputy Corker as much as admitted that that was what he was thinking as well."

"Really? What did he say about it?"

"He was very affected by the whole thing. I could see it in his eyes, and in the way he talked about it. This is what he said about it: He commented that his own wife told him that Coffin had plenty of time to have shot him as well as Speelman, and that she was surprised that he didn't. And then he asked me what I thought about it. It was as though he was trying to trick me into responding. So, I just repeated my original statement. That neither you nor I saw anything. We heard the shots, but we did not even know where they were coming from. I said we both ducked to the floor."

"Yeah," Kate said. "That makes sense. But, how does all this affect your case? Does it mean anything at all to the outcome of the investigation?"

"It sure does," Henry said through a huge cynical grin. "What I learned later was that Speelman had invested and reinvested all of the money in the Agnes Cross/Owens trust fund in his Bitcoin scheme. And then lost it all. There is no money left in the trust fund. Nothing at all."

"How could that be?" Kate asked. "There are safeguards built into those things to prevent that sort of thing. Right?"

"You would think so. But Speelman managed to find a way to get around it. It wasn't just the Cross/Owens fund that got raided. Several other accounts that firm was managing suffered greatly. Needless to say, the FBI is investigating."

"So, there's nothing at all left? How about insurance? Surely there must be some protections in place to protect against this stuff?"

"From what my cousin tells me, the lawyer he has looking into it says that Speelman's firm had Agnes Owens sign off on the investment portfolio, giving them too much power. Any way you want to view the transactions, the money is lost."

"So, your cousin is just out of luck?"

"That's how it would look to me. I thought I'd have Jack take a look at it when he gets back, and see how he thinks we should move forward, or if we even should. Hey, Kate, you're a lawyer. Right? In your early days? Your dad told me that you started out in law and then became a detective. What do you think about it? Do we have a chance of recouping anything?"

"I would certainly like to think so. I've been out of that game for a very long time, but trust funds are generally thought to be pretty safe against the type of mismanagement you describe. I'd say, have an attorney who specializes in trusts take a close look at the contractual agreement that is in place, and see how it reads. Speelman's law firm ought to have insurance to cover this sort of thing, but you never know. Just how much are we looking at? Do you have an idea?"

"Members of the law firm that was managing the fund were legally designated as a Certified Trust and Financial Advisors—just not very good ones. They also had an investment broker onboard. Everything appeared on the up-and-up—until Speelman joined them. From that time on everything went downhill. Now, I suppose, some if not all of them are going to jail.

"But, as for the money, it's all gone. Not just for my cousin, but just about everyone who invested with them. As far as my cousin specifically, initially Mansfield thought that there ought to be a couple of million. But she didn't know for sure. But now—nothing."

"Yeah. Have Dad take a look and see what he thinks. This all sounds a bit too iffy for a good attorney to even consider it on a contingency. Have Dad check out the paperwork in place, and I can take a look as well. Try doing that before you move forward. I think it would be the best—"

"Look who just walked through the door," Henry interrupted her when he spotted Jack. Kate whipped her chair around and took a look for herself.

"Dad!" she said loudly as she stood to her feet. She then quick-walked her way around tables until he reached him.

"Damn!" she said. "Am I ever glad to see you. Henry and I didn't know what to expect—you were gone so long. And we didn't know where, or what you were up to."

As soon as Henry saw him enter the bar he motioned for the waitress to bring another round of Ore Dock for each of them.

Jack took his time embracing Kate. Henry waited nearly half a minute, and then he walked over to them.

When Jack saw him coming he freed his right arm and reached out to shake hands with Henry.

Chapter 63

"Hey, old man," Henry said. "Good to see that you've still got two arms and two legs. What were you up to, anyway? Some sort of vacation?"

"I guess you could say that," Jack said through a grin. "Whaddya drinking over there? I could use something to wet my whistle."

"Ore Docks. She's bringing one over for you as we speak."

Kate pulled back and glanced over toward their table.

"Looks like she's got a round for each of us," she said.

"When did you get in, anyway?" she asked her father.

"Earlier today. I haven't had a good night's sleep in … how long have I been gone? Two weeks?

"The sheriff's been trying to reach me. Either of you guys got an idea about what that might be about?"

"No," Kate said. "How about you, Henry, have you heard anything?"

"I haven't heard a thing. How'd you learn about it?"

"I got a call," Jack said, checking his watch. "The sheriff called me about a half an hour ago. He said he needed to talk to me, and that he'd prefer not to do it over the phone."

"Are we in trouble?" Henry asked.

"No. I asked him if there was a problem, but he just repeated what he'd said before, that he didn't want to discuss it over the phone. But he did assure me that none of us was in any kind of trouble. I told him where I was headed and he said he'd come over to Timber Charlies and talk to me here. He should be here anytime now."

"I did get a call earlier today," Kate said. "But I didn't recognize the number, so I didn't pick up. It was a 906 area code. Might have been him, I guess."

"Have either of you heard from Millie and the boys?"

"I haven't," Kate said.

"Me either," Henry followed. "How about you?"

"No," Jack said. "But I had instructed them not to try to contact me for any reason, at least not until I reached out to her. I told her that in an emergency she could call one of you, but that I would be off limits until further notice."

"Then," Henry said, "they must be fine because she hasn't tried to call either Kate or me. That has to be good news. Don't you think? Where are they, anyway?"

"They were headed out east. Roger believes he has found a safe house for them to live in until this all blows over."

"Is it done now?" Kate asked. "Roger's mission, or your *vacation*, that is? Where is he? Is he staying with us on Sugar Island?"

"He's not in Michigan at the present. He had to have some work done on his arm, so he'll be enjoying the food at Bethesda for a little while."

"Will he be okay?" Kate asked.

"Oh yeah. I'm sure he'll make a full recovery. He didn't want to go in, but Bob insisted."

"Where the hell have you been—on this so-called *vacation*?" Henry asked. "And what happened to Roger's arm?"

Jack just smiled over his Ore Dock, but didn't answer the question. "I haven't had anything that tasted this good since we left the UP. How long have you guys been gone? After we parted ways in South Dakota? You headed back to Deadwood after you left Roger and me. Right?"

Henry hesitated, waiting for Jack to answer his question. When it became obvious to both Kate and Henry that Jack was quite serious about not discussing his activities for the past two weeks, Henry said, "Yeah—but we did not leave immediately, or directly. We both spent a couple more days in Deadwood. Then Kate got called back to New York. And I headed back to Sugar Island."

"How did you do there? In Deadwood. Did you learn anything?"

"Well, we stayed there long enough to see Speelman's boyfriend shoot and kill him. And then to witness Deputy Cocker shoot the boyfriend."

"You got to be shitting me! Right? You witnessed this? And who exactly is this Speelman character? Fill me in on this."

"He was the lawyer who was indirectly overseeing the investment—which, we have now learned, is all gone. Zero money in the trust fund."

"Oh my God. Tell me more about that—I'm talking about the shooting."

"It all went down pretty much like I just described. Except, we denied seeing it take place. We were more interested in getting out of town ASAP. Besides, there were plenty of other witnesses. Sheriff Miller didn't really need our input.

"Speaking of sheriffs," Henry continued, "Sheriff Bellere just walked through the door. And he's headed our way."

Jack did not look up immediately. Instead he tipped his Ore Dock up and polished it off. "Grab me one more of these, would you?" he said to Henry. "I've apparently got some work to do here. I'll be right back."

Jack arose from his chair just as Sheriff Bellere saw them.

"Sheriff," Jack said, reaching out to shake his hand. "Thanks for meeting me here. I think you've met my daughter Kate. And Henry."

"Yes," Sheriff Bellere said, nodding at both Kate and Henry. "We've all met before."

And then addressing them directly, he said, "I bring you greetings from the Luce County Sheriff's Office."

Kate and Henry smiled back, and each thanked the sheriff.

"I hope you won't mind if I borrow Jack for a few minutes, he and I have something important to discuss."

He then looked directly at Jack with the most sober of expressions.

Chapter 64

"Sheriff Bellere," Jack said, sensing the sober tone of his voice. "What's on your mind?"

"Jack," the sheriff said. "I'd like us to step outside for a minute. What I have to tell you is very private. Can we do that?"

"Sure," Jack replied. "Whatever you think."

"Excuse us," Jack said to Kate and Henry. "I'll be back as soon as possible. Don't know how long this might take."

Neither of the two men spoke another word until they were on the sidewalk outside the bar.

"Jack, there's no easy way to tell you this, so I'm just going to lay it out as simply as I can. Your boys were staying in New York. They were under the care of Millie Star. And Ms. Star's daughter, Angel, was staying with them. You are aware of that, right?"

"Yes," Jack said, grave concern now seizing his face. "Did something happen to my boys?"

"Your boys are fine. They were not injured at all. In fact, my deputy has them in his car parked in back. I'll return them to you when we're done."

"If the boys were not injured, who was? Not Millie, or Angel. Right? They weren't hurt, were they?"

"The girl, Angel, is fine. But I'm afraid that her mother, Millie, wasn't so fortunate."

"What the hell happened to her? Sheriff—just spit it the hell out!"

"They were staying at a house in Forest Hills—all four of them. That you knew about. Right?"

"Yeah! So what the hell happened?"

"There were intruders. Millie was wounded. Shot. She took three rounds. She's in the hospital in New York. At the Presbyterian Hospital in Queens."

"Is she going to be okay? When did this happen?"

"Last night. She is in a serious but stable condition."

"Holy shit! What exactly is her condition? Do you know? She got hit three times? Where? Is she going to make it?"

"I don't know all the details. But, I understand that the shooter fired a total of three shots, and all of them struck her. Two of them in her torso, and one—the last one—grazed her head. The last round was fired at close range while she was lying on the floor. Apparently, one of your boys caused the shooter to mess up his last shot. He lunged into the shooter's back. He knocked the pistol from the shooter's hand. Your other boy grabbed the pistol before the shooter could react. And then, it was all over. Both intruders ran out."

"She is still alive. Right?"

"Yes."

"Red and Robby—they're in the parking lot? I need to see them right now."

"I'll have my deputy bring the boys around. The girl, Millie's daughter, we don't have her here though. They tried to get her on the plane back to Michigan with the boys, but they said she wouldn't budge from her mother's side. NYPD's been trying to reach some of her mother's family, but, so far, they haven't had any success."

"Millie has no family—not out there, and not even in this area," Jack said. "I'll go get Kate. Bring the boys around."

As Sheriff Bellere radioed his deputy to drive around to the front, Jack hurried back into the bar to fill Kate and Henry in on what had happened. When he reached their table he laid three twenties down and announced, "There's been some trouble out east. The three kids are fine—the sheriff says. But Millie's been shot. Bad. We need to get out of here and back to the house. I haven't seen them yet, but the boys are here. The sheriff's got them with him. We need to get them over to the house—familiar surroundings, where they can feel comfortable."

He immediately turned around and headed back outside. Kate stood to her feet and followed after her father, and Henry squared up their bill.

By the time they left the bar, the sheriff was standing beside the open doors of the patrol car. The children had not yet got out. As soon as Kate hit the sidewalk she broke into a run, beating Jack to the car.

Robby was the first one out. Spotting Kate, he pushed past the sheriff and wrapped his arms around her. She threw her arms around him and held him. He was crying. And then Red slowly slid his feet onto the pavement and stood up. Kate reached out and motioned him to her side. Red joined them and hugged her as well. Red's eyes were swollen, but he appeared more angry than anything.

Robby ducked his face down so that his tears could not be seen.

"Are you guys okay?" Kate asked. "Physically. Are you okay?"

Red looked Kate in the eye and nodded.

"We're not hurt," Robby said. "We're all fine. But Angel, she's in pretty bad shape. She stayed at the hospital with her mother."

By that time Jack reached Kate and the boys, Robby had managed to stop crying. Jack wrapped his arms around all three of them. No one uttered a single word for a solid minute.

Finally, Kate broke the silence: "Where's Buddy?"

Robby looked up at her and said, "We left Buddy with Angel. She wanted him there to keep her company. And we did not want to put him on the plane. He doesn't like to fly."

"Oh, really," Kate said. "Okay, guys, I say we head to the house. You boys have to be exhausted. And hungry. We can do that, can't we, Dad? The sheriff wouldn't have a problem with our heading home, would he?"

"No," Jack said. "Go ahead and take off. You got your car here. Right?"

"Yes. And so does Henry. How about you?"

"I've got a rental. You get the boys and their stuff settled in your car, and then wait for me. I've got to get some things settled with Henry, and then I'll run over and fill you in on the details."

Jack broke away from the group and cornered Henry.

"I would like you to drive out to the island and stick around with the boys until they get to bed. And then come back over to the house for breakfast with Kate and the boys in the morning. Don't leave the area until I get back."

"Until you get back? Where're you going?"

"I've got to find a way to see Millie," Jack said. "I flew out on a charter arranged by Bob. I'm going to see if it's still waiting at the airport. If it is, I'll take it back to New York tonight. I can't believe that they'd leave a fourteen-year-old girl in the big city—there on her own. I've got to get to them as soon as possible. I'll leave my rental car at the airport."

Jack then shared his plans with Kate and the boys, and headed for the airport. On his way over he called Bob.

"I need to get to New York ASAP. Is the plane still at the airport?"

"Yes. I figured you'd be needing a ride. I just heard what happened to your friend—I am so sorry."

"I know New York can be a dangerous place," Jack said. "But, I think it's a bit of a stretch to separate our mission from the shooting. Don't you?"

"We're checking into it. Right now I can't say one way or the other."

"What sort of firearm was used?" Jack asked.

"That was my first question, too," Bob replied. "The detective in charge told me it was a .22 revolver, with a suppressor. They recovered it, you know. One of your boys apparently ended up with it. But no prints—except the kid's. The shooter was wearing gloves."

"That tells us a lot," Jack said. "We're dealing with a professional—probably associated with Deep State. That's what it speaks to me."

"Maybe. But I strongly doubt that it was carried out by an FBI agent. If it was a job perpetrated by Deep State, the shooter would most likely have been a private contractor—somebody a lot like you used to be, if you know what I mean."

Bob's brashness irritated Jack, but he knew that the former president's memory was accurate. Still, Jack did not appreciate the reminder.

"I trust that when you get some info you'll pass it along to me," Jack said.

"Oh. Right. You'll be the one who gets to deal with it. That's a given going in. When you get there, keep me filled in on your friend's condition. Okay?"

"Who first informed you about Millie?" Jack asked.

"It was Roger. He arranged the charter for your boys to fly home, and for the sheriff to meet them at the airport and to deliver them to you. He didn't call you first because he thought it best if you could see that your boys were okay right off the bat. And that you heard the news about your friend coming directly from the sheriff in person."

Jack heard Bob's words, but he would have preferred learning about Millie earlier. And then his phone vibrated. It was a call from Kate.

"Bob. I've got to go. My daughter's calling me. I'll keep you informed. You do the same. Okay?"

"Yes," he said to Kate.

"Everything's fine," she said. "I just thought you'd like to know that the boys saved some forensic evidence."

"No shit! What do they have?" Jack asked.

"You're aware that Buddy jumped one of the men and knocked the pistol from his hand? You knew that?"

"No. I understood that one of the boys tackled the one who fired the shots, and spoiled his aim. Buddy was in on this too?"

"Right. There were two men. Apparently after Red went after the shooter, Buddy grabbed the shooting hand of the second man. Between the two of them, they disarmed both shooters. The important thing is that Buddy not only knocked the gun out of the second shooter's hand, but he ripped the glove off. And that's what the boys brought back with them. It's got the man's blood on it—quite a bit, in fact."

"They didn't turn it over to the cops?" Jack asked.

"Red thought you would want to have it."

"Damn! That's a break. Here's what we do. Can't send it to your people in New York. If this ever got back to your boss, the boys would be in deep shit. Besides, the chain of custody is now corrupted anyway. This is all good. Send it to my friend in Chicago. Next-day it in the morning. I'll give him a heads-up. Tell him I need it right away—like immediately. I'll text you the address and details.

"How are the boys doing? Are they going to be able to sleep tonight?"

"No. As far as sleeping is concerned. We're going to be playing blackjack all night, I suspect. Every so often Red sends me a text about some new detail as it pops in his head. And Robby reads it, nods his agreement, and explains it in detail. It's all been very traumatic. …But I am documenting everything they tell me."

"I'm surprised that your boss let them out of his sight."

"He hasn't. I've been on the phone with him most of the time. He wants me to pull as much out of them as I can."

"You did the right thing with the glove. I don't want to see this thing drag through the courts. Never know what the outcome might end up being in a case like this, when it goes that direction."

"I thought that's how you'd see it. The boys are really quite amazing. They recognized the value in that glove, and immediately protected it in a zipper bag."

"You'll be up all night. I can see that happening."

"For sure," Kate agreed. "One nice thing came out of my talks with my boss. He's given me all the time I need to spend with the boys. With pay, even. He arranged it as a *Family Emergency Leave*."

To Jack the remainder of his journey to New York seemed interminable. During the course of it he called both Bob and Roger twice each: Roger, in an effort to draw out as much information as possible regarding Millie's shooting, and Bob, for pretty much the same reason. Bob did tell Jack that he would have a car waiting for him when he landed.

Jack was pleased to learn that Roger had assigned an around-the-clock Secret Service detail to protect Angel and Millie. As he prepared to de-plane, he fingered through his permits and credit cards until he verified to himself that he did have his NY Permit to Carry Concealed. Even though he was well aware of the advantages provided him by all of his "friends in high places," he knew that New York laws concerning firearms were among the most restrictive in the country. "Don't need any type of unnecessary hassle today," he told himself.

Jack's ride to Presbyterian Hospital was uneventful, aside from all of the conflicts occurring within his own mind. *I wonder if this is all over now?* Jack was asking himself. *POTUS is safe, and my job is finished. I should hope that, at this point, I should be able to just quietly fade away. I wonder how Millie's doing. Maybe I can fly her back to Michigan. I wonder if she's well enough. Bob might know. I think I'll give him another call.*

"Bob. I have another question. About Millie's condition. Do you know what the latest word is on that? Do you think she's well enough to fly back to Michigan?"

"Oh, hell, Jack. I don't know about that. She took three rounds. The last I heard she was in critical condition. As far as I know she's been unconscious ever since the round that grazed her skull. In fact, I understand that it did more than graze her. While it did not penetrate her head, it pulverized the skull where it struck her. She is fortunate to still be alive.

"The first two rounds that struck her did the most damage. One of them blew up some major blood vessels. She lost a lot of blood. They got those patched up, but the second round took out her left kidney, and did severe damage to her lower intestine. They had to remove over a foot of it. She is not in good shape—probably not good enough to travel for quite some time. At least that's how I see it. But, she is still alive. We can be thankful for that."

"I'm here to see Millie Star," Jack said to the nurse attending the desk on the sixth floor.

"Are you family?"

"Virtually. We're engaged to be married," Jack said. At first he felt a tinge of guilt for having lied about it. But, in his mind, it was true. He fully intended to marry Millie—it was just that the right moment to pop the question had not yet presented itself.

"Her daughter is in the room with her right now. She came out of surgery two hours ago, and has just been moved into the room—maybe half an hour ago."

"I believe Angel, her daughter, as well as a Care Dog named Buddy are there as well."

"The Secret Service agent, and the dog, are stationed in the corridor just outside the patient's room. Only the daughter is actually in the room."

"Just point me in the right direction. I want her to know that I'm here. And her daughter also needs to know that I'm in the city."

"Room 6012A. You can have five minutes. The woman is sleeping. She has not yet come around after her surgery."

Jack had what he was after—permission to enter the room.

"Five minutes is five minutes," he said to himself as he walked toward her room. Buddy made it easy for him to figure out where he needed to go. As soon as he had set foot in the hall Jack heard Buddy's barely audible whine. And so did the Secret Service agent.

"Excuse me," the agent said to Jack as he approached. "This room is off limits to all visitors."

"Yes, I know," Jack said as he reached down and petted Buddy. "My name is Jack Handler. Millie and her daughter Angel, they are both very close friends of mine. And, I believe it was Agent Roger Minsk who assigned you to this task. Is that correct?"

"Do you have some identification?" he asked Jack.

Jack showed him his Michigan driver's license, and said, "If you have any other questions I suggest you give Roger a call."

"It's all fine," the agent replied. "Roger told me that you'd be stopping by. I think the patient is sleeping. The daughter is probably asleep as well. At least she was the last time I looked in."

"Thanks," Jack said, opening the door to Room 6012A. "I'll make it quick."

Stepping in and closing the door behind him, Jack looked around the room. Lying on an upholstered, comfortable-looking chair was Angel. And just as the agent suggested, she was sleeping. Jack then sized up Millie—a full head bandage, needles and tubes in both arms, an oxygen mask, and at least two draining tubes. He walked over to her side and silently held her hand. It was cold. He then scrutinized the monitor beeping in the background. "At least her heart is still beating," he said to himself.

Jack could not recall the last tear his eyes had generated—but it was now happening. His eyes were growing moist and he could do nothing about it. "Millie. Millie. Millie." He silently mouthed her name. "Oh my God. What is happening to you?"

Jack realized that he was no doctor. But, her condition appeared to him to be much worse than he had anticipated.

With his free hand he wiped the tears from his eyes. *If she wakes up*, he was thinking, *I don't want her to see me like this.*

And just then her eyes opened. He could see her smile through the mask. Ever so lightly she squeezed his hand.

"Millie," he said. "If you can hear me squeeze my hand."

Again, she gently closed her fingers on his hand.

"I want you to know something," he said, with tears again forming. "With all my heart, I love you. I am so sorry this happened. I promise I will not leave your side until you walk out of this hospital. Anything you need … anything you want, just let me know. But, for now, you need your rest. Try to put everything out of your mind and let your body heal. Angel is fine. I'll watch out for her until you're back on your feet. All that you need to do is get well."

Again, she smiled. But this time she glanced over at Angel. And she did it in such a way so as to communicate her concern to Jack. He read her intentions.

"Yes. I will watch over Angel until you're up and around. I will be here for her."

With Jack's words Millie opened her eyes further and seemed to stare right through him. And then her whole countenance relaxed. Jack moved a little closer, but her eyes did not follow him. Seconds later the heart monitor alarm sounded.

Jack knew what that meant, but Angel didn't. It awakened her out of the deepest of sleep.

"What's happening?" she said.

And then she spotted Jack.

"Jack! I didn't know you were here. What's that noise?"

Right then two nurses and a doctor burst through the door. Angel sat up and looked around in astonishment. Jack stepped back from the bed to allow the medical team to do their work. Immediately they charged up the defibrillator and shocked Millie's heart. They repeated their efforts two more times. The doctor again examined Millie, and then looked up at the flat-line monitor. She stared at it blankly for a long moment, as though immersed in a deep sense of despair. She then looked down and shook her head. After reaching up to silence the monitor, she said, "What time is it?"

Millie was dead.

"Damn it!" Jack muttered under his breath. "How the hell can this be?

"That's it?" he asked the doctor. "No CPR?"

"Can't. Surgeon's orders, due to the nature and severity of the chest wound. I'm sorry, but I'm afraid we have lost her. Are you a relative?"

Jack did not respond. Instead, he turned around and stepped over to where Angel was standing, and he embraced her trembling body.

"Uncle Jack," she managed to utter between gut-wrenching sobs, "what's happening with Mom? Is she okay?"

Jack continued to embrace her, but did not answer.

Angel got the message.

Finally, she pushed back from Jack and said, "I want to see her. I want to touch her hand, and kiss her. She *can't* be dead. She just can't be."

As she left his arms, their eyes met briefly. Tears were now streaming down both of their faces. Neither of them had a word they could say. Angel slowly walked over to her mom.

Just then Jack's phone vibrated. He wasn't going to accept the call, but when he saw who was calling him he stepped over toward a corner of the room enough to respond.

"Yes, Mr. President, Jack here. Pleased to hear that you're back in DC. What can I do for you?"

POTUS had little to say. Only that he had heard about Millie's being shot and seriously wounded. When Jack informed him that Millie had just passed away, POTUS remained silent for an extended period of time.

Finally, POTUS simply thanked Jack for saving his life, and offered his sincere condolences. He closed by saying, "Jack. There's nothing I can say that will alleviate your grief at this moment. You are now my good friend. We'll talk later."

After disconnecting the call, Jack heard another phone ringing—it was Angel's. He picked up the phone from where Angel had been sleeping in order to limit the distraction. It was from someone he'd never heard of. Someone named Jessie. He disconnected the call and silenced the phone.

Jack turned and surveyed the room and what had just happened. He slid Angel's throw over and sat down. He pulled several tissues from a box on the small table beside the chair and blotted the tears from his eyes. He then leaned forward, and nesting his face in his hands, Jack wept.

Epilogue

For Jack, the next month was filled with immense sorrow at the loss of the woman he'd grown to love. He was torn between exacting revenge on those responsible, and fulfilling his promise to faithfully watch over Angel, Millie's fourteen-year-old daughter.

When the DNA came back from the bloody glove, Jack was angered to learn that the identity of the attacker was not provided to him from the federal database—something about the records being secured by the FBI.

Jack was not in a hurry. So, after a couple months he posed his request directly to his friend Roger. And, surprisingly, even as a career Secret Service Agent, Roger found that the records were sealed for him.

"What does that suggest?" Jack asked him. "Why can't you access them?"

"Not sure," Roger told him. "But, don't worry, I know someone who can open any file. Or, at least I think he can. Just give me a little time and I'll see what I can do."

Jack knew who Roger was referring to—Former President Bob Fulbright.

When Roger had told Jack that he would need some time to obtain the requested information, Jack knew that Roger could be talking weeks or months. And Jack also knew that it would be a mistake to rush the project. So, he set about tying up the loose ends of the cases he'd been working on. Because he had quickly become convinced that there was no financial benefit to be extracted from the Agnes Cross estate, Jack determined that he would gift the monies he had earned through his successful efforts on behalf of POTUS to Henry and to Henry's cousin—the one who had originally hired Henry and him to see what could be done on his behalf.

Not only did Jack wish to see Henry's cousin benefit financially from the family inheritance, he was adamant about rejecting any and all rewards for the job. First, because he felt it wrong to accept any payment whatsoever for his efforts on behalf of POTUS; and, second, Jack thought it unfair to receive any financial benefit given the fact that Roger, as a member of the Secret Service, would not be rewarded with any additional pay aside from his regular salary.

Immediately after the dust had settled, Roger handed over to Jack the keys to a brand new Mercedes Sprinter conversion van. It contained a dozen cardboard boxes, each of which held five thousand unmarked one hundred dollar bills—U.S. currency. As soon as POTUS heard about Fulbright's cash transfer, he personally called Jack into the Oval Office and matched that amount with an equal gift—less the "foreign-made van."

While Jack did keep the van, he had Henry distribute the cash to the cousin who had hired them in the first place. But he did tell Henry to keep enough to cover his costs and salary for the part he played in the Deadwood saga. Henry, however, chose to pass all the money on to his cousin, telling Jack that he regarded their trip to Deadwood as a "vacation."

Besides, Henry had charged all his costs off onto Jack's credit card anyway.

There was a third reason why Jack sought no personal gain for his effort. He believed that Millie's death was a direct result of his work defending POTUS against the Deep State. And, after five and a half weeks, the report given him from the Former President bore out Jack's suspicions—it identified Millie's killer as part of an elite two-man team known to be used by Deep State operatives to eliminate those who opposed them.

Bob Fulbright even provided Jack with the names of the two killers—Rick and Constable Applewhite. They were blood brothers, and they always worked together.

* * *

Keep your eyes open for Michael's next book (due out in 2020). The title of his new book will be "Sault"(as in Sault Ste. Marie). And, watch for *Emma*. Remember her?

A note from Michael Carrier:

In my opinion, there is no more intriguing place on planet earth than Michigan's Upper Peninsula. From its unique physical attributes to its amazingly diverse, tough-spirited population, the UP provides the perfect backdrop for the adventures of Jack, Kate, Red, Robby and Henry. If you would like to learn more about the UP, Check out the *U.P. Reader*. This is a collection of writings from the Upper Peninsula Publishers and Authors Association. Writer, Photographer and Videographer, Mikel Classen, is the managing editor for the publication (http://upreader.org).

Cast of Main Characters in the Jack Handler Thrillers

(Characters are listed in a quasi-chronological order.)

This book, *Deadwood to Deep State*, is the sixth book in the second Jack Handler series—Jack's Justice. Ghosts of Cherry Street—and the Cumberbatch Oubliette was the first book in the series. All told, at this time there are a total of thirteen Jack Handler thrillers.

While many of the characters encountered in this book have already made appearances in one or more of the previous Jack Handler books, if you want a deeper understanding about what makes a player tick, you can refer to The Cast to answer additional backstory questions.

Main characters are listed in quasi-chronological order.

Jack Handler:

Jack is a good man, in his way. While it is true that he occasionally kills people, it can be argued that most (if not all) of his targets needed killing. Occasionally a somewhat sympathetic figure comes between Jack and his goal. When that happens, Jack's goal comes first. I think the word that best sums up Jack's persona might be "expeditor." He is outcome driven—he makes things turn out the way he wants them to turn out.

For instance, if you were a single mom and a bully were stealing your kid's lunch money, you could send "Uncle Jack" to school with little Billy. Uncle Jack would have a "talk" with the teachers and the principal. With Jack's help, the problem would be solved. But I would not recommend that you ask him how he accomplished it. You might not like what he tells you—if he even responds.

Jack is faithful to his friends and a great father to his daughter. He is also a dangerous and tenacious adversary when situations require it.

Jack Handler began his career as a law enforcement officer. He married a beautiful woman (Beth) of Greek descent while working as a police officer in Chicago. She was a concert violinist and the love of his life. If you were to ask Jack about it, he would quickly tell you he married above himself. So, when bullets intended for him killed her, he admittedly grew bitter. Kate, their daughter, was just learning to walk when her mother was gunned down.

As a single father, Jack soon found that he needed to make more money than his job as a police officer paid. So he went back to college and obtained a degree in criminal justice. Soon he was promoted to the level of sergeant in the Chicago Police Homicide Division.

With the help of a friend, he then discovered that there was much more money to be earned in the private sector. At first he began moonlighting on private security jobs. Immediate success led him to take an early retirement and attain his private investigator license.

Because of his special talents (obtained as a former army ranger) and his intense dedication to problem solving, Jack's services became highly sought after. While he did take on some of the more sketchy clients, he never accepted a project simply on the basis of financial gain—he always sought out the moral high ground. Unfortunately, sometimes that moral high ground morphed into quicksand.

Jack is now pushing sixty (from the downward side) and he has all the physical ailments common to a man of that age. While it is true that he remains in amazing physical condition, of late he has begun to sense his limitations.

His biggest concern recently has been an impending IRS audit. While he isn't totally confident that it will turn out okay, he remains optimistic.

His problems stem from the purchase of half-interest in a bar in Chicago two decades earlier. His partner was one of his oldest and most trusted friends—Conrad (Connie) O'Donnell.

The principal reason he considered the investment in the first place was to create a cover for his private security business.

Many, if not most, of his clients insisted on paying him in cash or with some other untraceable commodity. At first he tried getting rid of the cash by paying all of his bills with it. But even though he meticulously avoided credit cards and checks, the cash continued to accumulate.

It wasn't that he was in any sense averse to paying his fair share of taxes. The problem was that if he did deposit the cash into a checking account, and subsequently included it in his filings, he would then at some point be required to explain where it had come from.

He needed an acceptable method of laundering, and his buddy's bar seemed perfect.

But it did not work out exactly as planned. Four years ago the IRS decided to audit the bar, which consequently exposed his records to scrutiny.

Jack consulted with one of his old customers, a disbarred attorney/CPA, to see if this shady character could get the books straightened out enough for Jack to survive the audit and avoid federal prison.

The accountant knew exactly how Jack earned his money and that the sale of a few bottles of Jack Daniels had little to do with it.

Even though his business partner and the CPA talked a good game about legitimacy, Jack still agonized when thoughts of the audit stormed through his mind. This problem was further complicated when Conrad was murdered in what was thought a botched robbery. Connie's lazy son, Conrad Jr., inherited his father's share of the bar.

A year earlier Jack had been convicted and sentenced for attacking a veteran detective, Calvin Brandt. The day that his conviction was overturned, an attempt was made on his life inside a federal prison camp. He believed at the time, and still does, that Calvin Brandt had been responsible for contracting the Aryan Alliance to carry out the hit.

Fortunately for Jack, Chuchip (Henry) Kalyesveh a Native American of the Hopi tribe, who was also an inmate at the prison camp, came to his rescue.

Kate Handler:

Kate, Jack's daughter and a New York homicide detective, is introduced early and appears often in this series. Kate is beautiful. She has her mother's olive complexion and green eyes. Her trim five-foot-eight frame, with her long auburn hair falling nicely on her broad shoulders, would seem more at home on the runway than in an interrogation room. But Kate is a seasoned New York homicide detective. In fact, she is thought by many to be on the fast track to the top—thanks, in part, to the unwavering support of her soon-to-retire boss, Captain Spencer.

Of course, her career was not hindered by her background in law. Graduating Summa Cum Laude from Notre Dame at the age of twenty-one, she went on to Notre Dame Law School. She passed the Illinois Bar Exam immediately upon receiving her JD, and accepted a position at one of Chicago's most prestigious criminal law firms. While her future looked bright as a courtroom attorney, she hated defending "sleazebags."

One Saturday morning she called her father and invited him to meet her at what she knew to be the coffee house he most fancied. It was there, over a couple espressos, that she asked him what he thought about her taking a position with the New York Police Department. She was shocked when he immediately gave his blessing. "Kitty," he said, "you're a smart girl. I totally trust your judgment. You have to go where your heart leads. Just promise me one thing. Guarantee me that you will put me up whenever I want to visit. After all, you are my favorite daughter."

To this Kate replied with a chuckle, "Dad, I'm your only daughter.

And you will always be welcome."

In Murder on Sugar Island (Sugar), Jack and Kate team up to solve the murder of Alex Garos, Jack's brother-in-law. This book takes place on Sugar Island, which is located in the northern part of Michigan's Upper Peninsula (just east of Sault Ste. Marie, MI).

Because Kate was Garos's only blood relative living in the United States, he named her in his will to inherit all of his estate. This included one of the most prestigious pieces of real estate on the island—the Sugar Island Resort.

Reg:

In Jack and the New York Death Mask (Death Mask), Jack is recruited by his best friend, Reg (Reginald Black), to do a job without either man having any knowledge as to what that job might entail. Jack, out of loyalty to his friend, accepted the offer. The contract was ostensibly to assassinate a sitting president. However, instead of assisting the plot, Jack and Reg worked to thwart it. Most of this story takes place in New York City, but there are scenes in DC, Chicago, and Upstate New York. Reg is frequently mentioned throughout the series, as are Pam Black and Allison Fulbright. Pam Black is Reg's wife (he was shot at the end of Death Mask), and Allison is a former first lady. It was Allison who contracted Reg and Jack to assassinate the sitting president.

Allison:

Allison is a former first lady (with presidential aspirations of her own), and Jack's primary antagonist throughout the series. Usually she fears him enough not to do him or his family physical harm, but she and Jack are not friends. She seems to poke her nose into Jack's business just enough to be a major annoyance.

On a few occasions, however, Allison's anger at Jack reaches he boiling point, and she strikes out against him. To this date, she has been unsuccessful.

Over a year ago Allison suffered a severely debilitating stroke, so her current activities have been dramatically limited, a situation which has provided Jack a bit of a reprieve in his having to worry about what she might be up to vis-à-vis his well-being.

Roger Minsk:

Roger is a member of the Secret Service, and a very good friend to Jack. Roger is also friendly with Bob Fulbright, Allison's husband, and a former president.

Red:

This main character is introduced in Sugar. Red is a redheaded fourteen-year-old boy who, besides being orphaned, cannot speak. It turned out that Red was actually the love child of Alex (Jack's brother-in-law) and his office manager. So, Alex not only leaves his Sugar Island resort to Kate, he also leaves his Sugar Island son for her to care for.

Red has a number of outstanding characteristics, first and foremost among them, his innate ability to take care of himself in all situations. When his mother and her husband were killed in a fire, Red chose to live on his own instead of submitting to placement in foster care.

During the warmer months, he lived in a hut he had pieced together from parts of abandoned homes, barns, and cottages, and he worked at Garos's resort on Sugar Island. In the winter, he would take up residence in empty fishing cottages along the river.

Red's second outstanding characteristic is his loyalty. When put to the test, Red would rather sacrifice his life than see his friends hurt. In Sugar, Red works together with Jack and Kate to solve the mystery behind the killing of Jack's brother-in-law (and Red's biological father), Alex Garos.

The third thing about Red that makes him stand out is his inability to speak. As the result of a traumatic event in his life, his voice box was damaged, resulting in his disability. Before Jack and Kate entered his life, Red communicated only through an improvised sign system and various grunts.

When Kate introduced him to a cell phone and texting, Red's life changed dramatically.

Robby:

Robby is Red's best friend. When his parents are murdered, Robby moves into the Handler home and becomes a "brother" to Red. Robby and Red are now virtually inseparable.

Buddy:

Buddy is Red's golden retriever.

Bill Green:

One other character of significance introduced in Sugar is Bill Green, the knowledgeable police officer who first appears in Joey's coffee shop. He also assumes a major role in subsequent books of the series, after he becomes sheriff of Chippewa County.

Captain Spencer:

Captain Spencer is Kate's boss in New York. The captain has been planning his retirement for a long time, but has not yet been able to pull the trigger. Kate is his protégée, and he almost seems to fear leaving the department until her career is fully developed.

Paul Martin and Jill Talbot:

Two new characters do emerge in Sugar Island Girl, Missing in Paris (Missing). They are Paul Martin and Jill Talbot. They do not appear in subsequent stories.

Legend:

Legend is one of the main characters in the sixth book of the series, Wealthy Street Murders (Wealthy). In this story, Jack and Kate work with Red, Robby, and Legend to solve a series of murders. Wrapped up in a rug and left for dead at the end of Wealthy, with Buddy's help he lives to play an important role in Ghosts.

Mrs. Fletcher:

Mrs. Fletcher, one of the caretakers at Kate's resort on Sugar Island, progressively plays a more prominent role as an occasional care-provider for the two boys. And, of course, she becomes embroiled in the intrigue.

Unfortunately, Fletcher and her husband are murdered in an earlier segment of this series: "Dogfight."

Sheriff Griffen:

The sheriff first appears in Murders in Strangmoor Bog (Strangmoor). He is sheriff of Schoolcraft County, which includes Strangmoor Bog, and Seney Wildlife Preserve.

Angel and her mother Millie:

In Strangmoor, the seventh and last book in the "Getting to know Jack" series, two new main characters are introduced: Angel and Millie Star.

Angel, a precocious fun-loving redhead (with a penchant for quick thinking and the use of big words), immediately melts the hearts of Red and Robby and becomes an integral part of the Handler saga. You will probably see Angel and Millie in other subsequent books in the "Jack's Justice" series as well.

Lindsay Hildebrandt and Calvin Brandt:

These two significant new characters are introduced in Ghosts of Cherry Street (and the Cumberbatch Oubliette). Lindsay, a rookie detective in the Grand Rapids Police Department, quickly becomes a special person in Jack's life. If you were to ask her if she is dating Jack, Lindsay (who is about two decades younger than Jack) would immediately inform you that people their age don't date. But she does admit that they are good friends and occasionally see each other socially.

They have in common the fact that they both lost their spouses in a violent fashion. Lindsay's husband, also a Grand Rapids detective, was shot and killed several years earlier. This crime has not yet been solved.

Calvin Brandt, a veteran Grand Rapids detective, does not get along with anyone. And that is especially true of Jack Handler. Jack would be the first to admit that he was not an innocent party with regard to this ongoing conflict.

Chuchip Kalyesveh:

Chuchip generally goes by the name of Henry because he has found most people butcher his Native American first name.

Jack first met Henry in a Federal prison camp where both were serving time. They became good friends when Henry saved Jack's life by beating up four other inmates who had been contracted to kill him. Jack says he has never met another man as physically imposing as his friend Henry.

Now that both are free men, Henry works for Jack at the Sugar Island Resort. And, sometimes, he partners with Jack (unofficially, of course) to help out with some of his tougher private security cases.

Expect to learn more about Henry as subsequent Jack Handler books roll off the press.

Emma:

Emma (Legs) is a very attractive thirty-someish contract killer. She made her first appearance in Dogfight. Expect to see her again.

* * *

Here are the Amazon links to my previous Jack Handler books:

Getting to Know Jack Series

Jack and the New York Death Mask:	http://amzn.to/MVpAEd
Murder on Sugar Island:	http://amzn.to/1u66DBG
Superior Peril:	http://amzn.to/LAQnEU
Superior Intrigue:	http://amzn.to/1jvjNSi

Sugar Island Girl Missing in Paris: http://amzn.to/1g5c66e
Wealthy Street Murders: http://amzn.to/1mb6NQy
Murders in Strangmoor Bog: http://amzn.to/1IEUPxX

Jack's Justice Series

Ghosts of Cherry Street: http://amzn.to/2n3lrRf
Assault on Sugar Island: http://amzn.to/2n3vcyL
Dogfight: http://amzn.to/2F7OkoM
Murder at Whitefish Point: http://amzn.to/2CxlAmC
Superior Shoal: https://amzn.to/2lolAmr

Made in the USA
Middletown, DE
15 August 2023

36809633R00354